Dear Oli

This is not biltong.

*I hope you savour the words though —
he's my top SA author.*

DANCING THE DEATH DRILL

Kent

Dancing the Death Drill

FRED KHUMALO

UMUZI

Published in 2017 by Umuzi
an imprint of Penguin Random House South Africa (Pty) Ltd
Company Reg No 1953/000441/07
The Estuaries No 4, Oxbow Crescent, Century Avenue, Century City, 7441,
South Africa
PO Box 1144, Cape Town, 8000, South Africa
www.penguinrandomhouse.co.za

First edition, first printing 2017
Reprinted 2017
3 5 7 9 8 6 4 2

ISBN 978-1-4152-0949-3 (Print)
ISBN 978-1-4152-0914-1 (ePub)

Cover design by Fire and Lion
Author photograph courtesy of the Khumalo Family Collection
Text design by Fahiema Hallam
Set in Minion Pro

Printed and bound by Novus Print, a Novus Holdings company

This book was printed on FSC® certified and controlled sources. FSC
(Forest Stewardship Council®) is an independent, international,
non-governmental organisation. Its aim is to support environmentally
sustainable, and socially and economically responsible global forest
management.

Also published in the United Kingdom by Jacaranda Books Art Music Ltd

To unsung heroes and heroines throughout history, in all wars known to man. But more specifically to those gallant souls who were aboard ss *Mendi* when she went down.

CHAPTER 1

France, 1958

When the two men entered the restaurant that afternoon, Jean-Jacques Henri, head waiter at the Tour d'Argent, was gazing out at the river, daydreaming about his impending retirement.

Quickly regaining his composure, Jean-Jacques took their coats and ushered the men to a table with a view of Notre Dame and the Seine flowing nearby. They *oohed* and *aahed* in appreciation. Although he exchanged pleasantries with the two diners in impeccable French, Jean-Jacques never tried to make eye contact with them. Some would have considered it rude; others would have thought he was shy. They would be wrong on both counts. Jean-Jacques had an embarrassing secret: his left eye was artificial. Because it had spooked some attentive diners in the past, he'd since contrived to avoid all eye contact while at work. This manoeuvre had worked perfectly, saving all parties concerned unnecessary discomfort. In all the years he'd spent at this establishment, he could remember only about six, seven faces that he had looked at intently. And these had been exceptional diners: Greta Garbo, who'd remarked on his expertly groomed moustache; General Charles de Gaulle, who'd mentioned he looked and walked like a soldier; Miles Davis, who'd told him in his raspy voice, on one of his early visits to Paris, 'I ain't gonna ask you how you lost that eye 'cos I know you ain't gonna ask me how I lost my voice!'

These were just some of the faces that Jean-Jacques remembered distinctly. Most of the others were blurs, silhouettes of stolen glances. To compensate for his failure to look patrons in the eye, he regaled his guests with saucy tales, and sometimes bowled them over with outrageous claims: 'I'm going to get you to try a special entrée that I had the chef create at the behest of Coco Chanel the last time she dined with us.'

Now, Jean-Jacques was just months away from retirement. It gave him joy that his forced daily interaction with people would be coming to an end. He was only fifty-seven, but he had had a long and eventful life. He needed the break, the solitude.

'Are you from Algeria?' asked one of the two gentlemen, breaking into his thoughts.

'Algeria is my original home; France is where I earn my bread, such as it is. But how did you make the connection?'

'Ah, with a complexion and hair like that ...' the man said, admiring Jean-Jacques' caramel skin. 'And also, Algerians are considerate people. Unlike the Europeans and the Americans, they don't look a stranger in the eye. It's considered rude in many parts of Africa. To look a person in the eye, I mean. I respect that attitude.'

Ignorant chatter like that drove Jean-Jacques up the wall. He could hardly wait for his early retirement in December – just eight months to go.

A few minutes later, he brought their drinks – two German beers. He poured these into tall, frosted beer glasses. The talkative man adjusted his monocle and then reached for his glass.

8

'Enjoy your drinks, gentlemen,' said Jean-Jacques, before remembering something. 'As a matter of courtesy, gentlemen, I am required to inform you that we'll be hosting Miss Édith Piaf this Saturday. She'll sing a song or two, as is her wont. Dinner time. Table reservation essential.'

Without lifting his eyes, he bowed and turned to go.

Jean-Jacques glided towards the kitchen. After a decent interval, he returned to ask if they were ready to order. The raconteur's order was simple: medium-rare steak with vegetables on the side. His mate ordered the restaurant's signature dish, *canard au sang*.

'What's that you just ordered?' asked Talkative One.

'It's literally pressed duck, where the bird is cooked in its blood.'

Jean-Jacques then asked if they wanted to select a wine from the cellar. Talkative One sighed and said, 'Well, well, well. Do we have the time to get up, walk to the cellar and explore its secrets? It could take us at least a year to view and understand the riches of your cellar, from what I've heard. A nice Burgundy will do. I think I can trust your judgement.' He spoke good French, but with an accent Jean-Jacques couldn't place.

'Thank you, gentlemen,' said Jean-Jacques. He proceeded to clear the table of their empty beer glasses.

Later, Jean-Jacques returned with their food, piping hot and aromatic. A wine steward stood aside while he put the food on the table. Jean-Jacques accepted a bottle of wine from the steward, who then disappeared back to the cellar. Having been instructed to go ahead and pour the wine, no ceremonial tasting, thanks very much, Jean-Jacques carried out the task.

Talkative One complained, 'This steak looks overdone.'

'But you haven't even touched it, monsieur,' Jean-Jacques

said softly. He was so absorbed in the act of pouring wine he didn't realise that the man's face was gradually turning red, and that his monocle had fallen off. Jean-Jacques continued, 'I suggest you cut it, if that pleases you, monsieur. That way you'll see how pink it is on the inside. Delectable, if I have to say so myself. Just let the blade of your knife rest on the meat, and it will simply and effortlessly slide through. That's how tender it is. Please try it.'

'A waiter doesn't remonstrate with a paying customer,' the man said, slamming his fist on the table, startling his dining partner.

Still refusing to look the man in the eye, Jean-Jacques said, 'I'm sorry, monsieur. I can take it back to the kitchen. Ask them to give you something else, if that's what you would prefer.'

The man sighed, then sliced the steak open. The knife did glide through the piece of meat as if it were a slab of soft butter. Just one bite and his eyelids fluttered in appreciation. He cut another piece, shoved it into his mouth and chewed slowly, rolling his food around his tongue to make the moment last longer. He let out an involuntary moan.

'See? I knew you would enjoy it, monsieur,' Jean-Jacques said in a soothing voice. 'It's done just the way you wanted.'

The man put his knife on the table and glared at the waiter. 'You may go now.'

Jean-Jacques bowed respectfully. He was in the process of removing an ashtray from the table when the talkative man turned to his mate and spoke contemptuously in Afrikaans, saying, 'Kaffirs are the same all over the world. Bloody cheeky, that's what they all are. Always backchatting their bosses. Look at this monkey, for example. Yackety-yack, yackety-yack!

Thinks he's better just because he's a light-skinned *houtkop*. What's the fucking world coming to?'

It was at this moment that Jean-Jacques, the bile rising inside him, felt compelled to look at the man whose words were like a hot poker in his heart, words spewed out in a language he hadn't heard in more than thirty years.

Immediately, his knees buckled. His ears buzzed, his head felt as if it was about to explode. Holding on to the back of the quieter man's chair, he inhaled deeply, his heart thudding violently, his eyes brimming with tears. That face mirrored terrors of his past. Had he made eye contact with the men when they walked in, he would have recognised the face instantly, a face, monocle or no monocle, that had remained etched in his mind for over three decades.

Suddenly the man's eyes lit up in a jolt of recognition. 'You! It's you!' He rose, his hand reaching for a knife on the table. Panicking, Jean-Jacques grabbed the diner's steak knife and plunged it twice – firmly, viciously – into the man's heart. Crimson ribbons of blood criss-crossed the white tablecloth. The man fell off his chair, thudding onto the floor. When the other man pulled a gun from his boot and tried to take aim, the waiter intercepted him, slashing his throat open in one move befitting his hefty size. The gun clattered to the floor. The man opened his mouth, but his scream was muffled by the gush of blood and air hissing out of his exposed oesophagus. Even as he went down, the man clawed the air in front of him, ripping the front of Jean-Jacques' white shirt with his sharp nails.

Jean-Jacques looked at the knife in his hand, the blood on his torn shirt. He dropped the weapon on the floor as if it had turned into a venomous snake. Turning on his heel, he walked calmly towards the kitchen. Some diners who'd witnessed the brief but vicious slaughter cowered behind their tables. Waiters and kitchen staff who had been brought to the scene by the screams of shock watched from a distance. No one tried to stop Jean-Jacques as he walked to the bathroom.

He stood in front of the mirror and stared hatefully at his face, his jaw muscles bunched. There was a distant, vacant look in his eyes. He did not recognise the man that stared back at him. Thinking the illusion would disappear, he blinked. But the stranger stared back at him defiantly, his eyes blank. As if mocking him. There was a large spot of blood on his left cheek, and a smaller fleck on his chin. His hands were caked in drying blood. He turned on the tap, then rolled up the sleeves of his shirt to wash his hands, his face. He then turned off the tap and straightened up. His gaze remained blank, pitiless. He spat at his mirror image. Once, twice, thrice. His spit slid down the face of the mirror. He reached out a hand to wipe the glass with his open palm, but then changed his mind.

Jean-Jacques sighed and trudged back to the kitchen, where he sat down heavily, buried his face in his hands, and waited for the police to arrive.

CHAPTER 2

As soon as the gendarmes were alerted, the place was crawling with reporters, who descended on Jean-Jacques' co-workers like vultures. They wanted to know what exactly had happened, chronologically, from the time the diners sat down. Was there a verbal altercation before blood started flowing? Were the diners loud and drunk? Were they belligerent in any way? What about the waiter himself? Where was he from originally? Algeria? Uh-oh! The Algerian War of Independence had moved to French soil.

Jean-Jacques' co-workers spoke about how shocked they were by the violence of it all, the suddenness. They spoke kindly of Jean-Jacques – a courteous gentleman, hard-working, focused – and, most of all, of his quirky, understated sense of humour. Even in the face of provocation by some of the restaurant's more famous patrons, who sometimes enjoyed throwing their weight around, making impossible demands on the staff, Jean-Jacques was always calm under fire, they said.

The gendarmes took a cooperative Jean-Jacques into a waiting police car. No scuffle, no tantrums, no raised voices.

When the other reporters had left the scene, Thierry Bousquet, a journalist on one of the lowbrow newspapers, stayed behind. He was a famous crime reporter, on first-name terms with many policemen. Even those who had never encountered him knew of him and his work, which is why the policemen at the scene tolerated his presence, even though the drama was over. Thierry overheard the officer in charge instructing two of his juniors to proceed to the waiter's house. When the officer in charge started his car, Thierry tailed him on his motorcycle.

The police car arrived at the apartment on Rue de Seine only a few minutes later. The two officers assigned to the task left the car in no hurry, taking their time as they fumbled for keys, and pushed opened Jean-Jacques' apartment door. They searched the apartment, with Thierry skulking in the shadows, until, as if only just made aware of his presence, one policeman asked him to leave. Thierry pretended to, but instead sneaked into the lounge, where his attention was immediately drawn to an easel, with a painting, a work in progress of some sort on it. Was Jean-Jacques a painter? What kind of paintings was he interested in? Thierry looked around the room for more evidence that the murderous waiter was also an artist. There was a cluster of artwork – charcoals, watercolours, linocuts – in a corner. Riffling through this treasure trove, he saw that most of the work was signed Jerry Moloto, explaining why it had attracted his attention. Thierry, an amateur painter himself, was familiar with Moloto's works which he had seen at some small, obscure exhibitions in Paris.

Moloto was a budding South African expat artist who'd been in France for a few years. Although not really a big name, he was one of the few African artists whose work serious Parisian collectors and appreciators of art were familiar with. Looking at the half-finished work on the easel, Thierry realised that the murderer had been trying to copy a famous painting by Moloto called *Donkey Song*.

'You are still here,' the policeman said in exasperation, startling Thierry.

'Pardon me, sir, I was just about to leave, but as an art lover I simply couldn't help myself. I just had to take a look at these pieces. I promise you I am not going to interfere with your work. I am just admiring the man's efforts.'

The policeman shrugged. 'Ah, suit yourself. But if the chief catches you here, you're on your own.'

After some prodding, the policeman told Thierry that they had found stacks of musical scores and notes.

'A very expensive-looking apartment,' observed the journalist.

'Grand piano, decent furniture. Hmm, all these unusual paintings and objets d'art. Decadent, wouldn't you say?'

'Especially for a mere restaurant worker.'

'You're reading my mind.'

'Who could this gentleman be?' asked Thierry, sensing the value of this story.

'We shall soon find out. Man could turn out to be a prince in his home country.'

'Bored out of his skull by Rich Father's demands on him. *When are you going to service your harem, Abdullah?*' Thierry said.

'Then it turns out poor Abdullah is more interested in Rashid or Bilal or Ahmed or whatever their names are. Harem forsooth!' laughed the policeman.

'Then Prince Farouk runs away from home, comes to Paris. Changes his name to Jean-Jacques. Lives anonymously, but comfortably enough.'

'*There's* a thought.'

'Just a shot in the dark, my friend,' said Thierry.

'Shall remember to mention that angle to my superiors.' The policeman then seemed to remember something. 'This fellow is somehow connected to a place called l'Échelle de Jacob. There are brochures from this Jacob place. Ever heard of it?'

The journalist had indeed visited this club about three months before, but he chose to plead ignorance. He wanted to be there first. It always helped to be ahead of the police.

He arrived at the club around 8 p.m. It wasn't hard to spot Moloto; he was the only black person in the thin crowd, sitting in solitary splendour at the bar, nursing a bottle of cider. Thierry had seen a picture of Moloto in one of the newspapers, and he noticed now that in real life the man was much lighter in complexion. Anyway, much lighter than the average African he had seen at the docks.

'Good evening, Mr Moloto,' he said politely in French. 'May I kindly have a word with you?'

'Speak to me, my brother,' Moloto said in English, showing the journalist a toothy smile, clearly happy to have company. He seemed to have had more than one cider already.

'I believe you are acquainted with Jean-Jacques Henri ...' It was a shot in the dark.

Moloto looked at his interlocutor, sizing him up. Then he said, 'Okay, let's get some things out of the way. You can speak French to me, but I'll respond in English. That fine by you?'

The Frenchman nodded.

'See, my home language is Sepedi. If you want to speak to me, you would speak in French, then I would consider what you're saying in English first. Then I'd translate from English to Pedi. Then my response would be formulated in Pedi, then translated to English. And from English to French. Tall order.

I've never tried to translate from Pedi to French, in my head, that is. It's always Sepedi to English, and from English to whatever European language I'm being spoken to.'

'I see.'

'Which makes me properly colonised property of the British Crown. My thought processes have to meet the approval of my British masters before they can be communicated to other Europeans. Ah, I'm losing the thread of what I was saying. What was your question again?'

'I wanted to know if you were friends with Jean-Jacques Henri—'

'Ah, yes. Jean-Jacques. That fellow is my bosom buddy, my intellectual sparring partner.'

The Frenchman leaned forward eagerly. Moloto frowned and got up, sensing the other man's appetite for a juicy story. 'Forget it, I shouldn't be talking about this.'

Thierry quickly said, 'My dear monsieur, I am not with the police. I am a journalist. I just want to get a sense of Jean-Jacques.'

'Forget it.' He walked towards the stage to join his colleagues doing the sound check. Thierry followed him gingerly.

'I'll have you thrown out if you continue like that. Stop harassing me,' barked Jerry.

The other band members looked up from their instruments. The owner-barman craned his neck in the direction of what was becoming a noisy exchange. He said, 'Do you have a problem, mister?'

Thierry raised his hands in resignation. He went to the bar and explained, 'No problem at all, monsieur. I was trying to have a friendly chat with my good friend Monsieur Moloto. Seems like I upset him somehow. That's all.' He ordered drinks for two. He took them back to where he'd been sitting with Jerry.

The band started playing Ellington's 'Mood Indigo', Jerry's fingers flying deftly over the piano keyboard. As the club began to fill up, the band broke into a spirited version of Cab Calloway's 'Minnie the Moocher'.

By the time the show was over, Thierry was thoroughly drunk. He had another go at Jerry when the band was clearing the stage. 'Monsieur, what I've been trying to tell you all night is simply this: your friend Jean-Jacques has been arrested. He's in big, big trouble.'

'What?'

'He murdered two men today.'

Members of the band raised their heads. Jerry shooed them away. He said to Thierry, 'I hope you know what you're talking about. I could hang you by your white nuts right now.'

'The story will be in the papers tomorrow morning.'

'What happened?'

Thierry smiled drunkenly. It was his turn to be difficult. 'Look, I am in no state to talk right now. Too drunk.'

'Come on, man, don't play games with me.'

'How about we have lunch tomorrow? Or dinner? By that time you would have read the papers, but there's always more to the story than what you'll see in the papers. And that's where I need your help. I have a few questions about things that won't be covered by tomorrow's papers, if you get my drift.'

Jerry stood for a long time staring at the journalist. 'Come to my place tomorrow, then. And your story has to be good, or I'll cut your balls off and have them for breakfast, you hear?'

'You seem to have taken a liking to white balls, monsieur,' Thierry laughed.

CHAPTER 3

A t eight o'clock the next evening, Thierry was at Jerry's place, an apartment building right behind the club. An upmarket building all right, but Jerry, who was the janitor in charge, lived – or maybe 'burrowed' was the right word – like a rabbit in the dingy basement. It was a biggish room which allowed for a kitchen table with two chairs, a gas stove, a fridge and a piano. A door led to what Thierry assumed to be a bedroom. It smelled of mildew. Thierry imagined that no matter how much you cleaned the place – and it looked spotless – the musty smell would never go away.

'So, you came,' Jerry said in greeting, with the undertone clear: *I'd hoped you wouldn't because you were talking nonsense last night.*

Jerry gestured for Thierry to sit at the table. He positioned himself on a chair on the opposite side. The journalist was hoping his subject would feel self-conscious and start talking. He was wrong. The man, booze from last night coming out of his pores, just sat there and stared at him with tired, bloodshot eyes.

Thierry was the first to look away, restless as a bumblebee on a leash. Dying to get started. Soonest. Now. But he didn't want to betray his eagerness, his desperation. He cleared his throat and tried to sound casual. 'Last night I said I would tell the story from my own perspective. I've brought you a copy of our latest edition so you can see what I wrote. It's simple and straight to the point. I mention that he is from Algeria, and what happened in that country – the French involvement, and so on. I also mention Jean-Jacques' art. My editor loved that bit. No one else came up with that angle.'

Jerry took the newspaper and dropped it on the floor without even looking at it. 'I've read all the papers.'

Many of the stories he'd read had highlighted Jean-Jacques' Algerian background, suggesting that he was a left-wing radical whose disaffection with the French stemmed from the Algerian War of Independence, which had left many young people angry.

Jerry repeated, 'I've read all the papers. And I think you don't know what you're talking about. The man all of you journalists have written about bears no resemblance to the man I know. I'm truly disappointed. Maybe it's time to set the record straight.'

'Of course. We absolutely need to get to the bottom of this.'

'Maybe my friend won't approve, but I think the truth needs to come out. The truth might just save him. You may have done away with the guillotine, but your courts are still stuck in the Dark Ages. Maybe my friend can use the story I'm about to tell as … what do you call it in proper legal language? Exterminating what – you know – factors that his lawyers can use to argue for a lesser sentence?'

Thierry's face was blank.

Jerry tried again. 'You write crime stories, man. You should know what I'm talking about.'

Thierry's mind was working overtime: translating from

Jerry's brand of English to French, and then trying to get colloquial French to bow to the dictates of French legalese.

'*Circonstances atténuantes*? Hmm, let me see … Extenuating circumstances?'

'That's the mother! *Extenuating* circumstances.' Jerry thought for a while, then started again, 'You see, my friend, I think this is more than a story. It's history, the history of a country. The full story of the Algerian War has yet to be told. I think, with your help and cooperation, we can show the effect that war has had on ordinary human beings, on young people trying to make sense of their country – hell, I'd be a fool to let such a morsel of history pass me by.'

Thierry retrieved his notebook from his knapsack and placed it on the table. 'I hope you don't mind if we record this.'

'You wait.' Jerry was silent for a long time. Then he said, half to himself, '*Quel poisson gelé.*'

Surprised, Thierry exclaimed, 'Why are you calling me a frozen fish?'

Laughing out loud, Jerry said, 'It's an expression I learned from Jean-Jacques when I first met him. He thought I was too cold and boring to make it as an artist in France. But I've defrosted since then.' He reached into the fridge, came out with some white wine, then he found two glasses, which he rinsed in the tiny sink, before he placed them on the table. He reached for a corkscrew.

He filled the glasses to the brim. 'You have to forgive me, my friend. I understand why you Europeans don't fill your glasses to the brim. I suppose it's on account of your sharp noses which tend to sink into the drink if the glass is too full. Fortunately, being a black man from Africa, with a nice, big flat nose, I don't have that problem.'

They laughed together and each took a sip from their glasses.

Then Jerry set his glass down and said, 'Okay, my journalist friend, and whoever you're going to share this story with. First things first: this is not my story, but the tale of a man I call a friend, a brother. Jean-Jacques Henri.'

Thierry saw Jerry's shoulder shake, until he exploded in laughter. 'Jean-Jacques Henri!' he repeated, oblivious to the Frechman's confusion. Still laughing, he got up from his chair, slapping his thigh as he did so. His outbursts of laughter hit Thierry like rolling waves pounding an unsuspecting ship. 'Jean-Jacques! Ooooh-wwwweeee! Jean-fucking-Jacques! Man, don't be fooled by that stupid name of his. He is a South African boy. Pitso Motaung is his true name.'

'What?' You could have knocked Thierry over with a feather at that moment.

Jerry continued, 'You know, when we come to Europe, from Africa, we sometimes have to assume new names, new identities, you see. Jean-Jacques fucking Henri! Ooooh-weeeee! And the French have fallen for it all these years.'

At last, Jerry began to regain his composure. He blew his nose on a handkerchief, and then wiped his face with the back of his hand. He reclaimed his seat, still sniggering quietly. 'As I was saying, when we arrive here in Europe, we have to be quick on our feet, and assume new identities. Especially those of us who are light-skinned. We know the French are more tolerant of North Africans – Moroccans, Algerians, Egyptians, etc. So, those of us who are light-skinned try to pass for North African-born bastards. That's how the world operates, my friend. So what would you like to know about our friend Pitso Motaung?'

Thierry's mind was reeling. So Jean-Jacques Henri was really a South African named Pitso Motaung? This was what you called news. He leaned forward.

'Man, you should be writing about me instead,' Jerry was saying now. 'I am a better pianist than Jean-Jacques. I sing well too. And I can outpaint him any day. Come to think of it, why haven't I assumed an Algerian-sounding name, seeing I'm also light-complexioned and my hair's curly enough?' Jerry laughed at his own joke. There was a moment of hesitation as Jerry remembered that his friend had asked him numerous times to speak in vague terms when matters of identity and country of origin came under discussion, especially with strangers. But now that Jean-Jacques was in prison, the truth about his identity would surely come out. Or maybe not?

Observing Jerry Moloto closely, Thierry sensed that there were many unresolved issues here. The whole incident had stirred some discomfort in the artist. As a cub reporter, Thierry had learned that long spells of silence made interviewees nervous, uneasy. Sooner or later, they would feel obliged to say something. So he decided to put this particular trick into practice. He waited.

Jerry Moloto got up from his chair. He paced the tiny kitchen, shaking his head. 'I *knew* it was bound to happen. I knew it. I told him a long time ago to walk away, leave France and its bad memories. Go to London, Amsterdam, New York, anywhere, and start all over again. I told him. I begged him, you know. He wouldn't listen. I knew that sitting here in Paris he was bound to bump into one of them. I told him, dammit.'

Jerry reached for a pile of papers he had placed on a small table next to the stove. His hand came up with a photograph, which he handed to Thierry. The woman in the picture had the body of a dancer, tall and slender. It was a black-and-white photo, so Thierry couldn't tell the exact colour of her hair, except that it looked dark. She was perhaps in her late forties, early fifties, hair cascading to her shoulders, a wide open face, a sharp aristocratic nose, flat forehead, penetrating eyes, thin lips turned into a provocative smile, tiny dimples in her cheeks.

Jerry tapped the picture with his index finger. 'This is the ghost that's been haunting my friend for a long time. He gave me this picture some months ago. Asked me to be on the lookout for this face whenever I travelled out of Paris. I do venture out into the provinces every now and then. To draw inspiration, you see. The French countryside is good for the artist. I think this woman here, this ghost of a woman – because I'm not sure she's still alive – is the trigger of all the mayhem you've just told me about. Since she went away, my friend has become unpredictable. You have to be careful what you say or do in his presence. Her name Marie-Thérèse. My friend can't leave France, thanks to this woman. She's got a hold on him. And she's powerful, well connected.'

'You're speaking in riddles, monsieur. Can you simplify that for me, please?'

Jerry was silent for a long time. He could easily have forgotten that he was standing in the middle of his own kitchen, with a journalist sitting there, watching and waiting nervously. At last, he picked up the threads. 'My French brother, I think you are a godsend. What's your name again?'

'Thierry.'

'Ah, Thierry. Jerry and Thierry. It rhymes. Should write a song about it one of these days. Jerry and Thierry, toyin' with a story. But Thierry gettin' teary, 'cos his story is a'changin' …'

Perry, J and C (eds). *A Chief Is a Chief by the People: The Autobiography of Stimela Jason Jingoes* (London: Oxford University Press, 1975)

Wreck Report for 'Mendi' and 'Darro', 1917:
http://www.plimsoll.org/resources/SCCLibraries/WreckReports 2002/21285a.asp

http://www.delvillewood.com/sinking2.htm

He laughed briefly, shaking his head, before getting serious again. 'My good friend Pitso's been asking me for a long time to help him write the story of his life, so he could make peace with his past. You know, I paint, I play music and I dabble in short-story writing. Sold some of my short stories to some of the American pulp magazines. One of my stories got published in the same magazine that published Dashiell Hammett and Raymond Chandler – tell me you've heard of them?'

Thierry's face was blank, but no matter, Jerry steamed ahead. 'Anyway, Pitso wants me to write about him. We can visit him in prison, get more meat from him. And then you can start running a series of stories in your paper. But to get the ball rolling, let me tell the story the way my good friend told it to me.'

Jerry started pacing again. He seemed to have rearranged his thoughts and come to a sudden decision. He spoke with urgency now. 'I, Jerry Mogodiri Moloto, want to get this off my chest as soon as possible: I am not about to give you a history lesson. On the contrary, I want to show you how Pitso Motaung or Roelof Jacobus de la Rey, who you know as Jean-Jacques Henri, was an accident of history. He was a complex character, Pitso was. I don't know why I'm speaking about him in the past tense. Pitso *is* a complex character. Three names already: Roelof de la Rey, Pitso Motaung and, of course, Jean-Jacques Henri. Complex.'

He paused, then said, 'Yes, my good friend Pitso. So, we will do justice to his story. As I said earlier, he is a complex man. But he is also an accident of history.'

CHAPTER 4

South Africa, 1900

Perhaps the best way to start, Jerry suggested to Thierry, was to imagine Jean-Jacques' father: standing at six foot seven on his bare feet, arms rippling with muscles, hands as huge as frying pans, a mane of flaming red hair, with a matching beard touching his chest, piercing grey eyes, an Irish potato for a nose. Cornelius de la Rey was an army commander's dream come true. He was big and, although he did not know much about the British, he hated them with a passion. That was why, in 1900, a year after the outbreak of the Anglo–Boer War, and just after Bloemfontein had fallen into British hands, De la Rey found himself in the bush of the Orange Free State, fighting the British, who were going about burning down farms belonging to his people, the Boers. His parents' farm, which was on the outskirts of the fallen town, had not been attacked yet. He wondered how long it would hold out.

In mid-March, the commando – a mix of trained soldiers and private citizens like him, the burghers – trekked towards Kroonstad in anticipation of British movements up north. Having vanquished Bloemfontein, the British had their eyes on the Transvaal, a province with riches of gold that had to be protected at all costs. There was even talk among the Boers of dynamiting the mines in order to thwart the redneck who wanted to get his greedy paws on the gold.

Like most burghers, De la Rey had recently gone for training and was ready to use his gun in defence of his homeland. Boer scouts had reported on British movements from Thaba Nchu towards Bloemfontein. Armed with this intelligence, four hundred Kroonstad and Bloemfontein commandos took positions along the route the Brits were to use. At dawn on 30 March, the commandos sighted a mounted British column. Typically of the British, it was bloated with ammunition carts and provisioning wagons, hundreds of horses and pack animals. It looked formidable, but the Boers were ready. Finger trembling around his trigger, De la Rey prepared to slice the enemy down. He was angry with the British, yet he also experienced moments of self-doubt. He did not believe he was born to fight; he'd far rather be home, working on the farm. He was therefore always startled that when the instruction to fire was sounded he did so with gusto.

Taken by surprise, the British were forced into a stampede. The Krupp field guns of the Boers spoke the language of violence until the sun came up. The Brits ran, with the Boers in hot pursuit. All told, the Boers killed a hundred and fifty men and captured four hundred and eighty prisoners. The field was carpeted with overturned provisioning wagons, injured horses and bloodied corpses.

'Bloody overfed rednecks,' exclaimed General Christiaan de Wet as he went about inspecting the harvest from the bloody carnage. 'Look at their provisioning wagons. Enough to feed the entire republic of the Free State. That's why their men are so fat.'

'General!' De la Rey called out. 'There're some Brits who are seriously injured here. They're not dead. They need medical attention.'

General de Wet walked over to have a look at the three British men with their faces crushed in by bullets.

'Ah, they won't make it, De la Rey. They won't.'

'So, what should we do? Do we leave them here to die?' asked De la Rey, unaware of the protocol in such a situation.

'No, you can't leave them here,' General de Wet said. 'You must finish them off.'

De la Rey looked at him, shocked. So did the British men who had been taken prisoner.

'Finish them off, De la Rey. After all, they are trespassing heathens. Greedy, godless creatures driving us off our land, intent on stealing our gold. Finish them off! Don't you know who you are? You are a De la Rey. You are a fighter. You are a liberator.'

The Boer men started chanting: 'De la Rey! De la Rey!'

De la Rey slowly took aim at one of the men.

'What are you doing?' cried General de Wet. 'You can't waste bullets. Use one of their bayonets. There's a fresh British bayonet. Use it.'

De la Rey looked up at his commander, and so did the rest of the men. De Wet glared back at them. De la Rey picked up the bayoneted weapon and walked gingerly towards one of the men, who was now sobbing.

One of the Brits put up a brave face, and started swearing. 'Yer fucking bastairds. Even the African savages are better 'n yer!'

De la Rey drove the bayonet in, once. The soldier shouted defiantly, 'Long live the Queen, yer bastairds!'

De la Rey drove the bayonet in again. Blood bubbled out of

the captive's mouth. Now the two other men were trying to crawl away from him. He reached one of them, drove the bayonet through his heart. The prisoner went limp immediately. By the time he reached the third man, De la Rey himself was possessed of an anger he had never experienced before. He stabbed the man six times – the stubborn mustard-eating, cucumber-munching, tea-drinking bastard – before he finally expired.

There was a momentary silence from the ranks. Then someone started chanting De la Rey's name. The rest of his comrades joined in.

As the Boers went about raiding the enemy's wagons, the chant resounded across the veld: 'De la Rey! De la Rey! De la Rey!'

Until he got drafted into the commando, De la Rey hadn't realised what a noble surname he had. General de Wet's allusion to the importance of his name had left him confused. The issue resurfaced when the commandos were sitting around a fire one day, eating the provisions they had inherited from the vanquished British in Kroonstad. One soldier said absent-mindedly, 'Ah, if General de la Rey were here, the Englishman would be shitting in his pants.'

'But we have Cornelius in our midst,' someone said. 'He should start leading us one of these days. He is a De la Rey, after all.'

'Yes, the De la Reys were born to lead.'

'Lead us, De la Rey!'

The soldiers broke into song about De la Rey's valour. Cornelius' face reddened at this. What made him most uncomfortable was that he did not know who this De la Rey was. He soon regained his composure, as he didn't want to betray his ignorance. He put out his questions carefully, tactfully, as one would lay traps for unsuspecting prey to find out more about the supposedly great man. Without realising it, his fellow soldiers taught him that there once lived in these parts of the country a brave soldier by the name of General Jacobus Herculaas de la Rey. Or, as he was famously known, Koos de la Rey, the Lion of the West. General de la Rey was one of the leading figures of the struggle for Boer independence from British oppression. A veteran of many battles; against the Basotho in 1865, against the baPedi, led by King Sekhukhune, in 1876.

Cornelius, who kept in his pocket a small book in which he drew pictures of people, would sometimes sit down, close his eyes and conjure up the face of General de la Rey, based on the rough descriptions handed down to him by the various raconteurs. Then he would painstakingly draw the figure of the general with an exaggerated moustache and strong facial features. He never forgot to include a rifle and a bandolier in all the pictures that he drew of General de la Rey. The drawings proved popular – in fact, so popular that some of the men offered Cornelius portions of their meals in exchange for drawings of themselves. These he rendered on pieces of paper brought to him by customers who wanted their portrait drawn. Many of his models were easy-going fellows who accepted the artist's interpretation of themselves. Others would moan, 'Why did you make me look sour-faced like an Englishman? Where are my lips? All I see here is a thin, mean line where my lips are supposed to be.'

'Surely I don't have a nose as flat as a kaffir's?'

'Everyone all over the Free State knows my beard is bigger

than Paul Kruger's. So, why give me a half-hearted beard? I'm not paying for this.'

One afternoon he quietly offered to draw a picture of the veldkornet's wife. The military officer, a tall, scrawny man with startled eyes and a fierce moustache, responded in his quarrelsome voice, 'How could you possibly draw a picture of my lovely wife, seeing you've never laid your eyes on her?'

'Sir, just describe Mrs Breytenbach for me. Tell me in detail what she looks like. And I shall render her beautiful face – I am guessing she's beautiful – on my piece of paper. Let me try, please, sir.'

Haltingly at first, Breytenbach started describing his wife's facial features. As he warmed up to the process, shimmering nuggets of description spouted from his mouth. And at long last, like someone coming to rest after a spirited sprint, he exhaled deeply, threw back his head and looked up at the sky.

Later, a beatific smile spread over the veldkornet's face as he leaned over De la Rey's shoulder to admire the magical feat the young man was performing with his pen and paper.

When the drawing was complete, Breytenbach showed it around. The men beamed at the image. After he'd left the circle of men drinking coffee, two soldiers who had actually met the veldkornet's wife in the past wondered aloud who had the more vivid imagination: the commander himself or De la Rey. The beautiful angel in that picture would run for cover if she were to meet the real Mrs Breytenbach.

For the next few weeks, De la Rey was the veldkornet's favourite. The older man shared his private bottle of brandy with him. He gave him generous cuts of biltong from his own knapsack. He waxed lyrical about the days he started courting Mrs Breytenbach. The beautiful drawing of Mrs Breytenbach inspired other men to make special requests. They asked De la Rey to draw pictures of their children, girlfriends, wives, favourite horses. In turn they rewarded him with their own share of food or drink. This activity offered De la Rey respite from the burden of being a De la Rey.

But De la Rey knew that the novelty of his drawings would soon wear off. The men would again remember that they were sitting with a somewhat reluctant warrior in their midst. For his part, De la Rey was spending sleepless nights trying to come up with a plan to make his comrades realise that he was not about to be leader of the commando, as they seemed to be suggesting. When he broached the subject one night, the soldiers shook their heads and said, 'Ag, shame, he is as modest as the General himself. Look at that beard. Look at those locks of hair. Look at those arms, those muscles, those sledgehammer hands, those sausage fingers.' And they broke into song, in praise of General de la Rey. Cornelius de la Rey sighed in despair.

By this time, the commandos, emboldened by their success in Kroonstad and Sanna's Post, had moved bravely southwards to meet the approaching Brits. Along the way, they could see the damage that the enemies had wrought. Some homesteads were still smouldering from British torches. At one stage they passed a village and noticed a group of men – clearly burghers by their dress – digging a trench. De la Rey thought it did not make sense, digging in the middle of the bush. What could they be planting? Then he noticed a mound of corpses nearby. The sweet-sour miasma of rotting flesh hit his nostrils and he recoiled, holding in his breath. His quick farmer's eye reckoned that the mound was perhaps ten metres by eight metres, the bodies piled four or five high.

De la Rey looked away from the corpses, towards the men who were digging what he realised was a mass grave. Arms rippling with muscles, bodies glistening with sweat, the men plunged their shovels into the soft, yielding earth. They moved like ghosts, mechanically, soundlessly, in the sweltering heat. There was something mournful, something ritualised about their movement. The loud buzzing of green flies muffled the rasp of shovels eating into the ground. Still holding his breath, De la Rey tried not to glance at the corpses, to look stoically ahead. But his eyes strayed and lit upon a tiny head. She could have been ten or eleven, with a heart-shaped face – now chalky and pale – her eyes staring pleadingly into space, her raven hair peeking out from beneath her off-white bonnet. De la Rey vomited and more men followed suit. Involuntarily, De la Rey's gaze returned to the child's face. He saw that she was resting on the chest of a black woman whose hair and cap looked to have been singed by fire.

Some soldiers walked towards the man who seemed to be in charge to find out what had happened to these Boer women and children and their servants. De la Rey recalled having seen one or two smouldering remains of farmhouses on the way and, like his brothers-in-arms, he wanted to know what was going on. But the veldkornet would have none of it. Before De la Rey's comrades could find out what had happened, Breytenbach gave the order for the men to move on, move on. They continued on their journey south. Their shock turned to anger. Their anger metamorphosed into impatience. They had to get the Brits.

A few days later, still in early April, they hit the Brits for the third time – this time at Reddersburg, about thirty-five miles south of Bloemfontein. Again, when the fighting started, De la Rey found himself inhabiting the body of a person he did not recognise, as he had when he'd killed the three British prisoners. He shouted as he poured bullets at the enemy.

At the end of the skirmish, five hundred and ninety rednecks lay dead. When De la Rey emerged from his trance, he looked at his hands and the corpses, and shivered. But when he remembered how scared he had been just before he started firing away, he smiled. It was with pride that he saw the arrogant British who had survived the slaughter handing themselves over. He wanted to cheer as they were driven at gunpoint to a farm controlled by the Boers.

With the British prisoners safely confined behind barbed wire, the victorious Boers broke into song as they invaded the provisioning wagons of the enemy. The leaders of the campaign had to remind the men that it was too early for them to become complacent. While De Wet's troops were making a few dents in the armour of the Brits, who were marching northwards and leaving a trail of destruction in their wake, the fact was that the Brits still had the upper hand in the republic of the Free State. The British scorched earth strategy – where they burned down properties belonging to burghers like De la Rey – intensified. Women, children and the elderly were being consigned to concentration camps.

The images of the dead men he had seen in the past three battles still loomed large in De la Rey's mind, as well as the picture of those men digging the mass grave. And the image of the little Boer girl's frozen, chalky face.

Haunted by what he had seen and his own part in the bloodshed, De la Rey began to think about the possibility of desertion.

The indignation against the British oppressors was the glue that kept De la Rey and his countrymen together, the potent pot of mampoer that they all drank from. It was what they had in common. Otherwise, the Boers had a mixed and varied ancestry. They descended mainly from the Dutch, but there was French Huguenot blood too, and some German and Italian. Some even had genes that bowed to the gods of the Khoisan or Bushman. Some had the blood of Malay slaves, which is why some had the lips, nose and buttocks of the black African that they so reviled. But now they were Afrikaners. Europeans in Africa. The white tribe of Africa rebelling against British colonialism and injustice.

De la Rey was becoming increasingly despondent and afraid the others would notice it. As the days went on, he realised that his mood was beginning to affect his comrades, yet his desperation continued to grow. Finally, he decided that he could no longer undermine the morale of his fellow countrymen: the only way out of this was to desert.

An opportunity offered itself one day when his company put up camp alongside a muddy stream a few days after their encounter with the Brits at Reddersburg. While his comrades slept, De la Rey crept away, grabbed a horse and fled. He rode in what he presumed to be the east, the general direction of Basutoland. At daybreak he found a clump of trees with a clearing in the middle, where he slept fitfully for the rest of the day, while his horse grazed nearby. He couldn't believe how much his life had changed almost overnight. From an innocent burgher whose experience of shedding blood had been limited to killing rabbits and antelope, he had become fluent in the language of violence. He had butchered men who, individually, had not done anything wrong to him. And now, he had deserted, although he knew that desertion was punishable by death.

When night fell, he resumed his journey. Even though it was

dark, he rode carefully in wooded territory, avoiding open spaces.

He was armed with his Krupp and his hessian bag with his prized possessions, which included a flask of mampoer, some food, a water bottle, tobacco, his sketchbook and some loose pieces of blank paper.

At daybreak, he hid in the bush again. He must have finally fallen asleep because when he next blinked his eyes, night had fallen. Time to move on. He got up stiffly and went to where he had left his horse. It was lying on its side, dead. He checked it for injuries. There were none, but foam pooled around its mouth. It must have died of sheer exhaustion. He'd ridden the poor thing to death. De la Rey collapsed next to it, sobbing. In between his bitter sobs, he spoke to the horse, apologising to it, begging it to get up even though he knew it couldn't. Stroking it, singing to it, telling it stories, weeping, until – his strength and resolve gone – he fell asleep next to it.

CHAPTER 5

The next thing he knew, De la Rey was being carried. Slowly, his mind began to clear. He could hear voices. His eyes opened gradually. Then he jolted, immediately remembering he was a soldier. The Brits must have caught up with him as he slept.

'*Los my! Los my, jou moerskont rooinek!*' De la Rey cried in his mother tongue for his tormentors to let him go.

To his surprise and mild disappointment, the Brits had not tied his hands together. Didn't they know he was a De la Rey? A clan made famous by the Lion of the West, whose name was spoken with reverence all over the land? Why hadn't they tied his hands together when they'd captured him?

'Ah, he is awake,' one of the voices said in Sesotho. De la Rey frowned, recognising the native language. So, these were no Brits, after all. Maybe Sesotho-speaking spies working for the Brits? De la Rey suspected the Brits were getting everyone to do their dirty work for them.

'Put him down,' said another voice. 'Let him be, let's hear him talk.'

He looked about him. One of his captors was pointing a gun at him; his own gun, the beloved Krupp which had served him so well in the past. One of the men was carrying his bag of provisions too.

'Who are you?' he said in his rusty Sesotho. 'Why are you selling me out to the Brits? I thought we were all in this together, the natives and the Boers against the Brits.'

They laughed at him.

Someone mimicked him, '*We're all in this together, the natives and the Boers against the Brits*. Did you hear him, my dear brothers? Since when are Boers calling us natives? Don't you usually call us kaffirs, heathens?'

The group of men were armed with spears and knobkerries. The leader motioned for one of the men to lead the way. They started walking.

The leader said, 'Morena, we pray and hope you don't try running away. Because if you do, you'll leave us no option but to shoot you. With your own gun.'

De la Rey swallowed audibly.

Tucked away at the foot of a mountain, the small village that they reached was one of the few that had escaped the attention of the British. Many other villages had been torched by the British, and the inhabitants rounded up and sent to concentration camps, their livestock impounded by the insatiable British army.

When they got to the village – a collection of grass-and-mud huts – the leader ordered some young girls to prepare drinking water, food and a bed for the stranger. The leader kept De la Rey's belongings. Two men were assigned to stand guard at the entrance to his hut at all times. De la Rey was left to rest for the night.

The following day, he was called to some kind of square where he sat facing the men of the village. The interrogation began, lead by the chief.

'I am Motaung, leader of the Bataung people of this village.

As I said to you yesterday, we know there is a war going on. We are not in the least interested in the fight. But we know that poor people like us, who have nothing to do with the fighting, are being punished by both sides. As they say, when two elephants fight, the grass suffers. I believe my own children, who were out there working for the white man, have been eaten by this war that we cannot make sense of. They are somewhere inside a concentration camp. If they are still alive. Now, we do not want any problems with the white man. With either the Boers or the British. You can see, I am an old man whose dying wish is to see this village remain untouched by this white madness. Are you still with me, Morena?'

'Yes.'

'Now, because it is not our intention to have trouble with either of the warring sides, we have to ask you some questions. We expect you to be as truthful as you can be. Do you understand?'

'Yes, I do.'

'Who are you?'

'Cornelius de la Rey ...'

'De la Rey? De la Rey?' the men asked in unison, turning to each other.

Leader Motaung raised his hand to silence the men and continued questioning his captive. 'Are you related to the famous General de la Rey?'

De la Rey smiled. 'I've never met the man, but I know of him. You could say we are related, seeing we're all Boere ...'

'So why are you here? You should be there in the war.'

De la Rey sighed. 'I think I've exhausted all the commitment that I had to the war effort—'

'I am disappointed!' cried one man. 'You're a born fighter, a

39

war machine, look at you. And you run away from the fight like a dog with its tail between its legs.'

'And you have in your possession such a big gun,' shouted another man.

'Hold it! Hold it!' Ntate Motaung said, raising his hand to restore order. He spoke harshly. 'We are not children here. Nor are we women. If you have something to say to this man, say it through me. Respect the rest of the men gathered here.'

The two men who had transgressed got up with their heads bowed. 'Oh, you Great Lion! You who grew up when we were but spittle in our fathers' mouths, do forgive us our transgression.'

Ntate Motaung motioned them to sit down. He turned to De la Rey. 'What else do you have to say for yourself?'

'One thing I can say for myself is this: I am not a traitor. I will never turn myself over to the rednecks.' He spat on the ground. 'That man Milner has spilled enough of my people's blood. Someone must stop him. But what I know is that I am not the one to stop him. I am not a fighter.'

'We are not questioning your commitment to your people's cause. All we want to establish is: are you truly who you say you are? Do you not harbour any other nefarious plans that might jeopardise this community?'

'I am not armed, so how can I harm you?'

'You can run away and go alert your friends about us.'

'I don't even know where I am, so how can I run away? I have no weapon to hunt or protect myself with. I would probably die in the veld.'

'Morena,' said Ntate Motaung with finality, 'we'll have to keep you under close guard. For your safety, and ours too.'

~

In the days and weeks that followed, the villagers were pleasantly surprised that De la Rey was friendly, open, and did not
seem eager to go home, which assured them he was neither a
spy nor a soldier sent on a reconnaissance mission. Nor did he
seem bothered by the endless questions thrown at him, nor by
what he was offered to eat or drink. He wanted to be one of
them, it seemed. Like them, he wanted to stay in this wilderness
that was still untouched by the war. Some of the old men who
could speak the white man's language thought he was not
right in the head – sometimes he would start screaming about
fire and guns. Nevertheless, they were impressed by his hunger
for knowledge, his eagerness to improve his grasp of their
language.

For his part, De la Rey began to feel at home in the village,
in Ntate Motaung's compound. Ntate Motaung was clearly a
man of means; his compound was almost a village on its own. It
had many houses in it, for he had many wives. Sotho culture
dictated that each wife be given an individual house for herself
and her younger children. Over and above his many wives,
Ntate Motaung had, over the years, acquired a number of
hangers-on – relatives who had been displaced by the war,
destitute widows of relatives, servants and their children,
grandchildren whose parents had been killed in the war or were
imprisoned in some concentration camp.

And now, De la Rey himself had been added to the detritus
that had gathered at Ntate Motaung's door. Everyone called De
la Rey Morena Rey – Morena being the local word for 'sir' or
'chief'. People in the village, as elsewhere in black Africa, always
treated strangers with respect and deference. They would make
sure to feed the stranger before they themselves ate, for they
believed their ancestors' adage, which held: 'the stomach of a

traveller is as small as a bird's kidney' – feeding a traveller will not make you starve.

Ntate Motaung took apart De la Rey one day and declared, 'In this community, my dear Morena Rey, we don't want men walking around with unruly beards and mops of hair where birds or snakes can nest. You have to do something about your hygiene.'

De la Rey's face turned red immediately, to the amusement of the chief.

The following morning, De la Rey was woken up by a noise he hadn't heard in a long time. But when it permeated his shelter, he recognised it immediately. It was the sound of someone sharpening a blade on a whetstone. It put his teeth on edge. When he pushed open the hut's door – a flap made of intricately woven grass – he was startled by what he saw.

Standing in front of his hut was one of the maidens of the huge household. All she had on was a skirt made of cowhide, which was not unusual, as it was how unmarried maidens were supposed to dress. It was, however, unusual for him to stand so close to what, in his culture, would be described as a semi-naked young woman. He tried to look away, but his eyes were arrested by her sharp-pointed breasts and flat stomach.

She said in her language, too fast for him to understand, 'You can't leave until I deal with you.' She had to repeat it slowly. Having grown up among the Basotho on his father's farm, De la Rey had a good grasp of the language, but he was not as fluent as he was in his mother tongue.

When the meaning of her short speech sunk in, he replied in Afrikaans, 'What do you mean you have to *deal with me*?'

She merely looked at him. He stared back at her. For the first time, he noticed she was carrying a sharp blade. So startled had he been by the sight of her, he had forgotten about the sound that had roused him. She explained, 'It's clean and efficient. I've just sharpened it. Papa said you can't venture out before I shave your beard.'

'What? No! A woman can't shave me.'

'I'm not a woman, I'm a girl. It's my job to shave you, seeing that you don't have a woman of yours here. My mother taught me how. Every time she shaves papa's beard, she calls me to come and observe. I've shaved him under mother's supervision – twice already.'

'I'm not your papa. I'm not your relative either.'

'Well, for as long as you stay here, you're one of us.'

'Let me go, girl.' He put his foot forward, but there was no way he could leave the hut without having to touch her body, to push her away. That he was not about to do. What if this was a trap? He had heard that these people had strange rules. In the native community, he had been told, you could be sentenced to death for *looking* at a person the wrong way.

Now he realised he was desperate to take his customary morning leak. But this girl was standing firmly in front of the entrance.

'I need to go and relieve myself.'

'Give me your word you'll come back so I can shave you. Because if you don't then I'll be in trouble with my *mme*. She said I had to shave your beard. Today.'

'Do you want me to relieve myself here in front of you?'

She giggled, covering her mouth with one hand, and made way. He ran towards the wood on the periphery of the yard. He saw some girls emerge from a section of the wood, laughing out loud.

When he came back, the maiden was waiting under a tree.

She had an old enamel basin with water in it. Next to it was an upturned drum which she had covered with a cushion for him to sit on.

'Sit,' she said sternly. One of the girls from earlier came towards them carrying a bunch of fresh green leaves. She gave the leaves to the girl with the blade, then left.

De la Rey sat down gingerly. The girl put her blade on a piece of cured cowhide. She took a handful of leaves and rubbed them vigorously together. Some sap oozed from the crushed leaves into the basin. She stirred the sap into the water, working up a lather.

One other girl brought another basin, a smaller one, with water in it. She placed it in front of the girl with the blade, who knelt on a sheepskin in front of De la Rey so that their faces were only a few centimetres apart. Her musky smell entered his nostrils.

He blurted out, 'How do the men around here manage ...'

'How do men manage what?'

He wanted to ask: *How do the men around here manage not to get aroused when they see women and girls walking around bare-breasted?* But he kept the thought to himself.

The girl shook her head. She scooped a bit of water and started wetting De la Rey's face, gently, careful not to flood his lap.

Next, she scooped a handful of lather and started applying it into the thick tufts of hair on his face. Her fingers penetrated the thick knots of beard, reaching the skin, rubbing and massaging it in deft strokes. He relaxed, closed his eyes, his back against the tree. She kept working the lather onto his face until it had formed stiff peaks.

Then she got up and took two steps back and stood there,

admiring her handiwork. He opened his eyes, disappointed that the soothing finger play on his face had come to an end.

She instructed, 'Stay put. I am coming back. The lather must sink in. Sit still.'

De la Rey frowned. Who was he now? Where was he? Allowing himself to be touched so intimately by one of them. By leaving him stranded, helpless among the godless ones, maybe God was punishing him for deserting, betraying his people.

When the young woman came back a few minutes later, he asked her name.

'Matshiliso. Everyone calls me Tshili.'

'How old are you?'

'Fifteen.'

He muttered to himself in Afrikaans, 'I would have thought eighteen, even twenty.'

'And how old are you?'

'I'm twenty-five.'

'*Iyhoo!*' she exclaimed. 'That old?'

De la Rey let out a short laugh, never having been called old before in his life. 'Do you go to school?'

'Have you seen any school around?'

'But you can count?'

'Yes I can. I can count to a hundred. Can you count to a hundred?'

Of course he could count to a hundred. Not only could he count to a hundred, he could also read the Bible, or at least some passages in Dutch. He had been told that there now existed a Bible in the Afrikaans language, but he had yet to see it. His mother frowned every time somebody mentioned the Afrikaans Bible. 'Ag, nee, Afrikaans is but a new language. I was born speaking Dutch. Now they want us to read the Word of God in Afrikaans. I wonder if God has learned Afrikaans yet. I'll stick to my *Bijbel*.'

When he recovered from his reverie, he realised that she was staring straight into his eyes.

'What's wrong?' he asked.

'Your eyes.'

'What about them?'

'I hadn't noticed their colour before … They're so … grey. So fierce.'

'So do you like them?'

'They look like a cat's.'

'That's not a nice thing to say.'

'At night, do they shine like a cat's? Or do they shine like a lion's?'

De la Rey decided to ignore her. He concentrated, instead, on her hips and firm legs.

Without wasting time, she reached for the blade. 'When I'm done with you, my brothers will stop calling you Makhupakatse.'

'What exactly does Makhupakatse mean?'

She laughed out loud. 'You like the sound of it?'

'Makhupakatse. Makhupakatse.' De la Rey rolled the words on his tongue. 'Maybe. What does it mean?'

'It means: man who's holding a cat in his mouth. On account of your big whiskers, you see.'

He could only laugh.

'Sit up straight now. Don't move, or we cut your skin.' Then she muttered in her mother tongue, 'Cat's eyes.'

He opened his mouth to say something.

'Shhh,' she immediately said. With her left hand, she pulled tight the area of his left cheek where she was to apply the blade, while her right hand dragged the blade across his skin. He was tense, his eyes watering. After a few strokes, however, he began to relax. He leaned back against the tree, eyes closed and was soon asleep.

The blade worked: whap-whap. A cow mooed out there in the distance. The blade worked: whap-whap. A cock crowed. The blade worked: whap-whap.

Deep in dreamland, De la Rey tensed. Matshiliso paused, lest she cut his face. The bad dream passed and he relaxed again. She resumed her task.

A little later, when her cousins and friends who'd been watching from their hideout had long since left, having lost interest, Matshiliso stood up and admired her handiwork. She was entertained by the contrast between the areas she had just shaved and the rest of his face. The newly shaved places were very light, while the rest of his face was darker, leathery.

The shave had softened his looks. But the huge mane of hair spoiled everything, it had to go. She'd never seen a white man with a clean-shaven head. It was a look that worked quite well among members of her own community – in fact, it was especially favoured by younger men. This man wasn't too old. Wasn't even married, from what she could tell. She decided to get rid of that unseemly fiery bush of hair.

She started stealthily hacking at his hair, unsure of how he would react. But she felt that the unruly locks of dirty hair, which smelled of wood smoke and God knows what else, and were possibly crawling with lice and other wildlife, undermined her artistic efforts. She wanted to be able to take unreserved pride in her work, to be able, when she saw him walking down to the river the following day, to point him out proudly to her sisters and friends.

When the long, flowing mane was gone, and the hair was shorter, but crudely and unevenly cut, she started working lather into his scalp. He snored away peacefully, so gentle was she. Then the blade started working again: whap-whap. She was humming a lullaby, softly under her breath, as she continued working the blade: whap-whap-whap. Pause. Hum. Whap-whap.

Finished, she stood up, stepped back and surveyed the results. She was struck by the fact that without the locks of hair, he looked just like somebody she knew. If she could apply some ochre to that face, it would look just like a regular Mosotho face. Pity she couldn't carve the nose into submission. She stepped forward and touched his left cheek, running her hand smoothly over it.

His eyelids fluttered open. He sat up quickly, confused, and touched his face. 'Ah, yes, you were shaving my beard. Feels good.'

Smiling, she backed away from him, creating a safe distance. He wrinkled his nose. Then his hand flew to his mouth, a feminine gesture that made her snigger. 'Oh, no, oh, no! No, you didn't. You did not. My moustache! What have you done? You said you were going to shave my beard, not my *moustache*. Not my *moustache*.'

She picked up the water basin and started backing away from him. He paused, feeling an itch on his head. His hand flew to scratch the itchy area. Then his two hands patted his head. '*My Here!*' he cursed in Afrikaans. *My dear God!* Then he switched back to his brand of Sesotho: 'What have you done? What have you done, you Jezebel, you Delilah?'

He stormed towards her. She immediately emptied the bucket of water into his face, laughing uproariously. Blinded by the suds, he halted and rubbed his face with his hands. Like a gazelle, she started running in zigzag fashion. Boiling with righteous indignation, he started after her, the wind whistling in his ears and caressing his bare scalp – an unfamiliar and not too unpleasant sensation. He was pelting her with his choicest insults as he bumbled after her: 'Bloody Dingaan's concubine! Queen Victoria's evil cat!' He was determined to get his hands on her. She deserved a serious spanking. How would he face the world without a moustache?

There clearly was no way he could catch her. He was a big man, and she was tiny and light on her feet. But his anger impelled him to carry on. As he put his right foot forward, it caught on a stump of a tree that had been chopped down a long time ago. He stumbled, almost landing face first on uneven ground, but he righted himself just in time.

'I'm going to chop your hands off, you donkey's jaw. You devil's daughter!'

She was laughing as she zigzagged forward, making him dizzy. Then, playfully, she turned to him and pelted him with her own choice insult: '*Marete a mmao!*' – *Your mother's testicles!*

She was running down the slope, with the river shimmering in the distance. Huffing and puffing, he thought he was catching up with her. The last time he had engaged in this kind of physical exertion was when a group of them – four, five members of the Boer commando – got chased by an enraged buffalo as they were walking to camp.

A group of boys driving their cattle from the river saw the man chasing the girl and shouted, 'Hey, who are you? Why are you chasing her?'

They pulled out their slingshots and started attacking him, but missed with each shot.

One of the boys recognised him. 'Stop shooting, stop shooting! He is the white man that lives with the Motaungs. But what's happened to him? He's got no hair. The beard is gone. Hey, Ralefahlana!' The other boys took up the chant, a popular insult for a bald man, 'Ralefahlana, Ralefahlana, who stole you hair?'

Hearing the derisive taunts, De la Rey turned his eyes towards the boys. It was then that he lost his footing. He tripped on a rock, fell, and started rolling downhill, landing with a painful thud along some rocks on the riverbank. He staggered to his feet, dazed. There was blood on his left cheek where a rock or a sharp tree stump had cut him. He touched his face, and saw the blood on his hand. He shook his head as if to clear his thoughts. He blinked repeatedly and saw Matshiliso standing fearfully on the bank.

She approached him, apologising. 'Morena Rey, *tswarelo, tswarelo!*'

He smiled at her. 'I don't know what I was doing playing children's games.'

'Come, let me clean that wound.'

'Don't worry, it's nothing.'

She looked at him sternly. 'I said come!'

He obeyed. She made him kneel on a rock near the water. She took off his shirt, tossed it on the grass, then scooped some water with her hand and washed the cut. Thankfully, it was not deep, it was only a negligible graze. 'You people have weak skin. It bleeds so easily. I thought it was a serious wound.'

When she'd cleaned the wound, she started washing his bare scalp. He enjoyed the feel of her fingernails as she raked them across the naked skin.

'*Tsamayang, lona!*' Matshiliso shouted at the herd boys, who were watching closely, to make them go away.

The boys did not move. She got up and picked up some rocks, which she hurled at them with deadly accuracy. Every time she threw a rock, it found a target. The boys went helter-skelter.

'Hey, you, Kamogelo, come here!' she said, addressing one of the boys.

'But you are going to hit me with a stone!'

'No. Peace time now.' She let the stones fall from her hands. 'Come here. I need to talk to you about something important.'

The boy hesitated, but then he came down the slope, running.

When the boy reached her, she spoke deliberately fast and in obscure Sesotho, so De la Rey couldn't understand. Kamogelo's eyes went big. Then he ran up the slope.

Matshiliso turned to De la Rey. 'Your clothes stink. Take them off.'

'What?'

'I said, take off your clothes so I can wash them here.'

'I'm not going to do that.'

'Then you're not going home.'

'Why not?'

She picked a pebble from a mound she had quickly collected and threw it at him, hitting him on the chest. It stung. 'If you don't take off your clothes I am going to pelt you until you bleed.'

'What are you doing?'

'Take ...' she threw a pebble at him, hit him on the shoulder, 'your ...' another pebble, 'clothes ...' another pebble, 'off.' She hit her target each time.

'Okay, okay, but what am I going to wear while you wash my clothes?'

'My brothers are bringing you a new fresh, beautiful outfit.'

'They don't know my size. I am a big man.'

'It's a one-size-fits-all outfit that they are bringing. Now, take your pants off.'

'Can't do that in front of you.'

'Fine, I'm not looking.' She faced the opposite direction while he quickly took off his veldskoene and pants.

She heard the splash as he dived into the water. She took his clothes, knelt on the flat rock and started washing them. Soap had become scarce since the war started, but a thorough washing with plain water still did wonders. Her hands were well seasoned and practised in washing coarse pieces of cloth. His trousers were tough, but not unmanageable. When the water had seeped deep into the fabric, she got up to pound them against the rock the way she'd been taught.

Months of dirt and grime were visible in the clear water as she bent to her knees again to continue with the last step of the washing process. Satisfied that she had done her best, she raised the shirt to her nose. It smelled of water. She smiled. She moved upstream where there were huge boulders on which the women of the village normally spread out their clothes to dry.

'Tshili!' a voice rang. She turned to see her brother. A mischievous glint in his eye, he said, 'Here's your husband's new outfit.'

'You little mouse, I'm going to get you! Who said he's my husband?' she said, addressing the wind. Her brother had disappeared into the bush nearby.

She sat down and watched De la Rey swimming in the distance. Finally, he started wading towards her. When the water was just above his waist, he shouted, 'Move away from there so I can get out of the water and get dressed.'

'What's wrong with me sitting here?'

'I am naked.'

'So what?'

'Stupid girl, I don't want you to see me without my clothes.'

'Why not?'

'I am saying it one last time: please move away so I can get out of the water.'

'Well, if it pleases you.' She got up and started walking upstream. When she was far upstream, hidden from his view, he quickly got out of the water and rushed towards where she had left the promised outfit. When he reached the bundle on top of the flat rock, his eyes widened. 'What is this?' He picked up the bundle and saw that it was a sack. Many of the men in the village walked around wearing sackcloth: they would take a normal flour or maize sack, cut a hole for the head, and two more holes for arms. In many parts of the Free State, poorer black people were most comfortable in sackcloth. It was only those who had converted to Christianity, those who had some schooling, who wore western clothes. However, he, Cornelius de la Rey, wasn't about to start wearing sackcloth. He was not one of them. Furious, he started shouting, 'Matshiliso!' before remembering he was still naked.

He heard Matshiliso's voice. She was singing a traditional song. Although she was still hidden from view, she was clearly moving towards him. Panicking, he put the sackcloth on. It scratched his bare skin.

Matshiliso, he now saw, was walking towards him completely naked, dragging her cowhide skirt with her left hand.

She beamed. 'That sackcloth was made for you. Isn't it beautiful? I always wondered how a white person would look in sackcloth. You look like an angel that my grandfather reads about in the Bible.'

He looked away, his face reddening. 'Girl, please hide your nakedness.'

'Why? I love the afternoon breeze on my bare skin.'

Still looking away, he repeated, 'Please get dressed. What are people going to say?'

'Your clothes are over there,' she said. 'We'll fetch them tomorrow when they are dry.'

He put on his veldskoene and started walking home up the hill. When she finally caught up with him, she had put her skirt back on.

'Matshiliso, you're a bit unwell in the head, that I can tell you. Anyway, what does that name of yours mean?' he asked in Afrikaans.

She merely looked at him. He asked the question in his shaky Sesotho: 'I know that in African society, every person's name tells a story. What does your name, Matshiliso, mean?'

'Condolences.'

He shook his head. She clearly had not understood him. He repeated, slowly, 'I said, what does your name mean?'

'It means condolences. You know when a person dies, we offer condolences to his family. Don't you white people also condole?'

'Yes, we do. But are you telling me your parents named you *condolences*?'

'A wonderful name, don't you think? Given to me by my grandmother.'

He tried the name in his own language: condolences – *meegevoel*. He chuckled at the thought of an Afrikaner mother calling out to her child to come and eat: '*Meegevoel, kom eet! Meegevoel!*'

As if reading his thoughts, she said, 'You are most welcome

to name your first child Matshiliso, so you can always remember me, this crazy Mosotho girl.'

He looked at her. They stopped walking and stared at each other for a long time. He looked away first. She took his hand in hers and they continued walking home.

'Matshiliso?'

'Yes?'

'What's the name of this river?'

'Oh, you want to know the name of the river so you can plan your escape?'

'Nonsense. Tell me the name of the river.'

'Mohokare.'

De la Rey was surprised it had taken him so long to find out where exactly he was. Mohokare was the Sesotho name for the Caledon River, which ran along the border between the Free State and Basutoland.

'Mohokare,' he said under his breath.

CHAPTER 6

Settling into the rhythm of village life took De la Rey a while. As a member of the Boer commando, he was used to waking up at four in the morning, at which time the camp commander would lead the men in prayer. They then would start their physical training, followed by quick ablutions. The senior soldiers would afterwards regale the men with stories – recalling the highlights of their careers or the achievements of brave soldiers of old – in order to keep everyone in high spirits. A simple breakfast, mostly bread with jam and coffee, would ease the men into the new day, as the sun began to climb. By the time the sun was nice and warm on the men's skin, the scouts who had left the previous evening to seek out intelligence on British positions and movements would appear on the horizon.

Now, having transplanted himself to this village, De la Rey did not know what to do with himself. By the time the village cockerels made their clarion call for everyone to get up, he would have long woken up. But he had no reason to abandon the warmth of his sleeping mat. To do what? So he stayed put, tossing and turning, and listened to the sounds of the morning. But, increasingly, his first thoughts were with Matshiliso.

As he lay on his mat one morning, he recalled how, two weeks ago, he had stumbled upon her one night by accident.

She was sitting on a rock down at the river, singing a sad song, her face turned to the sky. The song was almost a whisper, but there were occasions when her voice rose with sudden urgency before falling away mournfully. He had stood there, entranced, before he started feeling guilty, and walked away. The following evening, he had returned to the river. As fate would have it, she was there, on the exact same rock. It was as if she had been sitting there since the previous night. Again, she was singing. She abruptly stopped, and turned around. It was too late for him to hide.

'Morena Rey, why are you intruding on my private moment? Have you no shame eavesdropping on other people's conversations?'

'I ... I did not mean to ... Eavesdropping? But ... You were simply singing to the stars. Ah ...' He paused and looked up at the sky. 'I can see why you're so taken with the stars. They are beautiful.'

She stood up and started walking away. He followed at a safe distance, begging for forgiveness. She obliged, smiling privately to herself.

The following evening they found themselves back at the river. Except this time they were talking cordially. Matshiliso explained to him that this was her private moment with the parents she had lost. 'They are up there,' she said, pointing. 'Can you see them?'

'Yes, I can. They are moving slowly towards one another.'

'You can even tell they are moving?'

'Yes, I can.'

In the days that followed, they would rendezvous at the same spot. They told each other stories. They laughed. But mostly she sang, offering her song to the stars, and he listened.

As he listened to the sounds of the early morning, he thought of how beautiful those moments were, with her at his side, the stars looking on. Sometimes they held hands; other times he would sit on the ground with his back against their rock and she would lay her head on his lap. He would slowly run his fingers through her thick hair as she sang softly to the stars above. When the night breeze got too chilly, they would stand up reluctantly and walk back home.

De la Rey got up from his sleeping mat, stretched and yawned. In the distance, he could hear the river singing with undisturbed clarity, its monotonous music punctuated by the song of birds. Other noises soon emerged from all over the village, growing in volume as daylight began to declare its dominion over land: some young men whistling shrilly, as if in competition with each other, while others chanted praises to the cows that they were about to start milking. Soon enough, the air would be alive with a strange kind of melody: *klo-klo-klo*. De la Rey would soon learn that this was the music made by sharp jets of milk escaping the udder of a cow being milked, the streams of milk hitting the bottom of the wooden pail. *Klo-klo-klo-klo*, sang the pail.

Of course De la Rey had no idea what village life had been like before the war. What he witnessed when he arrived was a people unified in poverty and desperation. But soon enough, his impressions were replaced by those of plenitude and expansiveness. This touched De la Rey himself so that he began to wake up every morning with a smile, ready to face the day, and whatever it had in store for him. He would get up from his sleeping mat, stretch himself and yawn noisily. He would then gather his sleeping mat and the cured cowhide which he used as a blanket. He would put his sackcloth on, pound his sleeping mat and blanket against the wall of his hut and then roll them into a neat pile, which he placed alongside the wall. Before he left his sleeping quarters for the day, he would have a look at the latest drawing he had been working on the previous night. Then he would walk outside and inhale the fresh, crisp breeze.

On seeing De la Rey, the girls pounding the grain would pause from their labour. They would greet him shyly, covering their mouths with their hands as they gossiped about him. By this time, the young boys who looked after the cattle would have long left the compound, having taken the livestock to pasture. Older women would be sweeping the yard, or feeding wood into the communal fire. Old men would get out and inspect their horses, sometimes riding down to the river to water them. But riding long distances was no longer allowed, as the region was in the grips of war. It was better to roam around the confines of the village, hidden away from the rest of the country by the mountain and the woods which formed a natural perimeter wall around the settlement.

Having exchanged pleasantries with some of the girls and the old women around the yard, De la Rey would run down the slope towards the river, where he would take a bath in the shallows.

On this morning, he had left the village at daybreak. He was going about his ablutions when he felt something sting him on his exposed buttocks. He turned around to see Matshiliso with a group of her age-mates. They laughed out loud as he fumbled around the rocks for his sackcloth, in a desperate attempt to cover his nakedness.

Matshiliso said, 'How many times do I have to tell you not to wash your dirty self here? This is where we fetch our drinking water. If you want to wash, you go downstream. Over there.' She pointed in the distance. He mumbled an apology, put on his sackcloth and started walking uphill, back to the village. He'd finished washing anyway.

He decided to take a shorter route that cut through thick bush. There, he stumbled upon an old man squatting next to a tree, singing quietly as he relieved himself. De la Rey's hand instinctively went to his nose and he mumbled an apology.

'Why are you apologising, Morena Rey?' asked the old man. 'Haven't you seen a man emptying his bowels before? As a soldier, you surely must have squatted in front of other men. You know, Morena, daybreak is the perfect time for cleansing one's body of yesterday's impurities. You can't take breakfast while your body is still teeming with the impurities of the previous day. Why don't you join me here?'

De la Rey folded his arms across his chest to avoid his right hand's involuntary move towards his nose.

'Come on,' continued the old man, 'let's do our business at a leisurely pace, no hurry, and let us talk a bit. Pity I forgot my pipe at my house, otherwise I would light it now and we would enjoy it together. Yes, young man, nothing like emptying one's bowels in the presence of a friend. Your waste matter doesn't smell any better than mine, does it now? We are equals when it comes to these smelly matters.'

A carrion crow perched on a tree not too far from where they were. De la Rey shooed it away.

The old man continued, 'Ah, Morena Rey, so impolite of me. I don't think I've ever introduced myself to you. I know you see me around the village, but you don't even know who this old man is. I am Mokhele. Ntate Motaung is my cousin. We'll shake hands properly, some other time ...' His voice trailed off.

De la Rey grunted his acknowledgement.

Mokhele looked at birds flying in formation above, then he spoke, 'Looks like it's going to be a fine day. So, what are you waiting for, young man? Squat over there and rid yourself of yesterday's impurities before you go and take breakfast.'

'But I don't feel like … I mean, I am not pressed.'

'Nonsense. A man is never without some shit in him. Just squat right over there, and you shall see. In any case, this bush here is the communal toilet.'

'Why aren't you using one of the pit latrines? They are all over the village.'

'Ah, those things are for women. Men dispose of their manure right here. You can't just walk through this piece of ground without dropping some manure on it. The Christians would call this our holy ground, or something like that, where we dump that which helps nurture our soil.' The old man laughed at his own joke. 'Come on, squat, young man.'

In spite of himself, De la Rey obeyed. Before he knew it, he was groaning at the pleasurable effort of expelling a turd.

'See? I told you. Even your face is glowing with relief now.'

De la Rey allowed himself a smile of acquiescence. He didn't know what else he could do, or say.

'So, what is this I hear about you and Matshiliso?'

De la Rey looked into the old man's eyes and said, 'What is it that you have heard? Please enlighten me.'

The old man laughed briefly, shook his head, then said, 'You see, in these parts even trees have ears, eyes and mouths. What you do behind those *moluane* trees will finally reach our own ears.'

'Why is it that you always have to speak in riddles? Can't you just get straight to the point?'

'Aaah! The guilty are touchy.'

De la Rey let out a loud, fully rounded, earthy fart.

'I heard that,' the old man said. 'You are being dismissive of me, farting arrogantly like that. I heard that loud and clear.'

De la Rey stifled another one, face reddening.

Mokhele said, 'The tongues in the entire village are already wagging. Warawarawara! Yes, the tongues are dancing with some interesting truths. The village has seen you and the chief's granddaughter stealing into the forest together—'

'What are you—'

Mokhele checked him with an upraised hand, and continued, 'You see, Morena Rey, this is the chief's granddaughter that you are leading astray. From a long time ago, she was earmarked for one of the village sons, and now you come here and steal her purity.'

'But that's a lie.'

'It pains my heart to have to repeat such scandalous stories. But the village can't be wrong.'

'May I ask you to relay the message to whoever is spreading the rumour – I have done no wrong to Matshiliso. Besides, I can't betray your people after all you've done for me – feeding me, sheltering me ...'

'That's exactly why the village is disappointed in you: we shield you, feed you, and you thank us with a bowlful of shit.'

'I—'

'I have lived long enough to know the likes of you. Your brothers start a war. Cowardice takes the better of you. You show a clean pair of heels. Encounter helpless natives, and then take advantage of them. Now you're here playing saviour. Great white saviour. Tomorrow you will claim dominion over our village. Another Jantoni! *Gaat!*'

'You don't understand.'

'We should have killed you the moment we stumbled upon you. I told the others you were a bad omen.'

Mokhele gathered a handful of fresh tree leaves to wipe his behind, got up, and scooped up some soil and twigs to cover his smelly mound.

Then he said, 'The fire which will one day burn you is the same as that which warms you.'

'Wait,' De la Rey called, panic in his voice. The old man disappeared from view.

Finished with what he was doing, De la Rey realised, with shock, that he had not brought some leaves to wipe with. It had not been his intention to relieve himself here in the first place. He looked around for fresh leaves. There were none. He duck-waddled towards a tree and grabbed a branch with big, dark green leaves. He plucked a handful of these and used them to wipe his behind, wincing with pain as they cut him.

When Matshiliso came behind his hut to collect his empty bowl after breakfast, he looked up at her. He wanted to ask her if she had heard the rumours about the two of them. He wanted to ask her to sit down next to him so he could enjoy her presence, to ask her why her smile seemed to outshine the early morning sun and her eyes created in him a thirst he didn't know how to quench. He wanted to tell her that he believed the war would end soon, and things would go back to normal and society would turn over a new leaf. And on that new leaf would be written a new code of behaviour for mankind, where it would be normal for him to sit with her, even hold her hand, without his or her people finding the scene odd and unacceptable. He wanted to ask her so many, many questions.

But his heart thudded with fear when he remembered that

his relationship with Matshiliso was no longer secret. As difficult as it would be to leave her behind, maybe it was time for him to depart from the village. Maybe the war was over. He'd already been there for at least six months. There was not much food to go around, anyway.

After Matshiliso had left his hut, he started out on a fairly long walk. His bag slung over his shoulder, his club in one hand and his sharpened stick in the other, he took purposeful strides, his feet and legs cutting a swathe through thick undergrowth.

CHAPTER 7

When De la Rey arrived at the section of the river where women and girls fetched water for drinking and cooking purposes, he went down on his knees. He took a long leisurely drink of the sweet, clear water. Sated, he stood up and belched. He walked downstream. A fish broke the water surface, startling him.

He passed the spot where villagers took their daily baths. The sun was getting oppressively hot by the time he reached the place where boys watered their cattle. The rocks alongside the river were teeming with wild rats feasting on dried pieces of cow dung. Hours later, he found a cool copse where he put down his bag, club and spear. Sitting on the ground, his back against a tree, he started eating his dried fish.

Why, he wondered, didn't he just call this adventure off now, go back to his own people? Face the consequences of desertion. Confess to temporary insanity. He hoped he would be forgiven – the Boers loved the name De la Rey. Or he could simply surrender to the British – if he could find them. Had the chief heard the rumours about him and Matshiliso? What did he think? Somebody once told De la Rey the chief wouldn't hesitate to stone a man to death for stealing his granddaughter's virginity. Maybe he should simply run for it.

'Dammit, why am I being like this now?' he muttered to himself. 'Why am I even thinking about this? Is it cowardice? Haven't I told Tshili I want to make a wife out of her one day? Come on, don't be a worm! Be a man!'

He decided he would keep going along the banks of the river, keep thinking about things. He was conscious of the fact that he had walked a long way already, unarmed. No rifle. What if …? He let the thought hang.

When he finished his salty dried fish, he was thirsty. He regretted that he hadn't brought a gourd of sour milk. He got up and began to wade through the tall grass, towards the water's edge, then he paused. He had spotted a young steenbok. It was drinking, a mere ten metres from where he had been sitting, hidden from view. He instinctively dived to the ground, reaching for his club and spear. The antelope stopped drinking. It sniffed the air nervously. Suspecting that the breeze was wrong, and that the antelope would smell him, he stayed in a low crouch, coiled like a spring. He clutched his spear in his right hand, his club in his left. The antelope resumed drinking. De la Rey inched his way forward, his spear poised.

He lunged forward. The deer jumped as if shot out of a gun. In its shock and haste it collided with a tree. De la Rey sank his spear into its flank. The animal made a miserable cry as it leaped forward again. De la Rey finished it off with a clean club blow to the head. He knelt beside the steenbok, ensuring it was dead. He had not killed an animal in a long time.

He put his spear and club into his deep bag, which he slung over his shoulder. Then he grabbed his kill by its forequarters and lugged it over his other shoulder. A lesser man would have been forced to drag the dead animal behind him.

He must have been walking for about an hour when he saw

vultures circling in the sky above him. Soon enough there would be hyenas and other opportunistic scavengers, he thought. He stopped briefly and looked at the vultures. Let them come, I'll show them. Then he shouted, 'Come! You bastards, I am not afraid of you! Come and taste my spear and club! What are you waiting for? Come!'

The vultures continued circling, occasionally swooping down towards him, only to soar back up into the sky.

He resumed his walk. At some point, he dropped his prize on the ground and paused for breath. He took time monitoring the movements of the vultures. It gradually dawned on him that it was not he who was their target. They were interested in something else nearby. He followed their movements with his eyes. Slowly, they spiralled down until they settled on what looked like a small village. Not even a village – just a compound with a cluster of rondavels. Alarmed, he dived to the ground, hiding himself in the grass. He could not afford to be seen. Who lived in this village? What if the Boers had taken it over and were using it as their temporary base? From where he lay on his stomach, he watched the vultures as they settled on the open space in the middle of the compound. They started making a racket – shrieking and charging at each other. He stayed put, his eyes raking the scene from left to right. He expected the inhabitants of the compound to emerge from one of the huts and shoo the huge birds away. But, apart from the birds themselves, nothing else moved. After about half an hour, he decided to edge closer to the compound.

Then he understood what the birds were fighting over: a human corpse. He began to retreat, wanting to get away from the scene as fast as his feet could carry him. But he changed his mind. He stood there, trembling. Then, screaming at the top of his voice, he charged forward, his club clasped firmly in his right hand, ready to strike. Disturbed from their late-afternoon feast, the birds erupted into the air with a furious bang of their wings.

Satisfied he had scared the birds away, De la Rey turned his attention to the compound. 'Anybody home?' he shouted. He was beyond caring now, no longer concerned that there might be people watching him from their hiding places. He shouted again, 'Can you hear me? Somebody? Anybody?' No response. He was sweating, tears of anger and frustration blinding him. He couldn't help but take another look at the corpse. It was, by the look of it, the body of an elderly woman. The stomach had been ripped open, the entrails spilling onto the dusty ground. The eyes had been plucked out. The shrivelled breasts had been torn into shreds. There was a broken calabash next to the body. The old woman could have been trying to make her way to the river when she collapsed, possibly hungry, thirsty.

When De la Rey turned, he realised that a new group of vultures had settled on his steenbok, attacking it viciously. He ran towards them, shouting, his club making angry circles in the air. The vultures took their time to rise from the carcass. One of them – a monster with a wingspan of almost two metres – stood defiantly on top of the antelope, its sharp eyes daring him. De la Rey hesitated, but his anger triumphed over his fear. He charged forward, his club cutting a lethal swathe through the air. The bird banged its wings noisily and hurtled towards him, its sharp, blood-drenched talons aiming for his head. He ducked out of the way and hit the bird on the wing. It shrieked as it rose into the air. Then it lost its equilibrium and plopped to the ground.

De la Rey had no time for it. He dragged his kill to the door of one of the huts. Then he started running from hut to hut, shouting, 'Is there anybody home? Hello!' Still no response. He ran towards the next hut. Two corpses in there. Both elderly people – a man and a woman. Huge rats, almost the size of small rabbits, were gorging themselves on the corpses. He kicked with fury at a rat, sending it flying into the air. No time to listen with satisfaction as the rat's body splattered against a wall, exploding. Charging blindly forward, he came to the entrance of a hut. This was where the householders would have kept their grain. He poked his head around. Grain baskets lying in disarray on the floor, communities of rats having a market day on the floor. A bat blindly smashed itself against his face. He cried out in terror. Collapsing onto his knees, he vomited violently, repeatedly.

He ran from hut to hut. No life whatsoever. He had to get out of there. Fast, before dark. In the centre of the compound, the vultures were back, in even bigger numbers. He couldn't trust himself to fight them. He grabbed his steenbok and started moving as fast as he could. His head was aching badly, the noise in his ears growing in volume, drowning out the ear-splitting screech of cicadas and the calls of wild animals as they prepared themselves for the night.

The sun had long set by the time he arrived back at the village. He was drenched in sweat. He stank. Of fear. Of rage. Of death.

News soon spread that Morena Rey had caught an antelope. The older women supervised the cooking of the animal once the boys, working under the supervision of older men, had skinned and quartered the carcass so the pieces could fit into the pots.

While the meat cooked, De la Rey walked to the river, where

he took a long, thorough bath, scrubbing himself with a pumice stone until his body almost bled. He drank so much water his stomach nearly burst. Panting, he walked towards some thick undergrowth a few metres away from the river. There he knelt and drove two fingers to the back of his throat, inducing himself to vomit. When he had heaved almost every drop of water, every morsel of food, from his stomach, he walked back to the river. He drank some more water before trudging back home.

He was heading back to his hut when a figure emerged from the shadows, blocking his path.

'Morena Rey,' said Matshiliso. 'There's a fight brewing in the family.'

'What is it all about?'

'You're the cause. Rather, we are the cause. They want me to stop seeing you.'

He paused for a while. 'If it's unsafe to stay here, then I'll leave.'

'Yes, you must. But I am coming with you.'

'No, you can't do that. It's not safe out there. The war is not yet over. Travelling on my own, I should be safe. I can defend myself. But with you at my side ...' His voice trailed off.

'You don't understand. I think there's something wrong with my tummy ...' She paused. 'After what we did together, that last time.'

'You don't mean ...'

'I told my grandmother about what I was feeling, and she confirmed my suspicions and immediately called a quick meeting with the female elders. Now, they are going to tell the Fathers of the village.'

De la Rey nodded, accepting the situation. 'I understand

where this is leading. But I am sure they like me, and I am prepared to negotiate, make you a proper wife.'

'It will be too complicated and risky. We need to go,' urged Matshiliso.

'But how?'

'I've got a horse all saddled up. Your big gun is ready. We can go right away. We need to go.'

'Shouldn't we think about this a little more first?' De la Rey was flustered.

'If you can't make up your mind, I'll leave you behind with your beloved Elders. I am not prepared to enter into any negotiation with them.'

She made her way into the night, where De la Rey could make out the shape of a horse. He shrugged and followed her, ready to leave the village life behind.

CHAPTER 8

At daybreak the following day, De la Rey decided they should duck into a clump of trees and rest. When they dismounted, he was thrilled to find that Matshiliso had not forgotten his bag, which contained his drawings. She also had a bag of her own, made of goatskin. She dug into it and produced an ankle-length, off-white dress. As she unfurled it, she explained, 'This was made for me by a woman at a church. I'm not going to wear it now. I'll save it for when we get to your home. So they can see I am civilised. I even have a pair of shoes!' Glowing with pride, she showed him the shoes. They were old and weathered, but the soles looked good.

'So, you are well prepared for the journey,' he said, smiling.

They found a clearing in the middle of a clump of trees and laid down a blanket to sleep. When they finally woke up, night was just falling.

'No time for sleeping, man,' she said in a commanding voice. 'We need to move on. The horse is getting impatient.'

'Okay, let me just do something quickly. Sit on that rock over there.'

'We have no time for games.'

'I won't be long, love of my life. I have to capture this moment. Just sit on that tree stump over there.'

He sat on the ground, his back against the rock. Then, armed with a piece of charcoal and a pencil, he started working on his improvised sketchpad.

He saw the oval face framed by flowing braids. The heavy, expressive brows stood sentinel above piercing brown eyes. At first glance the eyes looked fiery and confrontational, but they soon softened and took on a flirtatious aspect.

His hand worked feverishly, transferring the vision onto the blank pages. He saw her high cheekbones, and then, in his mind's eye, her entire face suffused with the light of the many fires she had made to cook for her grandparents, for the entire compound; the fires she had sat around to listen to the village's folktales; the fires she would make in the future to cook for him, for their children, for his own dear mother.

He saw the bridge of her nose, vulnerable, a nose that was neither sharp nor too flat. The nostrils were flared just so, not angrily but somewhat petulantly. And then the lips. Thick, without being meaty. Slightly parted to reveal white teeth. A tiny gap between the front teeth. Below the lips, a sharp chin. Anchoring the head was a long, fragile neck. Collarbones you couldn't miss. A necklace of snail shells.

Just below the necklace the eye plunged into a valley. On either side of the valley were firm, tiny breasts, light brown in colour, with dark nipples.

He was breathless. Blushing, sweating, hands atremble. He had to pause, lest he spoil the entire drawing. He closed his eyes and shook his head.

His Calvinistic sensibility took over: he decided to dress the rest of the body in the flowing robes that some of the older black women wore, the ones who had converted to Christianity. But unlike the robes of the older women, which rendered their bodies shapeless, the picture that he imagined was that of a robe that clung to the contours of Matshiliso's body, making her breasts stand out and her hips more pronounced. And when the robe reached her thighs, it fanned out to the sides like a school bell.

What to do with her arms, her hands? He closed his eyes. He tried to recall the last conversation they'd had. Yes, her voice came back to him: 'When this war is over, I am going to leave this godforsaken place. Go to Bloemfontein itself. Or even Johannesburg. Before the war started, I was learning how to read the Bible and also to write. The church where they used to teach us to write and read is two villages away, but it was shut down when the fighting started. The white man who used to run it left. He did not belong to the Boers, nor did he belong to the British. He was from somewhere over the seas, but he has lived here and can speak our own language. I hope that when the fighting is over, I will resume my lessons in dress-making so I can produce clothes that townspeople can be proud of ...' She showed him what she was holding.

Yes! He started squiggling again. A long graceful left arm, which culminated in a hand holding a Bible. And then a right arm, bent at the elbow, ending in a hand holding an exquisite spear. He paused and smiled. Then the feet? The feet standing on a raised rock and covered with a garland of flowers.

He sat back, and admired the shape of her. 'Ah, my angel.' Then his hand moved quickly to add a halo just above her neat braids. He smiled. Done.

He folded the paper carefully, tucked it into his bag. They rode off.

CHAPTER 9

As they crossed the vast grassland, which was floodlit by a generous moon, De la Rey was floating on the wings of ecstasy. He had no care in the world. He knew the war was not yet over, but the British were way up north already, fighting their way towards the gold mines in the Transvaal. The only people he might bump into were folk like him, Boers on the run. Or black people who had escaped from British concentration camps.

He would fight to the last drop to protect himself and his woman. He couldn't believe the emotion coursing through him – the exultation of returning home with someone he loved. This was new to him, the sense of pride and complete trust in another. To be sure, it did scare him a bit that he had made someone pregnant, that he was capable of bringing to this earth a life. Was he capable of taking up the next logical challenge – raising and guiding the little human being through this increasingly complicated world? He would have to work hard on the family farm to provide for the family – his mother and now his wife and child. He was hoping for a son. After a devastating war, every family needed hard-working sons who would roll up their sleeves, plough the farms, rebuild the communities torn asunder by the conflagration.

He had left his home a young man, unwise in the ways of the world; he was going back there a man who had seen a world many of his friends and relatives could not even dream of. He had left his home a nervous young man being marched off to fight in a war he did not understand, and was now going back home a survivor who had a woman at his side, a woman he would lay down his life for. He came from a community where men never spoke about love. But with Matshiliso, he felt differently. He felt he could defy the unwritten rules of the community and parade his love for this woman.

On the border of his home village of Kareefontein, just forty kilometres south-west of Bloemfontein, they found a bush where De la Rey hid Matshiliso. Then he stealthily walked towards his parents' farm. It was a mystery how the tiny De la Rey farm had been left intact. Everybody knew that Lord Kitchener, the head of the British army – or Public Enemy Number One, to the average Afrikaner – had declared that every farm was an intelligence agency and a supply depot for the Boer rebels. The farms, therefore, had to be destroyed. The women and the elderly white men who'd remained on the farms while the younger men joined the rebels would be taken to concentration camps, which had mushroomed around the country.

After noting that the farm was intact, he stood and considered going into the house to check if his mother was there; to check if she was still alive. But it was dangerous. He had to go back to where he'd left Matshiliso. From their hideout they would watch for movement on the farm to determine if it was safe to enter the house. If, indeed, the house still belonged to his mother. If, indeed, she was still alive. He strode back to where he'd left Matshiliso.

'My bokkie, we are going to sleep in the bush tonight,'

De la Rey said. 'We don't want to wake my mother in the middle of the night.'

'That's sensible. We shouldn't alarm her,' she said, smiling to herself as she imagined the shock on his mother's face at seeing her long-lost son with a native girl on his arm. 'But are you sure the farm still belongs to your family? Perhaps you should wake up early in the morning, go and see if it's safe to show our faces there.'

De la Rey nodded. 'Always had a good head on your shoulders. We'll spend the night beyond the hills over there, where there are bushes to conceal us.'

Early the following morning, De la Rey crawled out of the bush and, lying on his stomach to survey the valley below, watched his family's farm intently. He was hoping for some movement on their farm, and on the one next to it. But nothing moved. There were no British soldiers. Not a single soul.

After two hours of observation, he detected movement. Heart thumping, he strained his eyes to assess the figure of a man walking from his family's barn towards the house. His heart swelled with joy as he recognised his Uncle Gawie. He wanted to rush down to greet his uncle, but he decided to bide his time. He saw Uncle Gawie talking to two black men, obviously giving orders as he pointed towards the barn. Uncle Gawie disappeared into the main house. Some time later, he emerged from the house and walked towards his own cottage, about two hundred metres west of the main house. De la Rey waited. A cool breeze blew wisps of dried yellow grass in quick, confused flurries over the area of veld where he was lying. A lone bird sang its early-morning melody. After more time had passed, during which nothing untoward happened, he decided to fetch Matshiliso.

Together, De la Rey and Matshiliso rode down the hill towards the house, as unobtrusively as they could. There was no one in the yard when they got there. He tethered the horse next to the barn and they walked towards the main house. Apart from a sagging zinc roof and glass missing from the front window, the house, desperately in need of a fresh lick of whitewash, looked just as he remembered it – a nondescript oblong structure with a verandah that led to the *voorkamer*. The front door was wide open. They walked in and he asked Matshiliso to sit on a chair in the kitchen while he proceeded towards his mother's bedroom. He wanted to surprise her.

At the door, he cleared his throat loudly. 'May I please come in?'

'Gawie ...?' His mother's voice was querulous. 'What is it now? What do you want?'

'I said, may I come in?'

'No, it is not ...' Her voice caught. 'It is not my boy ...'

In an instant, she was at the door, tears running down her sunken cheeks. Her wrinkled face peeked out from under a black bonnet. Her eyes, which had once been a piercing blue, had lost their lustre: they were now dull, peeking out from sockets like cockroaches tired from too much scurrying away from predators. The large blanket draped over her shoulders was clasped firmly together with a safety pin at her chest. Her voice trembled like the rest of her body. 'Oh, my boy, what have they done to you? Come in, come in, this is your own mother's bedroom after all. Come in and tell me about it. What a surprise!' She started sobbed loudly, burying her head in the folds of his huge coat. 'Oh, look at you. How you remind me of your pa, with that beard of yours.' Overcome with emotion, she embraced him tightly. When the shock started to wear off, she looked up and said, 'You must tell me everything, my son.'

'Ma, I must show you pictures of some of the men I was with on the front line.'

'Pictures?' she asked, suspicion written in her eyes. 'What do you mean, pictures? Do you now have those machines that take pictures? Where did you get the money to buy that thing?'

'No, Ma. I think Ma is getting on in years. Ma has forgotten that I am the artist of this republic. I can draw anything, from the big church in town to the most intricate rendering of President Paul Kruger's face.'

'Oh, you mean those play-play pictures that you doodled.'

'They are not doodles, Ma. They are real pictures. They are art.'

'So, while other men were busy fighting you were busy doodling?'

'When I am all cleaned up, I'll show you the pictures. I'll show you the face of our veldkornet. I'll show you the face of his wife. I'll show you the faces of the men I fought alongside of, complete with their rifles and things.'

'Which reminds me, just days after you went to war I found a whole load of those – um, er, cloths – those cloths that your father used to draw his pictures on. Those hard coarse cloths, man. They have a name …'

'Canvases?'

'Yes, I found a whole pile of them. And some oil paints your pa used to keep. All sealed, unopened. I know your father tried to discourage you from painting, said it would make you lazy, yet he himself used to paint like an angel, and still work like a slave on his own farm.'

They laughed together.

She continued, 'Anyway, those canvas things are in a box, in the barn somewhere. Maybe you want to have a look at them once you've rested and cleaned yourself up. Maybe you want to transfer your scribblings onto those big canvas things? Who knows about these things?'

'Thank you, Ma. I can't wait to start painting again.'

They sat down on the bed and she embraced him again. Her shoulders started shaking, her voice rose as she bawled like a child. At length, she regained her composure. Quietly, she said, 'How I almost lost my only son to a stupid war that still doesn't make sense to me. I know they want our gold, but couldn't they just discuss or negotiate with us? We are not heathens and savages, after all. We are reasonable. We know how to discuss, how to negotiate like civilised people. Ah, how I hate the British. They have reduced us to kaffir status. Rounding us up like cattle, locking us up. The kaffirs who are used to that kind of thing must have been laughing their heads off.'

'I'm glad you weren't in a concentration camp. You look healthy.' He touched her cheek. Her skin was cold to the touch, and pastry-white in colour. 'You should go out more often, sit on the veranda and enjoy the sun.'

'Hhhmphf! What is there to enjoy? Gawie has looked after me well enough, I must say. Over the past few months he's been working hard, getting the farm back on its feet now that the war is over.'

'He's always been a hard worker.'

'Yes, we're going to have a good harvest, thanks to him and those kaffirs. They're good kaffirs. Most others sided with the Brits, hanging onto the petticoats and coat-tails of the Brits the minute Bloemfontein fell into their grubby redneck hands. But Gawie's kaffirs have been loyal to us, you'll see them working hard in the fields.'

'That's good to hear.'

'But it's the other thing that bothers me with Gawie.'

'What thing?'

'He doesn't want to get married, settle down, start a family like any decent man his age.'

'But you're being hard on him, Ma. How could he get married in the middle of a war?'

'The war couldn't stop him chasing after those kaffir girls like a demented man. I think one of them is now pregnant with his child. What a disgrace. Soon this entire region will be run by half-kaffirs.'

'Ma,' he raised his voice, 'I wish you would stop using that word.'

She recoiled. 'What word? Kaffir? What has this war done to you?'

'These people are decent, Ma. You yourself have just told me how they stuck with you through the war, at the risk of being killed by the Brits. That's loyalty, Ma.'

He touched her hands reassuringly. There were liver spots on them. He lifted his eyes to her face. Around her cheeks, some veins had burst, leaving crimson webs.

'So, what do you want me to call these … these girls?'

'They are natives, Ma, natives.'

'That was before this war. This war has changed everything. This war saw people we mistook for fellow Europeans treating us like savages, like non-Europeans. Now we're not going to shrink from our new status. We are going to embrace it. We are of Africa. But the kaffirs remain kaffirs. They are godless. They have no culture. What do they know about diamonds? What can they do with gold?'

'We had no choice but to fight against the Brits.'

She looked at him with awe. 'So, you really fought? But what's this I hear about you joining the Brits?' She paused, then she added hastily, 'Ag, don't tell me. I don't want to know. I am just happy you are back in one piece. Now that you're back I think I'll go out more often. The other day I went out and sat on the veranda. And guess what?'

He shrugged his shoulders.

'I'm sitting there, and this antelope suddenly appears. Just up the hill, over there. It's just standing there, grazing. And I remember that I haven't eaten meat in a long time. And there's meat in front of me.'

He laughed nervously.

'So I get up, walk back to the house. I am stretching my luck, *mos*. I know that by the time I get back to the stoep, the bokkie would have long moved on. Anyway, I get your father's huge rifle. It's always well-oiled and loaded, since the war started. One has to be ready. Always. I get back on the veranda, with my rifle at the ready. This is my lucky day. The stupid steenbok is still there. I take aim. I think it takes a furtive glance at me. But it doesn't move. It must be thinking, "Ag, an old rickety bag of bones like that can't cause me any harm." I lower the rifle. The bloody thing still doesn't move. Now I'm taking it personally – I'm angry at the animal for not being scared of me. I take aim. I pull the trigger. Bull's-eye.'

'That was well done, Ma.'

De la Rey helped his mother up and, arm in arm, they left the bedroom. As they entered the kitchen, the old woman hesitated at the sight of the black woman seated at her kitchen table, dressed in an ankle-length dress, her head covered in a *doek*, as was the custom with married African women. She was wearing black, flat-heeled shoes. The older woman stared at the shoes for a long time. Her own feet were bare. Her only pair of shoes was reserved for special occasions – church, or some such. Her eyes travelled back to the younger woman's headgear, finally resting on her face. Her eyes were downcast, as was the tradition of African women when in the presence of their elders or social superiors.

De la Rey spoke hurriedly. 'Ma, let me introduce you to—'

'Why do you allow a *meid* to sit on my chair? What's this war done to you? Do you know how far back in the family this chair goes?'

'But Ma—'

'*Magtig!* You know my grandma passed it on to my own pa? And you're allowing a kaffir *meid* to *sommer* sit on it?'

'All I'm trying to —'

'Who said I need a housemaid, anyway? This war has bankrupted me. I can't afford a maid.'

'You are not listening, Ma!' he bellowed. 'This woman is my wife. That's why we are here. We are going to stay with you here until I am back on my feet and can start my own farm. And, as you can see, she is in the family way.'

His mother's face seemed to swell like a bullfrog. She muttered to herself, 'No, no, no.' She retreated to her bedroom and slammed the door closed. After about twenty minutes, she came out again.

'Out!' she hissed, pointing her big-barrelled rifle at her son. 'Out, off my farm. Out of my life. With your kaffir. Out.'

She squeezed the trigger, hitting a window.

'OUT! You have betrayed me. You're no son of mine. I don't have a son any more.'

CHAPTER 10

They were back to roaming the vast plains of the Free State, De la Rey and Matshiliso – riding by night, sleeping by day. Starving, tired, Matshiliso said, 'We could always go back to my village.'

'What?'

'When the baby comes, they will have no choice but to take us back. You will have to pay all the necessary penalties, and we can get married.' As an afterthought she added, 'That is, if you still want to marry me.'

'Of course we're going to get married. But in order to pay all those penalties I will need money. Hence I am saying, let's look for work on the farms, raise some money and then leave.'

'But you know that no farmer in his right frame of mind would take us on as a couple.'

'I know that. I think we stand a better chance of finding work in town. Bloemfontein itself. The Indian shopkeepers.'

She seemed to think about it. 'Do you think they'd be prepared to house us, thus bringing trouble to themselves?'

'You're not listening. We are not a couple. At least that's the story we will tell them. I'm a survivor of the war. I stumbled upon you, a poor pregnant black woman. And I thought, as a good Christian, I couldn't leave you behind.'

'Perhaps it could work. How far is town from here? I am totally lost now.'

'Let's ride. We shall be there at the break of dawn.'

Jerry paused, refilled his wine glass, then settled back and continued with the story. 'So now, De la Rey and Matshiliso find lodgings with an Indian shopkeeper in town. In those days, it was not uncommon for the so-called poor whites to work for Jewish and Indian traders. Of course the Indian is clever enough to see through their lies. He understands that they are a couple. But he provides separate sleeping quarters for the both of them. Just in case the authorities come sniffing around.

'They'd been working for the Indian for a few months when Matshiliso delivered a bouncy baby boy. They named him Roelof de la Rey. There was a celebration at the house, but it was a bit hush-hush as the Indian trader and De la Rey himself feared that the neighbours might start talking. The Indian trader Mr Saloojee and his wife came around to the shabby shack in which the baby had been delivered with the help of a black woman who did washing for the Saloojees. Again, De la Rey was discouraged from spending too much time in the shack where his fiancée and child were confined.

'One day De la Rey obtained a small loan from the Saloojees. He was going into town to buy some items – medicines, pieces of clothing – for the baby.'

Jerry took a sip from his drink, got up to stretch his legs. 'Turned out to be the longest walk ever. He never came back. Two weeks passed, a month. No De la Rey. Desperate now, Matshiliso decided she had to gather her things and go back to her village.' Jerry paused, gathering his thoughts carefully.

'Mrs Saloojee was livid. "What? With a young piccaninny like that? You can't leave." So Matshiliso stayed.

'And that, my friend,' said Jerry, 'is all Pitso's mother ever told him about his father, Cornelius de la Rey, and the circumstances of his birth.'

CHAPTER 11

Pitso must have been around six when he began to understand his station in life. The building he called home was quite popular in the neighbourhood. It was, after all, Salojee's General Dealer, where people bought their food supplies. It was also a place of gathering, where both black and white came to collect their post every Wednesday. The building was a two-storey affair. The bottom floor was the commercial hub, while the upper floor served as the sleeping quarters for Mr Salojee, his wife and four children.

After De la Rey left, and Matshiliso stayed, Saloojee had to do some swift thinking. At the back of the store was a warehouse where he stored extra supplies. He converted the storeroom into sleeping quarters for the newly employed young woman and her son. And he transferred his stock to the two shacks which he had used to accommodate – separately – De la Rey and his family.

The room was dark even during the day. It contained a bed in its corner, a table with a chair, and a suitcase in which they kept their clothes. That was it. Matshiliso ate her meals at the table, while Pitso preferred to sit on an upturned five-litre drum which he had rescued from a rubbish bin.

Mother and child soon acclimatised to this dreary world. It

mirrored their lives out there in the street, where they walked as if they were forever shrouded in darkness. No one noticed them. No one spoke to them. The only time they became visible was when a neighbour lost something – a chicken, a piece of clothing from her line. Then the neighbour would point fingers at the boy: 'They are always stealing, the mixed-race people. That's all they are good at.'

By that time, Pitso had been baptised at the local church and, on the advice of Mrs Saloojee, had been enrolled at the newly established school for mixed-race children. Mrs Saloojee had even encouraged Matshiliso to hand her child over to the orphanage for mixed-race children, but she refused.

Even though the child had been baptised Roelof de la Rey, his mother also wanted him to understand and appreciate his other cultural heritage – that of her own people. Thus, she had given him the name Pitso. She encouraged him to call himself by the surname Motaung when he was not at school.

'Roelof de la Rey is your school and church name. But your home name is Pitso Motaung,' Matshiliso would remind her son.

When Pitso turned three, and Matshiliso thought she had saved enough money to go home and face her people without fear, she took the long trip to the village of her birth. She thumbed a lift with a farmer's truck travelling in the general direction of her village. The journey took her the entire day, but proved a complete waste of time. Her people had been uprooted from their ancestral home. In fact, the entire village had been obliterated. In its place now stood what was clearly a hugely successful community of British farmers. They had taken advantage of the fecundity of this village along the banks of the Mohokare River and had turned it into the breadbasket of the region, as she would later learn. They planted maize, sunflower and all manner of vegetables. They kept cattle, sheep and pigs, providing a steady supply of carcasses for the butcheries in Bloemfontein and other smaller towns.

When she arrived at the farm closest to the road, she was met by a guard.

'My child,' the kind guard said, 'we don't have any job openings for now.'

'No, sir,' she responded, 'I am not looking for a job. I am looking for my people. But the entire landscape has changed. I know this is where my village used to be, but I can't seem to recognise anything here – not a tree, not a hill …'

'Oh, you're a descendant of the Bataung people who used to reign over this area? Sadly, shortly after the war, their land was taken over by the British government, and they were resettled.' She specifically asked the old man where he thought her immediate family had been sent to.

'Who was the head of your family?'

'Ntate Motaung was my grandfather. But my uncle Disemba, who spent time in one of the concentration camps, was also quite well known around these parts. He could read the Bible and teach people things. He was famous for that.'

The man nodded. 'Ah, I remember Disemba very well. Before the village was destroyed, he started a school. I've heard that he moved to Bloemfontein, where he is running another school. I don't know where exactly in the town. But if you go to any of the church people, they'll be able to point you in the right direction. He now goes by the name Paul Ontong.'

'What?'

'He goes under a mixed-race person's identity. He is a very smart one, that man. If I were much lighter in complexion and if I had some education, I also would adopt a mixed-race person's identity. Survival of the fittest, my dear child. Now, go back and find your uncle.'

That was years earlier. Pitso had since grown up. He was doing quite well at school. But in the neighbourhood where he stayed, his life was a challenge.

The black women who worked as washerwomen for local white families thought Pitso was a bad omen – a half person, neither white nor black. How would African ancestors in the land yonder communicate with these human bats? Yes, that's what mixed-race people were: neither bird nor mouse. Bats. Unpredictable. They looked at the world from a different angle, from upside down. When bats came out, the world got disturbed. They brought unease.

To the Salojees, Pitso was the child of a servant and therefore could not play with the boss's children. To the white families, for whom his mother washed clothes over the weekend to supplement her income, he was a mixed-race skelm, who might pollute their own children's brains. It did not help that Matshiliso herself was short-tempered and crossed swords with many women in the neighbourhood.

'You see, she's a kaffir like us, but she is behaving like mixed-race people who are always greedy,' her detractors would say. 'Why does she need so many jobs? It's greed, if you ask me.'

Matshiliso gradually lost the few friends she had around, preferring her own company.

Observant and resourceful, Pitso had realised that their neighbourhood was infested with rats. Initially, he started whiling his time away hunting down these rats, whooping with excitement every time he managed to kill one. But in due course, he decided to take his interaction with rats to another level. Seeing that he had no human friends, why not turn his four-legged enemies into companions? He took his time gaining their trust. When he saw them behind the Koekemoer property, where his mother worked at weekends, Pitso would approach slowly. Under the watchful gaze of the rats, he would slowly, unthreateningly, throw pieces of food in their direction. Suspicious at first, they would stop and watch, their eyes alert, whiskers and ears standing out. After a while, they would begin nibbling at the pieces of food. Then he would find a rock or an empty tin on which he would sit and watch them.

One Saturday afternoon he was in the company of his rat friends at the back of the Koekemoers' residence, as usual, while his mother toiled somewhere inside the house. By now, the rats were furiously rolling all over the ground, fighting or playing, shrieking with anger or enjoyment. He smiled and sniggered happily. To intensify the excitement, he threw more food into the circle. There was shrieking and the swishing of tails as the furry creatures fought.

Suddenly, a voice cried, 'Rats! Rats! The *verdomde* bastard boy is breeding rats in our backyard!'

It was Koekemoer himself, the master of the house. Pitso's mother was summarily dismissed from her job, which meant a reduction in her earnings once again.

But the Saloojees kept her very busy. By the time Pitso turned nine, his mother had finally managed to locate her uncle Disemba, who went by the name Paul Ontong and was a success-ful shop owner operating from just outside Bloemfontein.

To her relief, Ontong was still very much a Motaung. He slaughtered beasts in the proper Sotho tradition and taught his children how to be good Basotho warriors who had to use the system to their advantage – even if it meant the temporary indignity of lying about their true heritage.

Of course Pitso did not understand the constant fights that his mother and uncle used to have. Although he couldn't follow most of what they said, the gist of it was that his mother wanted them to return to their village, while his uncle said they should stay put in Bloemfontein and be part of the coloured community. They spoke good Afrikaans, most of them, and they were light enough in complexion to pass for coloured. Even though he could speak Sotho, sometimes the elder people spoke a far more complex vernacular which seemed to confound even Uncle Disemba's own children, who were slightly older than Pitso. His cousins had been born at one of the concentration camps during the war.

Happy as he was to have connected with his uncle at last, Pitso's world was about to become more complicated.

CHAPTER 12

When Pitso was around ten, he was subjected to his mother's nightly performances of remorse and grief, grotesque pantomimes that would embed themselves in his young mind, haunting him in his adulthood. In later years, whenever he thought of a love that was lost, he would find himself harking back to his childhood.

Their evenings would always follow the same routine. After supper, and a short session of storytelling, his favourite part, his mother would suddenly snap shut. Then she would start talking, first in a plaintive tone: 'I know, my dear Cornie, it was I who drove you away from me, from us. But, Cornie, you have to forgive me now.'

Her monologue would rise in pitch as she suddenly collapsed onto her knees, pounding the hard dirt floor with her fists until the knuckles were red. Every night, without fail, she would punish herself for her effrontery and impudence towards her man, her presumptuous nature in thinking the man she loved could stand up to his mother, or to the neighbours, and declare his love for Matshiliso and their young child. God knows she had tried to forget about him, to move on. But how do you unlove? How do you uncommit? How do you uncry the tears of hope?

It never occurred to Matshiliso that her outpourings of re-morse and endless tears and sometimes unintelligible fulmi-nations subjected her young son to unspeakable suffering. That each night's performance sent a dagger through him – daggers that he would wish to plunge into the person of his father if he were to meet him one day.

These long monologues that he was forced to endure, night after night, which constantly re-enacted his father's flight from the family nest, reminded him, perhaps unfairly, that his father had been a coward; he had run away from responsibilities. Daytime offered Pitso some respite from this reality. But at night-time, thanks to his mother's performances, the message was drummed into his head that he did not have a father and because of it he was a half-being, if not a complete nonentity. He would have liked to console his mother, or to politely ask his mother to be quiet, or even to shout back at her for her selfishness and pointless self-immolation.

Even at that tender age, thanks to the many hours he spent by himself, he had come to the realisation that thoughts needed to be dressed in appropriate clothing before being sent out to do the speaker's bidding. He had many thoughts that he wished he could communicate to his mother, but he was not mature enough to spin the appropriate words in which to dress them.

He also lacked the passion with which his mother's nightly doses of self-pity were delivered. So, while she raged and cried, he sat quietly and thought of other things. He thought of his rat friends, to whom he spoke endlessly, without fear.

He would be rudely awoken from these reveries by his mother violently reaching out for him and smothering his face with kisses. It happened every night without fail: tears streaming down her cheeks, her body heavy with fresh, warm sweat from her recent exertions, she would start kissing him all over, muttering to herself, 'Cornie, my dear Cornie, this boy is going to grow up to be a man. Just like you. You must see how big he is. He is going to go places, Cornie. Soon enough, he will be looking after me. But we still need you back, Cornie, to give this young man direction. We need you back to lead us, Cornie. I am a vile creature for having insulted you. Now my child plays with rats because you are not here. I deserve to die, Cornie.'

Then she would sob, 'Cornie, you remember the things you did back in my village. The boys you taught how to hunt. The girls and boys you taught how to grow food on our plantations. Come back, Cornie.'

At long last, when every bit of energy had been sapped from her body, she would kneel beside her bed, read from the Bible and say a prayer. She prayed with a sombre, solid voice devoid of her earlier emotionalism. After that, they would go to sleep.

But then, suddenly, everything changed: his mother grew big with child. There were whispers in the neighbourhood, accusing fingers jabbed in her direction when she was not looking. Who was the father, who was the father?

When the child, a girl, was finally delivered, she looked Indian. Saloojee and his family immediately left town, and Pitso's mother was taken to a place for the mentally ill. After only three months in the terrible conditions at this facility, Matshiliso passed away. Soon thereafter, Pitso and his younger sister were taken to the place of safety for coloured people where Pitso had been attending school. The girl died at the age of two, from tuberculosis. The death of his sister, his only remaining family, plunged Pitso into an abyss of depression.

He would go for days without eating, and he had endless nightmares in which his mother was always lamenting, apologising for leaving him all by himself, asking him to be strong.

By the time Pitso had reached his teens, the character of Bloemfontein and its environs had changed. Mixed-race people had suddenly come out of the woodwork. Like him, they were taught how to read, write and make things with their hands. They were trained in carpentry. They learned the art of the blacksmith, helping local farmers with horseshoes and other related requirements.

The centre where Pitso lived was laid out on a large tract of land. The residents kept livestock – pigs, cattle, mules, sheep and some horses. They grew their own food too: spinach, cabbages, carrots, potatoes, sunflowers, the lot. From a young age, children were drilled in the milking of cows, the grooming of horses, working in the vegetable fields. Pitso wasn't of much use in the vegetable fields, but he had to pitch in; it was the law of the centre.

'By the time you leave this place, you will be independent, self-sufficient adults,' the overseer, a man by the name of Fouché, would tell his charges. He was coloured, but so light-skinned many mistook him for a white man. He revelled in blacks cowering before him, calling him *baas*.

One of the survival skills the boys were taught was swimming. Mr Fouché personally trained them in a dam that had been constructed for irrigation purposes. Some teachers raised concerns that the water might not be clean, but Mr Fouché ignored their fears and took his charges to the dam, where he drove them hard. It riled Pitso that he never won any of the races that the boys organised among themselves. His boast, however, was that he could swim for the longest. Everybody agreed he had strong lungs.

Over and above their work in the fields, the children at the centre were made to read the Bible every day. Some of the children hated the Bible, but Pitso didn't. He'd grown up on it. He loved the stories. They took you to places you'd never been. They told you everything was possible: you could walk on water. You could see trees that burned ferociously, without ever being consumed by the flames. You could pass through the eye of a needle. You could build a ship so huge it could accommodate every animal on earth. It was a great book. That's why he also read the Bible in his own time. He knew other children would laugh at him if he told them that. They would think him strange – they already were finding him strange. He had the lightest complexion at the centre, yet he continued to speak Sesotho, against the advice of all the senior people, who encouraged the children to stay away from the native languages.

'English and Afrikaans are your future,' the teachers would say. 'Mainly English. African languages will only take you back to the bush. And remember one thing: we are a special people.'

Of all their activities at the centre, Pitso's favourite was when they sang church songs to the accompaniment of the church organ. Whenever he could get an opportunity, Pitso would tinker with the organ. Because he was everyone's favourite in this new environment – all the coloured people there admired his complexion and impressive build, similar to his own father's – no one minded that he was always fiddling with the revered instrument. In fact, they encouraged him to play and sing, which he did with gusto. In due course, he became the church organist's assistant, which meant that during the older man's absence, Pitso would play the organ. It was his duty to

97

keep it polished to a shine. When the centre for coloured children acquired a second-hand piano, Pitso was naturally the first person to play it. The official organist did not like this instrument with its funny short notes and less resonant sound, so it was left to Pitso to teach others how to play this new instrument. Soon, the coloured youth there had formed themselves into a formidable singing troupe. When Pitso was not playing the organ at the centre, he trifled with the accordion given to him by his mother years before.

He used to attract a small crowd on weekends as he took the long walk to his uncle Paul Ontong's house on the outskirts of Bloemfontein, playing his accordion and singing as he went, 'Mangoane nthekele serantabole sethiba letsatsi ... serantabole serantabole sethiba letsatsi.'

CHAPTER 13

A few months after the arrival of the piano, the teaching staff at the centre was joined by a woman straight from France, Madame Clinquemeur. She had been brought to teach history, English, Latin and music. She was slight of build, with long blonde hair and piercing blue eyes behind her spectacles. Immediately popular with both staff and pupils, Madame Clinquemeur took a special liking to Pitso. Long after the other children had left choir practice, Pitso would stay behind in the piano room, practising. Madame Clinquemeur remained in the room as well, so she could get an understanding of how much the students already knew. She believed she could glean this from Pitso, who seemed to be the students' obvious ambassador.

The friendship between the two soon grew beyond the music room. What Madame also enjoyed about this giant boy was that he had an aptitude for languages. She'd been at the centre for only a few months, but she could already detect that Pitso was picking up French and Latin faster than everybody else there.

During the day, the two of them could be seen sitting under a tree, drinking lemonade, talking, quizzing each other, laughing. Sometimes they took long walks in the sunflower groves on the periphery of the school. Walking next to a lumbering Pitso, the teacher looked tiny. Other teachers started talking: it was good to be friendly with one's pupils, but Madame Clinquemeur was going too far. A teacher couldn't and shouldn't allow her pupils to be too familiar. They must know their place: there was a fine line between familiarity and a reduced sense of respect for one's teachers. If these complaints ever reached Madame Clinquemeur, she ignored them.

Yet, for Pitso, these were possibly the happiest days of his life. As happy as he had ever been with his mother. In fact, Madame Clinquemeur, in a way, reminded him of his own mother. When not consumed by self-pity, Matshiliso had also encouraged him to come out of himself, to articulate his thoughts freely without being self-conscious, to dream aloud without feeling guilty.

'When you go back overseas I should go with you,' he told her one day.

She laughed. 'But why?'

'I want to be a voyager, I want to travel on ships, I want to discover new places, engage in long conversations with strangers, play with ideas, experiment with things.'

'But you don't need me to do that. You can get up right now and sail for India, for America, for Europe, all on your own. I know you're capable of taking care of yourself.'

'I need you by my side, madame. I want to explore the world with you.' He had not meant to say that. He bit his lip, feeling how tense the moment had become. Neither of them said anything more.

One evening they were together again in the piano room, singing and playing the piano. When they took a break, she said, 'You know what I like about you, Roelof?'

He looked at her, a question in his eyes.

'It's that you are not afraid of anything. You are not afraid of work. You are not afraid of challenges. You work hard in the field. You were the first to confront this monster of an organ, and gradually you are beginning to tame it. You sing out loudly, without fear. How did you become so versatile?'

'I don't know, Madame Clinquemeur ...'

'Maybe it's because you have the blood of adventurers flowing in your veins. You have French blood.'

'But how can that be? I am Afrikaans. At least, a part of me is Afrikaans. Our connection to Europe, as far as I know, is through the Dutch.'

'See? You still have a lot to learn. First of all, you, like me, are of French Huguenot stock, even if your people have been here for a few generations. Me? I came directly from France just after the war.'

'Yes, madame.'

'But don't let anybody mislead you, you're like me, part of the French Huguenot people, always resilient, always forward-looking, always brave.'

'Yes, madame.'

'You make me proud.'

'Thank you, madame.'

'Come, let me show you something.'

She sat him down on the organ stool and positioned his fingers on the keyboard. She cupped his hands, guiding them along the keyboard, and together they played the opening bars of Handel's *Hallelujah*.

Pitso was breathing heavily, not necessarily from his exertions on the organ, but from the pressure of Madame Clinquemeur's breasts pressing against his shoulder blades. He leaned as far forward as he could to avoid their rubbing against his back.

'Isn't that exquisite?'

'Yes,' he croaked. 'It is beautiful.'

Without thinking, he turned to her and wrapped his hands around the back of her neck, drawing her face towards his in readiness to kiss her.

She reared back. 'What do you think you're doing?' She pushed him with such force that he fell off the organ stool. On getting up, he fled the room, the door swinging violently behind him.

What had he done? Surely his teacher would report him to the authorities and he would be severely punished. Or forced to leave the facility. What would he do if they expelled him? He considered running to his uncle's house, but thought better of it. After creeping into bed, he lay frozen in fear and guilt. Tears of regret gushed out of his eyes and he sobbed silently. Eventually, spent from emotion, he fell into a dreamless sleep.

The following day, he expected to be summoned to the principal's office. But nothing happened. At lunch time, he was sitting with a group of friends under a tree when he saw Madame Clinquemeur approaching. He leaped away like a rabbit and fled. Over the next two days, he did his best avoid her and stopped going to music practice. But one evening, as he was walking to the dormitory, she appeared out of nowhere.

'Hello, Roelof.' Before he could respond, she said, 'Please come with me.'

He thought of running, but changed his mind, and followed her as she walked towards the music room.

When they got there, she lit the paraffin lamp. She instructed him to sit on the organ stool and then sat down opposite him on a chair.

'Roelof, I've been thinking about what happened the other night. And I suppose you, too, have had occasion to think about it, no?'

'Yes, I have thought about it a great deal, madame. I cannot find words to express my sincere apology. I do not know what got into me.'

'It's not your fault, my boy. I can see you are lonely. Everyone gets lonely every now and then. But you must learn to control your emotions, otherwise you will find yourself in trouble. I have not told anyone about what happened. Mainly because I do not want to see you fail, not after what you've been through in your life.'

Relief flooded through Roelof. 'Yes, madame ... Thank you for your kindness and consideration.'

'As I say, you must learn to control yourself. I know as a young man your blood is boiling with uncontrollable urges. But you're a danger to yourself. One day you will do to the wrong person what you did to me. And you can imagine what the consequences of that will be.'

Pitso shuddered.

'They'll expel you from this lovely place, where you stand a real chance of making something of yourself. Is that what you want, to be forced to leave this place?'

'No, madame.' Pitso was trembling now, blinking repeatedly to stop himself from crying. He couldn't cry in front of anyone. Especially not her.

She pulled her chair forward. 'You need to take charge of your life, control your urges.' She touched his face lightly with her right hand. Her expression softened. 'You have so much going for you, Roelof.'

He could smell her sweat beneath the sweet scent that she always carried on her person.

'Thank you for forgiving me, madame, for not reporting me … May I go back to the dormitory now?'

She did not respond. She appeared to be deep in thought, a conflicted look on her face. Then she inched her chair closer to the organ stool. Their knees touched. She leaned forward. 'Perhaps I can help you,' she said.

Their faces were inches apart. She reached for the paraffin lamp and snuffed it out. Pitso gasped as the room was plunged into darkness. His mind was reeling. She guided him to his feet and tried to press her lips to his, but he was too tall. So she slumped on the organ stool and roughly brought him to his knees. She pressed her lips to his and pushed her tongue into his mouth. Meeting no resistance, she probed deeper. In response, he pressed his tongue forward, nervously at first. His tongue gained confidence and assumed a life of its own; it began tussling playfully with hers.

Then she cupped his buttocks in her hands and started kneading them, feeling knots of muscles there. She started unbuckling his belt. He stood up and allowed his pants to drop.

He bit his lips in a desperate attempt to stop himself from crying out as she gripped his manhood as if it were a throwing spear. She shook it roughly from side to side and started tugging at his shaft as if it were an obstinate piece of weed that had to be removed from the ground. He had no choice but to moan.

She shrugged off her dress and removed her underwear, then got down onto the carpeted floor. He'd never been with a woman before, but instinct told him what to do. He positioned himself on top of her, and she guided him into her. When he started rocking fast, she grabbed his hips. 'Not so fast. Take your time.' He obeyed. They rocked gently, their murmurs and moans thick in the room.

Spent, he fell into her arms. A few minutes later, he felt his manhood hardening again. He groped between her thighs.

'Don't be greedy now.' She got up quickly, putting her fingers to his lips. 'Remember: control.'

'I'm sorry … I've never done this before.'

She brushed past him in the darkness. He heard the rustle of fabric as she got herself properly dressed again and prepared to leave the room.

'Roelof?' she said, as they stepped into the cool evening.

'Madame?'

'Please call me Christine, Roelof.'

'Please call me Pitso then.'

'Well, you know what, Pitso?'

'Yes, Christine?'

'I … *Deus tecum*. God be with you.'

She started walking away.

'I'll walk you home,' he called after her. Too late, she had disappeared, a fast-moving wraith in the shadows.

A soft rain began to fall, a welcome respite for Pitso's body, still hot and sweating from its exertions.

As he eased himself into his bed a short while later, his thoughts were consumed by Christine. He imagined taking her on his voyages over the seas, making sure she was by his side, come what may. He smiled in the darkness.

Then he muttered '*Deus tecum*' and slowly ran his index finger across his upper lip, below his nose, savouring the smell of Madame Clinquemeur. Christine. Sweet Christine.

CHAPTER 14

A week later, Madame Clinquemeur accosted Pitso as he was trudging home after a long day at the welding workshop.

Her face was crimson, the vein in the middle of her forehead throbbing visibly, her pert lips a pulsating pout. He opened his mouth to greet her. But before he could speak she dragged him behind the workshop and slapped him hard across the face. Tears welled in his eyes. She dragged him further until they were in the middle of the mealie field. The maize was the height of a full-grown man.

'Madame, what … I mean Christine—' Before he could finish, she slapped him hard in the face again. She was shorter than him, her head reaching to his shoulder, but the force of her slaps was that of a man almost his size. There was purpose behind those slaps.

He opened his mouth to speak, but she slapped him across the mouth. He could taste blood.

'How dare you!' The words were bullets coming out of the muzzle of a gun. 'How. Could. You?'

'What have I done?'

She slapped him again, but this time her attack lacked vigour. 'I risked everything … You lied to me.'

'What are you talking about?' He spat onto the ground. His saliva was red with blood.

'Why are you sleeping with that girl?'

'What girl?'

'Don't make me hit you again. You know, Saartjie. I heard her tell the other kitchen girls what the two of you have been up to. Says you two are getting married soon. Everybody around here is talking about the two of you. What do you take me for? So much for your proclamations of naivety. What—'

'But, I'm not—'

She pushed him hard in the chest, tears beginning to stream down her cheeks.

He moved to grab her, to stop her from hitting him again, then he checked himself. He searched her face. Her lips quivered. He could see that she was full of questions, that there was a lot she wanted to say. With shock, he realised that this woman really cared about him. She cared for him more than a teacher should care for her pupil. She cared for him more than a mature woman cared for an adventurous boy. Her face exuded a tenderness he'd never been exposed to before. She looked sad. She looked angry. She looked like one whose trust had been betrayed.

'I really don't know what you're talking about,' he said. 'I've never … That's not true.' He shook his head, bewildered.

Softening, she embraced him and murmured, 'Roelof, I mean, Pitso … I … I love you.'

In the days to follow Pitso realised that, unlike in the many books he had read, his love for Christine had not hit him like a bolt of lightning. It had entered his heart with stealth, like a sickness. Then, it had spread to his entire being, so that in every

107

wakeful moment, he could feel the pleasure-pain of this sickness throb with each thud of his heart, an illness he did not want to be cured of.

He wrote poems for her. He serenaded her after choir practice. He eased her into the intricacies of the Sotho language. She reciprocated with more lessons in French. She encouraged him to read more European history, to immerse himself in religious texts. His aptitude for French only encouraged her to escalate the pace and complexity of her lessons in the language. He learned his tables of conjugation, and his skills at composition improved. He was then working on improving his vocabulary.

At weekends, he was a regular presence at her rooms in the staff quarters. To assure the rest of the staff that the visits were innocent, they would leave the main door wide open. In fact, they mostly spent time sitting out on the veranda, the gramophone playing in the background. When she'd arrived, she'd been a hit with everyone who wanted to see the gramophone, this new wonder. She would play her limited collection of records on the contraption, mainly waltz and polka tunes. Pitso himself exulted in the machine and the music.

He asked her one day, 'Why didn't you bring recordings of classical music over from Europe?'

'Oh, my dear Pitso, those recordings are hard to come by. Even if I knew where to get them, I wonder if I could afford them. The gramophone itself is way beyond my pocket. It's only thanks to Grégoire that I'm the proud owner of this wonder machine.'

'Who's this Grégoire? Your brother?'

'A friend,' she said. Some red crept to her cheeks. 'A dear friend in Paris.'

The music played on, the two of them relaxed on the veranda, sipping their drinks.

But even with all these public assurances that there was nothing untoward in their relationship, people still talked. Mr Fouché cornered Pitso one day. 'Young man, people are talking. And I don't like the sound of it.'

'What are they saying, meneer?'

'Just stay away from the new teacher. I know you're a young man, hot blood and all, but for your own sake stay away from her. Stick to your own people, to your own kind. Saartjie, the cook, is going crazy over you—'

Pitso laughed out loud.

'You may laugh now, but tomorrow will be another story. If this thing gets serious and you must stick with Madame what's-her-name, you'd better leave Bloemfontein. Go to Johannesburg, Cape Town, a bigger town where you can live as a white man. Do that. Around here, everybody knows you're coloured and they will deal with you like a coloured man. In Johannesburg, you can easily pass for white. You are lucky that you're handsome too.'

Christine's accusation that he was seeing Saartjie began to make sense to Pitso. If Saartjie wanted him for herself, perhaps she had started spreading the rumours and even enlisted the help of Mr Fouché. Pitso decided to confront Saartjie.

CHAPTER 15

It was around 7 p.m. on a warm Wednesday. Pitso had been watching the door to the main kitchen vigilantly from his hideout. There were only three women in the kitchen: Saartjie and her two older colleagues. Thanks to his surveillance over the past eight days, he knew Saartjie was always the last to leave. Although he had never been inside the kitchen, he could imagine the three women finally sitting down to their supper after having dispatched food to the various sections of the centre.

He could picture them settling down for a hot cup of coffee after their meal. The gossip being exchanged between sips of coffee would be hot and spicy indeed. Every now and then, the laughter from the kitchen carried as far as his hideout – and he wondered what was being said about this or that man, or about this or that boss. He could hear the final rattle of coffee things as someone collected them. The task of washing the final cups would surely fall to Saartjie, being the youngest.

He could picture the other women taking off their aprons and wiping invisible breadcrumbs and balls of lint from their dresses as they prepared to go home. As the two elder women said their goodbyes, he could imagine Saartjie doing the final check-up – all windows closed, all plates, pots and dishes where they were supposed to be. The supervisor, who was always the first to arrive in the morning, was finicky about these things.

Having ascertained that the women were gone, he emerged from his hideout and approached the kitchen door, which was wide open.

Saartjie was sitting at the table, only now eating her supper. He hesitated. She was startled to her feet at the sight of him.

'*Magtig!*' she cried. 'You want to give me a heart attack?'

'My apologies.'

'You must always announce yourself. Don't move around like a ghost. *Magtig!*'

Behind the veneer of agitation and anger, however, her face was as exuberant as that of a cat which has just eyed a plateful of cream.

'Looks like I'm not welcome here, Saartjie?'

'Depends on what your mission is, Roeloffie.'

The anger he had been nursing as he stood in his hideout was gone. In its place, there was regret, guilt. He had disturbed the poor girl's supper.

'I wanted to speak to you about something, but seeing that you're still eating …'

'Speak. I'll listen.'

'But …'

'Matter of fact, why don't you join me for dinner?'

'I've already had dinner.'

'A man your size should never refuse a good meal. Especially from a lovely lady like myself.'

'I have to go now, Saartjie. Whatever it is I wanted to say can wait.'

'Do you want me to lose my temper and shout at you?' She got up, hands balled into fists.

He quickly sat down on a chair opposite hers. She smiled.

'You're lucky there's enough food for the two of us. And it is still very warm …' Her voice trailed off as she started dishing up.

'Smells good. What's this you've cooked?'

'Bobotie.'

'What's bobotie?'

'Come, I'll give you a taste.'

She took a dainty morsel with her spoon and held it out to him. He took the spoon from her and placed it in his mouth. He rolled the food on his tongue slowly, luxuriously.

'Hmm.' He chewed, swallowed. 'Sweet, yet salty. I taste some raisins here, and strange spices too. What is this?'

She explained the method of preparing bobotie and returned to the table with a steaming plateful of rice and bobotie. He grabbed a spoon and dug in as she watched with satisfaction. Then she crossed her arms and said, 'You've turned your back on your own people. You are running after, slobbering over white women who have no genuine interest in you.'

'You know nothing.'

'And you?'

'What I know is none of your business.'

'This is a grown woman you're dealing with. Not a child. She surely must have her own baggage, her own secrets, her own skeletons. Just like the rest of us.'

'I have no interest in anyone's skeletons.'

'And I hear you refer to yourself by that heathen African name. You must make peace with the fact that you are neither white nor black. You are coloured. The Africans despise us. They call us names.'

'You'd better stop now.'

'There are truths that must be told. And, just in case you didn't know, I am not scared of you. So, I will tell you straight: you are lost, you're confused, you need help. I think you need a person who cares. A person who'll help you come to terms with your demons, with your denial of who you truly are.'

'And you are that person?'

'What have I been saying all night?'

'And what gives you the right to go around spreading malicious rumours about—'

'There are no rumours, Roelof. What I have said is the truth: the two of us are in love, but one of us is still blind to the writing that is bright and clear on the wall. One day you'll wake up from your foolishness and realise you love me, Roelof de la Rey. You love Sara Beauchamp.'

He finished his coffee, shaking his head. 'Come, I'll walk you home. But stop hallucinating about me.'

When Pitso saw Christine at school the following day, he couldn't look her in the eye. Although nothing had transpired between him and Saartjie, he still felt guilty, as if he'd betrayed Christine merely by talking to the other woman. He felt naked. Felt as if she could see through him, as though he were a fraud, an imposter. Over the next few days, when she approached him, he was non-committal, evasive, gradually minimising their intimacy.

Undeterred, Christine invited him to a dinner party at her new house, one she had acquired without a word to him. Unbeknownst to Pitso, the evening would change everything.

CHAPTER 16

'This is my new home,' Christine said as she welcomed Pitso to the address he'd been directed to. It was an elegant house, some distance from the school.

'It's nice,' said Pitso, confused. He knew she'd moved to her own house, away from the staff quarters, but when he'd asked her why she'd just shrugged and muttered something about her independence. How could he complain, when it had been his idea to begin cutting down on the number of visits to her rooms?

Pitso was dressed carefully in long grey trousers with matching braces, a crisply ironed white shirt, and black shoes polished to a shine. His face was clean-shaven and he had on a dark-grey cap. Tufts of curly hair showed around his temples and smudged the lower back of his head.

Guests sitting in garden chairs under a jacaranda tree turned to look at Pitso as he walked with Christine up the path towards the house.

As Christine disappeared into the house ahead of him, a man called, 'Hey, boy, get me an empty glass, will you?'

For a moment, Pitso didn't move, bewildered. Then the realisation sank in: he was clearly mistaken in thinking he'd been invited as a guest.

'Yes, *baas*,' he said. 'Coming right away.' He walked around the house to the back entrance and found three servants in the kitchen. The three coloured women scowled at him. He greeted them in Afrikaans and asked for an empty glass, careful to explain that it was for the white *baas* outside. It was given to him on a tray and he took it out to the man, smiling as he held it out to him.

He went back to the house, using the same servants' entrance. After years of railing against the system, he was finally bowing to society's codes. He didn't know what else to do; Christine had asked him to come here, to her home. Perhaps it was simply her way of trying to see him outside of school hours. He stood in the large pantry, talking to the servants. They were from Kimberley and spoke what seemed to him a strange brand of Afrikaans.

Christine entered the pantry accompanied by a white man. 'Ah, found you,' she said to Pitso. The man beside her was wearing an apron, his shirtsleeves rolled up, his hands glistening with cooking fat. He was fairly short with a head of thick, dark hair. His eyes sparkled with friendliness.

Christine turned to the man and said, 'Darling, this is Roelof ...'

'Ah, the famous Roelof! Sorry, my hands are dirty; I prefer to prepare my own meat as many people do not know how to spice it properly.' He winked at Christine jovially. 'So, I can't shake yours right now.'

'Consider your hand shaken,' said Pitso in good humour. But he was confused. Who was this man, and why was Christine calling him 'darling'? Perhaps it was simply the way of the French.

'Come with me,' the man said, gesturing towards the kitchen.

As Pitso followed him, he couldn't help noticing that Christine seemed agitated, her eyes darting nervously between the two men as she walked with them. She seemed to want to say something and opened her mouth to speak. 'Eh, darling ...'

But the man's attention was focused on Roelof. 'I believe you can sing up a storm,' he said. He spoke perfect English, albeit with an accent. 'And I hear you can play the accordion better than a Frenchman. That we'll have to see. Once we've eaten, we're going to have to check the veracity of that claim. By the way, back home in Brittany, they call me Napoleon, on account of my height. And you, what do they call you, what's your nickname?'

'Some people call me the Lion. It's not exactly a nickname, but a praise name, derived from my surname.'

They moved outside, where coals on an open hearth glowed warmly. Pitso carried a tray of meat as requested. Napoleon started taking pieces from the tray and laid them on the grill.

As the meat sizzled, Pitso continued, 'But the name of De la Rey has got nothing to do with lions. My true surname is Motaung, People of the Lion.' Pitso proudly told him the history.

When the food was ready, the guests were invited to sit down at the beautifully laid dining-room table to eat. There was plenty of good wine. The three servants Pitso had encountered inside the house now hovered in the background, removing empty plates when required and bringing pitchers of water.

Pitso, who had been handed a plate of food by Napoleon, was not sure where he should sit, so he found a small outside table at the side of the house, hidden away from the guests. He sat down and began to eat. The servants nodded to him as they passed, but they still seemed uncomfortable in his presence, so they left him alone to his meal. He was focused on his food when Napoleon appeared with two glasses and a bottle of wine. 'Ah, there you are. Look, man, I am from France. Back home we don't do things this way, we don't tuck some guests away. I am sorry ...' He shook his head and looked genuinely upset.

'I understand that, sir. Thank you for the meal,' Pitso said.

Napoleon sat down next to him and poured wine into the two glasses. 'Well, Roelof, I've heard so much about you. Christine says you—'

'Ah, there you are!' A man appeared from around the corner. 'Monsieur, you're hiding from your guests.' As his gaze settled on Pitso, he recoiled and said, 'But it is the half-caste boy!'

Eyes blazing with anger, the Frenchman said to the man, 'That's a perfect display of the barbarism that I intend to fight against. Now, I'm going to ask you to apologise to my friend. Right now. Or leave this house.'

The man looked at the Frenchman, then at Pitso. He turned and walked away. When he reached the door to the dining room, he shouted over his shoulder, 'You're not going to bring your French ways here. You're not going to spoil our kaffirs and hotnots. You are not!'

An uncomfortable silence settled over the table. Soon the guests were whispering animatedly into one another's ears. Christine got up to play another record on the gramophone, but the atmosphere had been sullied.

One by one, people started leaving, although there were still mounds of food, and copious bottles of beer and wine.

'Monsieur, my presence here has completely ruined your party,' said Pitso. 'I shouldn't have come. The presence of one

French visitor is not going to change the mentality of this town.'

'Nonsense. I should be grateful for your presence. It has helped me set the tone, send a message to these people.'

Christine came out to the side of the house where the two of them were still sitting.

'Ah, there you are, Roelof. Has my husband been taking good care of you?' Although Christine tried to be casual, she was clearly anxious. Colour had risen in her cheeks. 'He can be so garrulous it's sometimes difficult to have a conversation with him. Grégoire, you do talk non-stop.' Christine put her hand on Napoleon's shoulder.

Pitso froze. His mouth went dry. Grégoire! The 'friend' who had sent her the gramophone. He looked at Christine wordlessly. Grégoire did not notice his new friend's sudden change of expression and resumed speaking, 'I've got a special liqueur that I want to share with my friend Roelof here. Excuse me while I go and get it,' he said.

The minute Grégoire turned his back, Pitso whispered to Christine, 'Why didn't you tell me?'

'I was going to tell you. But this doesn't change anything. I still love you ...'

'You can't love me and him. It's impossible.' His heart told him to cry out and beg. But his mind strangled that thought. 'You're greedy, selfish. You accused me of seeing Saartjie, yet you have another man that you love.'

'But Roelof, you knew I was married. I am Madame Clinquemeur, after all.'

'Yes, I did, but you gave me the impression that, perhaps, your husband was far away and therefore did not matter. Or that you'd come here to get away from him, start a new life.'

Christine's head dropped into her hands. 'It was wrong of me to get involved with you in the first place. You were a lonely, vulnerable young man, and I was lonely too. My husband was far away and he was not due to come for another year. But he changed his mind, decided to come early. I am sorry. I should never have allowed us to get into this mess.'

'Why did you bring me here, in the first place? Why invite me to your house?'

'Roelof, I'm so sorry. I brought you here out of guilt. I suppose I wanted to let you know about Grégoire ... to show you that he is a good man, that we have to put a stop to what we have. Because it is dangerous. I have betrayed my husband and I have hurt you. I have behaved most despicably towards both of you, Roelof.'

Pitso's lips trembled. He did not trust himself to say anything, so he kept quiet. He saw flies having a party on the table. They buzzed over remains of food, while others flitted about until they drowned themselves in the dregs of wine.

'Christine ... You can't just end things like that. I want you to tell him about us. Right now. If you don't, I will.'

'No, please, Pitso! There is too much at stake.' Her voice and eyes were pleading. 'I know I've hurt you, but please don't!' Christine got up and poured herself some wine, her hand shaking. She took a sip as Pitso stared, unseeing, into his own half-empty glass.

'My dear Roelof,' Grégoire cried as he emerged from the house, 'my dear Roelof, stop bothering yourself about those barbarians. It's not your fault that the party came to such a disastrous end. Let's just drink and be merry.'

Music had started playing again and the liquor flowed. But very little of this registered with Pitso. He had retreated to a corner of himself, that dark corner in which he used to seek refuge as a child, when his mother would cry herself silly and speak to his absent father, while Pitso would search in vain for words to comfort her, words to give meaning to the thoughts that were crowding in on him, suffocating him.

CHAPTER 17

On Pitso's sixteenth birthday, his Uncle Disemba threw a huge party for him. As part of the proceedings, the man slaughtered three sheep. People came from far and near to celebrate this important event. The party, which started on Friday evening, went on until Sunday. On the last day, Pitso was asked to give a speech, words which his relatives would cherish and take home with them. He spoke eloquently, thanking his uncle for keeping the family together after the war, for opening up business and educational opportunities for members of the community. He then startled many when he declared that he was no longer Roelof Jacobus de la Rey. He had officially become Pitso Motaung.

'If you ever call me a coloured person or a mixed-race person, I shall make you swallow your teeth. I am Pitso, the son of Motaung. The roaring cub of the Bataung people.'

Although many cheered and laughed, some of his relatives with straightened hair and artificially enhanced complexions were embarrassed at the young man publicly disavowing his mixed-race heritage, thereby giving the lie to the status they were aspiring to. Many of these relatives were much darker than Pitso. Unlike him, however, they refused to speak Sotho. Afrikaans was their first language, they declared to whoever wanted to know and to some who did not. Many felt Pitso's white good looks and higher-than-average education were wasted on him.

As a result, Pitso's speech left some of his relatives very angry, while others simply dismissed his speech as utterances of a drunken youth. After his disappointment with Christine, Pitso had been consuming huge volumes of alcohol – frequently and very publicly. Still wallowing in his loss, he moved like a sleepwalker. He bumped into things. He would not look people in the eye. He was always gazing into the distance, as if hoping that the love that he had lost would suddenly show its face on the horizon. As if his real Christine, not the one who had betrayed him, would come running towards him.

When it was time for him to be taken back to the centre for coloured children later that day, Pitso was nowhere to be found. He had simply disappeared sometime after his speech. Even the following day, nobody saw him. A messenger was sent to the centre, to check if he had perhaps returned there on his own. The messenger drew a blank.

Pitso was found four weeks later, hiding out at a distant relative's farm – one of the relatives who had refused to buy into this racial conversion charade advocated by his uncle Paul Ontong.

Against his will, Pitso was dragged back to the centre. He was not the same person any more: he fought endlessly with his teachers and classmates. Avoiding Christine, he sank into a cocoon of petulance and aloofness. When he was not playing his accordion or the centre's organ, he would have his nose buried in one book or another; English texts, old texts in Dutch and recent ones in Afrikaans. He even tinkered with some Latin texts.

Even though he tried his best not to think about Christine, he couldn't help recalling the works that she had recommended. He threw himself at these as if he were battling against Christine herself, to show her that not only could he understand these texts, but he could appropriate them for his own purposes. He read the commentaries of Jean-Jacques Rousseau, Plato and Socrates, and transplanted their thoughts to the South African situation – what these thinkers would have said about the application of justice in his country of birth. He read about the Atlantic slave trade, and his blood boiled with righteous indignation. Over and over, he read the story of Equiano, the famous slave. He thought he loved Equiano's story more than any biography he had read thus far.

One weekend, Pitso visited his uncle Paul Ontong again. He was serious about obtaining a new birth certificate, under the name of Pitso Motaung, and thought his relative might help.

'Uncle, I am not going to throw away my old certificate,' he assured the older man. 'It's a promise. I just want to have an African certificate as well. One never knows what the future holds in store.'

Paul thought he could see himself in the young man: a person with a long-term view of the future, a person with vision, a person with a mission. He decided to humour the young man. Over the next few days, he pulled a few strings, and Pitso, in due course, obtained a new birth certificate. As per the young man's request, the age on the certificate had been inflated by three years. Pitso could not stop thanking his uncle; he was now officially Pitso Motaung. How easy it was to shrug off the other identity, Roelof de la Rey, one that did not anchor him or make him feel complete.

During his spare time, he would also unfurl his father's

sketches from the war. Sometimes he would just look at them until tears came to his eyes; other times, he would start copying what he was seeing in front of him, on his own sketchpad, trying to imitate his father's strokes. Drawing soon became a passion. He drew things he had never seen in real life: buses and trains he had seen only in books. He conjured soldiers lying on their stomachs, their guns cradled confidently over their shoulders, the muzzles pointing into the distance. He brought to life a group of Zulu warriors armed with assegais and shields, clouds of dust boiling at their feet as they danced in a public square. He drew big, bright flowers; aloes standing guard at the top of a hillock; faces of old, wrinkled women smoking traditional African pipes, wisps of smoke curling to their eyes; scenes of men sitting under trees, drinking beer from huge calabashes, women dancing in the middle of the yard, and dogs fighting over bones strewn near the drinking men.

He drew a likeness of himself playing an accordion; a woman who looked like his mother, riding a horse. He drew endlessly, energetically. At the end of most of these sessions, he would study his efforts for a long time. He would speak to the characters in each drawing: 'Just what do you think you're doing? Tell me what you're thinking right now. Any plans for tomorrow?' He would laugh at his own futile questions, then tear up the drawing and throw the pieces into a rubbish bin.

Rummaging through his father's belongings, he stumbled upon a sketch showing an African woman resplendent in flowing robe, with a Bible in one hand and a spear in the other. His eyes widened when he recognised his own mother. His lips trembled, and he started laughing maniacally. Then he shouted, 'Mme waka! Mme waka!' My mother, my mother!

Tears flowed in torrents. He cradled the sketch against his chest and swayed sideways, weeping bitterly. '*Mme waka! Okae mme waka? Okae?*' *My mother. Where's my mother? Where?*

Soon, after that, it became his ritual to start his day by looking at the sketch, tracing his finger slowly along the lines of the drawing.

When the war broke out in Europe in 1914, Pitso followed it through the newspapers that were kept at the library. The newspapers were meant for teachers, but there were no regulations preventing pupils from sitting at the newspaper-reading desk. Besides, the newspapers were mostly outdated, meaning the staff at the centre did not place much importance on their contents. But to a young, inquisitive mind, what was happening in Europe was always intriguing, even if one could do nothing about it.

By the time the war entered its second year, local interest in it waned. The war was in stalemate. No one was winning. Pitso knew that, as part of the British Empire, the Union of South Africa had sent men over there – white men mostly. Which made sense, seeing as this was a white man's war: the German Kaiser and his friends on the one side, Britain, France and their friends on the other. What intrigued Pitso was that there were some black men from his own country also fighting over there. What did they stand to gain, fighting on the side of an empire that had taken their land, an empire that, not so long ago, had burned down their farms and taken their families to concentration camps?

Pitso was then already a big man, with a boulder-like build that resembled his father's. His face was the colour of vanilla and chocolate swirled together, complemented by a proud shock of black, curly hair. Although he had the sharp nose of a white person, this was offset by his thick lips. But he still could easily pass for white. That's what his mother had always said to him back then: 'You are the son of a white man – be proud of that. You are not a simple kaffir like your mother; you are going to get a good education and be like the white man, or even better than him, because you also have the genes of a Motaung, and we are a proud people. We can be wily in our own way, let me tell you that. We can outwit the white man. We are the Bataung, Children of the Lion.'

It was confusing, these divided loyalties. Then an event in 1916 offered him an opportunity to confront these divisions head on.

CHAPTER 18

The community hall in the centre of Bloemfontein had always been, at least as far as Pitso could remember, the preserve of white people. The only black people he'd seen entering the building were the cleaning women. To Pitso, the building looked like a church which, while still under construction, had been turned into something else instead. He had never seen anything like it. The only comparison he could conjure was the church where the white people congregated.

The hall was a huge rectangular structure, with a high, pitched roof and many windows on the sides. On the few occasions he had passed by, he had seen throngs of men, with stark faces and angry moustaches, speaking animatedly outside, gesticulating with their hands, which instinctively took the shape of impatient fists. These men had made him so uneasy he had decided to avoid walking past this building, even if it meant taking longer and more cumbersome alternative routes. Over the years he had noticed that his appearance always stirred strong emotions among white people. They always stared angrily. Many blacks assumed he was white and acted accordingly in his presence. The obeisance he received from blacks only managed to drive the whites up the wall. Or so Pitso thought. Which was why he avoided places frequented by whites, if he could help it.

But over the past two weeks, the town crier, who had been hollering his message up and down the streets, and deep into the villages outside of town, had invited all black men to gather at the town hall. A Very Important Announcement was to be made this bright Saturday morning. All able-bodied black men had to be present. The white farmers who employed the majority of the black men around there had encouraged their charges to attend.

By the time Pitso arrived, hundreds of black men were milling outside the building. Fidgeting with his hat, he stood outside a circle of men, and absent-mindedly kicked some stones while he surveyed the surrounding scene with one eye. He was dressed in khaki shorts, a black short-sleeved shirt, a black hat decorated with a yellow feather, and a pair of his school shoes, complete with knee-length socks. This was, after all, an important gathering, as his teachers at school had also observed. He could see the looks of envy from most of the other men. Many of them were in sackcloth. Those who were dressed in shorts and shirts did not have shoes on. But they all looked clean and groomed, clearly showing respect for the meeting that was about to begin. It soon became clear to Pitso that the other men were as nervous as he was. They spoke in quiet tones, as people would do at the graveyard, careful not to raise their voices above a certain tone.

When he felt a tap on his shoulder, Pitso spun around. His face broke into a nervous grin as his eyes landed on Tlali, a friend he had made recently.

'Do you have many enemies around these parts?' Tlali laughed. 'You should have seen yourself, almost jumping out of your skin when you felt my hand on your shoulder.'

'My friend, you must not tap people from the back, or you'll lose your teeth one of these days.'

They shook hands and laughed, before lowering their voices when they saw the other men's disapproving glares.

'So, you also want to go and fight in the white men's war across the seas?' Tlali said, without wasting time.

'Ag, my friend, I just want to hear what they have to say. Can't hurt to go to a meeting. How about you, are you ready to join up?'

'Depends.' Tlali shrugged. 'They are talking good money. One is not getting any younger, so one has to think about filling one's own kraal with one's own cattle.'

'True. One can't always be one's father's son. One needs to take a wife.'

'And they don't come cheap, these women. No self-respecting father is going to hand his daughter over to a man who doesn't own even a dog.'

'You—'

The loud, unmistakable sound of a bugle rent the air, startling the men out of their small circles of idle conversation. When the sound stopped, a nervous silence settled over the gathered men. They looked expectantly towards the entrance of the hall, where a tall, white man in British military uniform stood flanked by two black men in the khaki uniforms and big hats favoured by Boer commandos of a few years before.

'Oh, you great warriors of Mangaung, you sons of Bataung, you sons of Batsoeneng, you sons of the red soil of Africa, you beautiful brave Bafokeng, I greet you.'

Puzzled, the men looked at each other, uncertain as to what they had just seen and heard. The white man in a soldier's uniform had just greeted them, in their own language, singing praises to their ancestors. When that sunk in, they roared with pride, whistling and ululating, clapping their hands, shouting excitedly at each other, 'Did you hear the man from across the oceans showing respect to our fathers?'

A voice rang out, this time one of the black men flanking the white soldier: 'The great captain from across the seas can't tell his story to you brave people out here in the sun. Let us please move inside the hall, sit down on those shiny, comfortable benches, and hear what the great soldier has to say to you, great sons of Mangaung! There is a beautiful story to be heard. Let us move inside, please my brothers.'

Once they were all settled inside, various chiefs and local leaders rose to speak about the need for local men to join the war effort. The upshot of the speeches was simply that the war in Europe was in stalemate. Therefore, the King of England was appealing to his subjects to come forward and serve. The Crown, together with its Allies, needed to conquer the evil German Kaiser.

British victory up there in Europe would be victory for all concerned, for all the men gathered here and their families. After the war, the Crown would look favourably upon the black man in the Union. There would be jobs for all. The black man would walk proudly again. Besides, the Crown was going to pay all the recruits salaries of three pounds a month. This was far more generous than the average mineworker's monthly earnings. Some of the men nodded enthusiastically at the mention of the money. Others remained non-committal.

Later in the afternoon, the floor was open to questions from the audience. One man, who from his manner of speaking – he addressed the captain directly, looking him in the eye – had clearly had some dealings with white people in bigger cities, got up to speak. He talked in Sesotho, with some English words thrown in for good measure. 'It's well and good that we are being asked to go over there and fight. And, yes, the salaries are tempting. But what exactly are we going to be doing over there, seeing many of us have never handled a gun before, let alone fought in a foreign war in a foreign country? How are we going to fit in? Given the pressure that the Crown is under, how are you going to prepare us for what is going on over there? Look, most of us here are farmworkers – some have worked on the mines as unskilled labour, others, quite clearly, are snot-nosed boys who still herd cattle. How, then, do you see us fighting a war in a foreign land, given our lack of training and experience?'

The captain got up and addressed the man's concerns, although his voice had lost its earlier enthusiasm. 'My dear warriors, we are not sending you over there to die. You will be safe. You will be protected. You won't be on the front line. You are going there to offer support, to provide services to the fighting men—'

'You see!' The man who had posed the question was on his feet. 'I told you, men. I've been telling you to be careful. We are being sent there to cook for the white soldiers, to chop wood for them, to carry water for their camps, to wipe their behinds, even!'

Though the meeting ended in disarray, a message was shouted repeatedly for those who were still interested in enlisting to come to the hall the following day.

'I simply don't get you, child of my mother,' Pitso's friend Tlali Mokwena was saying as they chatted excitedly in Sotho, walking away from a War Recruitment office that had been set up in Bloemfontein a few days after the meeting at the hall. 'You have things going for you. You have an education, your uncle has his fingers in many dumplings. You have a trade, man, a trade. You can make cupboards, you can fix things made of iron. And, most of all, if you wanted to, you could get treated like a white man in this land. Why go and expose yourself to the dangers of war? This war is for poor, uneducated natives like myself. Not half-white boys like you.'

'The next time you call me a half-breed, child of my mother, you are going to eat this,' Pitso said, showing his friend a clenched fist.

'Come off it, man. God gives you a good complexion and heritage, and you spit into His face.'

Pitso's fist collided with Tlali's nose, which started bleeding immediately.

Men walking from the recruitment office stopped the fight, saying, 'Young men, you have to preserve your anger and strength for the real fight out there in the white man's land. Store up your fury.'

Pitso and Tlali were embarrassed by what they'd just done under the full gaze of neighbours who surely would soon start laughing at them: *These wet-behind-the-ears boys think they can fight the great white man's war across the seas when they can't even control their own tempers.*

CHAPTER 19

On 28 December 1916, Pitso, Tlali and many other men from Bloemfontein and surrounding areas were at the train station, ready for their journey to Cape Town. There was much excitement, and much shedding of tears, as wives and girlfriends hugged their loved ones for the umpteenth time. Pitso kept to himself, throwing only an occasional word into the conversation that swirled around him. Then, out of the corner of his eye, he saw a familiar figure. Christine was standing there, staring at him. She started walking slowly towards him and he saw that she was crying.

Conversations stopped. People stared as the white woman approached Pitso, clearly distraught.

She said, 'Why are you doing this? I'm sorry if I hurt you but don't go, please. I'm begging you. It isn't even your war.'

Even though Christine still taught at the school, Pitso had stopped taking music lessons with her. When they met on the school premises, their interactions were strained and formal. Now, here at the station, he did not know what to say or do. So he merely looked at her. When he turned to leave, she grabbed him by the collar of his shirt and kissed his lips passionately. Then she let go and, eyes filled with tears, said, 'Whatever happens to you over there, remember this: I love you, and I'm sorry if I hurt you … in the words of Horace, *Dulce et decorum est pro patria mori*.' She turned on her heel and walked away quickly. He watched her until she disappeared beyond the hedge that separated the railway company's property from the rest of public land.

Pitso slowly walked back to his companions. He did not bother to wipe the tears from his eyes, but no man said a word. The train staggered into the station, belching thick, black smoke and hissing like a thousand angry vipers. A festive mood floated in the air as people boarded, bundling their belongings inside the train. More tears were shed as women waved at the departing train. Others were ululating, as African women would when sharing their last words with warriors about to go into battle. Pitso saw Saartjie waving from the platform. He looked away.

There were already men from other towns inside the train. The men on board were from Pretoria, Johannesburg, Springs, Ficksburg and a few places that Pitso had never heard of. They were happy in their shared camaraderie, happy to be in the company of other recruits just like them – young, excited, scared, uncertain about what lay ahead, but committed to the cause of fighting the evil German Kaiser, or Mkize, as they had chosen to call him.

The recruits were from all over the country, from all language groups, from the Transvaal, Basutoland, Bechuanaland. Later, they would be joined by others from Natal, Pondoland, Cape Province. They spoke isiZulu, isiXhosa, isiNdebele, isiSwazi, Tshivenda, Sepedi, Setswana, Xitsonga. There were the smooth-talking city slickers from Johannesburg and its surrounds; educated, cerebral graduates from Lovedale College; tribal chiefs from Zululand and Pondoland; hard-working farmhands from the country's rural areas who had spent their lifetimes working on white people's properties for a pittance, people who'd never seen a train in their lives, let alone travelled on one; clergymen impelled by their consciences and a quest for justice on earth to throw in their lot with the Crown's troops; angry young men like Pitso who saw the war as their road to salvation and self-redemption.

'At the risk of getting my nose punched in again, what exactly makes you want to go and fight?' Tlali asked as the train chugged on.

'The money is good.'

'I know the money is good, but with you it seems to be beyond the money.'

'My father makes me want to go to fight.'

'You are speaking in riddles. You've told me before that your father went missing when you were but a piccaninny. You once said you hated him …'

'Hate is a strong word. I must have been angry when I said I hated him. It's just that I love him so much that I hate him. I hate him for not being there when I needed him as a child, to guide me, to advise me. I don't understand this war, but I feel I have to fight. I know he fought in the Anglo–Boer War, but did not see the war to its end. He ran away.'

'Maybe you're being unfair to him. You don't know what happened there.'

'All I know is that I don't want to be like him. I don't want to run away from responsibility; I don't want to run away from anything. This war is an opportunity to get out of my father's shadow and prove my worth as a man.'

Tlali fingered his necklace made of tiny bones – they could have been the bones of a monkey, as far as Pitso could guess.

Tlali's father had made the necklace for him as an amulet to protect him from evil forces. The centrepiece of the necklace was a gall bladder from some animal.

'That thing stinks,' said Pitso.

'You won't be saying that in Europe. When Mkize comes, all I have to do is to finger this necklace, and his bullets won't touch me. What about you, how are you going to protect yourself?'

'I will pray.'

'I see. And the bullets will bounce off your Bible.'

'Tlali, I know they say we won't be getting guns when we get there ...'

'Uh-huh, but I'll do my best to get myself a gun. Even if it means stealing one.'

Pitso laughed. 'Already thinking of breaking the law of the white man, even before we leave home.'

At intervals the hubbub of conversation would die down, and everyone would listen to the clickety-clack-clickety-clack music of the train.

As they rode, the recruits aboard the train began to feel superior to the rest of the South African populace. They were the Chosen Ones, the Anointed, the Untouchables. They were the ones who could change things.

Whenever the train nosed its way into a station, they would pour out onto the platform and take whatever they wanted from the rail-side stalls: fruit, food, cigarettes. The stall owners were too stunned to complain.

Back on the train, the men shared the spoils they had stolen from the traders at the previous station. In the midst of all the mayhem, Pitso noticed a group of men who sat quietly by themselves.

'Who are those men? Where are they from? Are they sick?'
he asked.

'They are Pondos,' someone replied. 'They are with their
chief. Even though he's a recruit just like everybody else, they
have to defer to him. They can't misbehave in front of him. It's
protocol.'

Pitso wanted to say something to his friend about superstitious, backward people, but suddenly remembered that Tlali
believed in lucky charms that turned bullets into water.

At another level Pitso had some respect for the Pondo chief
who, like some prominent figures in the black community,
believed that by taking the lead in fighting against the Germans,
they would gain the respect of the British. That upon their return
from the war, their loyalty to the Crown would be rewarded.

Every now and then Pitso found himself receding into his
own cocoon. Thoughts of Christine assailed him. Oh, Christine.
Dear, sweet Christine. The memory of her weighed him down,
dragging him into a pit of despair and depression. This was how
his mother must have felt at the departure of his father. Except
Christine had not just walked away from him – she had
pummelled him in the middle of his forehead with the hammer
of deceit.

When the train pulled into Worcester station, the recruits
found a stall packed with grapes. They pounced on the
cornucopia from the Cape, creating a mess. Some even dragged
the boxes onto the train. But the debauchery ended when the
train finally arrived in Cape Town. Then reality began to sink
in.

'Holy Modimo!' Tlali exclaimed. 'Is that what I think it is?'

'Yes, sir,' said Pitso. 'That, my friend, is the sea. We're going
to be floating on that for the next month or two, without ever

seeing the land. If we ever see it again.' Pitso himself had never seen the sea before. But he was a reader, and such was the power of the written word that beholding the sea with his own eyes was only confirmation of what he already knew, what he had already smelled, what he had already immersed his body in.

The recruits craned their necks to get a better look at this huge, endless body of water. Even though they had heard stories about the greatest river of all, they had never imagined what it would look like in real life. This was a new experience for many of them, apart from those who hailed from Zululand and Pondoland, situated along the coast.

As soon as they got off the train, they were met by a group of white officers who escorted them to waiting trucks. From the station, the trucks drove along the coast, evidently to give the recruits a taste of the city of Cape Town.

Pitso flared his nostrils and inhaled hungrily. The sea carried with it the subtle smell of dreams, hopes and ambitions that had driven the white man from his land of birth to the shores of Africa. The sea also smelled of crushed dreams and lost causes. It smelled of death; of frustrations. But it still carried with it the alluring scent of hope – hope that the journey he and his comrades were about to embark upon would be worth it.

They drove around for more than an hour, ending up at a place called the Rosebank Showgrounds, where they would be stationed until their final departure for Europe. There the recruits were to be checked by military doctors, inoculated and then tested for physical strength.

'Fall in line!' a white man with a powerful voice greeted them as soon as they had been disgorged by the trucks. 'Fall in line!'

When they had lined up, the men were issued with new clothing. The uniforms were dark blue melton, the same kind of clothing worn by members of the police force. Each recruit was also supplied with a strong pair of boots, two pairs of socks, one greatcoat, two shirts, two undershirts, four blankets, a towel, one belt, one hat or cap, one pair of braces. These uniforms were a novelty for the men, many of whom had never worn shoes or pants until they were recruited. At home, in the rural areas, they wore traditional outfits made of animal hide, or simply old sacks with holes for arms and a head.

Even so there were among them seasoned warriors who had fought in many battles against the white man, who knew how to manoeuvre against an enemy. In addition to being expert fighters using spears and clubs, some of them knew how to use firearms and dynamite. The challenge, however, was to unlearn the traditional African way of fighting. A whole new world awaited them across the oceans.

CHAPTER 20

Upon arrival, the recruits had been organised into battalions of two thousand men each, consisting of four companies of equal size. In terms of sleeping arrangements, tents had been organised for the men. Each tent slept ten to fifteen people.

The training started. Every day, the men were drilled and instructed on how to react when under fire, even though they would not be bearing arms in Europe.

The relationship between white soldiers and black recruits was tense. Many of the white officers in charge were highly agitated with these black recruits, whom they considered complete dunderheads.

'They can't master the simple art of marching in line, for crying in a bucket,' one white soldier was heard to complain.

The recruits were unable to grasp the most basic utterance in English. How, the officers wondered, was the white army going to work with these people in Europe?

The black recruits couldn't understand why they were being made to march in line. In their tradition, when you went to war, you didn't march around. You jumped about, ululating, singing at the top of your voice, wielding your spear and beating your cowhide shield with it. The dramatic singing and the screaming and the beating of the shield were meant to drive the fear of Satan into the heart of the enemy. Not this soulless, left-right, left-right, forward march, left-right, left-right, forward march. Even cows didn't walk like that.

An awkward scene took place on the training grounds one day. To ensure that they were physically fit enough to meet the demands of the tasks that awaited them overseas, where they would haul huge loads of cargo from ships and trains, the men were required to carry bags containing sand weighing a hundred pounds across a distance of a hundred yards. Each man had to carry this weight and walk steadily across the required distance to complete the exercise.

When it was Chief Mjongeni's turn to pick up the bag – the Pondo chief with the loyal subjects – his subjects would hear none of it.

'Our chief is not allowed to carry stuff like that. He's not a commoner. Please don't humiliate him, don't debase us,' pleaded one his subjects. 'I hereby offer my services to do his share of the work.'

The white officer asked the interpreter what the man was saying. The interpreter, a Lovedale-educated Xhosa speaker, did a straightforward translation.

Fuming, torrents of spit coming out of his mouth, the white officer said, 'Tell this monkey that the point here is not to simply carry a bag from point A to point B. Tell him we are testing everybody's strength – chief or no chief – to see if they qualify to go overseas. We can't carry sickly, burdensome bastards across the seas. We're going to war, not to a blooming picnic. Tell the blockhead what I've just told you!'

The Lovedale graduate who, like most educated black men, held the British-appointed tribal chiefs in utter contempt –

uneducated, polygamous heathens! – carefully twisted his whiskers, as was the habit of important educated people, and told the man: '*Uthi umlungu, hamb'onya. Akunankosi apha. Sonke singamadoda. Siyafana, sinamasende. Inkosi leyo yakho mayithathe langxowa iyibeke phaya phesheya kwebala xa ifuna ukuhamba nathi iye phesheya kwelwandle. Utsho umlungu.' The white man says, go and shit yourself. There's no chief here. We are all men, we all have balls here. We're the same. Your chief must lift that sack and carry it across the field like everybody else if he wants to join us on our journey overseas. The white man says.*

There were sniggers from those who'd overheard the exchange. The Pondos were angry that the white man had insulted their chief in such fashion. They vowed that they would arrange for their chief to take tea with the King of England so that this incident could be dealt with accordingly. Of course, it was a pipe dream. No such meeting would ever take place. In the end, the chief performed his chores just like the rest of the men.

The white senior officers had initially thought of keeping men from the various language groups apart. But after encounters such as this, it was decided to mix them up so that tribal chiefs couldn't count on their subjects to cover for them. This would later prove to be beneficial to both the officials and the men themselves – they began to trust and respect each other, despite their previously held prejudices. As a result of this mutual trust, they worked harder and faster together. During their breaks, men would exchange stories about their various traditions, only to discover they were not too different from each other. Significantly, Zulu speakers began to teach Sothos their language, and vice versa.

Pitso, even though he was a recruit himself, was working

overtime to translate to his comrades the white man's words. He had the good fortune of being able to speak Afrikaans, his father's language, which was spoken widely by the white people in Bloemfontein. But he could also speak his mother's language, Sesotho, and impeccable English, which he had of course learned at the centre for coloured children.

His linguistic interventions did not go unnoticed.

'Boy, where do you come from?' asked Captain Portsmouth, coming up to Pitso after a particularly demanding drill.

Standing at attention as he had been taught, Pitso briefly talked about his education. He never raised his eyes to look at the officer, but recalled that the man stood out from the rest because he walked with a limp, possibly an injury sustained in a long-forgotten war. His head and face were also clean-shaven, save for the tiny brown moustache which rested above his upper lip like an overfed caterpillar.

'You speak English so well,' the officer said at length, impressed by Pitso's story. 'But I also heard you speak Sesotho fluently the other day. What are you, a mixed breed?'

In the name of King Moshoeshoe, what was this paleface saying to him? Pitso's face clouded, his palms sweated, his lips twitched. If this man hadn't been an officer, he would have been tasting the young man's fist right then.

'Well, have you lost your tongue?'

'Sir, I am Mosotho, sir.'

'With looks like that, with hair like that? Do yourself a service, boy. Declare your coloured identity, and you will be accorded treatment befitting your status and moved to a coloured contingent.'

'I understand you, sir. But I'm still a Mosotho, as my papers say.'

'Ah, you're a proud Mosotho, then? Who is the founding father of the Basotho people? What's the original capital palace of the Basotho people?'

'I don't know, sir.'

'Would you like to find out?'

'To what effect, sir? The Basotho kingdom is as good as dead, so what would be the point of probing the past? That would only make me sad, wouldn't it, sir?'

Captain Portsmouth pushed on, 'Based on the evidence before me, I therefore conclude that you don't know yourself.'

'My father's white, my mother black, sir. But I am a human being. Classified as Mosotho, sir. Sorry, sir, my father *was* white. He is gone now.'

After a while, Captain Portsmouth said, 'We shall have another conversation, young man. I like your fortitude. But more importantly, I want you to teach me Sesotho. I used to be stationed in Basutoland some years ago. I started learning the language, but I stopped using it when I left that region. You know how it is; if you don't use the language often enough, you lose it. I need to brush up on my vernacular if I am to make myself useful to you fellows on our journey to Europe. But remember, you have just joined the army, not a debating society.'

The officer turned on his heel and walked away. Although he walked with a limp, there was pride and purpose in his stride. Pitso wondered if his father, the soldier he had once been during the Anglo–Boer War, had walked with such a sense of purpose.

CHAPTER 21

'Pitso,' started Tlali as they were eating dinner one evening in Cape Town, 'tell me I haven't died and woken up in the land yonder, the land of my ancestors.'

'What do you mean?'

'The food. White people's food on my plate. No boiled mealie-meal kernels and boiled cabbage here, no bitter wild spinach here. Look at this! The white woman who dished it up for me called it beef stew.'

'Come on, man, shut up and eat.'

'No, man! I won't shut up. The fact that I am eating so well is a sign of good things to come. Whoever thought the child of a humble African herbalist would be eating white man's food, off a white man's plate?'

Some of the men sitting not too far from them were probably thinking the same. They all came from poor backgrounds.

'At this rate, I think, maybe by the time I get to the land across the ocean, my own face would have changed to white.'

The other men roared with laughter.

What made the food even more delectable, Tlali said, was that it had been dished up for them by white ladies. He wished his father could have been there to witness the spectacle. With a smile as bright as the morning sunshine, the lady who dished up the food had generously placed a huge spoonful of meat onto his plate. He had been about to move to the next lady, who was dishing up vegetables, when the first lady asked him, gesticulating with her hands, if he wanted more. Of course he wanted more. Who could refuse a white lady's offering? So the white lady put more, and more, until his plate was as tall as the mountain overlooking their training grounds, the famous Table Mountain.

When the meal was over, an important-looking lady arrived. She was introduced to them as the wife of the Governor of the Cape. The men looked at each other, wondering what a 'governor' was. Speaking through an interpreter, the wife of the governor wished them well on their journey. She solemnly promised that she would be keeping them in her prayers.

The recruits were then asked to stand next to the governor's wife. A photograph was taken. Things happened too fast for Tlali to make sense of them immediately.

After dinner, as they were walking back to their sleeping quarters, Tlali was still in his element, telling stories and fantasising about life in Europe.

'Now that I've eaten my first white man's meal,' Tlali said, 'I think I am well on my way to getting myself a white bride.'

'Why would you need a white bride?' one man asked.

'Man, we're going to Europe! There are no black women over there. Besides, why would I want to go looking for a black woman in Europe when there are so many of them here at home? This war is freedom for us to explore, man.'

'Freedom,' one man assented.

Tlali continued, 'I'm just picturing my white bride. Perhaps with hips just so, wide enough to carry our children. Imagine the children. Grand, with a rich honey complexion, soft curly hair.' He saw Pitso's hands clench into fists and immediately fell silent.

One man argued, 'I know we've been told we can't touch white women over there. But what if the women want us?'

'Exactly,' said another man.

'I just hope,' Pitso said, 'that Tlali is not going to embarrass us over there in Europe.'

'What do you mean, I'm going to embarrass you?'

'Tell these men how you've never slept with a woman,' Pitso said to his friend, hoping to shut him up.

The men laughed and slapped each other on the back as they parted ways, each man to his own bed.

'Now, gentlemen, as you close your eyes to sleep, think of the white brides waiting for us overseas,' Pitso said, laughing.

As Pitso walked towards his bed, he was thinking what a wonderful, carefree friend he had in Tlali. The first time the two had met was at a tea room in Bloemfontein, where Tlali had been standing in line, waiting his turn to buy at a blacks-only window. The line had been long, the black lady serving them taking her time. Soon, Pitso had joined them, greeting those in line in their mother tongue, Sesotho. Then he had said, 'My mother's people, why are we standing at this window, in this heat, when we could go inside the shop and be served properly? We could sit down inside and enjoy our drinks on those chairs over there.'

There had been a hush, before somebody said, 'The inside of the tea room is reserved for white people.'

'Nonsense! A cup of tea is a cup of tea, whether you serve it from this window or from over there. I'm going to go inside and get myself a cup of coffee.'

Heads had turned and people were looking at him. One man said, 'Perhaps given your light skin they will serve you ...'

Pitso went inside, sat down and ordered a cup of coffee from a black woman who was wiping the top of a counter with a dirty rag.

Startled by the appearance of a non-white face inside the tea room, the woman stuttered and turned to a white man sitting behind the counter, reading a comic book. She said, '*Baas*, can I serve him from here?'

The white man looked up from his comic, adjusted his spectacles. His face turned red, and he growled: 'Hey, *fokof*, you. He's not white. He speaks the kaffir language. I know him, he's always causing trouble. Thinks he's white.'

'I'm not leaving this place until you serve me,' Pitso said quietly.

Now the blacks at the window started pelting him with insults: 'Hey, you half-breed cunt. Why are you always causing trouble for us? Don't you know the *baas* here will stop serving us altogether?'

'Leave our white man alone, you uppity yellow piece of shit, trying to show off!'

'The child of a black whore who slept with a cowardly white madman thinks he knows it all.'

One man held up his hand, asking his fellow customers to calm down. 'Maybe the young man has a point here. The shop is empty, and we are standing out here in the sun. Let's go in. I mean, we are regular customers here, the white customers are hardly ever here.'

The woman cleaning the tables smiled and winked at the man who'd said that. But the rest of the crowd started walking away from the shop. One of the men said, 'The *baas* will call the police, and we'll be in trouble because of your stupid vanity. Why don't you make peace with the fact that you aren't white, stupid piece of cow dung?'

Pitso shouted, 'Stupid dogs, all of you. You are an insult to the black race, to the whole human race.'

He stormed out, to the relief of Tlali, still standing in line, who'd been scared that the police would arrive and start beating up everyone.

A few weeks later, Tlali had encountered the troublesome boy again. Tlali had been sent by his father to the coloured children's school to find someone who could read him a letter he had received. None of the people in Tlali's village or the neighbouring villages could read it, as it was written in English. It looked important, and Tlali's father, always suspicious of white people, had been reluctant to find a white person from the town to read the letter for him, in case its contents could be taken advantage of by wily individuals. The herbalist had thought the Christian people who worked at the coloured children's centre were a better proposition.

When Tlali arrived at the centre, he was shocked to be greeted by the insolent mixed-race boy who had caused a scene at the tea room a few weeks before. What shocked him was that the coloured boy seemed to be in charge there. He was teaching younger boys and girls words in a language Tlali assumed to be English. The coloured boy recognised Tlali immediately and greeted him with a warm smile, speaking in Sesotho. 'I hope you haven't been sent by the white man to come and arrest me. I seem to recall that you and your friends did not take kindly to my performance the other day. By the way, my name is Pitso.'

Tlali introduced himself, then explained in detail his father's request.

'May I see the letter?'

He handed it over. Tlali noted that this young man called Pitso did not move his lips as he read the letter. He must be highly educated, Tlali thought. Only white people read letters or newspapers without moving their lips.

Pitso then explained that the letter was from a white man in Johannesburg, a Mr Whitlock, a former employer of Tlali's uncle Piet. Piet had died the previous month. Unable to locate his relatives until recently, Mr Whitlock had decided to bury Piet himself in Johannesburg. In the letter, Mr Whitlock was asking the family to advise him how he could send Piet's last wages and private belongings to his wife or members of the extended family. The family could decide what they wanted to do with these, as Piet had been a loyal and trustworthy servant.

Tlali snatched the letter from Pitso excitedly. He was in the process of running out the door when the latter stopped him. 'Tell your father that if he needs my English writing services to respond to this letter, I am available anytime.'

Indeed, Tlali's family invited Pitso to their huge household and watched him as he sat comfortably on a bench and wrote the letter. They were amazed at the ease with which he blackened a blank piece of paper with the 'white man's flies', as they called the letters of the alphabet.

A few weeks later, a telegram arrived inviting Tlali's father to come to Johannesburg to fetch his brother's money and private belongings. Ever since then, 'our light-complexioned boy', as Tlali's father called him, had been an important guest at all the family's traditional feasts and gatherings. He was considered the bringer of luck. As a token of appreciation,

Tlali's father had given Pitso a horse, a young colt which they duly named Lion, after Pitso's clan name.

Over the weeks that followed, Tlali had taken pleasure in teaching his friend how to ride. Pitso had his obligatory falls from his mount, but he soon proved to be a competent rider. The two of them could be seen galloping up the grassy knolls or hurtling down the various valleys of open country. They rode to the river where they washed their horses, swam together, picked wild berries. When they were not riding, Pitso would try to teach his friend basic woodworking skills, as he had been taught at the coloured children's centre.

Because Tlali's father was a hunter, he kept two old shotguns and a pellet gun. Thanks to his father, Tlali was a competent marksman, and Pitso was grateful when his friend started teaching him how to shoot. They ran after both small and big game. There were still large tracts of land that did not belong to anyone, on which ordinary folk could hunt. Amazing how the countryside had become peaceful once again, after the war.

Tlali and Pitso did have their differences now and then, as did hot-blooded young men, but they loved and respected each other like blood relatives. Tlali, who had never been to school, struggled to get into the mind of Pitso. His friend taught him the rudiments of reading and writing in his native Sesotho, but these basic skills did not equip him to fully understand what was going on in Pitso's head.

At the Cape Town Depot where they had started undergoing their training, Tlali watched enviously as Pitso engaged in what seemed to be a cordial exchange of words with the white officer. They smiled, shook their heads, gesticulated as close buddies would do. Imagine a black, young man having a casual chat with a white army official.

'One day I'll be like you,' Tlali said to his friend. 'One day I'll be able to read the Bible in English, and sing all those beautiful English hymns you've been teaching me. And I'll sing those hymns to my beautiful white bride in Europe.'

CHAPTER 22

It was a glorious day, the sun massaging the men of the Fifth Battalion's faces with its fingers of warmth as they stood at attention, in full uniform, at the Depot in Cape Town. It was 16 January 1917. A cool morning breeze blew from the sea and a group of seagulls hovered above the water, occasionally swooping to the ground below to fight over a morsel of food. There was very little talk among the men as they made their way towards the dock, laden with their kit. The boisterousness that had characterised their departure from their towns and villages, the loud mayhem they had caused on the train destined for Cape Town, the hearty singing that had accompanied many of their activities at the Depot, the naughty banter they had exchanged during their lunch breaks – all these things were behind them. The cheerful ribaldry had been replaced by a solemn resignation to the reality that lay ahead, waiting for them across the ocean.

Each man had good reason to wonder if this would be the last time he saw his country of birth, for he might die in combat, or the voracious sea might swallow him.

Before they left their homesteads, many of the men had slaughtered a beast – a cow, a goat, a sheep or even a chicken – to appease their ancestors. Having partaken of the blood of a freshly slaughtered animal, it was believed, the traveller would be protected by the ancestors, who would be at his side, acting as an invisible shield against all manner of danger. Some of the men had also burned heaps of the *impepho* herb as part of their farewell ceremony to the land. The *impepho* plant was considered sacred and many people made a point of burning a plateful of it before embarking on long journeys. But now that their journey was about to begin, the men's long-suppressed fears had been rekindled. The sea had to be approached with fear and respect. It carried many secrets in its belly. It was a realm inhabited by monsters never before seen by man. A world haunted by the souls of those who had drowned in these treacherous waters, or those whose vessels had disappeared without trace.

This was Pitso's final moment before he said goodbye to the land of his birth. He was clenching and unclenching his jaws, nervously trying to come to terms with what was happening, with the decision he had made. There was no turning back.

It was not often that Pitso found himself thinking about his mother, or mourning her. Now he was. Tantalising images of Christine, sweet Christine, also flashed in his mind's eye. But he shoved them aside, focusing on his mother. He found himself thinking of the little sister he only briefly knew. Where was she? Was she in heaven somewhere, watching over him? Where was his father? Did he even think of the family he'd left behind? What had happened to him? Was he still alive?

Pitso wondered if he even believed in this war. His friends had laughed at him, saying he was being wilfully manipulated by cowardly white people who could fight their own wars but were always looking for darker folks to use as cannon fodder.

Maybe his friends were right. How would he benefit from this war, assuming he came back alive? If he died, would it have been for a good cause?

Somebody started singing:

Ayanqikaza ayesaba amagwala,
athi kungcono sibuyele emuva.
The cowards are getting restless,
saying perhaps it's time we went back home.

It started as a slow hum by a handful of men, Zulu men to be sure, for this was a famous Zulu war song. The song grew in volume and momentum as more men joined in. Those who couldn't speak Zulu, and therefore didn't know the lyrics, first dipped their toes into this untested river of music. And then they were ankle deep in it. Before long, they had been swallowed whole by the thunderous, roiling wave of the song which they picked up with gusto:

… qiniselani nani maqhawe,
sekuseduze lapho siya khona
… stand firm, oh ye heroes,
For our destination is nigh.

The song soared; it swung low and then it swung high; it churned the men's emotions, swept them off their feet of self-doubt, landing them on the high clouds of certainty. Their voices rumbled and roared with a reborn sense of commitment, courage, hope; a joyous celebration of a new-found camaraderie.

Ayanqikaza, ayesaba amagwala
Athi kungcono sibuyele emuva.
Qiniselani nani maqhawe,
Sekuseduze lapho siya khona.

Some of the recruits secretly despised the fact that, even though the Zulus were in the minority, they were the most vocal, always imposing their opinions on others, always ready to usurp leadership opportunities. Pitso had read that, in the closing days of the recruitment drive, of the 25 000 men who had enlisted in the Labour Contingent, the land of the Zulus had contributed only 1 500. The final breakdown, by territory, would be as follows: Cape Province – 7 000; Transvaal – 13 000; Orange Free State – 800; Bechuanaland – 600; Basutoland – 1 500; Swaziland – 100.

Pitso wondered why the Zulu nation, historically a warlike people and numerically the biggest language group in the Union of South Africa, had not heeded the call to war with alacrity. After all, the Zulus liked fighting for the sake of fighting, or so it was said of them. Perhaps the reluctance of the Zulus to take part in the war stemmed from the fresh memories of their humiliation at the hands of the British at the Battle of Rorkes Drift in 1879, which finally put paid to the mighty Kingdom of the Zulus.

In the wake of that battle, huge tracts of land, which were originally the domain of the Zulus, were taken over by the conquering British and parcelled out to black chiefs appointed by the British Empire to carry out the nefarious mandate of the colonialists. Some lands fell under the authority of white magistrates, official appendages of the British Crown. It would take the Children of Mageba a long time, if ever, to recover from this sense of humiliation, let alone to forget it. They were a proud people, the Zulus. When they tried once again to rise in 1906, the ill-fated Bhambatha Rebellion was suppressed before it could gain traction. The ringleaders at the forefront of the campaign were dealt with ferociously. Bhambatha kaMancinza Zondi, the heart and brains of the revolt, was brutally murdered, and the victorious British chopped off his head and paraded it to sceptical followers who did not believe that the great warrior had succumbed to the colonialists. Under these circumstances, even those Zulus who had turned to Christianity during the time of King Cetshwayo, prior to the decisive Rorkes Drift battle, were still ambivalent about the British. They had not recovered from the shock of the violence visited upon their fellow Zulus by the agents of the British Empire.

But the Zulus who had heeded the call to join up with the British troops in their effort against the Germans had done so with pride and dignity. They had vowed to fight to the death for their belief in the justness of the war against the Germans, even if it meant dying at the hands of their fellow Zulus, who had violently tried to dissuade them from joining the conflict. There had also been hope in their heart that, at the end of the war, the British would reward them by reconsidering the status of their king. They couldn't wait to bask in the full glory of their monarch, once his powers had been fully restored by the British. The war in Europe was their hope for salvation and redemption. As the Zulu saying goes, *ithemba kalibulali – hope never killed anyone.*

> *The cowards are getting restless,*
> *Saying perhaps it's time we turned back.*
> *Stand firm oh ye warriors,*
> *For our destination is nigh.*

When they finally reached the vessel they would be sailing on, the men were breathless with joy and impressed by the size of the ship. The name emblazoned in bold script on either side of the vessel read 'ss *Mendi*'.

As they embarked, some men carried tattered bags and suitcases that contained their private clothes. Others carried small, decorative cowhide shields and fighting sticks. One man carried a concertina. An officer did the roll call, with each man climbing up the gangway as his name was shouted across the windy wharf: 'Geelbooi Dinoka! William Ditshepo! Saucepan Maake, Whisky Mahlaba ...'

Progress was slow, as many of the men had never been aboard a ship. There was a lot of laughter and nervous joshing – 'Won't this thing disintegrate right there in the middle of the water?' and 'Why did we sign up for these white wizards to play games with us?'

Once aboard the ship, the men proceeded to the holds below, which had been fitted as troop decks. The white leaders were ushered into cabins amidships, an area that could accommodate sixty people. Medical orderlies and interpreters were quartered near the hospital, which had its designated area in the second-class accommodation aft.

As the final provisions were being loaded onto the vessel – food, coal, clothing and so on – a rumour started circulating among the black recruits.

'The white man has loaded a ton of gold into the ship,' said one man in a conspiratorial tone.

'Why?' questioned another man, frowning.

'If we lose the war, we can simply hand over the gold to the victorious Germans, say we are sorry, and then they will let us go home,' the first man explained, proud to know more than his comrades.

'The strange ways of the white man. But what if we win the war?'

'Maybe the white man is going to chop the gold up into pieces, and we each get a piece.'

'What the hell am I going to do with a piece of gold?'

'Sell it and get money, or get money made out of it. You need money these days. Cattle are not enough. You need money to pay your taxes. Ah, there are so many kinds of taxes now. Hut tax, dog tax, poll tax. The gold is going to help us get money. That's how white men get rich.'

'Isn't this gold so heavy it can sink our ship?'

'Leave it to the white man, son. He's extracted a lot of wealth from the bowels of our country already and sent it to his native country. And his ships never sank. Maybe some did sink, but the majority reached their destination safely.'

On and on the stories about gold did the rounds. In fact, newspaper reports of the time confirmed that, before the ss *Mendi* sailed, gold bullion to the value of five million pounds had indeed been taken on board the ship. The war was costing the British Crown a lot of money and, due to the extraordinary situation, sailing international waters was high risk. German U-boats, submarines and armed cruisers had been dispatched to all the seven seas, attacking Allied merchant boats to prevent supplies from reaching their troops in Europe. Even passenger liners were not safe from the Germans. In these conditions, the ss *Mendi* had to sail in convoy with the *Kenilworth Castle*, also carrying South African troops and gold. Escorted by the armoured cruiser HMS *Cornwall*, the other ships in the convoy were the Orient liner *Orsova*, the White Star Liner *Medic*, the *Berrima* and the *Port Lyttelton*, all of which were carrying Australian troops.

Standing on deck, looking at the receding hulk of Table

Mountain and the mainland that they might be seeing for the last time, some troops wept.

'Look at that,' said Tlali to a group of men. 'The land is becoming smaller and smaller. Soon it won't exist. Isn't that a miracle?'

Thankfully, the weather was kind to the passengers of ss *Mendi* and the rest of the convoy. They sailed smoothly, and after looking at the land of their birth disappear from view, they went to their assigned tasks.

The commander of the *Mendi* was Captain Henry Arthur Yardley, a tall, gangly man with a ready smile and a well-trimmed white beard. An expensive pipe was always dangling from the side of his mouth, like a permanent appendage. Captain Yardley was a veteran sailor who had been a master of a number of vessels since 1901. Aboard the vessel was a crew of eighty-nine, including the master and officers, mostly British. The South African Native Labour Contingent consisted of five white officers, seventeen non-commissioned officers and eight hundred and two black troops. There were also a small number of military passengers; officers returning to Europe after wounds or leave.

Soon enough – amazingly quickly, in fact – the men adopted the routine of life on a troopship. They cleaned troop decks and laid kit out for inspection. During the day, they were encouraged to spend as much time as possible on the open decks. Taking advantage of his size and physical strength, Pitso applied for a job as a stoker in the engine room. He joined a group of strong, well-built men down there, recognising one of them as Ngqavini, the Zulu-speaking man who always led them in song.

Ngqavini glared at Pitso when he walked into the engine

room for the first time and picked up a shovel and started doing what the other men were doing – shovelling coal into the boiler.

'*Hheyi, msushwana ndini ufunani la?*' said Ngqavini. *Hey, you little Sotho boy, what are you doing here?* 'You think this is your mother's backyard garden? You will shit rocks and boulders here. Jesu-Maria-Josefa! We want men, not girls in pants!'

Pitso ignored the Zulu and continued shovelling the coal. The following day was the same, but Pitso sweated it out down there in the belly of the ship, Ngqavini's taunts and insults bouncing off his broad shoulders. Working down there allowed him the solitude he needed, the precious opportunity to be by himself with his thoughts.

On the fifth day of his service in the boiler room, Pitso suddenly felt the ship trembling and rocking wildly, the first time it had done so since they left port, scaring him.

To calm his nerves, he started singing:

> *When peace, like a river, attendeth my way*
> *When sorrows like sea billows roll*
> *Whatever my lot, Thou hast taught me to say*
> *It is well, it is well, with my soul.*
> *Though Satan should buffet, though trials should*
> *   come,*
> *Let this blest assurance control,*
> *That Christ has regarded my helpless estate,*
> *And hath shed His own blood for my soul …*

Ngqavini, his mouth agape, a spark of surprise, curiosity, joy in his eyes, rumbled, 'Hey, so are you a Christian?'

Pitso continued singing, ignoring the other man.

'*Msushwana*, are you listening to me? Are you a Christian?'

Exasperated, Pitso stopped singing and asked, 'So what if I'm Christian?'

'I was born into Christianity, but there were challenges ...'

They stared at each other wordlessly for some time.

Ngqavini seemed to change his mind about engaging in conversation. He picked up his shovel and cried, 'Back to work, *msushwana*. Jesu-Maria-Josefa! We came here to work, not to *perepereza* with our mouths like women.'

Frowning, Pitso picked up his shovel and went back to work. He broke into another song.

About an hour later, Pitso's rhythm was broken when he heard Ngqavini shouting, 'And what do you think you are doing here?'

Pitso, who was now used to Ngqavini's outbursts, most of which were unnecessary, decided to ignore the man. He continued shovelling coal into the furnace.

'Get the hell out of here, man. We have enough Basothos here as we speak. Get away from here!'

Enough, Pitso thought, dropping his shovel. When he looked up, he realised that Ngqavini was addressing Tlali, who had entered the engine room. Ngqavini moved like a dust devil towards Tlali, his fists clenched. 'I said get out of here. No more Basotho girls. Out.'

By way of reply, Tlali connected a right to Ngqavini's left cheek. A weaker man would have dropped like a bag of potatoes, but Ngqavini was a seasoned street fighter who'd done time at blood-spattered gold-mine compounds in Johannesburg. He merely shook his head, then threw a sledgehammer that caught Tlali on the jaw. Tlali was knocked back, slamming against a hot boiler. Screaming in agony, he shrank away from the burning metal.

Pitso couldn't just stand there and watch. He crouched and barrelled forward, meaning to ram his head into Ngqavini's midriff, but his opponent danced out of the way, and Pitso went crashing to the floor. He got up to have another go and saw Ngqavini charging at him with a knife.

Just in time, the black sergeant in charge of the engine room delivered a mighty right to Ngqavini's temple. The engine room resounded with a thud as the gangster fighter sagged to his knees, his knife clattering to the floor.

Three black guards rushed down, armed with billy clubs.

'Hardly a week into the journey, you're already embarrassing us in front of the white officers,' one of them said.

Ngqavini, Pitso and Tlali were marched upstairs. The trial, such as it was, lasted about five minutes: who did what to whom, yes, thank you very much, all three of you are guilty. Sentence? Twenty lashes each with a sjambok, and four days in solitary confinement for Pitso and Ngqavini. Tlali's burns saved him from a spell in solitary; he had to be taken to the hospital wing after getting his twenty lashes.

Captain Portsmouth heard about the fight and walked into the officers' mess just as the three prisoners were taking off their pants. Pitso looked up at him for a moment, then dropped his gaze in shame. After the sjambokking, which left their backs and buttocks with thick welts oozing blood, Ngqavini and Pitso were taken downstairs and bundled into the dark, windowless dungeon where they were to spend the next four days.

CHAPTER 23

By Pitso's rough estimation, the dungeon he and Ngqavini had been thrown into, down in the hold of the ship, was three metres by three. The ceiling was so low they could barely walk upright. Because there was so little room to pace about, they were to spend most of the time sitting or lying on their thin coir mattresses, staring into the darkness. It was so dark they could hardly see their own hands. The limited light they did receive filtered through an air vent at the top of the cell door. Inside the cell sat a night-soil bucket which they had to share. Next to the bucket was a generous supply of newspapers, but not for reading purposes. And next to this was a basin with water, in which they were to wash their hands and a bucket of water from which they could drink.

After only a few hours in the little cell, Ngqavini was attacked by a terrible bout of diarrhoea. Pitso cursed non-stop, Ngqavini cackling with laughter as he let rip. He hardly finished his business at the toilet when the door opened. A guard walked in. He had brought their food, he announced, trying his best not to breathe. For each person six thick slices of bread ladled with jam and a gallon of *mahewu*, a thick and very sweet drink made of mealie meal.

'Take care of this food, gentlemen, because your next meal will only be delivered tomorrow morning.'

'What time is it now?' Pitso asked.

'It is two in the afternoon.'

'How long have we been here now?'

'About two, three hours.'

With those words, the guard pulled the door shut after him and locked it.

They'd been there only three hours, yet it felt like a whole day. Now it was Pitso's turn at the bucket. Ngqavini roared with laughter as Pitso groaned in the dark.

Both men decided to keep their food for later. It was so hot down there they'd stripped down to their trousers. The air coming through the vent above the door was just enough to keep them alive. Apart from the sound of their own breathing, and the thudding of their hearts, it was quiet. The ride was smooth, with occasional bumps which reminded them they were not in their mothers' wombs but on the precipice of a cliff the depth of which they couldn't even imagine. Yet Pitso's imagination was running wild: what if the ship were to slam into another ship and start sinking? Who would remember them? What if the floor on which they were lying were to suddenly cave in, unbeknownst to the people upstairs? What if some sea monster, whose eyes could see through the walls of ships, was watching them right now, biding his time before carving a hole at the base of the ship and grabbing them both for his evening snack?

Pitso must have fallen asleep, for when he sat up on his mattress there was a strange sound in the cell. He strained his eyes, hoping to see something, anything, but it was useless – it was as dark as it had been when he'd gone to sleep. But the sound persisted. He listened.

'I knew you were bound to wake up,' a voice said in the darkness. 'Can't sleep on an empty stomach.'

Ah, it was his cellmate eating. Pitso grimaced, revulsed at the idea of eating food inside such a smelly place.

'Are you going to eat or what? If you aren't eating, tell me. I'll deal with your share. It's unchristian to let food go to waste. That's what my mother told me. Can't let food go to waste, that's what they teach you in jail.'

Jislaaik, Pitso thought, I'm thirsty as hell. He extended his hand to where he'd put his gallon of *mahewu*, reached for it, lifted the spout to his mouth.

'Easy on that drink. A sip at a time. Otherwise it will give you diarrhoea.'

Pitso was meditating on the different shades of darkness that he was aware of – dusky, gloomy, inky, indigo – when he finally fell, again, into a dreamless sleep.

When he woke up, he was famished. He fumbled around his section of the cell, looking for his food. He found the plate, but it was empty.

'You ate my food,' he cried out. 'You stole my food.'

'I thought you had no need for it,' Ngqavini said casually, belching.

Fists clenched, Pitso propelled himself forward in the general direction of Ngqavini's voice. But the latter, out of sheer instinct, ducked out of the way, and connected a punch to Pitso's stomach.

Doubling over and blinking his eyes angrily, Pitso crouched, listened attentively to ascertain the direction from which Ngqavini's heavy breathing came.

Ngqavini chuckled and said, 'Can you see my fist, friend?' Then he punched his cellmate in the stomach again.

Pitso staggered uneasily. Having regained his footing, he hurled himself forward, punching blindly. Ngqavini pushed him away, laughing. 'Remember, my friend, I still have that knife. You want me to use it now?'

Pitso threw a fist into the darkness. Luckily, it connected with Ngqavini's left temple. Ngqavini delivered a welter of punches to Pitso's face, until they both collapsed, exhausted.

On the day of their release, Ngqavini told the sergeant who had come to open for them how Pitso had almost killed him with a knife.

'He's got a knife?' asked the incredulous guard.

'Yes, sir. I managed to wrestle it away from him. Coloured people and knives are good buddies.'

'Bloody bushman,' the sergeant rumbled. 'I sentence you to one more day in this cell for carrying a knife.'

'It's not my knife. It's his,' Pitso protested.

'Liar!' cried Ngqavini.

The guard punched Pitso in the gut and pushed him back into the cell before locking it.

Ngqavini laughed, and shouted at Pitso in Afrikaans, a language he thought the Zulu-speaking guard probably wouldn't understand, 'Welcome to the world, fool!'

CHAPTER 24

One morning, as he was dozing in a chair in the hospital section, Captain Portsmouth was woken by a piercing scream. By the time he got to the source of the noise, a group of medical orderlies had gathered around two adjoining beds, whispering urgently between themselves. Portsmouth approached the beds and discovered two lifeless men lying there.

'Oh, shit,' the senior medical orderly exclaimed when he saw the dead bodies. He frowned, taking a closer look. 'Look at the faces; so black and almost brittle. What could have caused this? It looks like a contagious disease.'

'No time to wonder what killed them,' said Portsmouth. 'We have to get rid of the corpses, or the entire ship will be contaminated.'

Somebody ran to get the chaplain and the master of the ship, Captain Yardley.

A few minutes later, the captain and Reverend Isaac Wauchope Dyobha walked in. Tall, regal of bearing, Reverend Dyobha was one of those men who exuded power and charisma. When he walked, everyone got out of the way, including the white officers.

'I came as soon as I received your call, Captain,' Reverend Dyobha said.

'We need you, as a man of the cloth, to say a prayer for the two men ...' Yardley's voice trailed off.

'Couldn't we wait until we reached the next port, to give them a proper burial?' the reverend asked.

'I'm afraid we can't wait any longer. I don't want my ship contaminated,' said Yardley.

The man of faith nodded gravely. Captain Portsmouth volunteered to join Reverend Dyobha as he said a eulogy for the fallen men. Ngqavini and Tlali, who had joined the small group, started a song:

> Go tell it on the mountain, over the hills and every-
> where ...

The others joined him. When the song was over, Ngqavini shouted a Zulu war cry: '*Uyadela wen'osulapho!*' *Oh, how I wish I were you!*

'What's going to happen to the corpses?' Tlali asked quietly, as the men were walking out of the hospital section.

Ngqavini explained, 'The reverend and the hospital orderlies are going to throw the corpses overboard.'

Tlali was shocked. 'These men won't have proper graves? You are telling me their bodies are going to be eaten by the monsters of the sea? Ah, their spirits will never know peace. Their spirits shall roam these seas forever.'

As they were dispersing, Ngqavini bumped into Pitso. The two looked at each other, then Ngqavini spat on the floor, in front of Pitso.

Portsmouth caught him by the lapel of his jacket, and said, 'Soldier! Wipe that spit of yours off the floor.'

'Sorry, Captain, I will go and find a cloth.'

'With your tongue, soldier. On your knees! Now! Lick it up with your tongue, take it back where it belongs.'

Ngqavini got to his knees. Three white officers who were passing by – officers who had always thought Captain Portsmouth was soft on the kaffirs, always chatting cordially with them – smiled at what they saw.

'That's right, Captain. Put them in their place,' said one of them, who had the red face of a heavy drinker.

Captain Portsmouth ignored the comment and hobbled down the steps, towards his cabin, to rest for a while. But he couldn't find peace, thinking over the way Pitso and Ngqavini interacted with one another. So he went onto the deck, where most of the men were basking in the sun. Some were chatting excitedly, others staring into the distance in silence, possibly shaken by the recent deaths. Just then, they spotted a school of dolphins swimming about happily in the distance.

'Is that a shark?' someone called out.

'No, it's a whale. My God, it's going to topple our ship!'

The men laughed, as they could see that the whale was too far in the distance to do them any harm.

'Hey you!' Captain Portsmouth shouted at Tlali, who came running up to him. 'Where's your friend?'

'Down in the engine room, sir.'

'And the other man, Ngavuvu, or whatever his name is? The loud Zulu?'

'Oh, that would be Ngqavini, sir. He is also down there in the engine room, sir.'

'Go get them right this very minute. Get two men to replace them in the engine room. I want the two of them up here. Now!'

Tlali saluted and disappeared down the stairs, marching

proudly in his uniform, which he kept spotlessly clean. Captain Portsmouth paced up and down, deep in thought.

A few minutes later, Ngqavini and Pitso stood in front of him. He glared at them. 'You rotten lot are full of bad blood. We must drain it out of you before you infect everyone on this ship.'

He picked six men and told them to follow him downstairs. The four white officers who had been standing on deck, smoking and joking, paused to watch, as there seemed to be some urgency in Captain Portsmouth's manner.

When Captain Portsmouth disappeared downstairs, followed by confused men, the officers decided to follow at a distance, to see what was happening. When they reached the dining hall, Captain Portsmouth told the men to clear the tables and chairs away, and stack them in a corner. They obeyed. He hobbled away to his cabin. When he came back, he had two pairs of boxing gloves.

'Men! We are starting a boxing tournament today,' he said. 'To get the games started, I call upon Pitso and 'Gavini, to show you men how it's done.'

Pitso and Ngqavini exchanged stunned glances.

Captain Portsmouth threw the boxing gloves on the floor, in the middle of the improvised arena. He strode towards Ngqavini, grabbed him by the lapels of his shirt, and said, 'Pick up those gloves. Put them on. What are you waiting for? We need to deal with your anger.'

Ngqavini took off his shirt and reached for the gloves. He looked odd, fumbling his hands into these padded, oversized things. He would have preferred a bare-knuckle encounter.

Pitso stripped to the waist, picked up his gloves and put them on, by trial and error, as he had never touched a pair of boxing gloves in his life either.

There was a murmur of excitement in the crowd. Reverend Dyobha strode in, his face beaming. As a younger man, before he went to seminary to train as a priest, Reverend Dyobha had tried his hand at boxing.

'Brilliant move, Portsmouth,' one of the white officers said. 'Wonder why we didn't think of this earlier.'

'I bought the gloves in Durban because I suspected that we might need to start a boxing training club, to kill the long hours of our journey. Now is the time,' Captain Portsmouth explained. 'Used to be a keen boxer myself at military college in England. Bim-bam-bim-bam-bang! Love the sport, I do.'

He moved to the centre of the makeshift arena, held Pitso and Ngqavini each by the hand and said, 'Now, listen carefully, chaps. No holding, no biting, no kicking, no punching below the belt. The sound of the bell will mark the beginning or the end of a round. Understood?'

'Yes, sir,' they said in unison, preparing themselves for the fight.

Captain Portsmouth stepped back, reached for an enamel plate, which he banged with a spoon. The gladiators started dancing about. Pitso threw a left jab which caught Ngqavini on his right temple, stunning him.

Ngqavini cried out, 'Jesu-Maria-Josefa!'

He floated to the left and when Pitso closed in, intent on following his left jab with a right, Ngqavini dropped into a tiger's crouch. Pitso's right flew just above his head. Ngqavini bobbed back to the surface, bombarding Pitso's face with a welter of blows, to the excitement of the crowd.

Portsmouth banged the enamel plate. The fighters stopped.

There were whistles and shouts as the men retired to their 'corners'. Tlali had taken on the role of Pitso's coach. 'Pitso, you are fighting with your heart. You are angry. Take a deep breath, and watch the man's shoulders and fists, not his eyes. If you look at his eyes, you will get angry, but when you watch his shoulders, and his arms, you can tell which punch he's going to throw next.'

The bell sounded. Pitso ran into the arena as if shot out of a gun, stopped only by Ngqavini's left jab, which caught him on his right cheek. Ngqavini followed up with an uppercut to the jaw. Pitso sagged and dropped to the wooden floor. The fight was over.

The bout between Pitso and Ngqavini marked the beginning of a very popular weekly tradition. The boxing matches, in turn, paved the way for other recreational activities. Reverend Dyobha approached Captain Portsmouth one day and thanked him for his thoughtfulness in starting the boxing club. 'Through the boxing, you are catering to the physical needs of our men. But man is a more complex animal. I cater to the spiritual needs of these young fellows. Would it not be nice, however, to start a school for these men with literacy classes? Many of them can't even spell their own names, let alone read the Holy Book.'

A few days later, men started attending reading and writing classes in both English and their own languages. This kept everyone busy, from officers down to members of the crew, whose shifts had to be rearranged to give them time to attend classes.

The officers generally played bridge. Captain Portsmouth, when he was not busy with literacy classes or boxing matches, relaxed by playing the piano. He mostly played waltzes, especially those of Johann Strauss II – *The Blue Danube, Morgenblätter, Kaiser-Walzer*. The other officers used to laugh. 'The fucking Krauts started the war and you are playing their music!'

'Strauss was Austrian, not German,' he would respond.

'Even worse,' they would retort. 'It was Archduke Franz Ferdinand, an Austrian, who started this war by getting himself killed. And his cousins in Germany took umbrage. That's why we are all in the shit. Some of our men are probably going to drown in that Blue Danube you are busy celebrating.'

When they were not taunting Captain Portsmouth, the officers also boxed – but only with ranked opponents. No officer wanted to be humiliated by one of the 'boys', although they didn't admit to that. They simply argued rank didn't allow an officer to tangle with a mere member of the labour contingent. The 'boys' laughed themselves silly watching the officers, fat men dawdling all over the fighting arena with no sense of rhythm and timing. Captain Portsmouth and Reverend Dyobha had taught the men that boxing, like dancing, required rhythm. A typical fight sounded like this: Tap-tap, boom! Tap-tap, boom. Boom-boom-boom, bah!

In one of his inspired moments, Ngqavini, aided by four of his tribesmen, did a demonstration of a typical Zulu war dance, which was enjoyed by all. Captain Portsmouth was amazed at the similarities between some of Ngqavini's dance moves and the rhythm of a typical boxing fight: you charge forward twice, and you retreat one step. Move to the right, charge three times with your left hand thrust forward, and retreat two steps. You pause. You start the process all over again.

One night, after one of the officers' fights, Captain Portsmouth joined the others for a drink.

'The boxing seems to have raised the morale of our men,' one officer observed.

'Of course, boxing is good for them,' another said. 'You see, these brown races, that's all they are good at – physical exertion. They can't handle the bigger things in life – civilised governance, industrial innovation. It was ridiculous to even suggest that they should be joining us on the front lines. They know nothing about war, real war.'

'Yeah, good at monkey games. They want to draw blood, they want to see the next person suffer,' said the ruddy-faced officer who answered to the name of Haig. 'They shrink away from things that are cerebral, things involving proper strategy, am I right or wrong?'

'Speaking of strategy,' Captain Portsmouth broke in, 'primitive as they are in their methods, don't you think we have a thing or two to learn from them in terms of war strategy?'

All eyes turned to him.

'How did we lose the Battle of Isandlwana? They beat us purely on strategy. We had the technology, we had the international experience. But we were rigid in our strategy. My father told me in detail what happened there … it's not something I read in books. They used the bull-horn strategy. Simple yet very effective.'

The bull-horn or buffalo-horn strategy was a time-tested military maneouvre where the attacking army would face the enemy in front, on both flanks and in the rear. The 'horns' – the right- and left-flank elements – would encircle and pin the enemy before the 'chest', or the central main force, would charge forward to deliver the coup de grâce.

'Who's your father, then?' asked Officer Haig, pulling at his flame-red beard.

'Sir William Portsmouth.'

'By golly! *The* Portsmouth?' another officer said. 'I thought your name was Plymouth. So it's *Ports*mouth. Every military man worth his salt has heard of him. How did we miss that?

We've been thinking how odd you look for a soldier. Now we know you are old Bull Face's son. But I've heard only good things about the man. And we all know the Zulu victory at Isandlwana was a fluke.'

Portsmouth said, 'I can lay you down my last pound: in due course the European armies will be using the bull-horn strategy.'

'Whatever you say,' Officer Haig insisted, 'these Africans of yours are not ready for modern warfare. It's a good thing they won't be given guns in Europe.'

CHAPTER 25

'Land-ho! Land! I can see the white man's land on the horizon!' a man shouted from the upper deck early one morning. Soon the deck was overflowing with the crew. Their glad eyes beheld a smudge of land and vegetation in the distance. A flock of birds that they couldn't identify hovered just above them, occasionally swooping and touching the surface of the water with their wings.

While they were still in the grip of excitement, the ship was lifted high on a gigantic swell. A cold, salty spray rose high into the air, showering the men's faces. Some men cried out, others hit the deck.

Another towering wall of water rose ominously just ahead of them. Again, the vessel was lifted high, and crash! It bounced into a hollow. More cries and rushed prayers were hurled at the morning air.

After a while, the sea calmed down again. A light breeze rose, touching the skins of the sea-weary men. After a long, tense silence, they rediscovered their voices. They emerged as if from a trance, shook salty cobwebs from their eyes and listened to the wind whispering the secrets of the land they were approaching.

'We've done it. We'll get a drink or two as soon as we plant our feet firmly on the ground,' a man said excitedly.

They started singing, dancing and ululating. The ship was moving too slowly for the excited passengers. They couldn't wait to pick up a handful of sea sand and let it trickle slowly between their fingers onto the ground. They wanted to consort with the crabs moving up and down the beach, to drink fresh water from a tap or a stream nearby. To caress, with their eyes at least, the contours of women's bodies – the legs, the thighs, the flat stomachs, the jutting breasts. Ah, land!

'But the captain said the journey would take us more than a month.'

'We seem to have sailed faster.'

The excited chatter finally died down when Captain Yardley came up to the deck to announce that they were now approaching a country called Nigeria. The men listened attentively, without interrupting him.

As soon as he had disappeared, there was an explosion of excited chatter again.

'Is this Nigeria part of the white man's land?' one man asked.

'No, Nigeria is in Africa,' said Pitso.

'But when we left home we were sailing across the seas. Why have we gone back home to Africa? Is the white man lost?'

'No, brother, this is West Africa. It's on the *other side* of our own continent,' Pitso explained patiently. Many of these men were, after all, straight from the bush: no education, no exposure to the world apart from their own villages and the villages they grew up fighting against. Even those who had worked in the mines did not have a full appreciation of the vastness of the African continent. 'We have to dock, so we can fetch some fresh supplies of water, food and—'

'Well, we should have taken a train to Nigeria, then. From there, we could then have boarded the ship that would take us straight to the land of the white man. That would have saved us all these days and hours on the ship, don't you think? The train is faster than the ship. Plus you don't get sick on the train. Those two men wouldn't have died on the train. The sea is bad news. It's haunted by the spirits of men who died when their ships sank – men who never had proper burials, men whose spirits will never know peace until the end of time.'

Pitso gave up.

The ship was abuzz with arguments and complaints.

By noon, the equatorial sun was hammering down. Drenched in sweat, the men had stripped down to their pants. Moving restlessly on the deck, they looked like beached seals.

Late afternoon, the *Mendi* arrived in Lagos, along with the other ships in the convoy, the *Orsova*, the *Medic*, the *Berrima* and the *Port Lyttelton*. There was a near stampede as the men jostled for positions to get a better view of the city unfolding before them. They had to be called to order. The men, who had practised the boat drill and fire drill regularly, knew the formation they had to take before disembarking the ship.

Resplendent in their uniforms, the eight hundred black troops stood to attention as they were inspected by the officers, before marching in an orderly manner down the gangway. Once on terra firma, they were counted and divided into smaller groups. A white officer took charge of each group. At the harbour, the men were met and addressed by Sir Frederick Lugard, the Governor General of the Protectorate of Nigeria.

After his speech, Sir Frederick left with his entourage. The South African contingent allowed a respectable interval after the departure of the Governor General before they were guided into town by the officers, who showed them the sights. The men were highly impressed by the modernity of Lagos, how black people like themselves dressed in western clothes and wore shoes during the week. Back home suits and ties were only for rich, educated natives. Even then, the black native would wear such an outfit on occasions: special visits to the church, high-class weddings and the like.

'One day, our country will be like this,' Ngqavini said. 'One day, black people like us will walk about in suit and tie during the week, in broad daylight.'

'Look at that!' someone shouted. Heads turned. The men beheld a bridal party dressed in white dresses and frock coats, with the bride arriving in a smart horse-drawn cart – just as rich white people would do back home in South Africa. Mind you, not just any white people, but *rich* white people. Pitso, who had taken with a pinch of salt the stories he'd read about highly educated black people in Nigeria living like white people, was impressed. Here, at last, was proof of the value of reading. The things unfolding before his eyes did not seem entirely new – they were just confirmation of what he already knew.

While the men were walking, admiring the sights, they in turn were being hailed and admired by the locals who, through the local newspapers, had heard about a group of black troops from South Africa who would be passing through town on their way to fight the German Kaiser in Europe.

After the short walk about town, the officers guided the tour back towards the harbour. There the troops lined up for their early supper, which they ate from benches, the sea breeze cooling them after an oppressively hot day.

By this time, Pitso, Ngqavini and Tlali had become friends – but only after Tlali had sat the other two men down and asked them to find it in their hearts to put their differences aside. 'This is clearly a long journey that we are on,' Tlali had said, 'and we need each other. So you, gentlemen, find your humility. And at least show each other some respect.' It had taken Pitso and Ngqavini a while even to greet each other when they saw each other on deck or inside the engine room. However, because of Tlali's insistence, they finally got down to shaking hands. And they gradually began to listen to each other's stories and laugh at each other's jokes, which was not easy, for both men were proud and headstrong.

Now, as they sat next to each other, enjoying their meal, Ngqavini said, 'My friends, do you see what I'm seeing?' The two followed his gaze, which was directed at the two benches occupied by the chief of the Pondos and his subjects. Everyone was eating, except for one young man. His food was in front of him, but it remained untouched. He was visibly hungry, stealing glances at the food and swallowing his saliva.

Tlali explained, 'Oh, that young man is always the last one to eat. Sometimes they take his food away and give it to the chief, if the chief's belly is not full yet. Is it something we should worry about? Maybe it's one of those Pondo or Xhosa things that do not make sense to the rest of us.'

Pitso said, frowning, 'We have to put a stop to that nonsense.'

Ngqavini put his plate down, and started towards the chief's bench. Pitso got up and pulled him back to his place. 'Not in front of the officers. Let's do it in our own time. But, first, let's establish the facts.'

They watched in amazement as the young man took his own plate of food and gave it to the chief. The chief started eating his second helping. When he was halfway through this plate, he dropped it on the floor. The young man attacked the plate like a starving mongrel dog. Finished with the plate, he then ate the leftovers from the other men in the Pondo circle.

'That makes me sick,' Pitso hissed.

'Why? What's wrong with that?' Tlali asked. 'He is the chief, and he can do as he pleases with his subjects.'

'You just don't get it,' said Ngqavini.

'What is it that I don't get? The man is the chief, he can do as he pleases. Same as the white man in our own lives: he can do as he pleases, because he's in charge.'

Ngqavini and Pitso looked at each other. There was some sense in what Tlali was saying, but …

The troops were instructed to clean up and get ready to get back on the ship.

Supplies of coal and stores, including coconuts, were loaded onto the ship. One of the officers did the roll call: 'Paraffin Makilitshi, Majuta Makoba, Transvaal Masilo, Picennin Matlala, Thousand Matupu, Albert Nkomempunga Mbata …'

Two days later, they were in Sierra Leone. This time, the troops did not leave the harbour. Some of the staff helped transfer the consignment of five million pounds' worth of gold bullion to the HMS *Cornwall*, which was part of the convoy to Britain. Altogether, the *Mendi* spent three days in Sierra Leone, during which time the whole crew performed exercises at the boat stations on board. Forever conscious of the safety of the men, Captain Yardley ordered that the boats be lowered into the water, where they were found to be tight and in order. In addition, a couple of rafts were thrown into the water and found to float satisfactorily.

The *Mendi* had seven lifeboats capable of carrying a total of two hundred and ninety-eight persons. She also carried forty-six life rafts, each fitted with lifelines round the structure and intended to support about twenty people in the water, holding on to these lines. The rafts consisted of airtight copper tanks enclosed in a wooden grating, on average six feet square, with a total capacity of about nine hundred and twenty persons. Further, the *Mendi* had fifteen lifebuoys placed round the rails and a total of 1 319 lifebelts. All troops had to carry their lifebelts with them at all times. The black troops mostly used them as pillows at night.

With all the exercises completed, and all the new stores having been taken on board, the *Mendi* left Sierra Leone. While the troops stood on deck, waving at the locals, Ngqavini found the opportunity to sidle up to the young man whose food had been eaten by the Pondo chief.

'What's your name?'

'Milkota. Milkota Nyawuza,' the young man replied, his eyes shifting to avoid Ngqavini's gaze.

'Can I talk to you in private?'

'It's not possible.'

'Why not?'

'My chief won't allow it.'

'Relax, I won't get you in trouble. We'll be discreet. When you've done your cleaning duties tomorrow morning, come to the engine room downstairs.'

'But I'm scared.'

'Listen,' Ngqavini growled. 'I need to speak to you, even if it means beating up your chief. Tomorrow morning, in the engine room.'

CHAPTER 26

To look at Milkota, you would think he was trying very hard to be a black version of Charlie Chaplin. His height and his jerky, uncertain gait were reminiscent of the comedian, as was the moustache. Not to mention his ability to twist his neck almost a hundred and eighty degrees to look over his shoulder – which he did a lot, as he was such a nervous fellow. If you happened to suddenly materialise at his side, he would almost jump out of his skin. His voice was squeaky and quarrelsome. And, also like Chaplin, he could be a melancholy figure – his face perpetually downcast, as if he would break down into tears any moment.

The morning he went down to the engine room for his rendezvous with Ngqavini, he cried out when he was startled by two rats noisily mating on the steps. It had been a difficult decision to make: come and meet Ngqavini, thus risking the wrath of his chief and the rest of his tribe? Or defy Ngqavini, and thus risk being beaten up by the man?

'You look like you've just seen a ghost,' said Ngqavini in greeting. 'Pull yourself together. Here, have a drink.' Milkota accepted a jug of *mahewu* with his two hands. He put it down on the floor, wiped his lips with the back of his hand and squatted on the floor, making a huge ceremony of it. He drank noisily, slurping like a hungry dog. Ngqavini, Pitso and Tlali watched him sympathetically.

'That evil chief of yours is surely starving you, boy,' Pitso said above the roar of the engine.

'Men,' Ngqavini shouted. 'I think it's rather too noisy here. Let's go up on the deck and chat for a few minutes. I'll get some boys to relieve us here in the engine room.'

'But, Brother Ngqavini, with due respect,' Milkota said, 'we can't be seen together. The chief will not like it.'

'"The chief will not like it, the chief will not like it,"' Pitso mimicked him. 'What is wrong with you? Does your chief own you? He isn't God. While you're on this ship, your God is the King of England, or the captain of this ship.'

'But,' Ngqavini spoke quietly, 'I could also be your God. I have owned people before – I've been in charge of their souls. I don't see why I shouldn't do it again. In any case, I'm going to deal with your chief once and for all. Today if need be.'

All three looked at him sharply.

'Let's go up there and get some sun,' said Ngqavini cheerfully, ignoring his fellow men's stares.

The deck was flooded with the bright gold of the morning, the sun just coming up. Some men were exercising, stretching their limbs, others sitting and enjoying their morning *mahewu*, still chatting about what they'd seen in Nigeria.

Milkota spotted his chief and his acolytes in a remote corner. His eyes met those of one of the chief's lieutenants, who then said something to the men in his circle. They all turned their eyes towards the young man.

'Hey!' Pitso shouted at the Pondo men. 'Have you lost your manners? Why don't you greet before you start gossiping?'

One of Pondo men walked hastily towards him, his hands balled into fists. Pitso decided to meet him halfway.

'The chief wants that boy,' the man said.

Tlali finally found his mouth. 'Tell your chief we are still speaking to the boy.'

The man retreated to his tribe's corner and whispered something into the chief's ear. The chief scowled and spewed a brown jet of saliva onto the floor.

'So,' Ngqavini said, 'why is it that you are donating your own food to the chief? Look at you. You are skin and bones already.'

'From here on, gentlemen,' said Milkota, 'I will be at your mercy. Not only will my chief officially disown me, but his men will try their best to make my life miserable, or even kill me. They are ruthless bastards, I know them.'

'You haven't answered the question,' Pitso said. 'Why do you allow them to take your food from you?'

'I don't deserve to eat my portion, until the chief is nice and sated. You see, I am not a full man. So I have to do everything I can to please the chief, to apologise for the fact that I am not a full, complete man.'

'What the hell do you mean you are not a full man?' Ngqavini said. 'You don't have breasts that I can see. You have a moustache. Speak some sense, man, before I lose my patience.'

'Gentlemen, what I mean to say is that, in our Pondo and Xhosa tradition, you can't be a man until you've been to the mountain where you get circumcised and get yourself immersed in the sacred secrets of our culture—'

Pitso jumped at him, grabbing him by the lapels of his shirt. 'Are you calling me a woman, then? Are you calling all of us women just because we haven't done your stupid, backward, superstitious bush circumcision?'

Everyone on deck was gawking in anticipation of a fight.

Ngqavini and Pitso could always be counted on to offer some entertainment.

'No, gentlemen, please bear with me,' Milkota whimpered. 'I do understand that Zulus and some of the other ethnic groups stopped this circumcision thing a long time ago. But those of us in the broader Xhosa community still use it as a measure of one's commitment to one's culture. We believe that a man has to enter into a covenant with his gods by going to the mountain to get circumcised. Now, I was on the verge of going for my circumcision when I heard the call to enlist with the King's troops. So I had to make a tough decision. How I would prove myself – through going to the bush, where I would be circumcised and taken into proper manhood, or by fighting against the Kaiser's men in Europe? I have tried to explain that to my chief, but he won't hear of it. He says I can't fight alongside men because I am not a man. I have to endure all the indignities and insults, simply because I am not a man.' He paused. 'Can't you see, gentlemen, I am dirty. I am not worthy of your company. I have yet to be cleansed and accepted into the ranks of real men. I will only bring tears, sorrow and the gnashing of teeth on this ship. I should have stayed home until I was ready.'

Tlali spoke, 'But how do they know you're not circumcised? Do you go around showing them your weapon?'

'No, they don't have to see my penis to know that I am not circumcised. They have their way of finding out. The whole bush secret society has its own language.'

Pitso stormed away from the group. When he reached the corner where the chief sat on an upturned tin, he said, 'You pieces of cow dung say we are not men, simply because we haven't been to the bush to get our dicks messed up? You know what? I am challenging you, dear Chief, to a boxing fight.'

The chief's spokesman shot to his feet, shouting, 'You can't speak to my chief like that, you half-breed piece of shit.'

Just then Officer Haig appeared. He looked around and shouted, 'What's all this noise about?'

Ngqavini spoke in a mixture of Zulu and English as they did in the mines. 'My chief, the chief of the Pondos has expressed his fervent wish to tear the half-breed boy apart and have his liver for breakfast.'

'Is that so now? Well, we should settle it in a boxing fight. I haven't seen you boys boxing in a long time,' Officer Haig said. He raised his voice. 'Tonight the Pondo chief and the half-breed boy are entertaining us, no?'

'Yes!' the men said in unison.

Having been told of the fight, Captain Portsmouth decided that a fight between the Pondo chief and Ngqavini would make more sense and declared that it would take place the following week. Both men were popular and headstrong. Ngqavini, everybody knew, was a hardened criminal from the Johannesburg underworld, a man whispered to have killed other men. This would be a fight to end all fights.

Over the next few days, Milkota found himself spending more time with Ngqavini's group. He ate his meals with Ngqavini, helped him make his bed and would sit on the Zulu man's bed until lights out. Naturally, this caused some men to snigger. Stories started swirling around: 'Hey, have you heard? That Pondo boy is Ngqavini's wife.'

'Oh, yes, I heard, after lights out he tiptoes from his section and sneaks into Ngqavini's bed.'

'Yes, that Ngqavini learned all these dirty habits in prison.'

'They are going to bring the wrath of our ancestors up-on us.'

'Let's throw them overboard.'

'Let's tell the white captains.'

'The white captains won't care. They do it too. It's part of their culture.'

'Somebody must get the cook to poison their food.'

'I am not getting anywhere near that crazy Zulu.'

The rumours took a toll on Milkota, who avoided sharing the hurtful stories with Ngqavini.

One day Pitso and Ngqavini saw Milkota squatting in a corner on the deck. He had his back turned to them, engrossed in something that they couldn't see. When they craned their necks to look, they saw he was playing with a sparrow, feeding it pieces of bread.

'This fellow has been with me since we left Cape Town,' Milkota said when the two men joined him in his corner. 'He's my lucky charm. Every time I come up on deck, he suddenly materialises. I don't know where he sleeps, but he's always there when I need him. Always ready for bread. I've got a small water container for him to drink from.' He showed them, tucked discreetly in a corner, an empty pilchard container which he'd filled with water. The sparrow was chirping merrily, as if in conversation with him.

The two men exchanged glances and waited. Milkota took his time feeding the bird. They decided to let him be.

The night of the fight came at last. Ngqavini entered the ring barefoot in the usual fighting gear – sleeping shorts and boxing gloves. The chief had decided to enter the ring wearing a vest and his long pants, rolled up to his knees, to keep a modicum of respectability befitting his status.

Officer Haig, the referee, formally introduced the fighters to each other and reminded them of the rules: no holding, no biting, no kicking, no hitting below the belt, and so on.

And off they went. Ngqavini started dancing about the ring, throwing jabs at the chief. The chief stood firmly on his feet, with only his upper torso swaying this way and that as he effortlessly evaded Ngqavini's jabs. Ngqavini couldn't get the hang of the chief's fighting style because he did not assume the usual fighting stance. The chief stood with his feet slightly apart and his arms raised high, like the horns of a buffalo, leaving his entire body exposed. This to the merriment of the city men, who shouted, 'Hey, the chief thinks this is a stick-fighting match! Chief, assume a proper fighting stance, or Ngqavini will have a field day on your exposed stomach and face!'

Indeed, that's exactly what Ngqavini was trying to do, crouching low and attempting uppercuts to the chief's face. Unperturbed, the chief swayed his upper torso to evade Ngqavini's welter of jabs.

The crowd roared, 'Hail the chief! Hail the chief!'

Realising that the chief was agile enough with his neck and head, Ngqavini decided to concentrate his efforts on the man's midriff. It is a way to tire an opponent, pounding the hell out of his midriff. But when Ngqavini crouched low and threw his left jab around the chief's midriff, he didn't realise that he was leaving his head wide open to the chief's right fist, which descended on his left temple. Wham-wham! Startled by the double blow, Ngqavini staggered to his right, out of harm's way. Too late. The chief intercepted him with a left which caught him on his neck.

The crowds roared again, 'Hail the chief! Hail the chief!'

A seasoned street fighter, Ngqavini had encountered adversaries of all stripes and experience, but the chief was too unconventional for his liking. Those buffalo horns were driving him crazy. Then Ngqavini had a moment of inspiration: he appropriated the chief's fighting stance. The crowd hollered approval when he raised his arms in the air like the horns of a buffalo, and immediately landed two blows to the chief's face.

Smiling at him, the chief danced away and assumed the conventional southpaw posture, with his right foot forward, and his right hand delivering jabs powerful enough to flatten a banana tree. Ngqavini, who had fought left-handed people in the past, was happy that the chief had fallen for his trick. He moved with speed, delivering a rain of blows on his opponent. But the latter was a skilled fighter, who knew how to parry blows, duck out of the way, and continue to deliver dangerous jabs.

The chief assumed his buffalo-horn stance again, with his feet planted firmly on the ground, his upper torso swaying like a cobra responding to a snake charmer's flute.

'Hail the chief! Hail the chief! Hail the chief!'

The gong went. Ngqavini's body was soaked in sweat, and a trickle of blood was snaking out of his left nostril.

'Ngqavini,' said Pitso, who was Ngqavini's corner man, 'you are exposing yourself too much. In the next round, don't take the fight to him. Just hold back. Provoke him into making the first offensive move and then pin him. Those buffalo horns are for show. They only work when he is on the defensive. He can't sustain an offensive move using that strategy.'

'Rules,' Ngqavini cried in exasperation. 'There must be rules. Where's Captain Portsmouth? I think it's against the rules and regulations to raise your arms like that. We are not fighting with sticks here.'

'I already asked Captain Portsmouth, *mfan'omdala*,' Pitso said flatly. 'He says there's nothing wrong with that stance. Just stick to what you know.'

Milkota was standing close by, trembling. He said, 'My big brother Ngqavini, you can't let the chief win. You can't. Or I am dead. Please win this one for me.'

Pitso wiped the thread of blood trickling out of his friend's nostril. He gave him a sip of water.

The gong went again.

'Where's your blanket, my boy?' the chief said quietly as he edged towards Ngqavini. 'You're going to need it now. I'm going to put you into a very long and peaceful sleep.'

'Keep that shit to yourself, you heathen,' Ngqavini growled, and charged forward like an enraged bull. But punches to the older man's midriff were easily, almost effortlessly, parried away.

The chief started wiggling his upper torso playfully, stamping his feet on the ground like a Xhosa warrior dancing at a wedding party. The chief's men started singing a popular traditional song that matched their leader's movements. Buoyed by this, he moved in for the kill. He delivered a left-right-left-left combination to Ngqavini's face, causing snot and tears to spring from his nose and eyes.

Ngqavini's body thudded to the wooden floor. The referee gave a count. At the count of ten, Ngqavini still hadn't recovered. Portsmouth poured a jugful of cold water on his face, at which the fighter trembled back to life, his eyes blinking. They helped him to his feet, and he staggered drunkenly towards deck, in search of fresh air.

The chief's supporters were singing at the top of their voices. One of them approached Ngqavini and his entourage, saying, 'That's what we Pondos do to men who sleep with boys. Bloody devils!'

Tlali lurched forward, landing a punch on the man's

stomach. Pitso moved swiftly to stop the fight. 'You boys don't want to go down to that dungeon.'

Pitso and Tlali led Ngqavini away from the melee, and they all repaired to the deck above. Once there, the vanquished boxer found himself an upturned drum, on which he sat heavily, not saying a word. A few men gathered around him. Someone gave him a jug of *mahewu*. He gulped the thick, sweet liquid hungrily, and stared long and hard at the orange setting sun in the distance.

'I think these white people are lost now,' he said after a while. 'When last did we see a piece of land?'

'You know, I've been told that when you are dying a certain kind of peace descends upon you,' one of the men said. 'You don't seem to have a care in the world. That's how I am feeling right now – I can feel it in my bones, that I'm going to die. I'm going to die before we reach our destination. I don't know how I'm going to die. Maybe one of you is going to kill me in my sleep. All I know is I am going to die. And nothing can change that now.'

'Don't speak like that, man,' Tlali said. 'We are almost at the end of our journey, gentlemen, and we've travelled so regally and so peacefully. From here on, it can only get better.'

Milkota stood among the men, his sparrow eating breadcrumbs off the palm of his hand. He was muttering to himself, 'Eat, my boy, this might be your last meal.'

Tlali spoke, 'Ngqavini, our reputation is in tatters. We need a return fight before we reach the white man's land.'

'That's the spirit, my boy,' said Ngqavini. 'Ngqavini *always* has the last word.'

The men were soon distracted by the sight of a school of dolphins playing in the water.

Somebody suddenly cried, 'Hey you, boy, what are you doing?'

Everybody followed the gaze of the startled speaker. Milkota had scaled the railings and hung precariously over the water. He screamed, '*Ndiyindoda! I am a man! Ndiyindoda! I am a man!*' And he plunged into the churning surf.

CHAPTER 27

Days later, the captain announced that they were about to enter the English Channel.

'These are choppy waters, gentlemen,' he continued. 'It can be a bit uncomfortable. So, brace yourselves. I don't want anyone on the upper deck. It's dangerous. And remember to put on your lifebelts at all times. *At all times!*'

The men received the announcement with a mixture of excitement and trepidation, but went about their duties as usual. Not long afterwards, a light rain began to fall. The distant rumble of thunder could be heard. Weak strobes of lightning criss-crossed the darkening sky. Within minutes, the bolts of lightning had become more forceful, illuminating the sharp needles of rain which were now coming down ferociously.

A gigantic swell rose just ahead of the ship. The vessel was lifted into the air, the propellers screaming. And then the ship plunged into a deep valley, a thunderous noise reverberating all round. There were ear-shattering cries from some of the men.

Ngqavini bellowed, 'Jesu-Maria-Josefa, *kuyafiwa namuhla!* We're dying today!*

Pitso fell to the deck and started vomiting. Tlali was soon at his side, trying to support his friend. Tlali fingered his lucky charm, the necklace made of monkey bones, chanting and muttering. More men joined Pitso in a frenzy of vomiting. Others cowered in corners, crying out in alarm as the sky broke into a dance of lightning and God coughed angrily.

There was a moment of calm, during which the ship cruised confidently forward. Men started breathing normally again, wiping sweat from their eyes. Then those on the starboard side cried out as a mountain of water came crashing down on that side of the ship, sending it spinning once again. Some lifeboats were so rattled they broke loose from the davits.

Just when the men were beginning to recover again, with the wall of water behind them, a series of angry waves started pummelling the vessel from almost all directions.

Pitso crawled across the deck. He reached the stairs and slid down them until he reached the lavatory below. Inside the lavatory, he continued to retch until his stomach was completely empty. He kept on heaving, his bowels threatening to come out of his mouth. His ears were ringing, tormented by the cracking, roaring thunder. He got back to his feet, holding on to the lavatory wall for support as the ship continued to rock, but before long he felt a strong urge to sit down. The roiling contents of his stomach came out in a torrent. Dizzy and disoriented, he reached for the toilet paper, cleaned himself and got up. He wanted to get out of that lavatory as soon as possible. He lurched forward drunkenly, trying as best he could to reach the stairs.

The gale thundered towards them, the angry hooves of a thousand buffaloes.

Suddenly, the ship was airborne again. It remained suspended there for a while, before pivoting its nose down a steep watery slope. Pitso fell onto his knees, hitting his head against the railings of the stairs. Tears welled in his eyes. He stayed on the floor for a while, catching his breath. He started muttering to himself the last words Christine had said to him at the station, '*Dulce et decorum est pro patria mori, dulce et decorum est pro patria mori.*' Yes, it is sweet and beautiful to die for one's fatherland. He knew he was about to die, had to make peace with it.

Moving erratically, falling to his knees every now and then, Pitso finally made it into the holds where the other men were cowering, praying loudly.

'*Dulce et decorum est pro patria mori.*' There was no going back now.

A loud crack of thunder rose above the din that already enveloped the ship's interior. The lights went off, plunging the interior into an inky darkness. More shouts followed.

'*Dulce et decorum est pro patria mori.*'

The ship pivoted into yet another valley, angry mountains of water towering on all sides. When it resurfaced, fresh bolts of lightning seemed to slice the vessel into a thousand pieces. That illusion soon vanished, as the *Mendi* found itself on a relatively calm stretch of water. Like a person startled out of a nightmare, the ship panted.

But then a gigantic, angry fist of water rose on the port side, slamming the vessel with such immense power that the ship jackknifed crazily before finding its bearings again.

The roar of the engine sounded louder than usual. The men were silent, staring fearfully into the dark. One by one, the lights sputtered back to life. Somebody shouted the Zulu war cry, '*Hebe! Usuthu! Hebe! Usuthu!*', which was taken up by more voices, '*Hebe! Usuthu!*'

Medical orderlies started moving about the ship, attending to men who were seasick, of which there were many. The medics fed them spoonfuls of sugar and made them drink some water. The vomiting and groaning subsided at last.

The men started singing and chanting again. The nightmare of the storm was now behind them.

CHAPTER 28

Someone shouted, 'Land-ho! Land-ho! Land-ho!' and most of the men scrambled to the upper deck. They had to strain their eyes to see the smudge of land they were approaching. Everything was cloaked in mist.

After the horrific storm, the men were relieved they were about to touch God's soil once again. Ngqavini started teaching the men a simple war chant that would keep them calm and focused:

Ngqavini: *Uph'uMkhize? Where's the Kaiser?*

Troops: *Usebhoshi! He's in the toilet!*

Ngqavini: *Wenzani? What's he doing?*

Troops: *Uxov'amadede! He's kneading dough from his own turds!*

Ngqavini: *Uzowenzani? What's he going to do with those turds?*

Troops: *Uzowadla! He's going to eat them!*

Ngqavini: *Uzowenzani!*

Troops: *Uzowadla!*

Ngqavini: *Uzowenzani umhlathi kanina?*

Troops: *Uzowadla!*

Ngqavini: *Uzowenzani umgodoyi?*

Troops: *Uzowadla!*

Captain Portsmouth, who had come on deck, had a good laugh at the Zulu warrior infusing the spirit of anger and war into his fellow troops. They were about to arrive in Europe. Energy levels needed to be kept high. The men had to be alert, ready. The army needed men like Ngqavini as officers, Captain Portsmouth thought, men who could lead and inspire. He planned to recommend him for a senior position once they got to France.

More white officers soon came onto the deck. For the first time in a while, there was a shared camaraderie between the men and their officers. Some of the officers – all of whom were conversant in at least one African language – engaged the troops in such friendly conversation that the troops were shocked that these were the same men who had seemed aloof all along, to the point of being hostile. Perhaps it had finally dawned on them that the enemy's bullets would not discriminate between whites and blacks, officers and ordinary troops.

It was late in the afternoon when the ship arrived at Plymouth, followed by the other vessels in the convoy. Some passengers of the *Mendi* – retired officers who had hitched a lift – hobbled off the ship, relieved to be on terra firma at last. The troops were disappointed when told they were not to leave the harbour. They were only allowed to disembark and stretch their legs on the quay under strict supervision.

Reverend Dyobha asked the officer in charge for a moment with the men. He asked everyone to kneel on the ground and close their eyes. They said a quick prayer, thanking the Lord that the ship had arrived safely in England, the King's country. Now, they were in for the last lap – final destination, France.

Ngqavini broke into song: 'Oh, what a friend we have in Jesus ...'

~

Late in the afternoon, Captain Yardley called for final inspection. The men moved like ghosts, taking orders from their officers as if in final rehearsal for the task that lay ahead of them in France. Then the *Mendi* set off, sailing from the port of Plymouth, escorted by HMS *Brisk*, a destroyer, since the English Channel was awash with submarines. As the *Mendi* sailed, the weather was overcast, with light mist, but the sea was smooth. By 5.30 p.m., it was completely dark.

The men were singing and talking now, already imagining themselves as decorated heroes going back home after the war. Their spirits were high.

'This Mkhize bastard,' said Ngqavini, 'must ask the English about Isandlwana ...'

'That's the spirit, boys,' said Officer Haig, who had been sitting nearby, unnoticed. 'We are going to show Fritz his mother.'

'*Hhawu*,' said one man. 'Officer Haig, I thought we were going to fight Germans. Who is this Fritz?'

'Same people, my boys. Another name for Germans is Fritz.'

'Oh,' the men said in unison. 'Then we will show this Fritz his mother.'

Aware that these waters were busy and treacherous, Captain Yardley was not taking any chances. He had stationed one man in the crow's nest, and two on the forecastle head as lookouts. Several of the troops were scattered around the ship, assigned at strategic positions, and a quartermaster stood with the officers on the bridge. At around 7.30 p.m., the oil sidelights and the stern light were lit – they used oil lamps because Yardley believed that they provided better visibility in the fog than electric lights.

But the officers kept cursing the growing lack of visibility outside. One of the men, by the name of Hertslet, had been on duty from 10 p.m. He would later record in his memoirs how it had been 'a weird experience visiting the men on watch at midnight, the ship heaving and rocking in the choppy seas of the Channel, the whole sky dark, the fog increasing the invisibility of everything, the ship's siren booming every minute making one jump at every hoot and the guards giving the challenge and taking the password at each strategic point on deck'.

Ngqavini, Pitso, Tlali and a handful of other men were on night shift in the engine room. At 4.30 a.m., they were ordered to go to bed. They took their time about going up. As they ascended the stairs, they could hear no voices; apart from the roar of the engine and the sound of water as it lapped against the hull of the ship, there was silence. They knew then that everyone, except for the guards, was sleeping. The officers and NCOs in their cabins amidships; the crew in their quarters forward; the black soldiers in the troop decks. They were mostly fully dressed, covered in blankets against the biting cold and using their lifebelts as pillows.

Still walking up the stairs, Pitso and his companions were startled by a loud cannon-like bang.

'Wooo-haaaa!' shouted Ngqavini. 'Mkhize, we're getting closer to you. Our guns will sound like this when we get to you.'

'You pig-raping, twisted devil! We're coming for you!' cried Tlali.

The three of them had felt the tremor that coincided with the noise, but they'd dismissed it as a massive wave, or whatever happened in English waters. The commotion was nothing compared to the storm that had hit them as they entered the English Channel.

As they emerged on deck, however, they found themselves in the midst of pandemonium. Men were shouting, crying, running about in panic.

'Calm down, you cowards!' Ngqavini shouted. 'This is plain sailing compared to the storm from the other day!'

'Indeed,' agreed Pitso.

Then the three men began to hear what sounded like the endless scream of the ship's alarm whistle. The serenity that had possessed them began to lift off, gradually. But they still couldn't make sense of what was happening. The ship was calm again, unlike the time they had encountered that memorable storm.

They saw men in full kit scurrying for the upper deck, defying the captain's instructions, who had specifically told them *not* to go to the upper deck whenever the sea lost its temper.

Pitso, Ngqavini and Tlali felt like they were waking up from some dream. Things were not making sense at all. The frightened shouts that had greeted them as they ascended the stairs now came from everywhere.

'I think we should find out exactly what is happening here,' Tlali said.

'Are you also getting cold feet?' smirked Pitso.

'These monkeys are cowards,' Ngqavini said. 'Imagine how they are going to behave when we finally get to the front, and the bombs start dropping.'

Two men came rushing past them. Tlali hailed them, 'Where's the party, my friends? Why are you rushing around like this?'

"Think this is a fucking joke?' a man shouted as he took the stairs two at a time, running for the deck.

'We've collided with another ship!' somebody else shouted. 'We're sinking!'

It was only then that Pitso began to feel the irregular movement of the ship. He couldn't stand still. The ship was rocking this way and that; he had to hold on to something. But still, this was nothing compared to the first storm. This was not how he imagined a sinking ship would behave.

The three of them finally got to the upper deck and were met with chaos and the clamour of voices against the incessant scream of the ship's whistle. Men were pushing and punching each other out of the way. No time for good manners, decency. The fight for survival had begun. Survival at all costs.

Pitso turned and ran down to his cabin to take whatever he could of his belongings – things he could slide into his pockets, just in case. But mostly to get his greatcoat, as he was mainly concerned about the cold on the upper deck.

Soon, he was back on the top deck, with his lifebelt on. He saw men in the freezing water, shuddering and thrashing about. Screaming. Cursing. But for some reason he still didn't believe they were in serious danger. The captain had not spoken. It had to be a false alarm.

His mind began to race. So did his heart. The stampede intensified. It was time to plunge into the water. *No. Wait.* He turned back to the deck. Men were standing at attention there, clearly waiting for orders.

Do the right thing. You've never done this before. Wait for orders. You're a soldier, after all. The captain hasn't said anything. So wait.

It was true that the ship was tilting. But what if this was something temporary? That would explain the captain's decision not to make an announcement. Unlike when they endured that horrific storm, the ship was not flying in the air. There were no canyons of water besieging them. False alarm. It had to be.

So he stood. Looked around. No officer in sight.

'Brothers, what is happening?' he asked.

No response from the men standing at attention.

Then he saw a white man, an officer, at the other end. He was leaning against the rails. He seemed relaxed. Pitso ran towards him.

Pitso saluted him and shouted at the top of his voice, 'Sir, the men are waiting for orders. What should we do?'

There was no response from the officer. It was as if he were alone; the action around him did not seem to register, to penetrate the bubble he was in. He seemed hypnotised by some force just beyond his line of vision. Pitso wondered if he was in a state of shock.

Pitso ran towards members of his company who were now untying one of the lifeboats that hung on the side of the ship. He wanted to tell them to stop what they were doing. They were behaving like cowards. They were overreacting. Then he saw Tlali, in tears, shouting, 'Pitso, my dear friend, we are about to die here. But one of us must not die …'

'Shut up, you fool!'

A scream in the distance. The continued wail of sirens. Still no word from the captain.

Tlali was still shouting, 'But if I must die, I shall die. Die for my country, I die for the King!'

Ngqavini was running towards the white man who had ignored Pitso and shouted, 'Sir, we need direction. Jesu Maria-Josefa, we are waiting for orders!'

The white officer descended some stairs, went into a cabin.

Then the unmistakable crack of a gun rang from inside the cabin. Ngqavini froze, beads of sweat on his forehead.

'No, no!' Pitso cried out.

The ship was listing. Some white officers were running towards the flooded holds. Men trapped there. Muffled cries. Some men so shocked they could not move. Not even shout. They just stood there. Screaming impotently. Holding on to whatever there was to hold on to. Many could not swim, a fact discovered back in Cape Town when they were being drilled. They also did not seem to have any confidence in the lifebelts that they were already wearing. They stood frozen. Some of them had to be kicked or punched to get them out of the trance of shock and fear, so that they would do something to save themselves.

Pitso cried, 'Where is Portsmouth?'

'Come on, man,' screamed Tlali, 'save your own life!'

'I have to know he's safe!'

Pitso decided there was no point in waiting for the captain to make the announcement to abandon ship.

He ran towards the officers' cabins. But as he sprinted down the stairs, water lapped at his feet. The cabins were already underwater. He flew back towards the deck, cursing.

He bumped into Ngqavini, who shouted, 'I'm going down to the prison. People are trapped there.'

'Too late. The place is flooded!'

Ngqavini rushed towards the hold where the dungeon was. He plunged into the darkness and disappeared.

'Portsmouth!' Pitso shouted. 'Captain Portsmouth!' He was running up and down like a man possessed, bumping into people. 'Portsmouuuth!'

Somebody pushed Pitso out of the way, sending him sprawling on the deck.

He got up. It was dark in the hold. He tried to find his bearings. There was a struggle in the obscurity to lower the boats. Pitso was finding it difficult to think because of the shouts. The whistles. The pushing and shoving.

He elbowed his way through a wall of men, then helped launch No. 3 boat. While he was busy, he saw a group of men lowering No. 4 boat. When the boat reached the water, a full load of men jumped into it. Just when Pitso thought the boat was stable, more men jumped on top of the men already in the boat. The boat capsized. Screaming and cursing, the men scrambled to stay afloat.

No. 6 boat was launched, but the bottom fell out of it as it hit the water. Some men must have been knocked out by the boat as it bucked. More screams.

'He's biting me!' a man shouted.

After the boats had been disposed of, work went on to get out the forty-six rafts, each capable of supporting twenty people.

Pitso ran from where he'd been helping push men onto the boats below. He wanted to make sure that all his comrades were safely out of the forecastle. On his way back, Pitso noticed that the men he'd seen standing at attention were still there, still standing. He saw Reverend Dyobha, the big reverend towering above the men, also standing at attention.

Pitso shouted in all the major languages of the ship, 'Reverend! *Mfundisi! Moruti!* We need to get on the rafts! Are you out of your mind, standing there like that? There's no Jesus here. Save yourselves! Release those men! The ship is sinking!'

In his thunderous preaching voice Reverend Dyobha cried, 'Be quiet and calm, my countrymen, for what is taking place is exactly what you came to do ...'

Somebody screamed. Somebody shouted. Somebody wailed.

'You are going to die ... but that is what you came to do ... Brothers, we are drilling the death drill.'

The music of the alarm whistles shrill and thick.

'I, a Xhosa, say you are my brothers. Swazis, Pondos, Basutos, we die like brothers. We are the sons of Africa. Raise your war cries, brothers, for though they made us leave our assegais in the kraal, our voices are left with our bodies ...'

Two gunshots were heard above the din.

'We are drilling the drill of death, we are drilling the drill of death, we are drilling the drill of death, *nasi isporho! Hamba sporho!*'

Pitso ran towards Reverend Dyobha, tried to pull him away from the scene, hoping that this would break the trance that these men were in. But Reverend Dyobha, a big man, simply pushed Pitso away. Pitso fell on the deck, grazing his cheek against a pillar.

The reverend then joined the rest of the men as they took off their boots. Still in a trance, they started shuffling their feet on the ground as they would have done at the funeral of a king or chief. *Shhhhm! Shhhhhm!*

'You are going to die ... but that is what you came to do ... Brothers, we are drilling the drill of death. *Asikoyiki sporho ndini! Hamba!*'

Like a well-rehearsed troupe of dancers, they lifted their right feet into the air. In thunderous unison, they thumped their feet on the deck – boom! – in time with their muffled cry of 'Aji!'

Drilling the death dance. Not crying, not panicking, not screaming at the approach of death. In Africa, even in times of death, people celebrate. Death becomes a spectacle, a moment of defiance, the defiance of death itself. Staring death in the face, challenging it to a duel. Come and get me, death. I am not afraid of you.

'Brothers, we are dancing the death drill. We're going to die.'

They lifted their left feet into the air. In unison, their feet thundered across the boards, in time with the loud chant, 'Aji!'

'Aji! Aji! Aji! Brothers, we are dancing the death drill. We're prepared to die.'

They moaned and repeated the reverend's words: 'Brothers, we are drilling the drill of death. We're drilling the drill of death, we have no choice but to die ...'

The uniform explosion of their feet sounded a tattoo on the deck, gaining momentum with each second, each minute.

'We're drilling the drill of death!' That was the men's resounding cry of selflessness, men daring death, men resigning themselves to their fate, men taking the idea of war to another level. Their dance was their fight, the ship deck their last battleground. They were not going down without a fight. They were going to fight death through their dance.

Boom-boom! Aji-aji!

Pitso tried to disrupt the crazy dance of death by shouting at the reverend, '*Mfundisi*, you are mad! You are possessed!' before giving up on them and running away.

Boom-boom! Aji-aji!

Elsewhere on the ship, a loud shout came, 'All overboard ... boats ... she's sinking!' That would have been Captain Yardley, the man in charge of the ship. Why had he waited so long?

On the deck, Pitso noticed that about fifteen to twenty yards from the ship's starboard side, lay one of her boats, fastened to the ship by a rope. With a pang of joy he realised that his friend Tlali and Portsmouth were among the men who were already sitting in the boat.

Somebody from one of the lifeboats was shining a bright light on the water to increase the visibility of those trying to swim towards the boat. Someone else unfastened the boat in which Tlali and Portsmouth were sitting. It started moving away. The sea was suddenly a boiling mass, the rescue boats being swept upward by the rising swells. The ship was sinking fast. Those people still on board were sliding as they ran towards the railings.

Pitso shouted as he jumped into the water. It was freezing cold. He panicked as he went deep under the waves, wondering if he was going to come up again. But the lifebelt held him up and he resurfaced quickly. His teeth began chattering with such violence he thought they were going to break. He could barely see through his salt-encrusted eyes as he started thrashing about in the water, slicing the surface with his strong hands as he swam as fast as he could in the general direction of the rescue boats. He had never in his life experienced such cold – and this was also his first experience of the sea; he had never braved such a strong, frenetic body of water. As his body acclimatised to the cold, he began to see other men thrashing about and shouting in the water. Some had resigned themselves to their fate. They were singing dejectedly; others were praying.

Pitso's hands and his feet inside his boots were completely numb. But he pressed on. His chest was burning, his heart thudding violently. Strong and fit as he was, he began to feel the enemy of fatigue overpowering his arms. His greatcoat, which had protected him from the severe cold on the top deck, was weighing him down, sapping the last remnants of energy. He struggled to keep his head above the surface, and water was washing into his mouth.

His first thought was that he had to get rid of his greatcoat.

But how? His lifebelt was cinched over it. He couldn't think straight. A combination of cold and fatigue was slowly taking possession of his body. He was making peace with the fact that he was going to take his eternal rest. He was no longer scared, just contented with the way things were. He fell into the arms of a strong, comforting silence, a quietude that blocked out all the noises that had filled the morning air.

He could picture himself smiling and mouthing the words 'Dulce et decorum est pro patria mori.' How sweet it was that he was indeed dying for his country. At least he was dying going towards the trenches of war – unlike his father, who had run away from battle, from commitment, from fatherhood, from being a breadwinner.

'Dulce et decorum ...'

His journey had come to its end.

Oh, God of love, peace and mercy, the words came to his mind. My journey has come to its end. I'm now beyond all the suffering. But I go down as a soldier, fighting, fighting a different battle ...

His head exploded with pain as someone kicked him, startling him from his watery bed. He was shocked to discover that he was underwater. Still alive! He kicked furiously. A new and potent energy boiled inside his arms, which were now working vigorously, pushing the heavy blankets of water from his path as he finally resurfaced. He inhaled the cold air in huge, hungry gulps.

He was alert and hungry for life once again, albeit disoriented. Treading water, he looked sideways, trying to find his bearings again. The roiling waters were alive with the noise of screaming men and ear-splitting whistles and sirens. Through the fog he made out one of the rescue boats. It was a long way off. He had no choice but to swim the distance. As he was fighting the strong, stubborn water, he caught a glimpse of another figure swimming just ahead of him. His heart singing with relief and joy, he realised that the figure was swimming towards a greyish smudge in the water, a smudge that took the shape of a raft as he got closer to it. In that instant, numerous heads mushroomed all around him, all swimming in the direction of the raft. Many were well ahead of him. But that only spurred him to swim even faster.

With a shock, he saw that as the men tried to climb onto the raft, the man who had got there first was kicking them back into the sea. One after the other, he kicked them away. Through the darkness he thought he recognised the wavy mop of hair. Could it be? No, it could not. He squinted his tired, salt-bitten eyes and tried to focus. His vision was blurry, his arms heavy with fatigue.

As he drew nearer, he saw two more men being kicked in their faces as they tried to clamber onto the boat. He squinted once again. Yes, it was him. How could a trained and seasoned soldier like him stoop so low? That little boat could carry easily twenty people without taking strain. As the beam of a powerful torch from one of the ships licked the man's face, Pitso's fears were confirmed. He thought of forging ahead, of confronting the miscreant, but realised that, in his tired state, he did not stand a chance of overpowering the man. He had to change course. His heart pounded with anger as he started swimming towards the bigger boat, occasionally having to push people out of the way – those who had given up, who were just floating, not even making an attempt to paddle or swim.

Getting close to the boat, and thanks to the light that somebody was shining in his direction, Pitso saw a figure he thought he recognised. The man turned out to be one of the subjects of the Pondo chief. Then he saw another figure bobbing next to the man, and recognised the chief himself. Pitso shouted at the chief, '*Nkosi, uphila njani na?*' *Chief, how are you?* The chief answered, '*Akukabiko nto.*' *There is nothing the matter yet.* Pitso shouted encouragement at the chief and his subject as he finally reached the boat.

Some men dragged Pitso aboard. Shivering with a combination of fatigue and relief, he started vomiting. When he'd recovered his breath, he joined the men who were rescuing others from the water, helping them onto the boat. Then he saw the Pondo chief. The man was stiff, quiet and very heavy as they dragged him aboard. Water came out of his mouth as he lay on the floor of the boat. He was not breathing. They dragged him into a corner, swaddled him with some blankets, but it was too late. He was dead.

One of the men, a crew member, called out, 'We have to paddle as far away from the ship as possible. Let's get moving …'

'We can't go!' Pitso cried. 'There are men who need help.'

The crew member, helped by some of his more experienced colleagues, started slicing the surface of the water with the oars, determined to create as much distance as possible between themselves and the sinking ship.

Angry at their cowardice and heartlessness, Pitso got up and looked into the middle distance, to check if he could still see the *Mendi*. One of the boats kept shining a light across the water surface to assure those floating in lifebelts that they were not alone – and in that light, Pitso spotted the ship.

At the exact moment he recognised the *Mendi*, she was swept upward – at least the bow seemed to shoot upward – before she staggered into a huge hollow. A thunderous sucking sound reverberated across the darkness. Then a strong current swept across the confined space where the boats and rafts were bobbing up and down. In the ensuing whirlpool, Pitso saw one boat and a number of rafts getting sucked down, sparking a new wave of shouting. The boat in which Pitso stood shook violently. Exhausted, Pitso himself slipped into unconsciousness.

As the hours dragged by, many of the men from the rafts were rescued onto the boats just released by the *Brisk*, the vessel which had been escorting the *Mendi*, assisted later by the *Sandsend*. Even as these vessels moved about in a desperate mission to save the men, they had to sail cautiously in the dark, foggy waters, lest they cause another accident.

When the boats reached Dieppe in France, Pitso, Tlali and other exhausted survivors were rushed to hospital. Pitso learned that his friend Captain Portsmouth had already been admitted to one of the hospitals in France. As reports of what had happened started to flow in, it was revealed that, of the original crew of eighty-nine, thirty-one were lost, as were two of the South African Native Labour Contingent officers, and seven of the seventeen non-commissioned officers. Out of a total of eight hundred and two black troops on board, only one hundred and ninety-five survived.

CHAPTER 29

Pitso had never been admitted to a hospital in his life. While he'd expected a hospital to be a place of hope and comfort, Dieppe Hospital turned out to be more like a slap in the face. Still startled by the screams and shrieks, the groans and gurgles that had greeted him as he was wheeled in, he was soon enveloped in a cloying putrescence of disease and death. It was a smell that reminded him of the stink of a dead dog left on the side of a road for a number of days, only to be picked up and dunked into a bucket of disinfectant, and then pulled out, to be left in the sun to dry.

On his second day at the hospital, they brought in a soldier whose legs had been blown off by a mine. The man had been stationed in Rouen. Even though they were comrades-in-arms, fighting on the same side, Pitso took solace in the fact that the man was British and not South African. It was a mental game he would continue playing with himself for the duration of his stay in hospital. Whenever they brought a body, or a severely injured soldier, he would sigh with relief upon learning that the deceased or injured man was British, or Australian, or from some other colony. As long as he was not South African, it was fine. It meant, he hoped, that South Africans were removed from danger. These thoughts made him feel guilty – made him feel like a coward. After all, they had not travelled thousands of miles from Africa to come and hide in hospital wards.

When he arrived in hospital, he had been running a high fever. It had abated over the three days since he'd been admitted. Only his leg was keeping him confined to a hospital bed. In the agitated fight for space on the rescue boat after the sinking of the *Mendi*, he had broken an ankle and dislocated a kneecap. He had only discovered his injuries when he regained consciousness, a day after the shipwreck. Although he could not walk, he couldn't wait to be sent to camp, to see what exactly he had come to do in Europe. He owed it to his country. He owed it to his fallen comrades.

What made his life in hospital bearable were the nurses. He found that, unlike the white women back home, they did not talk down to him. There was no distaste and suspicion in their voices, or in their interactions with him. The French lessons he had received from Christine back home were to stand him in good stead. Of course, his French was rusty, and his vocabulary limited, but he could understand what the nurses were saying. Sometimes he could even respond confidently, in a full sentence. The nurses would arch their eyebrows, impressed, their smiles full of human warmth.

It was thanks to these nurses that he began to piece together the story of the sinking, which had thus far been a jumbled collection of images, noises and cries in his mind. Through the nurses he learned that the ss *Mendi* had collided with a large cargo steamship called the ss *Darro*, which had been sailing from France to Liverpool. The *Darro* had failed to see the smaller vessel in the thick mist that morning and had collided with the troopship. The nurses had obtained this information from newspaper reports, which further declared that an official inquest into the accident would be held. Even though Pitso did not want to be reminded of that horrific morning, he needed to hear the full story. Justice had to be done, even though it was not going to bring back his friends and comrades. They were gone forever.

He was happy to have these generous nurses as friends. There was one fly in the ointment, though: the white officers who always seemed to hover around the ward when treatment was needed. The official regulation, which had been drummed into their heads even before they left Cape Town, stipulated that black troops could not fraternise with white women in Europe. To ensure that the regulations were observed, white soldiers had to be present whenever a black soldier was being attended to by a white nurse. The soldier did not even have to be an officer, as long as he was white. Pitso knew none of the men. He assumed the white officers who had come on the *Mendi* were already deployed to the various camps.

Before long, Pitso found that he was developing a warm rapport with one of the nurses in particular. She had introduced herself as Marie-Thérèse something-or-other.

'You have such lovely hair,' Pitso said one day, admiring her strawberry-blonde hair tied in a bun. Her eyebrows shot up, then she blushed profusely.

The white soldier present, who hadn't heard what Pitso had said, looked at her crimson face and smiled, thinking she was blushing on his account.

'I can feel myself recovering already, in the company of such beauty,' Pitso continued softly.

'You speak such good French,' said the nurse generously, also lowering her voice. 'You can't tell me you only learned the language when you got here?'

'Ah, it's a long story, my dear lady. Perhaps one day I shall be able to relate it to you.'

The nurse finished what she'd been doing and hurried away. On her next visit, she sneaked him a bunch of grapes when the white officer wasn't looking. When the following time, she sneaked him a packet of cashews, he reciprocated with a pencil drawing depicting a woman in a nurse's tunic, accepting a bunch of flowers from a man kneeling next to a bed. Nurse Marie-Thérèse looked furtively at the image on the piece of paper, stole a fleeting glance at Pitso and sped out of the ward.

The next time he saw her, she walked into the ward accompanied by two white men in uniform. One was the usual run-of-the-mill corporal charged with the responsibility of supervising nurses' visits to the black troops. The other had captain's stripes on his uniform. The men in the ward who could stand, did so and saluted him.

Pitso hastily whipped his legs over the edge of the bed, stood unsteadily and saluted.

There was a momentary silence as the two men sized each other up, before a whoop of laughter exploded from Portsmouth's mouth. 'By Jove! The old rogue is indeed here! I thought you were in Rouen. I am sure somebody said you'd been sent to Rouen.'

'*Jislaaik*, Captain, I thought you were dead.' Pitso looked at Portsmouth, at his close-cropped hair, his clean-shaven face. The other men in the ward stared uncomprehendingly at the emotional exchange between the white captain and the coloured recruit. 'Every time I asked about you, no one knew who I was talking about. I was beginning to fear the worst. Almost every day one sees corpses from the front and one counts one's blessings.'

'That's true. We're all mixed up with members of the battalions that got here before us. Sit down, soldier, we need that leg of yours to mend as soon as possible so we can send you over there. Some men are at Mendicourt, Hebreuve, Olhain—'

'Those names mean nothing to me. Where are you stationed, sir?'

The white corporal who'd come with Portsmouth was taking in the exchange like one watching a fast game of tennis.

Portsmouth addressed the soldier, 'Corporal, please give us some privacy, will you? Ah, there's a good chap.'

The soldier saluted and disappeared.

Portsmouth turned back to Pitso and said in Sotho, 'I am stationed at Arques-la-Bataille, which is just a few miles northeast of here. When they release you, you're going to join some of the *Mendi* comrades at the base over there at Arques. We are digging quarries.'

'That sounds wonderful, sir. Just wonderful. Not that I've ever dug a quarry before. But it sounds wonderful that I'll be in the company of familiar faces. Your Sotho is still impeccable, by the way.'

The nurse, who had been watching the exchange with growing amusement, asked Portsmouth, 'Moroccan or Algerian?'

'*Non, mademoiselle*,' responded Portsmouth. '*D'Afrique. Afrique du Sud.*'

No sooner had Portsmouth left the ward than some of the other patients crowded around Pitso's bed. 'So, is it true? You're from that ship that sank?'

He told his personal story to soldiers from all over the British Empire until his voice got hoarse. With the war now at stalemate, the sinking of the ship became an exciting distraction, a source of much excitement not only to those directly involved in the war, but also to ordinary people in various countries. The newspapers, especially in Britain and in the rest of the Empire, went on and on about the *Mendi*.

Even though he was far from the front line, Pitso still witnessed the horrors of war. One day they brought in a young man whose entire body had been covered in bandages, so that he looked like a mummy. His face was a sickly yellow, and pus was oozing from his eyes. Pitso would later learn the young man was a victim of mustard gas.

When the nurse wheeled the bandaged man past Pitso's bed, Pitso looked away.

'Why don't they just kill him?' Pitso muttered to nurse Marie-Thérèse, who was massaging his ankle.

'He'll live. I've seen many like that.'

The following day, they brought in a man who had lost an arm. He was South African, and black. Pitso developed an immediate interest in him. When the nurses were done with him, Pitso hobbled over to his bed. The man was high on some drug, which made him animated and loquacious. As he spoke, he seemed unaware of his missing arm.

'I'm from a base in Dieppe,' the man said after Pitso had introduced himself. He had arrived in France with the Third Battalion, a year before the sinking of the *Mendi*. He sounded like one of the so-called 'Lovedale boys', the educated Xhosas who had studied at the famous college of the same name. 'I don't know how many miles Dieppe is from here ...'

'You are in Dieppe Hospital, my friend.'

'How can that be? I seem to have travelled hundreds of miles over the last two days. Are you sure we're in Dieppe?'

'As sure as Mkhize is our dinner-table guest.'

The man laughed until tears started coming out of his eyes. Then he started sobbing, crying for his mother.

'Shut the fuck up, you negro!' someone, who according to the nurses was Australian, shouted from the furthest end of the ward. 'Why'nt you go home and look after your cattle, you stoopid cowardly cunt.'

Pitso's new friend eagerly tried to sit up, looking in the general direction of the voice, but Pitso calmed him down.

'By the way, my name is Joseph Vundla,' the man said. He spoke in a quiet voice, just as if he hadn't been crying his eyes out a few minutes before. 'From the Cape.' Vundla pointed at the stump where his arm used to be. 'Just the other day, we are cutting some trees by the forest. Pine trees and gum trees up there. And we see British chaps running to their trenches. Our captain shouts orders, shouts that we too must run.'

Vundla broke into a long fit of coughing. When the coughing stopped, he continued his story. He had switched to English, speaking as loudly as he could, for the benefit of others so they could marvel at his gallantry. 'So our officer shouts orders, says we must run. This is a funny war. The British chaps are armed, on account of being white, and we are not armed, on account of being who we are. But Mkhize and his boys don't give a damn. They shoot anything that moves. You can't say, "Hey, Mkhize, I am black and unarmed." Mkhize shoots everything that moves. There's gunfire everywhere. We start running. But Lieutenant Gardner changes his mind. It seems he's just realised we are too far from the trenches. So the fast-thinking lieutenant says, "Fall down flat, and once you're down don't fucking move!"

'But there's this chap. From Swaziland. At least that's what he tells us. Name of Seven. Or is it Eleven? Anyway, he's a big chap with the build and bearing of a born soldier. But it soon turns out Seven or Eleven is yellow to the core. He does not seem to hear Lieutenant Gardner when he says we mustn't move. This chap, he is running, and he is screaming, "*We mammmme! We mammmmme! Siyafa! Siyafa namuhla!*" *My mother, my mother, we're dying, we're dying today.* Another chap called Majola, from the Cape, feisty with big fists to match, connects a mighty punch to the Swazi's jaw. It's the only way we could contain the screaming piece of shit who was going to betray our position. Pig-raper goes down like a sack of potatoes.

'The bombs start dropping. Bha-bha-bha-bha! Gunfire. Boom-boom-boom! Mkhize dropping those bombs. Our guys – the Brits and the other Allies – are firing away at the German planes. Bha-bha-bha-bha! I like the sound, man. Wish I could take that sound back to my home village. So they can hear what a European war sounds like. Bha-bha-bha-bha! Our boys are shooting like crazy. How I wished I had a big gun in my hands, so I could start firing away as well.'

Vundla started coughing all over again. He lifted his hand, to assure his audience the story was not yet over.

He picked up the thread. 'Anyway, the planes evade our shots. They disappear, only to come back a few minutes later. Now there's only three of them. Diving low, skimming over the tops of the trees. You see the pine trees and gum trees up north? There. One of our guys starts firing again. He hits one of the planes. Vrrooooom! It twists and turns in the air – vroom-vrooom-vrooom! – before finally crashing onto the ground. When we run up to the wreckage, we find three men. But two are dead. One is still alive. Talking, laughing derisively at us. The Basotho chaps in our group want to kill the German bastard. I could have throttled him with my own hands. That's how angry I was. The bugger and his friends made me soil my pants. No man alive made me soil my pants.'

The entire room vibrated with laughter.

Vundla continued, 'I wanted this Fritz to die. But Captain Geddes says no, let's spare him. Let's get as much information as we can get out of him. Which makes sense. Much as we hate Fritz, he's got information we need. Anyway, the prisoner is taken to hospital. This very hospital. Dieppe Hospital. On being interrogated, he apparently told our men that their instruction was to wipe Dieppe off the face of the earth. Why? Because Dieppe is where the troublesome blacks are based. The blacks are fast in handling the supplies on the docks, the same supplies that have breathed some new life into the almost comatose body of the Allied forces. So, my brother, that's what we blacks are doing here. That's how we've changed the pace of this war. But the bastards still won't arm us.'

There were snorts from some sections of the room. Pitso spoke some more with Vundla about the attack in which he lost his arm. He was still enjoying this raconteur's tales when Vundla drifted off and started snoring.

Weeks later, on his release from hospital, Pitso had finally made peace with the fact that this war did not discriminate: whether you were British, or a native of India, or a white South African, or an unarmed black auxiliary from any of the colonies, as long as you were on the side of the Allies you were in shit. Mkhize was out to get you. Pitso shuddered at the thought.

CHAPTER 30

After the bleak, overcrowded confines of the hospital, Pitso was happy to be breathing the crisp, fresh air of the coast. To the west, beyond a gauze of fog, he could see the sea. And to the east the land unfolded in a steady incline towards the dark heavy sky. Everything was blanketed in snow – the stunted, dejected trees, the flat open country. It was depressing, inspiring a slight shiver in him even though he was swaddled in layers of clothing – long johns, thick army uniforms, a greatcoat, snow boots, undershirt, thick shirt, windbreaker, gloves, a scarf which he had contrived into a mask that covered his entire face, leaving only space enough for the eyes to peek out. His head was covered in a heavy woollen cap with thick earmuffs.

An officer with some British accent he didn't care for was giving him a ride on horseback to a warm hut at a camp in Arques-la-Bataille, which he'd been told was about ten miles from where they were.

The officer said, 'Should learn to dress appropriately for this kind o' weather, son. This here is not Africa. Yer goin' to freeze yer balls.'

Pitso merely grunted.

The horse was having a hard time, its hooves sinking into

thick mounds of snow. Every now and then they had to pause so the poor creature could catch its breath. Pitso's heavy coat was gradually feeling thinner and thinner. His teeth started chattering. The officer did not appear to be in a hurry.

'We get to camp, they'll teach ye how to dress properly and yet be able to move about, make yerself useful. As it is, you look like a mummy. Cain't be very comfortable, can ye? Cain't be a useful soldier dressed like that.'

The horse trudged on. 'At the camp they got hot showers, boy. Ever taken a shower in yer life?' Silence. 'I didn't think so. They got water from the tap. They got taps in Africa?' Silence. 'Didn't think so. At the camp they got hurricane lamps.'

Pitso closed his eyes. He was roused from his doze by the man speaking again. 'But what they don't have at that camp are nurses. No white nurses for ye over there. I believe some nurse was doing more than massage yer broken leg at the hospital, ye old rogue, ye.' Pitso threw a panicked look at the back of the officer, whose laughter rang across the wide-open expanse of land. 'Word travels fast, boy. We know ye randy lot from Africa don't waste time, do ye now? And, listen to this, they have heated huts for ye lot. Ye don't have to go looking for wood out there in the freezin' cold. At least not just yet.'

Pitso chose not to respond. Mainly because he was at the mercy of the bugger, but also because it was so cold he feared if he opened his mouth his teeth would freeze. He shuddered at the memory of some patients he had seen at the hospital – sufferers of chilblains, trench foot and frostbite. A lot of amputations had taken place there.

He cast his mind to the warm, pleasant climes of home. His mouth salivated at the thought of biltong. When were the French ever going to discover biltong – the salty pick-me-up that a healthy body demands as a matter of course? Oh, biltong. And he missed mangoes. Mangoes which tasted like sunshine. Home. He could see African women in twos and threes, sashaying in deliberate languor down a winding footpath. Pots of water balanced on their heads, their arms folded across their buxom breasts, their hips swinging. Their tongues dancing with stories, the women would every now and then stop to look each other in the face, and joyous laughter would explode from their lips, dancing all the way to the deepest valleys.

'Soldier,' the voice startled Pitso out of his African reverie, 'behold yer new home.'

The camp was a sprawling settlement of timber huts which, in Pitso's opinion, would have done a South African village proud. Once inside the gate, which was guarded, they tethered the horse to a stunted tree and started walking towards one of the huts. The white officer consulted a notebook before he went to another hut. The minute they entered the hut, the warmth inside slapped Pitso in the face with such force his eyes watered. He removed his scarf from around his face. His ears buzzed. His lips, previously comatose, woke up. Confused by the sudden change of temperature, they began to tremble. His armpits itched. The hospital smells he'd got used to came to be replaced by the welcome aromas of warm peasantry, tobacco, stale alcohol, horseshit and woodsmoke.

The twenty-odd men who had been playing cards and lazing about snapped to attention at the appearance of the officer next to Pitso.

'At ease,' said the officer. 'Now, boys, we have a new member. He has been allocated a bed in this room somewhere. Do give him a warm welcome, will ye?' He saluted and left.

Most of the men went back to their game of cards or whatever else they'd been occupied with. But some looked at Pitso expectantly, not unlike prison inmates sizing up a new arrival.

One man sniggered. 'What a nose he has, the new one.'

'Hawk-like, wouldn't you say?' his mate offered.

Pitso did not care for these comments. He put his mild irritation aside and greeted the men with a warm, but shy, 'Good afternoon.'

The men started speaking together in Zulu. One of them cried, '*Ha, labelungu! Basilethela esinye isilwanyana futhi!* These white people! They have brought us another creature!' 'Why is he speaking to us in English?'

'It's because he can't speak an African language. Can't you see he's not like us? Look at his hair, his eyes,' another replied.

'I thought the half-caste ones had their own battalion. Why is this one here, with us?'

'Have you noticed that it's usually the camps occupied by the whites, the coloured and the non-Ngunis that are susceptible to Mkhize's attacks?'

'Now that you mention it, us Zulus and Xhosas have remained unscathed thus far. But why is that, my brother?'

'It's because we still pray to the African gods. Before we came here, my people slaughtered a beast to ask my ancestors to be with me on my journey to the white man's land.'

'Same here. Now, the other people, the whites, the mixed-race and others, they've forgotten that though he may sojourn long in the branches of the *umganu*, the partridge will never forget the nest of lowly brush where he was hatched.'

'True. They've forgotten their roots,' the first man said. 'Now these whites in charge have brought us this creature who will bring misfortune to our section. My friend, can you tell him we don't want him here? You know I can't speak English. Get someone who can speak English to tell him straight away, before he even sits down.'

Standing near the entrance, Pitso had an epiphany: he was going to like these chaps; they were honest, laying it all out there in front of him, not sniggering behind his back. But some business needed to be taken care of first.

Harking back to his Zulu lessons from Portsmouth and his late friend Ngqavini, Pitso said, '*Bafowethu, nakhuluma ngami ngikhona! Kanti ngiyini kinina? Ngiwumsuzo?*' *Brothers, you speak about me as if I am not here. What am I to you? Am I a fart?*

They stopped playing cards. One man got up. 'Who are you to speak to us like that?'

'I am Pitso Motaung, the cub of a lion that roars across the dusty plains of the Free State,' he said in a mishmash of Zulu and Sotho. 'I am the stone that the builders refused.'

The man pushed Pitso back. Pitso threw a punch that floored the man immediately.

'Hey, you two!' a thick voice bellowed from somewhere in the room. 'This is not prison, you ill-brought-up sons of bitches! We are soldiers here. We are united. Forget your past and focus on what's in front of you.'

The owner of the voice approached Pitso. He was a dark man, almost as tall as Pitso himself. The other men suddenly snapped to attention.

'At ease!' The soldiers relaxed. When the man was directly in front of Pitso, he spoke to him in Afrikaans, 'Where do you come from, soldier?'

'Who wants to know?' replied Pitso. The other men sniggered.

'Sergeant Major Madosini, King William's Town, Cape Province. Junior Certificate holder, Lovedale College.'

Pitso was startled, but tried to mask his surprise by shouting as loudly as he could, 'Corporal Pitso Motaung, Mohokare, Free State, Standard Six Certificate holder, Centre for Coloured Children, sir.' He saluted.

'Your bed is in the corner over here. All your belongings are there, properly labelled.' He switched to English, mixing it with some Sotho. 'Your exhibition of physical prowess was impressive, albeit a bit excessive. I think you broke the man's jaw. How do we explain that to the senior white officers? I'm only a lowly native sergeant, how do we explain this incident?'

'I don't know, sir. I didn't start it, as sir is my witness, sir.'

'It was a rhetorical question, soldier. Do you know what a rhetorical question is?'

'It's when someone asks a question to which he doesn't expect an answer.'

'Ah, this man is educated.' He clapped him on the shoulder. He turned to the other men. 'Troops! We have another educated man among us. What do we have?'

'An educated man, sir!'

'Now, the labels on your belongings say PITSO MOTAUNG, but the man standing in front of me looks more like a Van der Merwe or something.'

'I'm a product of these long-running wars of conquest, sir.'

'He has a sense of humour to boot. Troops! The man has a what?'

'A sense of humour, sir!'

'Now, soldier Motaung, feel at home. We are currently on break. We shall resume duty tomorrow at six in the morning. Seeing as you've just come out of hospital – is that correct?'

'Correct, sir.'

'Seeing that you're straight from hospital, you probably don't know about rations, daily food rations?'

'No, sir, but I do know your food can't be worse than what they serve in hospital, sir.'

Some men laughed.

'I've never been to hospital, so I would not know, corporal. Anyway, in terms of our regulations, our daily rations are as follows: one pound frozen meat, or nine ounces preserved meat. One pound mealie meal, one pound bread, one ounce coffee, one ounce sugar, half an ounce salt, eight ounces fresh vegetables, two ounces of English tobacco per week, three ounces of South African tobacco per week, one box of matches per week. Any questions, corporal?'

'Yes, sir. Any alcohol, sir?'

More men laughed.

'Ah, yes, we are allowed to brew our sorghum beer. But the strength and quantity is closely supervised by group commanders. Pity you have repudiated your white blood, or you would be drinking brandy just like the white officers and their coloured cousins.'

Even Pitso joined in on the laughter.

Officer Madosini continued, 'They say the weather is gradually improving, although I'm not seeing any improvement. By the way, which battalion are you with? When exactly did you arrive in France?'

'Fifth Battalion, sir.'

'Fifth Battalion, Fifth Battalion,' the sergeant major said, toying with his moustache. 'Fifth Battalion.' He suddenly snapped to attention. '*Thixo wamazulu!* You wouldn't be one of the *Mendi* survivors, would you?'

'Yes, one of them, sir.'

Everyone sat up at the mention of the *Mendi*. The room was suddenly a cauldron of excited voices. 'What did he say about the *Mendi*?'

'Said he survived the *Mendi*.'

'Fucking ghost!'

'Order!' shouted the sergeant major. 'This man is exhausted, utterly exhausted. He needs to lay his side on the bed and rest. But, Corporal Motaung, would you mind sharing your story with us?'

Pitso grinned benevolently. 'You'll tell this story to your grandchildren, if you live long enough …'

CHAPTER 31

Spring arrived. The landscape, long buried under thick blankets of snow, woke up from its slumber. Trees threw up their fists of triumph into the warm air. Brooks started gurgling. Birds – thrushes and blackbirds and other variously hued types – filled the air with song. They flitted among the chestnuts and the elms and the pine trees. Bees buzzed from one bright flower to the next.

A relatively festive mood reigned at the various camps. Only the distant explosions reminded the soldiers that they were still at war, that they were far away from their loved ones. The appearance of an ambulance on its way to the hospital also helped sober the men up – reminding them that the game of death was far from over.

Pitso was among the men who, one day, were told to dress sharply and climb onto the back of a big lorry. They were going into town, a town called Rouen, to take advantage of the beautiful weather. The lorry was to be part of a convoy of five, each carrying about thirty men. Two huge drums of *mahewu* were mounted onto the vehicles. For many, this excursion was going to be their first trip into a French town.

As the lorry rolled into motion, the men sang and danced in the back of the truck. Equally excited, Pitso devoured the passing landscape with his eyes. Being from the Free State, which was largely arid flatland, he was enthralled by the rolling hills and the broad valleys of France, the landscape blanketed in a profusion of trees whose leaves were so green they reminded him of spinach. The valleys and flatlands alongside the road were carefully cultivated. Every now and then an old chateau showed its elegant face, speaking of a bygone era. At every hamlet they passed, the roads would be lined with people who waved excitedly at them.

The lorries slowed down and a hush fell when they entered a small town whose most conspicuous landmark was a broken cathedral tower. A statue of the Madonna holding the infant Christ surmounted the ruined tower. They were told that the partially damaged figure had been rescued from falling by local engineers. The townspeople seemed intrigued by the soldiers, who, in turn, were entranced by the ruined cathedral. The convoy moved on.

When they finally arrived at Rouen, they were mobbed by locals. Women threw garlands at them and sang. The children reached out and touched the soldiers. It was clear they had never seen black men before. Many wanted to feel the texture of their hair. The men obliged them, bowing their heads and letting the children stroke their hair.

The men who wanted to buy fresh supplies of tobacco were allowed to. The troops then walked around to get the feeling of a French town. Before long, the soldiers had taken over the entire main street. The white officers stationed themselves at the various cafés along the street. An instruction was sent for the drums of *mahewu* to be offloaded from the trucks and set up on the pavement. The men were ordered to stand in line and received their rations of *mahewu*, while the officers drank their beer and wine in the cafés.

A local man came out in a huff and said, in rapid-fire French, 'What the hell is happening here? Why are these men drinking from pig troughs, while the others are sitting on comfortable chairs, on the porches of our cafés? What's happening, where are you from?'

The white officers grinned stupidly since none of them could speak French. Pitso saw an opportunity. He said to the man in French, 'Monsieur, we're from the Union of South Africa. Back home, this is how we do things. People of your colour are not allowed to mix with *les noirs*.'

'What? Tell your officers to get out of our town then. They are not welcome here.'

Now the local people had gathered around to watch.

An officer who had seen Pitso talking to the man said, 'Corporal, you know the rules: only under an officer's supervision are you people allowed to speak to locals.'

'Sir, with respect, sir. But the man needed some urgent help. The man is trying to sell us prostitutes, but I told him we are soldiers from Africa, and we're held in highest regard by all the nations involved in this war. We do not sleep with syphilis carriers. That's why he got highly agitated and said we must leave his town. I hope that I represented the South African army well.'

The officer hurried towards a group of his colleagues. They had an animated discussion before they gulped their beers and got up.

It was time to go back to camp. The men were counted, as usual, and their names checked against a register. Someone had gone missing. The senior officers communicated this to the officers in the other lorries. The men in charge sprang into swift action, moving from shop to shop, from café to café.

About two hours later, the recalcitrant man was brought back and pushed into the back of a lorry. He'd been found in the company of one of the local ladies. On the way home, the mood was muted. When their camp came into sight, there was a sudden roar above them. Everyone scrambled for cover. It took them a few minutes to realise what had just happened – a German plane had whizzed past, raining pamphlets on them.

Many of the men who had managed to catch the light green pamphlets could not read them. Luckily for those next to Pitso and other literate soldiers, the mystery was soon solved. Pitso took one of the pamphlets and started reading. 'Okay, brave men, the German Chief, Mkhize, has a message for us. Listen very carefully, he says:

'*I hate you, Uncle Sam* …' Pitso paused to explain, 'Uncle Sam, my friends, is America.' Then he continued, '*… because I do not know what caused you to come and enter this war. I hate Belgium, and I will crush it, because I have already taken most of it. I hate France. I hate England the most, because she takes other countries into her Empire. But in this war, I hate the black people the most. I do not know what they want in this European war. Where I find them, I will smash them!* So says the German ruler, my friends.'

'Come here, you dog Mkhize!' some of the men shouted, pointing at the skies. 'Come, let my spear drink your blood!'

Back at the camp, the men filed into their respective huts. The man who had tried to elude the troops was to be transported to the native prison in Dieppe. He would probably face a charge of consorting with a white woman, which carried a sentence of twenty-eight days, as provided for under Field Punishment No. 1 regulation. There would be no proof that he had tried to desert.

'What was that fool trying to do?' one man asked at the dinner table that evening. 'Say he managed to give us the slip, where would he go? He doesn't speak the language, doesn't know exactly where he is, doesn't have money – I mean, it doesn't make sense at all.'

'When you're desperate, you don't spend too much time thinking. You act when you see an opportunity.'

'But it's not as if we were forced to come here,' the first speaker continued. 'I don't know about you chaps, but many of us were attracted by the money.'

'And the promises that we would get the vote back home once the war is over.'

'Promises, promises.'

'But to go back to this chap … what's his name?'

'Mjoli.'

'Sounds like a Cape surname.'

'Yes, from Qumbu somewhere.'

'So, I'm still intrigued by what he did, or tried to do.'

'Maybe Mjoli wasn't even trying to run away. Maybe he wanted time with his lady,' suggested someone with a grin.

Pitso ate his dinner quietly, listening to the conversation without bothering to join in. Not that he wasn't interested in what was being said; he was. But the subject that had more weight for him was the delivery of the German pamphlets.

He finally spoke, eager to discuss the enemy's strike. 'What do you think of Mkhize's pamphlets?'

'Mkhize has balls. Flying into enemy space just like that.'

'Have you stopped to think – what if Mkhize had dropped, not pamphlets, but bombs?'

He had their attention now. 'Think about it, gentlemen – there we were, out in the open, unarmed, with nowhere to hide. Proverbial sitting ducks. What kind of death is that? A soldier dying unarmed, right there on the front.'

'So, what are you suggesting?' a man asked.

'I'm not suggesting anything. All I'm saying is that we're at Mkhize's mercy. He knows that the blacks are not armed. He's laughing in our faces. That won't be his last visit to the black-dominated side of Allied lines.' Pitso finished his mug of *mahewu*, let out a long luxurious belch, then said, 'Me, I'm not going to die with my thumb up my behind like a fool. I'm going to get myself armed.'

CHAPTER 32

Since his days of shovelling coal into the furnace aboard the *Mendi*, the callouses on Pitso's hands had hardened into shiny crusts. His nails resembled tortoiseshells. His arms, naturally big and thick, now rippled with muscles as he raised his axe in his steady attack on a tree trunk. While some of the men from his camp had been sent to work at a quarry, he had been assigned to a team of tree fellers. After felling the trees, they would cut up the trunks. These would then be dragged by specially trained horses onto wagons, which would cart the cargo to the trenches.

The survivors of the *Mendi* were just a tiny fraction of a huge workforce from the Native Labour Contingent, which comprised a total of 20 887 black men deployed all over France. The contingent had been broken down into forty-three companies involved in a variety of tasks. The principal classes of work were ammunition (discharge of ships, train loading and unloading, building and traversing of hangars), provisions (discharge of ships), petrol (discharge of ships, train loading, ropeway work), Royal Engineer stores (discharge of ships, train loading), and, of course, forestry.

Pitso loved the rhythm of his new assignment in the forestry section. Like his stoking duties aboard the ship, tree felling

238

allowed him to think, rather than spend time talking to his comrades – although, in fact, he had learned a number of things from them. One of his comrades, who had been on a road-building chain gang back home, taught them some agreeable ways of working. With the permission of the officer in charge, he showed them how to stand at the base of the tree that needed to be cut. And then, when he screamed '*Nazo-ke!*' each man would start hacking at his own tree. This was done in a coordinated manner, the blades of the axes falling in unison at the base of the tree, so that there was a musical cadence to the sound reverberating across the forest. With each strike, each man would cry, '*Abelungu oswayini! Basincintsh'itiye, basibize ngoswayini.*' Whites are swine! *They refuse us tea, and call us swine.*

All morning long, the chant would ring across the forest as the axes rose and fell. Without breaking the rhythm, a man would use the chant as a springboard from which to launch a poem or short song which spoke of his love for the woman he left back home. So it went:

> *Oh, girl if you were to see what they are doing to us here …*
> *Abelungu oswayini, basincintsh'itiye basibize ngo-swayini*
> *Out of old buckets we eat some mishmash they call food*
> *Abelungu oswayini, basincintsh'itiye basibize ngo-swayini*
> *You should see our axes making love to huge formidable trees*
> *Abelungu oswayini, basincintsh'itiye basibize ngo-swayini*

> *When I chop down a tree, I am chopping down a*
>   *German thug*
> *Abelungu oswayini, basincintsh'itiye basibize ngo-*
>   *swayini*
> *From you girl, I draw my strength, I derive my*
>   *focus*
> *Abelungu oswayini, basincintsh'itiye basibize ngo-*
>   *swayini*
> *I use an axe, for the whites refused me a gun.*

On and on it went, the chanting and chopping and the singing and cursing. Insects and rivulets of sweat blinded the men, but they didn't slacken their pace, for their concentration was intense. Enemy shells that dropped with shattering noise in the distance soon became part of the songs of the Arques forest. *Abelungu oswayini …*

At noon they would break for lunch, which was usually a hasty affair of mealie-meal porridge with some vegetables, chased down with a huge mug of *mahewu*. This was strength-giving food. After lunch some men, indolent of body, heart and mind, would flop on the ground and take a nap. Others would venture deep into the forest to lay traps for animals, which they would check before work began the following day. They caught rabbits, sometimes antelope whose names they didn't know, but which reminded them of the impala of home. If somebody caught something, he would come and finish it off before work began. When work was over, the man would carry his catch back to camp. The walk back was always filled with song and storytelling and joshing around.

Immediately after dinner, some of the men would break into small groups and start teaching each other songs which reminded them of their various villages back home. Others engaged in stick fighting. Those with some missionary-school education performed theatrical sketches they had learned at school. Pitso sang in one of the groups, but he sometimes preferred watching the various activities. It gave him an insight into the lives of his comrades. It also was then that he had time to concentrate on his drawings. Like his father many years before, he soon became popular among fellow soldiers for his realistic drawings. They would pose for him during the performances, or as they skinned an antelope they'd caught in the forest.

The one face he couldn't stop reproducing over and over again was that of Marie-Thérèse, the nurse. Marie-Thérèse on horseback; Marie-Thérèse in a bright pink dress, floating down a glade ablaze with brightly coloured flowers; Marie-Thérèse walking hand in hand with him down a street in Rouen. He wondered how she was and if she ever thought of him.

CHAPTER 33

O ne Saturday, at the height of spring, the various companies stationed in camps on the outskirts of Arques-la-Bataille marched into town, singing lustily. Proud in their uniforms, they swung their arms, their boots thudding on the dusty stretch of road. The June sun touched their faces with fingers of warmth. The green countryside rolled steadily past them, nicely rounded hills and knolls. On a hill before them they saw a sprawling feudal ruin – their destination.

When they finally reached the ruins, they were made to sit down on the grass. The morning dew had evaporated. A makeshift platform rose in front of them, at the entrance to what looked like an old fort.

A Catholic priest welcomed everyone and opened with a brief prayer. Then a local French soldier in uniform got up and took the podium. He introduced the various speakers who would appear before the soldiers that day – prominent local citizens including shop owners and minor politicians. They each spoke of how, ever since the arrival of the South African soldiers in town, business had been brisk, the town had found a new sense of purpose. The locals had never felt safer. They were grateful for the soldiers' good neighbourliness and positive attitude.

The French soldier translated from French to English. Taking initiative, one of the South African soldiers quickly got up and offered to translate from English to Xhosa and Sotho, the main South African languages represented there.

Pitso almost had a heart attack when the next speaker was introduced. Marie-Thérèse ascended the stage. *His* Marie-Thérèse. She greeted everyone present, then began, 'I take pride in being a native of Arques, and in welcoming you to our small, but historically rich town.'

The sunlight still had the magical golden hue of early day, touching her face lightly as she continued.

'The full name of this town is Arques-la-Bataille, named after the Battle of Arques, which is dear to every self-respecting French person. The battle broke out in September 1589, between the French royal forces of King Henry IV and the troops of the Catholic League, during the eighth and final war of the French Wars of Religion. You gentlemen came all the way from Africa to defend your Crown, to uphold international justice and democracy. So you will readily understand what it means to be proud of one's nationhood, one's culture, one's religion.'

Pitso looked at her lips as she took a sip of water from her glass.

'Henry IV stood no chance against the 35 000 troops of the Catholic League, so he fled to this city you see at the bottom of this hill, the city of Arques. These here are the ruins of just some of the fortifications left by Henry IV.' She waved her hands to indicate the formidable ancient structures, complete with a moat. 'The Catholic League attacked Arques and the surrounding areas on numerous occasions, but when Queen Elizabeth sent about 4 000 English soldiers to support the French, Henry IV was left victorious.

'So, my friends, we have strong ties of history that bind us together: back then, the English rescued and protected Arques; today, the British Crown is protecting not only France, but international democracy and justice. And you are the foot soldiers of that righteous army. You should be proud of yourselves.'

She paused to allow for applause. At that time a new company of soldiers arrived, but Pitso did not bother to look at them. He hated latecomers.

Marie-Thérèse concluded, 'As you sit with us in this town, you must be secure in the knowledge that we are fighters. You must be secure in the knowledge that we respect history, much as we hope you do. On behalf of the mayor, I wish you a warm welcome here. I know you have been here for quite a while already, but today the mayor wants to officially welcome you and thank you for what you have done for our town.'

Everyone applauded.

A group of men from the Cape were next on stage. Dressed in leopard-skin traditional outfits and wielding ceremonial sticks, they took the stage by storm. Their voices, coming from the pits of their stomachs, resounded around the hill and poured down the slope to the town below. The ground thudded and shook as they stomped their bare feet, provoking ghosts of dust into the air.

Soon, the number of people in attendance had swelled as more townsfolk ascended the slope to see, first-hand, what the Africans were doing.

As the celebration continued, Pitso sidled up to Marie-Thérèse, catching her as she was taking a stroll just behind the ancient chateau. But as he was about to catch up with her, he realised she had a rendezvous with someone else back there. His shoulders dropped.

As he was turning to go, she called out, 'Hey, where do you think you're going? Come and join us.'

He realised she was talking to him and followed her wordlessly. Turning the corner, he was surprised to come face to face with Captain Portsmouth.

'Fancy seeing you here,' said Portsmouth, laughing.

'When did you arrive, Captain?'

'Just as mademoiselle here was regaling the audience with the history of this illustrious town.'

The men paused, looked at each other. Then, in turn, they looked at Marie-Thérèse, who had a shy smile on her lips.

She said to Portsmouth, 'You're the senior officer here, will you kindly give this young man permission to go to town and get some tobacco? In other words, can you play escort to him, as per your army regulations?'

Pitso opened his mouth, but changed his mind.

'Why, sure.'

'Well,' she said, starting her descent back to town, Portsmouth in tow, 'what are we waiting for?' Pitso followed them down the steadily sloping hill.

Portsmouth shouted to one of the senior officers, 'Just going to the town for a roll of tobacco. When you're finished up there, you may join us for a drink at the main bistro. And from there we'll push for home.'

When they got to the town, they walked to an inn. 'This is my elder brother's establishment,' explained Marie-Thérèse, meeting Pitso's questioning gaze. 'He is currently in Saint-Nazaire, on the northern coast. So, I spend my free time here when I am not working at the hospital.'

They sat at a table on the veranda, sipping soft drinks and discussing what they had been doing since Pitso was released from the hospital. A young woman soon joined them. 'Gentlemen, this is my sister Geneviève.'

The resemblance between the two women was striking. The men shook the lady's hand politely before sitting down again. Their conversation turned to the usual banalities – weather, never-ending war, shortage of stocks at the shops.

Marie-Thérèse then got up and assumed a businesslike tone. 'Excuse me, Corporal Pitso, may I have a private word with you?'

Pitso looked at Portsmouth, who nodded assent. The young soldier got up and followed Marie-Thérèse inside, through the restaurant to a door that led to the inner recesses of the building. Marie-Thérèse closed the door behind her. Pitso looked around and realised they were now in some kind of corridor.

'You looked rather shocked when you saw me give that speech earlier.'

'I didn't expect to see you there, let alone giving a speech.'

'You clearly haven't done your research,' she teased.

'What do you mean?'

'Our family is highly regarded in this town. My brother, who owns this inn, is a famous lawyer. He has a practice in Paris, as well as some businesses in different parts of the country. Were it not for his law practice, he probably would have been mayor of this town.'

She opened a door, led him inside, and closed the door behind them. He looked around at the nicely appointed, typical hotel room – with a bed, a writing table, a comfortable chair.

'I know you've been wanting to speak to me. Now's your chance,' she said.

'I thought I wanted to say something to you, yes, but ... I thought you and Captain Portsmouth ...'

'I knew you'd misread the picture, much as he has misread it. He is interested in me, and I am interested in you,' she shyly explained.

Butterflies exploded in Pitso's stomach, who was relieved his feelings were reciprocated. But, remembering his bitter-sweet experience with Christine back home, Pitso could not help but change the subject. 'I enjoyed your speech very much. It opened a new window for me into European affairs.'

Embarrassed, Marie-Thérèse got up, and said, 'Let me get us some drinks.'

When she came back she had a tray with a half-full bottle of white wine and two glasses. She put the tray on a side table. He got up to pour the drinks.

'Thank you,' she said. They clinked glasses. Pitso sat down in his chair and took a small sip of his wine.

'Well, Mr Soldier, a proper welcome to France!' she laughed, raising her glass.

'Thank you. I'm beginning to get the feeling that before the war, you were not the humble nurse you are now ... that there's a lot of power behind you?'

She smiled and told him about her family, about the businesses they had in different parts of the country, about their history as part of French nobility.

'I thought nobles did not mingle with lowly plebeians like us!'

'You're misunderstanding me. We were nobles a long time ago, before the revolution. Now we are just businesspeople. If you are still here by the end of the war, you will probably meet my brother and cousins. They are highly successful in business, but humble human beings.' She paused. 'But do tell me about yourself.'

Pitso gave her a rough biography, without emotion, without dwelling on the racial tensions at home. He sensed that that part of his story would not make much sense to this lady who was so much at ease with him. He remembered that she had raised her eyebrows in suspicion and confusion whenever there were unpleasant exchanges between Pitso and white soldiers back in hospital. But she had not brought these issues to him; so why dwell on them?

They spoke about history, about books. He commended her on the natural beauty of her country. She gasped in surprise when he told her it had taken his ship one full month to sail from Africa to Europe. 'That long? I couldn't survive it. I would die of fear, or exhaustion!'

He drained his glass and put it down on the small table, feeling more courageous after their exchange. 'Do you know how to dance?'

'Yes, but there is no music,' she replied, frowning slightly.

'Come.' He got up, and helped her to her feet. 'Let me show you how to dance to the music of our hearts.'

She laughed. 'Why, you must be mad!'

'Listen to it, listen to the music. Can you hear it?'

'No, silly, are you drunk already? One glass of wine and you're imagining things. What are we dancing, anyway? Waltz, polka, foxtrot?'

'Part waltz, part heart. A new dance, just for you and me.'

Again, she giggled. 'I have never heard such foolishness.'

'Close your eyes,' he said, drawing her close to him. 'If you follow the dance with your heart, if you listen to the music, you will find my message to you, my words to you, hiding in there. Close your eyes.'

Slowly, they began to move. Then their movements and twirls around the room gained momentum. They twirled and twirled. Her eyes remained closed. On passing the drinks table, her dress got snagged on his trousers. She panicked, opened her eyes. He looked down at her, his arm holding her tight. 'I won't let you fall.'

They started moving again, Pitso leading her gracefully. She was an experienced dancer, her movements gracious and minimal.

Then she rested her face on his chest. Panting, they stopped. He touched her chin, and her eyelashes fluttered shyly. He lowered his face to hers. Closing her eyes, she obliged him with a kiss on the lips.

At that moment there was a soft knock on the door. She started, patting her hair. 'Who is it?'

There was a polite cough from the other side of the door.

'It's your colleague,' she said. 'I think you have to go.'

'Will I see you again?' he said, standing up and smoothing his uniform.

She looked away and shrugged, fingering a bunch of flowers on her windowsill. Until now, he hadn't noticed the flowers. They were bright yellow in colour. Now he could detect their spicy scent in the air. He moved closer to her, kissed her again. He then bent forward and breathed in the blooms on the windowsill. Perhaps that unusual shade of yellow was the colour of hope.

They met again a week later. He'd come to the inn unannounced, with a friend. They sat out in the sun, the four of them – Marie-Thérèse and her sister, and the two soldiers. They drank, told stories and laughed until it was time for the soldiers to leave. A few days later, Pitso and his friend returned. Pitso was bearing a bunch of yellow flowers, an approximation of the ones he had seen in her room. Again, the four of them sat in the sun, drinking and laughing, until Pitso looked meaningfully at her. She nodded surreptitiously. They excused themselves, and went to her quarters.

They sat next to each other on the bed, and kissed. Then he went on his knees, and touched her shoes. 'May I?'

She smiled approvingly. He took off her shoes carefully, then stood up and reached around her torso to undo her corset. She froze. He hesitated, then sat down next to her, his hands on his knees.

'I'll undress myself, if you don't mind,' she said, after a short pause. She kissed him again on the lips and got to her feet.

As she removed her clothing, he took off his boots, then his uniform. They lay down on the bed, side by side, kissing, exploring each other's bodies. He could taste her saliva, which had a tinge of the wine they'd just enjoyed. Then he smelt her perfume, subtle, intoxicating. Her breasts were pert, pointed and hard like fresh pears. Like the rest of her body, her breasts were so pale it seemed they had never been touched by the sun. By contrast, the nipples were a very dark pink, reminding him of strawberries, with the areolas a lighter pink.

He gently spread-eagled her, and then knelt in between her outstretched legs, his face dipping into the valley between her breasts. He spent some time stroking the area with the tip of his tongue. Then he gently bit into her strawberry nipple. She gasped, then shivered.

Taking his time, he moved from that breast to its partner. Her voice rose in a low moan. Then he traced his tongue from the valley all the way down to her navel, which he attended to with his tongue. She moaned, raised her knees, and bucked rhythmically. Her sharp nails dug into his shoulder blades.

From her navel, his tongue went south until it found her oasis. She couldn't wait any longer. She dug her hands firmly beneath his armpit, pulled him back on top of her and received him. Their movements were measured, unhurried. It was as if they were long-term fellow travellers on this road to mutual pleasuring.

He varied his movements from fast, furious thrusts to the slow, rolling motion of the hips. She wrapped her legs around his back, her heels drumming his buttocks, egging him on. All the while they were both moaning and muttering each other's names.

She felt she was reaching the point of no return, but held back. She wanted to prolong the pleasure.

Pitso felt he was about to explode. To distract himself, he closed his eyes and listened to someone playing an accordion somewhere outside.

They rocked as one entity. An electrifying wave rose from deep inside her, growing into a huge swell which collided with his throbbing deposit of himself into her. Their bodies convulsed. Then, spent, they lay next to each other, their sweating hands locked together in a passionate clasp. Sleep stole over him.

Standing in front of a mirror and smoothing his uniform back into shape, he turned to her. 'Please tell me: are you married?' he asked, thinking back to his first love.

'No,' she said, frowning.

'No steady boyfriend on the front line somewhere?'

'No man, no parents, just my sister and brother. No cats, no dogs, no children. If you want to be my beau, you are most welcome.' She giggled nervously, looking down.

There were tears in his eyes as he walked outside, leaving her behind, still tidying herself. He hoped he hadn't insulted her by asking those questions about boyfriends and husbands.

The cool afternoon breeze smacked him in the face, bringing him back to alertness. Captain Portsmouth was standing there, an inscrutable expression on his face. Marie-Thérèse's sister was nowhere to be seen. Pitso's heart sank, as it dawned on him how he had kept Portsmouth waiting while he was enjoying himself. He steeled himself for a serious rebuke.

But for now, he tried to be jovial, 'Captain, my Captain, how's the afternoon treating you?'

Portsmouth looked at him long and hard, and started walking almost angrily towards him. Then he suddenly broke into laughter. 'Corporal, my Corporal, you're such a rascal.'

The two men left the premises, heading back to camp. The rest of the troops were still in the town, most of them gathered at the public square where the joyful singing continued.

CHAPTER 34

On 9 July, a call was sent out: the King was in town. He would be inspecting his troops the following day. The officers were nervous, and the soldiers laughed at them behind their backs. From what Portsmouth told Pitso, not a single officer had met the King before. They did not know what impression he would have of the troops, or of the officers themselves, leaving them jittery.

After a quick breakfast the next morning, the men gathered at the parade square in Arques. The agitated officers inspected their individual companies and made the men rehearse 'God Save the King' a number of times. At 9 a.m. sharp, they got into trucks, and off they went to the town of Abbeville. An hour later, King George v, accompanied by Queen Mary, arrived on the lawns in the garden of an officers' club at Abbeville. The men could not help but feel impressed at finally meeting the sovereign they would be fighting for. The King's delegation included some distinguished individuals – in the persons of Sir Douglas Haig, the commander of the British Expeditionary Force, and Colonel S M Pritchard, commanding officer of the South African Native Labour Contingent. Colonel Pritchard introduced the King to senior officers of the Contingent. Pitso was intrigued when he learned the identities of some of these men. They included

Lieutenant Colonel J C Emmett, a Boer General during the Anglo–Boer War, and Lieutenant Colonel J Jacobsz, previously a staff officer with General de Wet, the very general who had fought alongside Pitso's own father during the Anglo–Boer War. Pitso thought it was amazing how these white people played the game of war. Also in attendance were some leading chiefs from black South Africa, among them Chief Mamabolo from Pietersburg, who had sent several hundred of his men to the Labour Corps. During the Anglo–Boer War, he had been a scout for the British, captured by the Boers, only to be released when Pretoria fell into British hands.

Under the pleasantly warm morning sun, the King walked slowly along the lines. He stopped occasionally in front of a man and asked a question through an interpreter. Pitso was sweating, praying His Majesty would not stop in front of him because he did not know how he would sound speaking to the King – would he respond in English, or would he use the services of the interpreter just like everyone else? The King did pause in front of Pitso, but only took a long look at him, smiled and moved on.

The King then walked to the centre of the square. He cast his eyes across the sea of faces eagerly waiting to hear from him and spoke: 'I have much pleasure in seeing you who have travelled so far over the sea to help in this great war. I take this opportunity of thanking you for the work done in France by the South African Labour Corps. Reports have been given me of the valuable services rendered by the natives of South Africa to my armies in German South-West Africa and German East Africa. The loyalty of my native subjects in South Africa is fully shown by the helpful part you are taking in this world-wide war. Rest assured that all you have done is of great assistance to my Armies at the front. This work of yours is second only in importance to that of my sailors and soldiers, who are bearing the brunt of the battle.

'But you also form part of my great Armies who are fighting for the liberties and freedom of my subjects of all races and creeds throughout the Empire. Without munitions of war my Armies cannot fight. Without food they cannot live. You are helping to send these things to them each day, and in doing so you are hurling your assegais at the enemy and hastening the destruction which awaits him. A large corps such as yours requires drafts and reinforcements, and I am sure your chiefs will take upon themselves this duty of supporting your battalions with ever-increasing numbers. I wish them and all their peoples to share with all my loyal subjects that great and final victory which will bring peace throughout the world. I desire you to make these words of mine known to your people here, and to convey them to your chiefs in South Africa.'

After his address, which was followed by a response from the delegation of traditional chiefs, the King, in keeping with African custom, presented a white ox to the soldiers for good luck. The ox was to be slaughtered the following day. Sadly, Pitso and his comrades from Arques-la-Bataille were to miss the feast. Nevertheless, they revelled in the day's festivities before travelling back to camp late in the afternoon, having enjoyed a sumptuous lunch and some traditional dancing.

On the way back home, some of the men were talking excitedly. 'Did you hear what the King said? He said we are here to fight for our liberty, our freedom for all the people in his Empire.'

'It's a good thing we came here. When we go back home, we will be proud and free.'

'We will be equal to the white South Africans. We shall have the vote – just like the white man.'

Pitso knew this was wishful thinking. But, all the same, the King's words had given him hope.

The inquest into the sinking of the *Mendi* began on 24 July. In maritime law, it was not called an inquest, but a Formal Investigation. In charge of the proceedings was Mr J G Hay Halkett, a magistrate who had much practical acquaintance with this type of investigation. He was assisted by three assessors, also selected for their experience in maritime matters.

Summoned to appear before the inquest were the masters of the two vessels that had collided – Captain Yardley of the *Mendi*, and Captain Stump of the ss *Darro*. Also in attendance were some of the officers of the Native Contingent. Various interested parties – including the South African government – were represented by their lawyers.

Pitso, like many other troops, would have liked to attend, but that was not possible. There was a lot of work to be done: ammunition to be offloaded from ships and channelled to wherever it was needed; fuel to be provided for the various camps; food to be cooked; trenches to be dug; medical support to be provided when needed. The troops were grateful that the authorities had seen fit to disseminate as much information about the proceedings as physically possible. They promised newspaper reports would be disseminated among the officers, who would then appoint some literate members to hold public readings at regular intervals. The authorities believed that this would keep the morale of the men high. It would show that the authorities cared about the men and that the proceedings were transparent.

The public readings soon assumed legendary status, remind-ing some men of the fireside tales they had been raised on.

Because of his reading abilities and his grasp of various languages, Pitso was selected as one of the public readers. He received his regular supply of material, which he would first read quickly by himself and then summarise so that it was succinct, accurate, but as dramatic as possible.

The first two days of the inquest were largely a review, based on submissions by various witnesses, of what had happened before and during the collision. On 20 February, the *Mendi* sailed from Plymouth, escorted by the HMS *Brisk*, a destroyer, in misty weather. By 11.30 p.m., the vessel was going at full speed. Because it had become foggy and visibility was poor, the whistle was sounded at one-minute intervals to signal their position, as required by regulations. Yardley mostly remained on the bridge, except during short intervals when he went down to the chart-room under the navigating bridge to fix his position by chart.

At 4 a.m., Second Officer H Raine and Fourth Officer Hubert Frank Trapnell came on watch. On account of the weather, they decided to reduce speed. The HMS *Brisk* was having trouble keeping up, also because of the thick fog.

Unbeknownst to Captain Yardley and his crew, another ship was fast approaching. The SS *Darro* was a much larger ship than the *Mendi*: five hundred feet in length, sixty-two feet in the beam, gross tonnage of 11 484 tons. The *Mendi* was a single-screw steamer of 4 230 gross tons, three hundred and seventy feet in length and forty-six feet in the beam. The *Darro*, under the command of Henry Winchester Stump, had sailed from Le Havre in France, and was on her way to Liverpool. Later reports would show that the *Darro* had been moving at a speed of thirteen knots, while the *Mendi* was moving at six knots. The *Darro* had lookouts on the forecastle, in the crow's nest and on top of the wheelhouse. But it was treacherously foggy.

At about the time the ss *Mendi* was slowing down, the *Darro* hurtled on at full speed, with Captain Stump on the bridge with the officers of the watch and the lookouts still in position. It transpired that, although the *Darro*'s masthead lights and electric sidelights were on, her whistles were not being sounded as required by regulations.

On the *Mendi*, Fourth Officer Trapnell, who was at the starboard end of the bridge, heard another vessel coming through the water. He alerted his colleague, 'Raine, I think there is a vessel near us.' He then proceeded to sound the *Mendi*'s whistle numerous times. Just then, he saw the masthead light of another ship so close that the other vessel seemed right over them. Raine blew three blasts of the whistle, but the other ship remained silent.

It was already too late. The *Darro*'s bow crashed into the starboard side of the *Mendi* at exactly 4.57 a.m. on 21 February 1917. The crash happened just about eleven miles south to south-west of St Catherine's Point on the Isle of Wight.

Needless to say, the spotlight during the hearing fell largely on Captain Stump, master of the ss *Darro*. He had been blamed for negligence and everyone, especially the press, was baying for his blood. On the third day of the inquest, Captain Stump took the stand, cross-examined by Sir Reginald Acland, King's Counsel, representing the Board of Trade. The questions regarding Captain Stump's failure to make any attempt to save the men in the water began like this:

Acland: What steps did you take to save life?
Stump: I took no immediate steps.
Acland: Why not?

Stump: I considered my own ship was in
danger of sinking … She was a
tender ship, I consider.

Acland: Did you hear anybody singing out?

Stump: I heard some shouting out … Very
shortly I could hear the oars of a boat
coming alongside. I naturally thought
that it was shouting from the boat that
had a crowd of men. It was a tramp so
far as I knew, an ordinary cargo
steamer. I had no idea that there were
800 or 900 men in a ship with 6 boats
or anything of that sort.

Stump did acknowledge that, after the first boat arrived about
half an hour later, he received a report that the collision had
been with the *Mendi*, which had black troops aboard. He denied
hearing cries from the water after the second *Mendi* boat had
come alongside. Other *Darro* witnesses heard shouting much
later than that, two of them until daylight, which would have
been about 6.30 a.m. Stump argued he had insufficient crew to
man the boats and work his ship if the need arose. He had a
crew of one hundred and sixty-three men. He claimed that if he
had put out boats, they would have been lost in the fog.

Pitso paused here, looking at his audience. 'Gentlemen, you
have to listen carefully to the next part. Listen carefully. This
Captain Stump says he had not known for certain until noon
that the *Mendi* had sunk.' Pitso waited a few seconds. Some men
were shaking heads, others were fidgeting with their hands.
'That's why he left the scene. He thought he could leave the
work of rescue to the navy patrol boat.'

'How heartless!' one man shouted.

'It's because he'd been told the men on the *Mendi* were black,' Pitso said. 'That's why he left us.'

A white officer who had been listening got up. 'Corporal! You are inciting these men. You are making them angry.'

'With due respect, sir, I'm only doing my job. I am reading what has been prepared for me.'

'Very well,' said the officer. 'You've come to the end of today's presentation in any case, haven't you?'

Pitso nodded and the crowd slowly dispersed, muttering about the dishonesty of the captain of the *Darro*.

The next presentation, which Pitso delivered the following day, covered the interaction between Captain Stump and his own counsel, who said, 'Having been a Master all these years in a large company it is now suggested by Sir Reginald that you wanted to leave men who you knew were in the water to drown.'

Stump replied, 'No one could regret the circumstances more than I do myself.'

After Stump had described how he finally left the scene of the collision at 6.45 a.m., heading for St Helens Roads, Isle of Wight, this exchange followed:

> Acland: It would be interesting to know whether you went full speed in that fog.
> Stump: No I did not.
> Acland: Why did you not obey the Admiralty instructions which you say you received …?
> Stump: I had got into enough trouble already.

From various witnesses during the inquest, it appeared that there was much confusion, which extended to members of the Court, about the expected behaviour of a master of a ship in times of war. It appeared that instructions from the Admiralty in time of war differed from the standing regulations relating to safety at sea. A lot of questions arose, including: should a ship be driven at full speed in fog in a danger zone, and should it sound its whistle? Stump argued that sounding a whistle in a danger zone in time of war could render his vessel vulnerable to enemy attack.

Pitso had never been to court, but he was shocked to learn that on the third and fourth day the proceedings were already being wrapped up. He had expected the hearing to last longer, considering the gravity of the subject and the number of lives that had been lost. Also, having read Plato and his account of the trial of Socrates, Pitso had imagined court cases, especially where death was involved, to be long, rambling affairs.

He wished Ngqavini were around. After all, his friend had been a veteran of many court cases. Ngqavini could have given some insight into these proceedings.

On the fifth day, the magistrate, Mr Halkett read out the Report of Court. Attached to the report was an annex containing its finding of facts, covering the various aspects of the inquiry. On the question of travelling at high speed in foggy conditions, the annex declared:

> The Court has every desire to make the fullest allowance for the anxious position in which masters are placed by the dangers with which they are beset at the present time; but in its opinion, these dangers, frequent as they are, do not justify

masters in taking the responsibility of running their vessels into other dangers, and more certain, in the absence of authoritative Admiralty orders compelling them to do so.

With regard to Captain Stump's failure to save lives, the annex pronounced:

> The facts of the case are such that the Court is unable to find any excuse for the Master's inaction. He knew that his powerful ship, going at full speed, had struck another vessel a heavy right-angled blow and, very soon afterwards, that this vessel was the *Mendi*, with troops, the crew of which had been compelled to take to her boats. He must have heard, for much longer than he admitted, the cries proceeding from the water, as they were heard generally on board his ship, for hours, by competent witnesses on duty. There was nothing to have prevented him from sending away boats, in the then smooth water, to ascertain what had happened to the other vessel and what the circumstances were of those whose cries were heard.

The report concluded:

> The Court having carefully inquired into the circumstances attending the above-mentioned shipping casualty, finds, for the reasons stated in the Annex hereto, that the collision and consequent

loss of life, loss of the ss *Mendi* and material damage to ss *Darro*, were caused by the wrongful act and default of Mr Henry Winchester Stump, the master of ss *Darro*, in not complying with articles 15 and 16 of the Regulations for Preventing Collisions at Sea, as to sound signals and speed in a fog, and by his more serious default in failing, without any reasonable cause, to send away a boat or boats to ascertain the extent of the damage to the *Mendi*, and to render to her, her master, crew and passengers, such assistance as was practicable and necessary, as required by section 422 (1) (a) of the Merchant Shipping Act, 1894. The Court suspends his certificate, No. 017169, for 12 months from the date hereof. Dated this 8th day August, 1917.

When Pitso read the last words, a hush fell over his audience. Summer birds called from their perches, a light breeze blew from the sea in Dieppe. Then a siren sounded, and the men got up slowly from their haunches.

CHAPTER 35

Much as most men were disappointed with the outcome of the inquest, the inquiry at least bore some positive news for Pitso. His courageous conduct had been commended in the inquiry. The Committee for the Welfare of Africans in Europe arranged for some tangible recognition for the members of the crew who had distinguished themselves on the night of the sinking. Although Pitso was not a crew member, some officers who had witnessed his bravery confirmed that he was deserving of recognition. He received ten guineas, alongside others who had distinguished themselves.

'So proud of you, old chap,' Captain Portsmouth told Pitso on his visit to the camp on the day the announcement had been made.

'Thanks, my Captain, but I don't really know what exceptional things I did on that morning.'

'Well, according to witnesses you did excellent work. You selflessly stayed behind on the ship to make sure many of your shipmates were safe.'

Pitso also received a copy of the Bible, courtesy of the Archbishop of Canterbury. A few weeks after the citations, Pitso was appointed as a fully-fledged interpreter and clerk. The position came with a number of privileges, chief of which was a change of diet. Instead of mealie meal, he now qualified for rice and a lot more meat. He recalled, with a chill, how the issue of food had sparked a riot at one of the camps in Dieppe.

While still in hospital, he had heard about a disciplinary hearing involving one Stimela Jason Jingoes. Originally from Lesotho, he had arrived in France with one of the earlier battalions. This man, articulate and not scared of whites, had stood up at breakfast one morning, lifted his porridge bowl to his nose and said, 'Hmm, yummy! Maize-meal porridge with weevils! A black soldier's breakfast in France.'

Then he proceeded to dump the contents of his plate on the floor. More men followed suit, shouting, 'No more weevils! No more weevils!'

White officers came rushing in, wanting to know what the ruckus was all about.

Some of the black soldiers, who didn't want to be associated with the 'troublemakers', had sat at their tables dutifully picking their way through the weevil-infested sludge.

At the height of the heated exchange between the soldiers and the officers, Jingoes started giving an impassioned address in English, obviously meant for the ears of the officers. He said many things, but the words that got him in trouble were these: 'We Bantu are often treated like dogs here by the white people from home, yet they forget that we are all here at war against a common enemy. Actually I made a mistake in saying that they treat us like dogs, because usually they treat their dogs very well indeed. They ignore the fact that we have left South Africa for the moment. We are in Europe, and we are at war, and we were promised decent treatment if we would fight the Germans.'

Jingoes was suspended from duty for the day. The following day, he was summoned to appear at a hearing.

As his opening salvo, the captain officiating at the hearing said, 'You are a lance corporal. Yet you have been charged with making mischief here yesterday. I have to consider your case in terms of martial law.'

Martial law. The scariest words on the front, for they meant possible death by firing squad.

In response to the captain's opening remarks, Jingoes said, 'I said yesterday, sir, that in Europe we are not *natives*. Is that an offence, sir?'

'Did you say that?'

'Yes, sir.' Then he immediately went on to the issue about the food. 'Sir, our meals have been changed from the usual rations to mealie meal, which we are given from morning to night, sir, Monday to Monday, and the mealie meal we get is bad. There are weevils in it. It is for you, sir, to judge where justice lies in this matter.'

The captain stormed out of the room, and went to the kitchen. He scooped up some porridge and some uncooked mealie meal in bowls. Both bowls had weevils wriggling about in them.

Enraged, the captain turned to the man's accusers – a sergeant major and the sergeant of the man's platoon, both of them white men – and addressed them. 'After you heard this man speak so strongly against his officers, and after you heard the men complaining about their food, did you go to the kitchen to check on whether they were telling the truth?'

The accusers said they had not.

'What did you do, then?'

'We did nothing, sir.'

The captain asked the two accusers to look closely at the food. They did and admitted there were weevils in the food.

The captain said, 'Why do you complain when your men tell you that their food has weevils in it?'

'As natives, we did not think they were telling the truth …'

'What do you mean by this term *natives*?'

The two officers squirmed. 'We mean these black people.'

The captain got up and started pacing the room. Then he said, 'Then your complaint is that this man said black people are not natives in Europe, thereby implying that whites are *natives* here?'

'Sir, I am a European, not a *native*!' one of them exclaimed.

The captain shook his head and told the accused they were free to go.

That afternoon, the black soldiers were served potatoes, meat, rice, bread and, of course, their beloved *mahewu*.

Pitso smiled and shook his head at the memory. Now, alongside other clerks and newly appointed black chaplains, he was allocated new accommodation, which allowed the clerks and chaplains the privacy necessary for their work. But this new situation also meant that Pitso would have to be transferred to another camp – which he regretted, seeing as he had grown to love his camp at Arques. He was going to leave behind a lot of good friends he had made there.

Imagine his surprise, then, when he arrived at the new camp, also in Arques, to be greeted by Portsmouth and some of the survivors of the *Mendi*. The other survivors, including his friend Tlali and Officer Haig, were at the camp next door. He rejoiced in being able to reconnect with his old comrades. He spent the first day getting used to his new surroundings and tasks.

'You're an old skelm, Captain Portsmouth,' said Pitso when he ran into him, two days later.

'I don't know what you're talking about, old chap,' replied Portsmouth, looking away.

'This is all your doing, sir, the promotion, then the transfer. It bears the unmistakable Portsmouth signature.'

Portsmouth's face was inscrutable. He changed the subject. 'There's a rumour doing the rounds here. A grave rumour.'

'I hope it doesn't involve me, sir.'

'On the morning of the sinking? As we were all scrambling to safety, one of the men found a raft. But as soon as he was on the raft, he kicked into the water whoever tried to join him on his perch.'

'I did catch a glimpse of that man. But I think his raft was sucked into the whirlpool when the *Mendi* was going down, sir.'

'No, old chum, the man is still with us.'

'How would you know, sir?'

'I'm privy to a lot of things that *need* to be known. Don't forget about my father and his military background; my eyes and ears are wide open, my dear lad. What I can tell you with certainty is that the man is one of us. What a shame.'

Pitso looked away. 'Sir?'

'Yes?'

'Between the two of us, sir ...'

'I'm all ears.'

'I think I recognised the man.'

Portsmouth searched Pitso's eyes. Then he started pacing up and down. 'If you are sure you recognised the man, keep it to yourself. One day you might need to reveal his name, but certainly not now. We're in the middle of a war. And, who knows, this might be a secret you want to take to the grave. I certainly don't want to know what you know. I don't like peddling rumours – I'm an officer, after all. Can't afford to sully my name and reputation. As a battalion we've acquitted ourselves so well. As the survivors of the *Mendi*, we have a reputation to protect. For posterity's sake, we need to remove this stain.'

CHAPTER 36

Pitso took to his new assignment as interpreter/clerk with aplomb. Every now and then he could be seen on horse-back, clip-clopping from this point to the next, fulfilling his duties.

His new job also gave him more time and excuses to be with his friend Portsmouth. The latter, in charge of a company that worked the quarry, spent a lot of time with the cooks after there'd been complaints about the quality of food. Portsmouth's epicurean tastes were legendary, his culinary skills having been cultivated, on the side, while he was at military college in Britain – skills which he would later refine when he served as a lay preacher. He ate and drank only the best if he could.

One day Pitso found him with his sleeves rolled up, with the black cooks looking on in surprise and amusement. He wasn't in the kitchen to give instructions but was actually doing the cooking himself, explaining every step in preparing his dish.

'Gentlemen,' said Pitso, greeting the cooks, 'why do you allow this man to poke his long European nose into your pots? Ever heard of food poisoning?'

'I thought I knew how to cook,' said one of the cooks in Sesotho, 'until he started showing me all these things called spices. The only cooking powder I've ever used is salt. Now these colourful powders and the leaves he's got are an eye-opener. They smell good, I must admit. Can't wait to taste them.'

'Hey, Pitso, you old thing,' said Portsmouth without lifting his eye from the saucepan, 'what are you doing here? Aren't you supposed to be on duty somewhere?'

'A little bird tells me you need my services here, Captain.'

'Well, yes and no. These gentlemen here are good cooks, or at least they show some potential. Now, trying to impart my knowledge to them is proving rather difficult. They don't understand my brand of Sotho.'

'That's because they speak Sepedi, which you white people call Northern Sotho. But I can help with that. So, what are you cooking, sir?'

'Don't worry, the chaps here have already cooked the regulation meal for the troops. What we are now conjuring is for my own private consumption – though of course I'll share with them, so they can experiment with my recipes at their leisure.'

'Good for you, sir.'

'Okay, let's start here: can you cook at all?'

'Well, I'm not a top-class cook like you, Captain, but my bobotie will make your taste buds stand up and cheer. The traditional braai is my specialty. A simple beef stew with rice is not too much of a challenge, either.'

'Well, if you can cook a creditable stew, you'll get a hang of the rogan josh. That's the dish I'm taking these gentlemen through.'

'Josh what?'

'Basically, rogan means fat, and josh means heat. What you're doing is you're cooking meat on the bone, slow-cooking it in its own fat. But you use lots of spices here – chilli powder, cardamom, Kashmir shallots, cinnamon or bay leaves, coriander, fennel powder, and, of course, stewing lamb or chops.'

'But we don't have any lamb here, sir.'

'We improvise, my boy, we improvise. Remember, our boys now have full and official permission to lay traps in the forest.'

'So, what of it, Captain?'

'We catch antelope, and we pretend it's lamb, that's what. I've never been too much of a hunter myself, so I don't even know what these animals here are called. But they've got just the right amount of fat, just like a sheep.'

'I get the picture. But the dish you're cooking today sounds … Indian? I lived with an Indian family when I was a child,' Pitso said.

'Of course it is Indian. Kashmiri, to be exact. It is a curry. Back at military college in England, we had this great chef from India – gigantic whiskers, nostrils always a-twitch, sharp piercing eyes … Taught me everything I know about Indian cooking, the old codger.'

'And where do you get these Indian spices from, in the middle of a war?'

'British officers. Many of them are so addicted to Indian cooking they can't leave their own country without these spices. When they go to war, the spices become part of their arsenal.'

'I have yet to see an undernourished British soldier, Captain.'

Portsmouth laughed good-humouredly.

'But it's true, sir,' insisted Pitso. 'In all the war books I've read, the Brits will, in the middle of a ferocious skirmish, take a break for "a spot of lunch", as they call it.'

It quickly became a Friday-afternoon tradition: Portsmouth

at the pots, cooking rabbit vindaloo, or antelope rogan josh, or antelope shank korma, the cooks beginning to get the hang of it, and Pitso pretending he was only there in his capacity as an interpreter, when in fact he also was an eager student. Not to mention that he relished the resulting meals.

Every now and then during the week, Pitso would ride to the hospital, ostensibly to perform an assignment, when in fact his primary motive was to see Marie-Thérèse. When he was supposed to be working, he would sneak into town and spend time with her at her house, whenever she was off duty. He knew it was risky even though his new-found status offered him a sense of immunity from close scrutiny. He could go to many places unaccompanied by a white officer, but going into town was pushing it. All the shopkeepers in town knew the rules: don't serve a black soldier if he is not accompanied by a white officer. The second rule, though unwritten, was: French citizens should not hesitate to report an unaccompanied black soldier to the authorities.

One day, after Pitso had spent a sizzling afternoon inside Marie-Thérèse's bedroom, he was untying his horse from a pole when a familiar voice said, 'And what are you doing here?'

He wheeled around to see Officer Haig, his eyes bleary and red.

Officer Haig switched from English to Afrikaans. 'Answer me – what are you doing here unaccompanied?' When the officer spoke for the second time, Pitso's suspicions were confirmed: the man was drunk.

'You know I can have you court-martialled?'

'But why would you want to do that, sir?'

'The rules are simple: a black trooper can't enter town un-accompanied by a white officer.'

'But, sir, you're here. I am not unaccompanied.'

'Are you trying to be funny with me? You know I can get you punished for that. That's insubordination.' He took a step forward.

Three passers-by slowed down to watch the exchange between the two soldiers.

'Sir, I think you're attracting attention to yourself. These people can see that you're drunk. You wouldn't want another senior officer, say, Captain Portsmouth, finding out about this ...' He allowed his voice to trail off.

Officer Haig turned to the onlookers and grinned foolishly. Pitso got onto his horse.

'Hey,' Haig shouted after him, 'will you give me a ride back to camp?'

'With pleasure, sir.'

Getting Officer Haig on to the back of the horse proved to be a challenge. His drunkenness and unruly belly did not help at all. Pitso wondered what the passers-by were making of these clownish men in uniform. How had Officer Haig passed the physical test with such an unwieldy body?

They rode in silence for a while, before Pitso said, 'Excuse me, sir, but why are you speaking more Afrikaans these days? On the ship you spoke English to everyone.'

'English is a good language for playing cricket or polo. Afrikaans is the language of war. Zulu is the language of war. *So waar as wragtig!* We're in the trenches now; we need to communicate in an inspiring language, such as Afrikaans.'

Pitso wanted to laugh, but he remained guarded in the presence of this man.

'More seriously, I'm an Afrikaans-speaking person by birth. But we're Cape Boers. And as you know, the Cape Boers have always sided with the English. All about convenience, my man ...'

'I didn't know that, sir.'

'Well, listen and learn. My grandfather moved over to the English side a long time ago, in exchange for huge tracts of land in the Cape, in the Grahamstown area. We have ever since been more English than Afrikaans – at least in the public eye. At home we speak Afrikaans. Needless to say, during the Anglo–Boer War, we were officially neutral, but our sympathies were with the English.'

Perhaps sensing he'd revealed too much to a mere corporal, and a black corporal at that, Officer Haig clammed up all of a sudden. They continued in silence. At some point, Pitso realised that Haig had fallen asleep and allowed his mind to travel back to what had happened at Marie-Thérèse's house that afternoon.

As they were getting dressed after making love, she had said, out of the blue, 'Pitso, I can see blood. Blood flowing. And you're in the middle of it.'

'What are you?' he had said casually, as he pulled on his clothes. 'A clairvoyant or something?'

'Gosh, no, not a clairvoyant!' she replied in alarm. 'It's just that when something terrible is about to happen, I dream about it. Sometimes my dreams come to fruition.'

'*Sometimes.* This won't be one of those times your dream comes true, my dear. Nothing will happen to me.'

She ignored him, continuing, 'Avoid unnecessary confrontation over the next few hours – or days. I know this is all vague but ... It was in the dream.'

'You're just anxious, my dear. That's only natural. And it's also only natural that when you dwell too much on something, it tends to weave itself into your dreams.'

'But I see lots of blood!'

'Blood is inevitable. We're in the middle of a war, after all.'

'Try and avoid all confrontation,' she repeated, 'even in its mildest form.'

Officer Haig's groggy voice startled Pitso from his musings. 'Tell me, have you heard the rumours about what happened as the ship was going down?'

'I don't know anything about any rumours, sir. All I know is what I saw, sir, and what I heard at the inquest.'

'What did you see?'

'One could write a book about the whole thing, sir.' Pitso stayed non-committal.

They rode past the dilapidated Norman chateau. Some children waved at them from the side of the road. Pitso waved back.

'Somebody is spreading malicious rumours ... rumours that can destroy a man's life.'

Pitso was silent. His mind flew back to the day of the sinking.

'Trooper.' Haig broke into his train of thought. 'I know you're close to Captain Portsmouth ... I think he is behind the rumour. Maybe you could politely ask him to stop, to desist.'

'What is the rumour about, sir?' Pitso could now vividly see Haig on the raft, kicking desperate men back into the water as they tried to clamber onto the raft.

'Are you listening to me, trooper?'

'Yes, I am.'

'The captain says ... they say I was the man who kicked people off that raft as the ship was sinking.'

'What raft?' Pitso was trying hard to control his rage.

'Apparently there was a raft. And ... and this ... this person climbed onto the raft. When the other people tried to join him on the raft, he started kicking them back into the water.'

Even though he was seething, Pitso said calmly, 'Why wasn't it mentioned at the inquest, sir?'

'I don't know. I don't know why they are raising it only now.'

'But why does it bother you, sir?'

'I just told you. They say I was that person. They say I must be court-martialled. But they have no evidence against me.' Haig's voice rose, almost to a wail.

Startled by the sound, the horse came to a halt and clopped the ground hard with its right front hoof. Pitso brushed its mane reassuringly. It started moving again.

'Trooper, I am a good man, a better soldier than most. Do you think I would do that?'

If Pitso had had any doubt about what he'd seen that night, Haig's fear and anxiety only confirmed his suspicions.

'For what it's worth, I'll speak to Captain Portsmouth about it, sir.' Pitso was relieved to drop Haig off at his camp.

That night, Pitso went to bed, with Officer Haig where he didn't want him – sitting on his mind.

CHAPTER 37

Two days later Pitso got an urgent message to make his way to the native prison in Dieppe. There had been a disturbance at one of the camps, and some men had been arrested. They were to appear before a court martial that day and the services of an interpreter would be needed. As he was leaving his hut, he made sure to bring with him a set of pencils, sheets of drawing paper and some of his older drawings. He found that, on these assignments, the wheels of officialdom could not always be trusted to start spinning at the appointed hour and minute. The best way to kill time, and thus keep himself in good humour, was to work on his drawings while he waited – either retouching older drawings, or embarking on entirely new pieces.

His horse was sweating and foaming at the mouth by the time they arrived at the native prison. Pitso introduced himself to the two officers in charge. They assured him it was not going to be a long trial, which could mean anything. He was told to sit down as they were still awaiting the arrival of an officer who was an accuser in the matter.

Although Pitso had never seen the two officers before, there was no mistaking their South African accents. They must have come with earlier battalions. They were cordial and polite, cut from the same cloth as Portsmouth, not as boorish as Haig and some of the others.

It was his first time at the prison, which was a rudimentary structure – a huge hall, really, with a partitioning of iron bars right down the middle. The prisoners' side was gloomy, pale shafts of light filtering from tiny windows that were set high up. In the gloom, he could see that the floor was completely bare. The prisoners' sleeping mats and blankets had been folded and lined up in neat piles against the walls. For toilet purposes, the prisoners used three buckets, placed next to each other in a corner.

On the jailers' side of the building, towards the entrance, the floor was of dark, smooth cement, polished to a shine. There were two sturdy tables side by side, with a chair allocated to each table. A large grey typewriter sat in the middle of one of the tables, a neat pile of white paper next to it. The other table was completely bare, except for a huge copper-bound register, a record book of sorts, which was shackled to one of the table's legs. There were two benches for visitors against the wall, facing the officers' tables.

The officers asked Pitso to join them for a cup of tea. He gratefully accepted, noticing how the officers poured the tea from their cups into the saucers, slurping it from the saucers, tilted just so. It was an affectation Pitso had observed among the Brits. He smiled to himself, reflecting how his own friend Portsmouth had become more English ever since they'd arrived in France.

When the officers finished their tea, they excused themselves and left the room, presumably to go over the final strategy for the day's proceedings.

Quickly, Pitso moved towards the bars and asked the men to

come forward and brief him before the officers returned. It was only then that he spotted Tlali among the men.

Pitso almost shouted for joy at seeing the friend he hadn't laid eyes on in months. They had last met each other when Tlali's company had driven past Pitso's own camp – a quick glimpse during which they had called to each other. But excited as he was now to see his friend, he checked himself and simply looked at Tlali. He had to exercise restraint here. Like the other prisoners, Tlali was wearing a white vest, government-issue trousers, no shoes. Tlali was uncharacteristically sullen, his face sporting dark unseemly bumps.

'What happened? Speak quickly before they return.'

'There was a fight at camp last night. I fought with Officer Red Beard' – Officer Haig – 'and he stole my money.'

'What?'

'I gave him money, as I usually do, to go and get me some tobacco from town. And a little bit of white man's liquor as well. He always buys it for me.'

'Are you out of your mind?' exclaimed Pitso, unable to recognise his friend's behaviour. These were all new habits for Tlali, who had never drank or smoked before.

'When I asked for my money back, he attacked me. The other men rose to my defence. That's why we're here.'

When the two officers came back, Pitso was back on the bench where he had been sitting earlier, studying his drawings. The one that always stood out was that of his mother as drawn by his father those many years ago. It had been one of the works in the pocket of the greatcoat he'd been wearing on the day of the sinking of the *Mendi*, and he had since restored it.

One of the officers interrupted his thoughts. 'I don't expect this to be a major hearing. Just going through official motions, to remind our troopers that we're watching them. Levels of discipline among our troops have been nothing but praise-worthy.'

'Quite commendable, Captain Moffett,' added the other, 'if you consider that these are not trained soldiers. They've had to deal with the whole issue of … uhm, cultural adjustment. The snow, the sea and the diet, which must be largely alien to them. It must have been a shock to their system. But they rose above it all, and acquitted themselves admirably.'

Pitso merely nodded.

'They'll probably only receive a reprimand,' said Captain Moffett. 'And everybody can go home.'

'Discipline is important,' said Pitso quietly.

Suddenly the morning air outside was filled with song – throaty African voices, singing, chanting. As they got closer, the words of the chant became clearer: '*Bakhululeni, bakhululeni.*' *Free them, free them.*

The two officers – Captain Moffett and Lieutenant Benjamin – instinctively reached for their guns.

The voices grew closer. Pitso, joined by the two officers, rushed outside. In the distance, from the direction of the barracks, they saw the black soldiers, in full uniform, half running towards the prison.

'They are not supposed to be here,' said Lieutenant Benjamin. 'These hearings are private matters. They are not court cases.'

'Look, lieutenant, these are not regular soldiers. They don't understand procedure like you and I,' said Moffett.

'But rules are rules, Captain.'

'Maybe we should let them sit in, just to assure them that everything is above board. It will also give them an under-standing of how our justice system works.'

Pitso chimed in, 'I don't think they mean any harm. I don't know the entire rule book myself, but I think what the captain is saying is reasonable enough.'

'It's your call, Captain.'

The men, who could have numbered anywhere between thirty and forty, were now at the gate, remonstrating with the guards who wouldn't let them in.

The captain said, 'Lance Corporal Motaung, why don't you go over and tell the men to stop singing? Tell them to walk in an orderly way into the building and get seated while we wait for the officer who is the main complainant in this matter.'

Pitso hurried to the gate to explain the situation to the guards. Then he spoke to the men in Sotho and broken Xhosa. They immediately stopped shouting and followed him back into the building. But their spirits were still high, peppering their muttered conversations with angry words.

Because the front of the prison had not been designed with large groups of visitors in mind, there was not much space for sitting. The men decided to stand and wait. The minute they saw their colleagues waiting in the darkness behind the bars, they chanted, '*Siyekhaya! Siyekhaya.*' *We're going home, we're going home.*

Pitso called them to order. They obeyed.

The captain spoke, 'Just for the record, gentlemen, this here is not a court of law. You are not supposed to be here. The hearing that is about to unfold was supposed to be a private matter between the accused members and the officer in question. But in the interest of justice and openness, I see no harm in allowing you to stay.'

After Pitso had interpreted the captain's words, the men cheered and sang praises to the captain. Pitso knew there was no sincerity in the captain's words. He thought the man was being oh-so-polite and reasonable because he realised he had a possible mutiny on his hands. He was saying now, 'But as you know, I am not the chief of chiefs here. I'm only one of the many small chiefs. There are many chiefs above me, who will be very upset if they discover that I've broken the rules. In order for them not to find out, I am asking for your cooperation. I am urging you to respect my position but, most importantly, to respect the proceedings that are about to unfold. If you don't shout and heckle, this matter will never reach the ears of the big chiefs. If you have problems or complaints about our procedure, there are channels you can follow. You can appeal the sentence, or ask for a review of the sentence – that is, if someone gets sentenced. Which I doubt very much.'

After Pitso had finished translating the captain's words for the group, the five men behind the bars were moved to the front. They were made to stand next to the table with the typewriter.

No sooner had the accused men taken their place than the door opened. In walked Officer Haig, in full uniform.

Some of the men roared with fury, 'Here's the dog! Here's the dog!'

'Order,' cried Pitso. 'Order. Show them you're civilised.'

The roar was reduced to a murmur.

Officer Haig was clearly shaken by the sight of the men. He took his place next to the captain.

'Ah,' said the captain consulting his watch, 'Officer Haig has finally decided to grace our humble little event with his great presence. Seeing as we've already run out of tea, we shall go straight into the matter at hand ...'

Pitso noticed that even though Officer Haig had tried his

best to look sharp – with nicely pressed trousers and his beard neatly trimmed – there was still something haggard about him. His face looked puffy, as if he hadn't slept in a week. His thin lips were cracked, his eyes bloodshot.

'My apologies, Captain,' said Officer Haig, but he was looking at Pitso. 'What is this man doing here? He's not from my camp, the camp where the … unfortunate events took place. And I was not expecting any spectators, either.'

'Lance Corporal Motaung is an interpreter,' said the captain. 'He is here in that capacity.'

Officer Haig switched to Afrikaans. 'With due respect, *agbare kaptein*, could we not have an interpreter from another battalion? Not the Fifth Battalion. Certainly not a survivor from the *Mendi* …'

'Why not from the *Mendi*?'

'The *Mendi* people are biased against me, *en dis die waarheid*. This man, in particular, is a notorious agitator who's been spreading malicious rumours about me. In the interests of justice, I would urge you to consider getting another interpreter. Not this man.'

'Ah, this is getting more complicated than I anticipated,' said the captain in his shaky Afrikaans. 'Can we …'

Pitso had recoiled from Haig's words. The captain looked sharply at him. 'Everything all right, Lance Corporal?'

'Everything is fine, sir.'

'You don't look fine.'

Pitso was sweating and trembling. He could hear Marie-Thérèse's words resounding in his ears: 'Try to avoid all confrontation. Even in its mildest form.'

The captain addressed Pitso directly, 'Lance Corporal Pitso, did you hear what Officer Haig had to say, or do you want him to repeat it?'

'Captain,' Pitso said suddenly, surprising even himself, 'I'm prepared to recuse myself. I can arrange for another interpreter to be sent, if that pleases this hearing.'

One man shouted, 'We can't understand what you're saying. Tell us in one of our African languages. We didn't come here to watch you speaking through your nostrils like this.'

The other men laughed.

Pitso turned to the captain. 'The men want to know what's happening. Do I have your permission, Captain, to give them a summary?'

'I see no harm in that.'

Pitso translated Haig's words to the audience.

'He can't change the rules!' one man cried.

'Order!' shouted Pitso.

'*Hy lieg soos 'n koerant, hierdie rooibaard!*' said one of the Free State men. *He lies like a newspaper, this redbeard!*

'Order!' shouted the captain.

'He killed our people on the *Mendi*, the piece of shit!'

'The truth must come out!'

The two armed guards, disturbed by the noise, ran from their posts at the gate and burst into the hall.

'Everything is under control,' shouted the captain. 'Everybody stay calm. Guards, go back to your posts.'

'Stop behaving like monkeys!' screamed Officer Haig.

One man launched himself forward, ramming his head into Officer Haig's midriff. The officer's belly proved formidable, for the assailant bounced off it and fell. As Officer Haig staggered backward, another man slammed a fist against his temple. Haig bellowed in fury and pain.

A guard fired a warning shot in the air, hitting the roof. One man snatched the rifle from the guard's hands and started firing indiscriminately above the men's heads, shouting, 'Let our men go!'

The captain shot the man in his shoulder so that the rifle clattered to the floor.

'Order!' cried Pitso, looking around with panic in his eyes.

Tlali jumped on the captain, punching him so hard his nose broke and a cascade of blood poured out of his nostrils. He then picked up the captain's weapon and charged towards the centre of the room.

Officer Haig reached for his own pistol, aimed it and pulled the trigger. Spatters of blood exploded from Tlali's chest, vivid against the whiteness.

Screaming with rage at seeing his friend fall, Pitso leaped on Haig, grabbing his throat. The two crashed against one of the tables. As he was going down, Haig pulled the trigger again. The bullet went wide. A guard came hurtling towards them, hitting Pitso with the butt of his rifle, catching him in the face, the force of the blow sending an explosion of pain through his left eye socket.

Somebody slammed a chair into the guard who'd just attacked Pitso. There were more gunshots. Officer Haig was tussling with yet another man on the floor, while the other men were trying to disarm the guards.

Pitso was fully conscious, but he decided to stay on the ground for a while, to catch his breath and find a way to escape. It was clear to him that the fighting was not about to end. The room reeked of gunpowder. Slowly, he dragged himself towards the door, which was wide open. Once he was there, he tried to stand up. A surge of dizziness overpowered him and he collapsed onto the floor. He could taste his own blood, which was gushing in torrents from his injured eye. He licked the bloodied saliva that had collected in the corners of his mouth and spat it out. With great effort, he heaved himself to his feet and staggered out into the dusty yard, putting his left hand on his damaged eye in an attempt to staunch the flow of blood. There was no pain there, just the fast, dull thumping of the blood, as if his heart had relocated itself to his eye socket.

He tried to run, but fell on his knees. As if it could sense trouble, his horse neighed animatedly. With his hand still firmly pressed over his injured eye, Pitso blinked with the other. He saw the horse stomping the ground impatiently. The desperation of the animal gave him renewed hope. 'I can do it, I can do it,' he muttered to himself. With his last ounce of strength, he heaved himself to a standing position, then started hobbling forward drunkenly until he reached the animal. It took great effort to mount his horse.

Once he was astride the animal, he galloped away at a furious speed.

He knew that sooner or later someone was going to call for reinforcements. There was no doubt that the mutineers would be court-martialled. They would be dead before the day was over. Even though he was confident of his innocence, and could justify his action against Officer Haig that morning, his chances of winning the case were slim. He did not want to take the risk.

It would be sad to die in front of a firing squad when he knew he hadn't done anything wrong and that the war was slowly crawling to an end. What would he tell the angels in heaven: that he had travelled all the way from Africa to succumb to the bullets of his own comrades in Europe? That he had given up so easily on his dream to fight to protect his dignity? That he, like his father, had refused to see the war to its conclusion?

As soon as he thought about his father, he felt a twinge of

guilt. Many of his friends at the camp had looked to him for advice, for friendship, for leadership. Yet, here he was, running away. Riding like a madman, not back to camp. He felt that there must be another way to continue fighting this war. But how, how? He brought his horse to a slow canter, tears of shame blinding his good eye. He felt dizzy and his head was throbbing. He brought the horse to a halt and dabbed his injured eye with his handkerchief before starting to wail loudly. He was angry at what had just happened, but ashamed of his reaction. How would he live with himself? He had spent his life mocking his father for running away from war, from his responsibilities. Yet here he was doing exactly that. He dismounted, collapsed on his knees and bawled for a time, not caring if there were men pursuing him. He clawed the earth with his fingers, hoping for the ground to collapse under him, to bury him and his pain, anger and shame.

It was only when he was nearing Marie-Thérèse's inn that Pitso felt truly excruciating pain. He was now drifting in and out of consciousness. Marie-Thérèse rushed to meet him and he quickly explained the situation, feeling all his energy leave him.

'We can't stay in this town. The military police will be after him,' Marie-Thérèse told her sister Geneviève, as they helped him off his horse and into one of the bedrooms.

'Let's attend to his bleeding first. He might die of blood loss.'

'I'll make a poultice to staunch the bleeding. He also must take lots of liquids. Then you are going to get him out of town, as soon as possible,' urged Marie-Thérèse.

'What? Why me, why not you?' Geneviève asked.

'When the military police come knocking on my door, and find me here all by myself, it will confuse them. They will want to subject me to a long interrogation. They will do a thorough search of the inn, and the house. That will give you enough time to reach Amiens. Cousin Bernard will take care of him.'

'Why don't we take him to Saint-Nazaire? It's a busier place, where he won't stand out.'

'Saint-Nazaire would have been ideal. Problem is the distance – too far for a person in his state. Plus, Bernard is a surgeon – he can help. Once Pitso's fully recovered, we can reassess the situation.'

'What do I tell Bernard?'

'He already knows about me and Pitso. All you need to emphasise is the need for vigilance. No one should know Pitso is there – or that he even exists. My poor darling. His eye looks horrific.'

'Bernard should be able to fix it. He is a magician with those hands of his.'

'Pitso must stay indoors at all times. Tell Bernard I'll be in Amiens in a few days' time,' instructed Marie-Thérèse.

Pitso spoke in a slurring voice, '*Dulce et decorum est pro patria mori.*'

'What did he say?' asked Geneviève.

Marie-Thérèse translated it into French: '*Il est doux et beau de mourir pour la patrie.*'

'You think …' asked Geneviève hesitantly, '… you think he's dying?'

'No,' replied Marie-Thérèse, knowing how tenacious Pitso really was.

CHAPTER 38

Nine weeks later, Pitso was sitting on the veranda of a well-appointed house in Amiens, watching the river Somme as it flowed gracefully by, about six hundred feet from him. The gardens, which sloped gently towards the riverbank, were profuse with chestnuts, plane trees and wild lilacs, offering the inhabitants of the house privacy, protection from prying eyes. Pitso could sit for hours on the end of the veranda, or take short strolls up and down the garden, without having to worry about being noticed by people sailing past in their boats, or fishermen slumped over their fishing rods further up the river.

Now that it was autumn, the lawn and the gardens were covered in a russet carpet of fallen leaves. The smell of the river was sharp, and its cold breath even sharper on Pitso's skin. Birdsong was still in the air, but not as clamorous as it would have been at the height of summer. A group of ducks, of a breed Pitso had never seen before, floated by. He wondered what they would taste like. His exposure to wildlife at Arques-la-Bataille's bountiful forest had sharpened his appetite for game meat.

This was a house of understated opulence. The gardens stretched for some distance on all sides and the stables were sizeable. Next to the stables were coach houses, where Pitso saw the finest collection of carriages, and then there was an automobile – a wondrous monster, gleaming black in the coach house. He spent time admiring the emblem with its two gleaming letters: RR – Rolls Royce.

Though he was grateful for the shelter, he found that he was missing camp and his tree-felling duties – the hypnotic music of his axe as it swung towards a tree, the querulous voices of birds from nearby trees, as if they were challenging the tree fellers to stop what they were doing. And the song of the tree fellers – *Abelungu oswayini! Basincintsh'itiye, basibize ngoswayini!*

In all the weeks he'd been at the house, he had not once looked at himself in the mirror. Bernard, Marie-Thérèse's cousin, had been good to him. A retired surgeon and good spirit rolled into one, he had been taking care of Pitso ever since he arrived, changing the delicate dressing around Pitsos's injured left eye with his own hands on a daily basis. He couldn't risk sepsis setting in.

Pitso had tried on numerous occasions to get a better understanding of Bernard: how was he 'related' to Marie-Thérèse? Why was he spending so much time and money on a stranger? Pitso's experience with Christine had taught him to be always on the alert when it came to women: they would put you on the pedestal of happiness, then knock you down into an early grave. Was he Marie-Thérèse's husband? If he was, why would he expend so much care on a young man who was cuckolding him? Pitso thought he would never understand the ways of the French.

When Pitso asked about his damaged eye, Bernard would only say, 'Yes, it is in bad shape. But modern medicine can surprise you. Once the war is over – which I believe is only a matter of months – we'll go to Paris. There are some highly accomplished eye specialists there – they'll know what to do.'

Every time Pitso recalled the events of the day he got involved in the bloody mutiny, he shivered. A lot of questions were floating in his head, keeping him up at night. How could he have acted differently, to bring the situation to a different conclusion? How many people had died that day? Who were the survivors? What had they said about him? Portsmouth would have heard about his involvement in the mutiny. He must have been disgusted and disappointed by Pitso's despicable behaviour. What had he told the military police about him?

Most importantly, why had he run away? Shouldn't he have stood his ground and faced the consequences? Isn't that what he'd vowed to do: to take responsibility, to stay in the war and fight to the last, unlike his father, who showed a clean pair of heels when the heat became too intense?

He was grateful that Marie-Thérèse had saved him from capture. Indeed, she had saved his life. He could have bled to death. But what was the next step? Surely the military police were closing in. Amiens, after all, was only a few towns away from Arques. It was only a matter of time. In wartime, he knew, the army could become a law unto themselves. There was nothing stopping them from embarking on a house-to-house search. Now that he was fully recovered, albeit with a huge patch on his left eye, he felt confident enough to go out there in the bigger world and find his feet, fight his own battles. Except that he didn't know France, apart from the things he'd read in books and the maps he'd consulted. But his plans would have to meet Marie-Thérèse's approval: she had the money. She could also easily bring the military police to his hideout, if she chose; she had so much power over him. He hadn't heard a word from her since he'd left Arques.

As he sat on the veranda, deep in thought, a familiar sound wafted towards him in intoxicating ripples. He strained his ears. The waves of sound came in richer swirls now, with more urgency. He thought he was dreaming. Warm tears welled in his eyes, as he recognised *The Blue Danube*. The music sent his mind back home to Bloemfontein, to Christine's house, to her gramophone, to the two of them whirling and twirling about to this waltz, to them making love to the enchanting flow of the music.

Pitso got up and went inside. In the middle of the huge ballroom, he found Marie-Thérèse and Bernard waltzing. They were so engrossed in the music that they did not immediately see him, at least not until he stumbled into a chair.

'Ah, there you are,' cried Marie-Thérèse, coming towards Pitso with outstretched arms. 'We thought you were taking a walk down by the river.'

They embraced, then she stepped back, stood on tiptoe and gently pressed her lips across the patch over his left eye.

Pitso simply said, 'Let's dance. Bernard, play something up-tempo, will you?'

Taking her by the fingertips, he led her to the middle of the ballroom. Bernard inserted the disk into the gramophone, then went to stand by the staircase, a glass of red wine in his hand and an amused smile on his face.

The sound of Johann Strauss's *Luxury Train* filled the cavernous ballroom. The dancers glided and twirled. As the music slowed down, then speeded up again, the vivacity of the violins and the fury of flutes and the thud of the tuba made them understand, once again, why the song was called *Luxury Train*. The train was barrelling between Viennese mountain passes, swooping past deep verdant valleys, crossing shimmering rivers, snaking along the banks of smiling lakes and nosing its way through endless blonde cornfields.

Pitso's bare feet made a squeaky sound when he swivelled on the shiny, highly polished floor. Marie-Thérèse knew he did not wear shoes if he could help it. He'd told her walking with his feet bare made him feel at one with the earth he was treading; he loved the comforting softness of rotting leaves under his soles when he walked in the garden, or the cold morning dew in spring and summer.

Marie-Thérèse noticed he was crying, tears running down his right cheek.

'Don't worry, dear,' she said, her voice raised slightly above the music, but not so loud as to reach Bernard, 'we'll get your eye fixed.'

But she did not understand. These were tears of joy he was shedding. He hadn't been sure how soon he would be touching her hands again – if ever. Every now and then, his heart was constricted by a suspicion that, like Christine in the past, Marie-Thérèse might just stab him in the back. His comrades were knee-deep in the mud, German shells falling all around them, but he was still alive, his snout in the trough of splendid food. That was why he was crying. Not because he was missing his eye.

When the music came to an end, she was breathing fast, pebbles of sweat gathered on her nose. 'You waltz like this in Africa?'

'That was a polka, dear, not a waltz.'

'You get my meaning, silly.'

'*Ex Africa semper aliquid novi!*' Out of Africa, always something new.

Later that evening, after dinner with Bernard, Marie-Thérèse suggested a walk in the gardens. Pitso was happy to be out and about, as he had been sleeping in the bunker ever since he got to the villa. He found it claustrophobic, but he had to abide by Bernard's rules. Pitso helped her into her cape, took her arm in his, and they breezed into the night. The sky was clear, dotted with stars, the natural light just enough for them to slowly trace their path down towards the river.

'Tell me how you've been,' he asked.

A night bird called out. The Somme murmured.

'It has been tense, as you can imagine. I've been interrogated numerous times by your military police. They're convinced I am hiding you somewhere.'

'Very perceptive, aren't they?'

'The one who has been persistent to the point of being a nuisance is the one with the red beard, Officer Haig. He's been at my door countless times, cajoling me, badgering me, threatening me with arrest if I didn't tell him your whereabouts. It got to a point where I had to remind him who my brother is, what kind of influence our family has, not only in Arques but in Paris as well.' She paused. 'That man is ... how do you people select your soldiers back home? That man is always drunk, always. His demeanour and physique don't say *soldier* to me. They shout *vagabond*.'

Pitso wanted to tell her how he had considered leaving. It wouldn't have been difficult — there were no guards at the house. But where would he go if he did decide to leave? Yes, he had looked at the map of the region he was in, Picardy. He'd looked at the map of France, of Europe. But he didn't know how deep the rivers were. And the mountains and the valleys – were they penetrable? He felt torn about his reasons for leaving. He didn't trust Bernard, but Marie-Thérèse had sacrificed so much for him, had risked her own skin in order to protect him. Did that not count for anything? He wasn't sure.

If he did escape and was caught, there was no doubt they would send him back to South Africa, where he would serve a long jail term. Or, worse still, they would simply kill him here, on European soil, to send a message: this is how we deal with traitors. He had been central to a murderous mutiny, after all. He had also deserted. The more he thought about escape, the worse he felt about himself, his own integrity. He was overwhelmed by shame. Hadn't he joined up in order to fight?

He admitted, 'I thought you were never going to come for me. I really was getting scared. Knowing your family's connections with the French authorities, I thought I'd been sold out to the military police.'

She pushed him angrily away from her. 'What do you take me for? What do you take my family for?'

'Sorry, I didn't mean it. You know the mind of a desperate man is full of poisonous thoughts, always suspicious, always on the lookout for conspiracies. And it's been almost two months since I last saw you,' he explained with desperation in his voice.

Her shoulders dropped. 'I know, my dear. I had to defer my visit, seeing I was under strict surveillance. I did not want to lead them to you. Even coming up here I had to be extra careful. I took a train from Dieppe down to Rouen, where I spent two days with a friend.'

They were walking along the banks of the river, carefully

picking their way through rocks and undergrowth. A fish broke the surface, landing back in the water with a loud splash, startling both of them.

'Anyway, after two days, I took a train back home, except I didn't get off at Arques, or at Dieppe. I proceeded to Abbeville, spent the night, sneaked out of my hotel at dawn, and my chauffeur drove me all the way from there.'

He laughed at her ingenuity.

'Anyway, tell me your story,' she said. 'How have you been?'

'I've been eating, eating, eating, in between long moments of missing my love. What else is there to say? I can't leave the house, can't do anything that normal people do. So, I sit here, eat, read, listen to some music, and eat again.'

'That's why your face is so pudgy and your shoulders so round,' she laughed.

'Don't start with me,' he said, squeezing her arm playfully.

'My darling,' she said, enjoying their back and forth, 'I think we'd better get back inside. It's getting rather chilly.'

Before they turned in for the night, she said, 'Your friend Portsmouth visited me once, to give me support. He was very nervous when he appeared at my house one night. He wanted to give me a letter for you. I wouldn't accept it. Two days later, my sister Geneviève gave it to me. I was so angry with her – I told her, if we accept it, it only confirms that we know where Pitso is. Anyway, I brought it with me. If they visit me later and want to know what I did with the letter, I'll simply deny knowledge of it. They can't court-martial me, or do any of those crazy things they do to soldiers. I've heard some horrible things—'

'May I see the letter?' Pitso cut her off, eager to know what his friend had written.

'Of course. I have it here.'

With unsteady hands, Pitso opened the sealed envelope, almost tearing the letter in two.

CHAPTER 39

My Dear Old Prune!

I know your body and soul are still intact, which is why I'm not going to waste time asking you about your health. What I am going to ask is: are they feeding you well, wherever you are? And do you have a good doctor/nurse tending to your injuries? Pity you don't have a strong witchdoctor to protect you from those who are hunting you down. As you know, Tlali's own witchdoctor and charms did not protect him that day, and he is no longer with us.

Things are not as they ought to be, and I write to you with a heavy heart. The Germans would laugh themselves silly if they were to learn about the blood that has been shed at our camps, about the mutinies and court martials. It makes my heart ache.

It's a good thing that you went there to do your job, to translate for your comrades during that hearing. A sign of good leadership. You see, leaders do not fall from the sky. Leaders come from families, from communities. Leaders embody the dreams of their people, but they also channel their people's energies in the right direction. Leaders are the source of light, but they also are the fuel that keeps a communal body going. You are all that. Because of it, you are a living nightmare for the likes of Haig. Yes, he survived the bloody mutiny. The two officers who were there both died, as well as three of the guards. But Haig survived. And, for some reason, he has made it his life's mission to hunt you down.

I have faith in you. I am confident in your ability, once all this is over, to make a life for yourself among people from all walks of life. I have lived with top military men – my father being one of them. I have hobnobbed with titled people: earls, barons, counts, etc. Highly educated, well-travelled, refined people. But you have a depth of humanity I have rarely been exposed to.

I know you must realise that the cards are currently stacked against you. Yes, we're in a war right now, but there are men in our midst, men who have been distracted from the real war, and are expending their energies and time on hunting you down. It is as if we have transferred the racial war from South African to French soil. What is happening right now is ridiculous, and sad. Black men are being singled out for court martials. Men are being cut down for raising their voices in protest against bad food. They are labelled mutineers, getting shot as if they are antelope. Our camps are burdened with the smell of gunpowder, and the smell of our own men's blood, when the gunpowder should, rightfully, be reserved for the enemy.

Pitso, you fought your fight, and I know you still haven't stopped fighting. Neither have I. When we were on the ship, and you kept telling me that you were going to fight in Europe, no matter what, I dismissed you as a delusional black man consumed by his own anger and impotence. How wrong I was: now I can see that fighting is such an all-encompassing concept. It's not confined to the actual trenches, to the gun, the limpet mine, the bayonet.

I don't want to know where you are, but I hope and pray you are safe. Keep your head down. Don't taint your good name by getting caught. You're cleverer than that. I know we shall meet again once this is over. The end of the war is nigh, and, in Europe, you will be able to disappear with a new identity. You speak good French, and you have many skills: you can work on a ship or in the forestry industry, you can cook, you can play music, you can build things with your hands. You can teach people how to write – yes, there are many Frenchmen who can't write their own names. You even have the aptitude to go to university if you so choose. So you don't have to worry too much about the future, old man.

My parting shot: store up your anger, keep your head down. There's a future waiting for you beyond the blood-drenched trenches that choke this country now.

I remain, your friend.

Pitso folded the letter, closed his eye.

After a beat, Marie-Thérèse asked, 'What is it?'

He got up wordlessly and went to the liquor cabinet in the drawing room.

Back in their bedroom, he sat down on the bed next to her, gave her her drink. They drank in silence for a few moments.

Taking in a long breath, she touched his shoulder. 'Are you going to tell me what the letter says?'

He searched, in vain, for the appropriate French expression to convey what was on his mind. He shrugged, and said in English, 'A curate's egg.'

Seeing her confusion, he tried to explain himself. 'This real war is eluding me – I'm getting sidetracked by nonissues, side-shows.'

'You must count yourself lucky. The war is actually at your doorstep, but of course you won't see it. You are safe and protected where you are.'

'The sound of shells is so distant I wonder why Bernard insists I sleep in the bunker.'

'When the war started back in 1914, this town was under brief German occupation,' she explained.

'Really?' he said.

'They took some men prisoner. They ransacked some of the businesses. But they pulled back because the British were pressing in …'

'You're not serious.'

'Ask Bernard.'

'Who is this Bernard, anyway? Why is he so reticent, so evasive?'

'Bernard is my uncle, my father's half-brother. Biologically he is Austrian, you might say German—'

'I'm living with a German?'

'My grandfather adopted him from an orphanage when he was ten, and raised him as his own son. He trained and worked as a doctor for a very long time. Now that he is retired, he is very much involved in the family businesses. Sadly, he's still very conscious of his Austrian roots, hence his discomfort in the presence of strangers.'

'But can I trust him?'

'As a matter of fact, he is the one who suggested we create a new identity for you. I have spoken to my brother in Paris, who says he can help.'

CHAPTER 40

Nothing could have prepared Pitso for what he saw on arriving in Paris on 15 March 1918. He had been expecting a smouldering, broken city – rickety buildings tottering to the side or completely on their knees, their walls blackened by shellfire, windows like the hollow sockets of a sun-bleached human skull. But when he got there, the wide boulevards opened their arms to him. The city was truly alive, and it was like nothing he had ever seen before. There were massive libraries everywhere, museums and art galleries too. The cobbled avenues smiled indulgently at him and offered to share their million secrets with him – the very secrets they had whispered to Voltaire, Rousseau, Balzac, Zola, Flaubert and other dreamers. Notre Dame, the Champs-Élysées, the Arc de Triomphe, the Eiffel Tower – all tributes to human innovation and commitment to *liberté, égalité, fraternité* – stood defiantly, proclaiming the indefatigability of the human spirit.

While the buildings were still standing, however, the city's inhabitants had been touched most profoundly by the war – psychologically and emotionally. The deserted streets and shut-up businesses spoke of fear and uncertainty. Behind the curtains, behind the shutters, men and women lurked about – a loaf of bread in exchange for cash at this shop; across the road, at the butcher's shop, a pound of horsemeat proffered to grateful hands. Further down the street, a man might push a door open and shut it behind him, taking off his gloves, rubbing his hands together. The men inside would look suspiciously at the new arrival. He would order something to drink. One by one, the others would go back to their glasses, drinking beer, knocking back absinthe. Life had to go on. In the evening, the city became livelier as the bars filled up with men and soldiers of all nationalities.

Pitso observed these things gradually, over the weeks. He still maintained his anonymity – bulky in winter clothes, refusing to surrender his cap and greatcoat whenever he entered an eating or drinking establishment. Under no circumstances would he ever take off his cap, which had large external flaps for his ears and a visor that stuck out like a hard tongue, casting a long, dark shadow over the top part of his face. Looking at himself in the mirror, he'd realised that his new incarnation looked more European than African. The curly locks of hair cascading down his neck, the beard, the moustache, a nose which had assumed a curious red hue – all this combined to give him a satisfyingly rebarbative look. No one would be inclined to give him a second glance.

When he'd arrived in Paris, Pitso was accompanied by Bernard, the two of them sitting in the back of a chauffeur-driven Rolls Royce. Bernard had then escorted him to a small but distinguished house on Boulevard Raspail, owned by Marie-Thérèse's family. This was going to be his home until further notice.

'Marie-Thérèse told me you're an artist,' said Bernard. 'Is it true?'

'That's putting it rather strongly. I just do a bit of sketching, that's all.'

'Well, I hope you won't be disappointed,' Bernard said,

leading him to one of the rooms in the house. The room contained an easel and a generous supply of sketching pads, a forest of pens and pencils, palettes, and other art-related paraphernalia Pitso had never had the pleasure of touching. One corner of the room was dominated by an upright piano. This, Pitso realised, was Bernard's own acknowledgement of the long hours the soldier used to spend on the piano back in Amiens.

Early the next day, Pitso was visited by Marie-Thérèse's brother Sebastien. Big-boned, and as tall as Pitso himself, Sebastien was a congenial fellow with an easy laugh, speaking English with a fruity accent that reminded Pitso of the white captain who had addressed the group of recruits gathered at that hall in Bloemfontein back in 1916. Sebastien invited Pitso to join him for breakfast at a bistro just a block away from the apartment.

'How do you like your new house, then?' asked Sebastien.

'Can't express in words my sense of gratitude for what you and your family have done for me so far.'

'Marie-Thérèse says you're a good human being, and she is the best judge of character I've ever known in my life. And she loves you to bits. I'll do anything and everything to keep her happy. You break her heart, I will not hesitate to break you, tear you to pieces. Understood?' Smiling insincerely, he'd looked across the table at Pitso as he tucked into his breakfast of coffee and croissants.

After breakfast they'd gone to the offices of Sebastien's law firm. He showed Pitso around and introduced him to some of the senior staff. Then he led him to a small office next to his.

'This is your new office. I can offer you work as a filing clerk, if that's acceptable to you.'

'What?' Pitso asked, overcome with gratitude.

'Isn't that what you wanted? Something to keep you busy?'

Later that day, Sebastien, accompanied by one of his business associates, came to Pitso's office.

'Pitso,' Sebastien said, 'we know that you are likely to start encountering problems with our immigration officials.'

'I'd appreciate any help from you, sir. I am a stateless individual, an alien.'

'Bernard told me as much. Which is why I've brought my friend and colleague Charles to see how he can help you. Great lawyer, Charles. Was my intellectual sparring partner at Cambridge, where we both read law. A very flexible Englishman, for a change. Right, Charles?'

'You don't have to patronise me, you old frog-muncher!'

They laughed, clearly used to throwing friendly gibes at each other. Sebastien turned back to Pitso, 'Look, I've got other business to attend to. Why don't the two of you sit down and talk about this, and see what comes out.'

At the end of the interview, Charles asked Pitso to carefully think about his preferred new identity. Without hesitation, Pitso said, 'My first name is Jean-Jacques.'

'After Rousseau, I suppose. But, hey, give it some more thought. You have plenty of time.'

It came to pass, then, that after a visit to the immigration offices, accompanied by Charles, who had helped 'smooth things out', Pitso came back bearing a new identity: Jean-Jacques Eugene Henri, born 20 January 1901, in Tangiers. Brought over to France as a child of ten, raised in Lyons, where his parents worked as labourers for a wealthy French family. When he came of age, he also worked for the French family, but stayed behind when his parents went back home. Adopted by that same family after his parents and one known sibling were killed during the Algerian War.

It was May now. The city had thawed completely, physically and psychologically. With the streets devoid of snow, more people emerged from their houses – initially nervous, tentative, not unlike hedgehogs emerging from their burrows, sniffing the air for threats, adjusting their eyes to sudden brightness.

Then there were automobiles. Hundreds of them crawling up and down the streets. Unbelievable. Tlali would have loved this, Pitso thought. Ah, Tlali. Ah, Ngqavini. His heart ached for his friends who had lost their lives in such senseless ways.

On Sundays, Pitso would wake up to the ringing of church bells. This was it. He was at the heart of civilisation, not somewhere on the fringe. There was so much to do and see, that he drew up a strict schedule for himself. He visited museums and galleries, spent time drawing and practising the piano, attended morning mass at Notre Dame. Pitso Motaung in Paris, who would have thought? The lion was finally out of its cage. The lion tore thick chunks off its freedom and swallowed greedily. Yes, the lion knew that there were stalkers in the shadows, hunters with hateful eyes, devilish members of the military police. But that was the reality of a lion. It thrived on adrenaline. Expectation, not fear.

But the dawning of summer also meant a number of new adjustments. The long-deferred procedure on his left eye would now take place. The Parisian eye specialist who had examined him, based on a referral by Bernard, had advised against having the operation in winter, fearing complications. Also, Pitso couldn't hide behind his bulky winter clothing any more. He had to think of other disguises suitable for the summer. The most important change was that Marie-Thérèse would be coming up to Paris to live with him.

Two months later he had recovered enough – both physically and psychologically – to look at himself in the mirror without recoiling. There had been a time when an encounter with his mirror image filled him with shame and self-loathing. His missing eye was a constant reminder of how he had run away from his friends, how he had betrayed them. It was also a reminder of how he had been wrong, right from the outset, to enlist in this war. Many of those he had met on the ship had sound reasons for enlisting. Some, like his friend Tlali, had done so out of financial necessity; the money being offered was simply irresistible. Tlali had a clear plan: serve in the war and save enough money to buy a head of cattle that he would put down as a bride price upon his return. Others, like Ngqavini, were fugitives from the law; men who'd enlisted to run away from their crimes back home. Yet others, like those educated Lovedale boys who spoke good English on the ship, had signed up out of sheer idealism. They'd hoped that, by throwing in their lot with the British Crown, they'd establish their credentials as proud subjects of the King, humble citizens of the Union who deserved the right to vote, and a rightful claim to the land that had been taken from them during successive wars of conquest. By contrast, Pitso's initial motivation had been vague. He'd enlisted partly out of anger at his own father. There was a part of him that had hoped he would be killed in France so he could get away from it all. His father's betrayal of his mother, her subsequent mental illness and death, his sordid, ill-fated affair with Madame Clinquemeur – all of these things had weighed him down, robbed him of proper perspective on life, and the ability to think logically.

But all of that was behind him. He might have come to France by default, but he now knew, with clarity, that he was here to stay. He would work hard to prove himself not only to Marie-Thérèse and her family, who'd granted him a new lease on life, but also to all those he'd interacted with in this country. He felt a sense of belonging he'd never experienced in his country of birth. He felt respected, valued. He felt like one who had been emotionally lame, but was now walking with charisma and sophistication in his gait. When he spoke people listened, really listened.

He felt free.

Every time he woke up next to Marie-Thérèse he felt blessed. He'd look at her sleeping form, her serene face, her even breathing, and a surge of mixed emotions would course through him. Yes, there were moments of self-doubt when he believed he did not deserve this beautiful human being sleeping next to him, moments of fear that he had nothing to offer her, that one day she would wake up and change her mind about him.

'Stop being a coward,' he said to himself one Sunday morning as he contemplated himself in the mirror. 'Tell her what's on your mind!'

After a particularly stirring service at Notre Dame, where he and Marie-Thérèse had become regulars, they went on their customary Sunday-afternoon walk along the Seine. There were other couples like them, walking hand in hand, pausing every now and then to laugh, to look into each other's eyes, a man removing imaginary fluff from his partner's frock, a woman adjusting her beau's collar.

Thirty minutes into their walk, Jean-Jacques took a breath and gripped Marie-Thérèse's hand so firmly she flinched.

'Ouch! You're going to cripple me!'

'Sorry, my dear, I didn't mean to hurt you.' His mouth suddenly went dry. His lips quivered, but words failed him.

'Darling, is there something the matter? Are you feeling dizzy?'

'Yes,' he croaked. 'No, I'm not feeling dizzy. But let's find a bench. Let's sit down for a while.'

After sitting down on a nearby bench, Marie-Thérèse's brow knotted in worry and she looked into his eyes. 'Maybe we should go home so that you can lie down?'

'Yes, good idea. But let me recover my breath before we proceed.'

'All right, no hurry. Is it something you ate?'

He did not respond. He closed his one good eye tightly and bowed his head. When he finally recovered, he swallowed before he spoke. 'I don't know what you'll make of what I'm about to say, but it has to be said ...'

'Say it, darling, there's nothing to fear. It's just the two of us.'

'Yes, it's about the two of us ...'

'Yes?' She sat back and searched his face. There was a slight tremor in her voice when she spoke. 'What is it?'

'My darling, I have not a cent to my name. Even the clothes on my back are not my own. You bought them.'

'But why are you speaking about this now? I know, with your skills, it won't be difficult for you to find a job once this war is over. We have enough reserves to take care of your ... medical condition. I couldn't live with myself if I failed you during your hour of need.'

'Please, hear me out.'

'But you're not yourself. Your eyes look glazed, as if you've just seen a ghost. You need to lie down.'

'*Jislaaik*,' he said in his mother tongue, 'can't a man state his case without being interrupted?'

This silenced her.

'What I am saying to you, sweetheart, is I am coming to you on my knees. I am asking if you could please, please take pity on this beggar and make an honest man of him. Will you marry me?'

CHAPTER 41

It was with shock that Jean-Jacques learned from Sebastien that Amiens, the town in which he had spent time recuperating, had fallen under German bombardment on 8 August. Bernard had fled to Arques-la-Bataille, leaving the exquisite mansion deserted. Jean-Jacques gestured animatedly, pacing about the room.

'This is ridiculous, Sebastien, absolutely ridiculous,' he shouted. 'Here I am, an able-bodied man, a soldier who crossed the seas to come here and fight. But now I am following the progress of this war through newspaper reports.'

Sebastien who, like his brother-in-law-to-be, was trembling with anger after reading about the devastation that had been wrought on the town of Amiens, picked up a bottle of wine and smashed it against the wall of his office.

His Scottish secretary Elspeth poked her head through the door. 'Anything the matter, monsieur?'

'Sorry, Elspeth. Tell everyone to go home. Take the rest of the week off. All of you.'

'But it's only Tuesday, sir.'

'I know. Just go home. What's the point of what we're doing when the rest of the country is in flames? Go home. All of you.'

'*Oui, monsieur. Merci beaucoup.*'

It later turned out that Sebastien's despair had been premature. In fact, what had happened was that on 8 August, the first day of what would later be called the Battle of Amiens, Allied forces advanced over seven miles. This was one of the greatest advances of the war, marking the end of trench warfare, which had been the phenomenon on the Western Front for the past three years. The British Fourth Army took 13 000 prisoners, while the French captured a further 3 000. Germany lost around 30 000 men. On the other hand, the Fourth Army – comprised of British, Australian and Canadian infantry – suffered 8 800 casualties. These did not include tank and air losses or those of their French allies. More positive news about Allied victories was to come over the next few weeks.

Emboldened by these developments on the front lines, developments which seemed to indicate that the war was drawing to a close, Jean-Jacques and Marie-Thérèse proceeded with their wedding plans. Growing up, he'd dreamed of an elaborate wedding ceremony that would be attended by hundreds of well-wishers, including relatives and neighbours, as was the norm in the Bloemfontein of his childhood. He'd dreamed of a ceremony where a number of beasts would be slaughtered and where there would be singing and dancing. Sadly, he had no relatives here in France and, apart from the people he'd met through Marie-Thérèse's family, he did not have many friends either. He was sad that his mother, uncle and cousins would not be there to witness this momentous occasion. What would his mother's neighbours in her village say when they heard that 'their son' had got married without their blessings? But of course that was a crazy thought. They'd never hear of him ever again. The old Pitso was now dead.

As it happened, the ceremony, which took place on 10 December 1918 – almost a month after Germany had surrendered – was attended by Marie-Thérèse's close family, and some of the people from Sebastien's office. The food was good, the music splendid, but it still lacked the carefree spirit that he associated with weddings in Bloemfontein.

Nevertheless, he was thrilled. Marie-Thérèse was now his wife. They planned to start a family together. Every night before he fell asleep, he prayed: *I'll do my mother proud, wherever she is. I will honour and respect my wife. Together we shall have a brood of happy, contented children. No one taught me how to be a father, but with God's guidance and grace, I'll do my best.*

Three months later, Marie-Thérèse broke the news that struck Jean-Jacques like a bolt of lightning. She was pregnant. The tears of joy that rushed to his eyes soon turned to tears of worry: he was still unemployed. While he still helped at Sebastien's law firm, he did not regard it as a permanent appointment. How was he going to take care of his family? He knew that Marie-Thérèse did not necessarily want for money, but he felt that it was his responsibility as a man to take care of his family.

He rushed to a timber shop, where he bought cheap castaway pieces of wood and planks.

The shop owner was curious. 'Whatever it is that you think you can make with this junk?'

'A cot, sir, I want to build a cot for my son.'

'I'm not much of a carpenter myself – I just sell timber – but I do tinker a little and I too have a baby on the way. I'd be curious to watch you put a crib together. May I come to your workshop?'

'As a matter of fact, I do not have one, sir. I don't even have tools.'

The man looked surprised. 'How were you hoping to make a crib if you don't have tools?'

'I was hoping you'd direct me to a place where I could rent them.'

The shop owner looked at him long and hard. 'I have a suggestion for you. I have some tools here on site, but I can't let you take them home. If you like, you can work from here until you finish the crib.'

The arrangement suited them both: the shop owner, who duly introduced himself as Agostino, would learn by observation how to build a crib, and Jean-Jacques would work on the project away from his wife's prying eyes.

A week later, the two men loaded the cot onto a truck and transported it to Jean-Jacques' home. Marie-Thérèse was overjoyed when she saw it.

'Your husband is a true craftsman,' said Agostino. 'Look at this piece of work. It looks like it is store bought!'

Three days later, Jean-Jacques brought home a bucket of white paint and a smaller tin of cherry-coloured paint. He painted the crib completely white. When it had dried, he set about decorating it with elaborate sketches of cherubic angels bearing garlands of cherry blossoms.

'You're a magician!' Marie-Thérèse exclaimed. She couldn't stop admiring the elaborate drawings. 'It's exquisite.'

'Only the best for my loved ones. I draw my inspiration from your love.'

When Jean-Jacques's son was born on 3 November 1919, Marie-Thérèse named him Victor, after one of her maternal uncles. His father loved the name, and added a second one: Motsomi, the hunter.

By the time Victor Motsomi Henri was six months, his father had been supplied with a new artificial eye, which looked more like the real thing. It felt more comfortable and never fell out of its socket, embarrassing him.

With a new mouth to feed, Jean-Jacques was feeling even more pressure to find himself a job.

'Anything, Sebastien, absolutely anything,' he pleaded with his brother-in-law one day.

'You are under no obligation to find work, J-J,' Sebastien said. 'You're still recuperating, man. Take your time. Marie-Thérèse can cope.'

'I am not a charity case, Sebastien. I want to work. Just give me an opportunity. I won't disappoint.'

It came to pass that Sebastien pulled some strings and Jean-Jacques found employment at the restaurant the Tour d'Argent in June 1920. He started out as a general assistant in the kitchen – chopping vegetables, cleaning, running errands and doing whatever it was that was required of him.

He worked hard and was always eager to learn. An easy-going person by nature, he endeared himself to the head chef, with whom he soon became friends.

His son was growing fast. Marie-Thérèse was happy that, although both father and son had explosive tempers, they were very close. Over the years, what brought them even closer was their love of art and music.

But then war broke out once again, and life as the family knew it was disrupted.

CHAPTER 42

Paris, 1946

'It's a miracle this house is still standing!' Marie-Thérèse was beaming, having disembarked from a car that had driven her and Victor from Dieppe, where they had sought refuge during the long war years.

Jubilant, that's how Jean-Jacques felt as he embraced his wife so tightly that he could feel her heart beating against his stomach. Then he felt her body break into rattling sobs.

'You're back home, now, you are safe,' he whispered. Her tears seeped through his thin shirt, bathing his chest. She did nothing to stop the flow. He repeated soothingly, 'You're safe, sweetheart, home at last.'

When she had unburdened herself, she stepped back, a shy smile on her face. He wiped her tear-stained face with his white handkerchief. She took the handkerchief and blew her nose. Then she looked into his eyes, with relief, with love, with indulgence. He, in turn, took her in greedily. Her skin was healthy and luxuriant, her complexion clear, if slightly pale, thanks to staying indoors while the war had raged on. There was a new heaviness around her jowls.

Victor, who'd been standing a few feet away, shyly looking at his parents, now moved forward. 'Enough of that now,' he said. 'I too want to say hello to my father.'

'Careful, now, young man,' his mother teased.

'My hero!' Jean-Jacques cried, giving Victor a hug. Jean-Jacques then stepped back, looked into his son's face and kissed him on the forehead. The young man blushed, wiping his forehead with the back of his hand. 'Am I not too old for that, father?'

'How you've grown up!' Jean-Jacques said, playfully punching the young man's arm.

'So glad to see you again, father,' Victor said in his quiet voice, a smile touching the corners of his mouth. He was indeed a man now. When the war had started, Victor was in the third year of his law degree in Nice.

After intense debate, it had been decided that Marie-Thérèse and Victor would see the war out at the coast. Sebastien would go and fight, while Jean-Jacques would remain in Paris. Marie-Thérèse had pleaded with her husband to come with them to Dieppe, but Jean-Jacques had prevailed. It helped his sanity that the Tour d'Argent stayed open even during the war. He had something to do, to calm his nerves, to keep him focused.

Now, after several long years, his loved ones were back for good. He knew he would have to work hard to re-establish his relationship with his son, but his plans to spend more time with Victor were thwarted when Victor was accepted to the University of Massachusetts Amherst on a full scholarship. While disappointed that his son would be leaving again so soon, Jean-Jacques was proud that his son was going to the United States of America, a country everyone was talking about.

The Americans had gained in popularity during the war. With the war now over, some of them had stayed on in Europe. They could be seen at night spots in the Saint-Germain district, one of which was a place called l'Échelle de Jacob, where Sebastien decided to take his brother-in-law and sister in April 1950.

As they entered the dark bar, a beautifully harsh sound seemed to tear into Jean-Jacques' flesh. This was the unmistakable sound of a saxophone, but he had never heard it played this way. He hadn't realised that such sounds could be coaxed out of this humble horn.

When they were seated, Sebastien could see his brother-in-law was taken with the music. 'I don't know what you make of it, but this is a new sound they call jazz. It's new to us here, but I believe it's been around for a while in the USA.'

'Shhh,' Jean-Jacques said, now listening to the piano gurgling out a torrent of notes. What a sound. He would soon learn much more about this music called jazz – a sound from the southern states of America. What a chapter in human civilisation, he thought. He sat back, closed his eyes, and allowed the sound to envelop him, drifting back to the sounds of his childhood. Music holds memories, rekindles memories, creates memories … Jean-Jacques wondered how a song from his youth, 'The Song of the Sun', would look dressed in the clothes of this new sound. It was a thought that preoccupied his mind for some time.

One Sunday afternoon in June, he went on his customary walk along the Seine. He used these walks not only for exercise but to have time by himself. To think, to dream. Sometimes he walked briskly, pausing every now and then to feed the birds. Other times he would walk until he found a nice quiet spot, where he would sit down, take out his sketchpad and pencil or piece of charcoal, and proceed to sketch a quick scene, or a face he'd encountered somewhere in the city during the day.

That afternoon he'd decided to bring his new concertina. Once he had found a nice quiet copse, away from prying eyes, he sat down on the ground and started playing. He was trying to imitate the new jazz sound he'd been hearing at the club. He knew the concertina was not the perfect instrument for these sounds but, what the hell, he wasn't performing for a paying audience. He was just experimenting.

The sun had just set, leaving the sky a pure cobalt blue. Occasionally, birds would fly by, in impressive formations. He continued playing. Without even realising it, he started playing 'The Song of the Sun'. The song that he'd heard in the villages around Bloemfontein, that young Basotho men picked up from their fathers and let grow on them, so they could pass it on to their own sons in turn. Slowly, softly, just the notes of the concertina with no singing. A warm spring breeze wafted towards him, bringing with it the smells of the Seine. He closed his eyes and continued playing. Soon enough, he was seeing the mountains of home in his mind's eye. The smell of roasted maize assailed his nostrils. A shimmering blanket of sunflower plantations danced on the horizon. He played on. He could hear the voice accompaniment to his playing, the voice of a village singer walking home after a long day out there in the fields. The voice rose and fell, rose and fell. Eyes closed, he played on. His fingers picked up speed. The instrument obeyed. The music came out in quick sharp bursts now; the voice of the village singer kept up as well. He opened his eyes slowly. The voice crescendoed. He realised he wasn't imagining it. It was coming from behind him. No, it couldn't be. He continued playing, hoping the voice dream would go away. But no, it only rose with a new intensity. When he turned to his left, he saw a man, head thrown back, eyes closed, singing his heart out.

When Jean-Jacques stopped playing, the man was jerked back to attention. He looked around like one who'd just woken up from a dream.

'Who are you?' Jean-Jacques asked in French, glowering at the man.

'Wow, my brother,' the man said in English, 'I did not know music from Africa could travel so far.' He paused, then said in broken French, 'Excuse me, sir, I couldn't help but join you. You play so well ...'

'Thank you, my brother, but who are you?'

'Sorry, my brother, I am Jerry Moloto, an artist from South Africa.'

'Welcome to France. I hope I'll learn something from you one of these days, Mr Artist-from-South Africa.'

'Ah, this brother is mocking me!'

They looked at each other. Then Jerry, staring straight into Jean-Jacques' eyes, spoke in his mother tongue. 'I could have sworn this piece of shit was from home. Looks like a Boesman from home, I swear to God.'

Jean-Jacques looked at him impassively, unblinkingly. At length, he said, 'What language was that supposed to be?'

'My mother tongue, sir. Sepedi, from South Africa. I was just reminding myself of something.' He paused. 'You sound like a Frenchman, sir, but—'

'I *am* a Frenchman, by way of Algeria.' He smiled.

'Yes, sir, I know that. What I mean to ask, if I am not intruding, sir, is where did you learn that music from? That is a song from my home, from South Africa.'

'Music has no home. It is of the world, it belongs to the world.'

'Well said, sir. But there's always a source?'

'A source, he says. A source. Well, I learned this from one of the African sailors. I'd been having dinner at one of the bistros along this river and was walking back to my apartment when I encountered this man playing this song. I fell in love with the music immediately. I paid him some money, asked him to play it again and again.' He paused. 'A lovely song, isn't it?'

'Sir, you must hear the story behind the song. They—'

'I must be on my way, my brother,' Jean-Jacques said, but he did not move.

Jerry shrugged, and said in his home language, 'He even has the short temper of a mixed-race. Ah, to travel is to see.' He started walking away.

Jerry hadn't got far when he heard hurried footsteps behind him. Striding purposefully towards him, the concertina player seemed agitated. Now that he was on his feet, he looked quite imposing.

'You said you were an artist?' the brown giant asked.

'May I speak in English now? My French is really, really horrible. May I?'

Jean-Jacques shrugged.

'I paint, I carve wood, I do some writing, I play some piano. But mostly, I paint,' explained Jerry.

'Are you with a band?' Jean-Jacques asked, still speaking in French.

'No. But an acquaintance has invited me to some club called Jacob's steps or something like that.'

'L'Échelle de Jacob?'

'Yes, that's the one. Have you been there?'

Jean-Jacques opened his mouth, but decided to curb his enthusiasm. 'Tell me, how long have you been here now?'

'Three weeks, four. Why?'

'Listen.' Jean-Jacques looked at the man long and hard. Then he looked away, before saying, 'Maybe our paths we'll cross again. Maybe at l'Échelle de Jacob, who knows?'

Indeed, two weeks later the two men bumped into each other at the club. Jean-Jacques was polite, but remained distant. They regularly enjoyed drinks together, discussing music and art. But it took another month before he felt he could trust Jerry Moloto enough to tell him who he really was.

Jerry was overjoyed. 'I knew it!' he said. His initial suspicions had been confirmed.

Now that all cards were on the table, their friendship blossomed. Jean-Jacques took it upon himself to acquaint his countryman with the hot places in the city. Jerry, in turn, was delighted to fall under Jean-Jacques' tutelage. They both became regulars at l'Échelle de Jacob. After a while, Jean-Jacques took an additional job as a part-time bartender at the club, just so he could be close to the music. The owner was thrilled to discover that Jean-Jacques could also cook – which he did on special occasions, surprising guests with the Indian dishes he'd learned from Portsmouth and with African cuisine from home. And whenever he was free, he would jam anonymously with the band. He played piano, mostly. But as time progressed, he took to the alto saxophone. Not entirely proficient on the horn, but his sound was tolerable, listenable.

He still kept his job at the Tour d'Argent. And there he stayed, until a certain day in 1958, when two men walked into the restaurant, and one of them said something to the other in Afrikaans.

'So you see, Thierry,' said Jerry, as he arrived at the end of his story, 'me and Jean-Jacques know each other pretty well.

He showed me the ropes when I was still new around here. I often wonder how my life would have turned out if I hadn't met him here. Not only did that brother open doors for me, he also gave me the confidence to stand on my own feet as an artist, to think beyond the next meal. And his story ... his story showed me that life could be a field of limitless possibilities.'

CHAPTER 43

Jean-Jacques did not regret his actions in the restaurant. Haig had deserved to die. He had kicked numerous desperate men back into the water during the *Mendi*'s sinking, and he had killed Pitso's friend Tlali. Moreover, he was the reason for the mutiny that had almost killed Pitso. Truth be told, however, he had been shocked at the men's sudden appearance at the restaurant, and had acted on pure instinct. He had had the fleeting, half-formed thought that they were members of the military police looking for him after all those years. They would take him home where he would be tried for deserting. He had heard that there was a new regime in power back home; a government that upheld a system called apartheid; a government that was even more vicious in its dealings with black people. With the men now dead, he thought he would feel safe. No one would ever know his true secret: that he was a South African who had deserted.

While Pitso felt justified in killing Haig, he felt remorse for the other man's death: his only sin had been to be with the wrong man, at the wrong place, at the wrong time. He was prepared to stand before a court and tell his story. He knew he had done wrong, and was willing to be punished according to French law.

But he should have listened to Marie-Thérèse – listened when she'd warned him all those years ago to avoid confrontation of any kind. Her dreams, which he had dismissed, had been followed by a mutiny during which he'd almost been killed and had lost an eye.

In later years these dreams had come and gone, always followed by some mishap – a car accident, a burglary at the house in Amiens, a sudden illness. Now he could see that he should have taken her dreams seriously all along. They were rooted in something; they had a logic of their own. For over a year, she had been begging him to stop working at the restaurant because she kept seeing, in her nightmares, a bloodbath taking place there, at the centre of which was her own husband. But being the stubborn man that he was, he had ignored her warnings. He would take his retirement as planned, in December.

Then, one morning, he'd woken up to find Marie-Thérèse gone. She'd left a brief, cryptic note, which he carried with him everywhere, even in his cell.

Dearest,

I cannot take the torment any more. I think the best thing for me, for both of us, is for me to leave. Long before we got married I told you that I was a bringer of bad luck. My dreams are a curse. Somehow, they bring pain, even death, to the people that I love. You barely survived that mutiny, years ago. You might not survive what I am seeing now. You know I have been having these endless nightmares over the past year. Believe me, my darling: there will be violence.

Lots of blood. At least two people will die. If you are not willing to listen to me and walk away, I will.

I do not know how long my absence from you is going to last. I will wait until I get a message from wherever these things come from. And, please, darling, do not try to find me. It will simply complicate things for everyone. I do not know where I shall go, nor do I intend telling members of my family, even our beloved Motsomi. I will return when the time is right.

Until the day he killed the two men, Jean-Jacques had been tormented by regret and sleepless nights, trying to imagine where his wife could have gone. Was she hiding at the house in Amiens? Had she left France altogether? Had she secretly fled to Boston, where their son Motsomi, now a lawyer, was based? No matter where he searched, Jean-Jacques could find no trace of her, nor did she send word. Where could she have disappeared to, and when would she be back? The questions had tortured him, making him moody and unpredictable, with a temper he could barely control.

Ever since his arrest, he had refused to be interviewed by investigators about his motive for the murders. But how long could he go on like this? How sustainable was the game that he was playing? With the passing of each day, worry weighed heavily on his mind. He knew the French could hang him for double murder.

He also worried about whether his story would be heard. Would the case be adequately covered? He doubted it. Without the story reaching as wide an audience as possible, the murders would not have been worth it. Although he hadn't had time to think before he killed the men, a public court case would give him the forum he needed to tell his story, with maximum effect.

It heartened him to learn that no one had come forward to claim the bodies of the men he had murdered. In fact, the authorities had discovered that the men, who had been identified as Stephen Humphrey Monash and William John Scobie of Australia, were not who they claimed to be. Their passports were fake. A huge stash of diamonds was found in their luggage at the hotel – hence, perhaps, the fake passports, and the gun in the man's boot.

Inevitably, this revelation would delay the investigation. And the most obvious course of action for Jean-Jacques would be to cooperate with the authorities and apply for bail. But would they grant him bail in the first place, since his papers stated that he was an Algerian, a flight risk according to the authorities? He doubted it. Perhaps, he thought, making this as public a case as possible might influence the court's decision. He did not know. He lived only on hope. Hope that the story he would tell in court would offer enough extenuating circumstances.

Then, one day, he received two unexpected visitors.

'Who are they?' he asked the guard who was escorting him to the front room where prisoners awaiting trial met their visitors. 'What do they look like?' Could it be the military police? How had they tracked him down? Why now, after so many years? As far as he knew, no picture of him had appeared in any papers. Even if it had, his appearance had changed completely over the years. 'What do they look like?' he repeated.

'One is a Frenchman, the other sounds ... like an Englishman.'

'Black? White?'

'The Frenchman is white, the other is black. The black one says he's your doctor, the Frenchman says he's your lawyer or something.'

If these were members of the military police, they would simply take him away. He was going to face them, he decided, but he would only leave the premises in a body bag, or a coffin.

As he entered the visitors' room, Jean-Jacques' body was humming like an engine, his mind on alert, his muscles tingling with anticipation.

'Yooowwweeee, brother, look at you!' A familiar voice shouted. Jean-Jacques turned and was startled to see his friend Jerry Moloto. Tears of relief and joy welled in Jean-Jacques' eyes.

He half-whispered in Sesotho, 'Child of my mother! What are you doing here?'

'Relax, brother, relax. I think you'll need me, you'll need my friend here. Your story needs to be told to the world, before it's too late. Telling your story might just save your life.'

The three of them followed the guard, who ushered them onto three uncomfortable seats, then withdrew to a discreet distance.

'You were the last person on my mind, my brother,' said Jean-Jacques. 'Given your immigration status, I thought you wouldn't want anything to do with officialdom.'

Jerry switched to English, keeping his voice very low. 'My brother, this here is Monsieur Thierry Bousquet. He is a journalist and an author.'

They shook hands. Jerry continued, 'We don't have much time with you, so let's cut straight to the chase. Thierry and I have been doing a draft of your life story. We've covered a lot of ground as it is—'

'What the hell are you doing? You can't publish my life story—'

'Wait, let me explain. We do realise that we need your permission to go ahead and publish. Which is why we are here. But the reason we thought of documenting your story in the first place is to help build a defence for you. Admittedly, we are not lawyers so we'll need some guidance.'

Jean-Jacques sighed and sat back. 'All right, go on.'

'Now, I know that your brother-in-law Sebastien runs one of the biggest law firms around. But I also know that you've never told him your full life story. Having worked with Thierry on this story since your arrest, I believe we could be of use to Sebastien. We could fill in whatever gaps there are in your history – assuming you're engaging him as your lawyer, that is.'

'I haven't spoken to him.'

'What do you mean, you haven't spoken to him?'

'He hasn't been here.'

'What? So, who has been here?'

'No one.'

'Shit. Why not?'

Jean-Jacques shrugged. He had no idea why his brother-in-law, one of the most respected lawyers in town, hadn't visited him since his arrest. Had Marie-Thérèse instructed him to stay away? Was he now an embarrassment to the family?

'My brother,' Jerry continued, cautiously, 'I hope you won't be angry with me, but I want to know why you killed those people. Who are they?'

'Take a guess. I've told you my story so many times you should be able to put two and two together.'

'Are they members of the military police?'

'You might say so.'

'How did you know they were military police? Did they say, *You're under arrest*?'

'No. Had they not started speaking Afrikaans, I wouldn't have recognised them. When one of them started saying insulting things about me in Afrikaans, I couldn't hide my curiosity. I had to look at them. And guess what? There is Officer Haig staring at me right in the face. He tried to reach for the knife, but I beat him to it. There was no time to think. It was all instinct.'

'What about the other bloke, who was he?'

'I don't know who he was. I only killed him because he tried to pull a gun on me,' explained Pitso, shifting in his chair uncomfortably.

'A gun? I wasn't aware of that.'

'Yes, he had a gun hidden in his boot.'

'Damn, brother. But you're still in shit. Deep shit. Now, tell me, how has the South African government reacted to this?'

'These pieces of cow dung were travelling incognito. False Australian passports.'

'The story gets better every day …' Thierry spoke for the first time.

Jean-Jacques said, 'To chart the way forward, gentlemen, I suggest you contact Sebastien on my behalf. Tell him you have my blessing to work with him, and ask him, please, to get in touch with me. I am all alone. My wife is somewhere out there in the world …' He paused and thought for a moment. 'Why are you two taking so much interest in this, anyway?'

'Come on, man, I am your brother. I should look after your interests. This story must come out once and for all.'

'Jerry, I know you. What else is of interest here? Is there money to be made?'

Jerry looked at the floor. 'Naturally, my man, a brother has to eat. Thierry is going to run a series in his newspaper. And the series is going to culminate in a book – your life story. We split the proceeds. Man, it's not as if I am taking bread from your mouth now. I am helping you. People must begin to appreciate who you truly are, not a demented Moor of no consequence.'

Jean-Jacques laughed out loud. 'I knew it. Have you taken care of my documents and drawings?'

'Naturally.'

'Look, Thierry, once you chaps have spoken to my brother-in-law, please come back to me and let's discuss this further. I appreciate everything you've done so far.' He got up.

'Wait!' said Jerry. 'Our visiting time isn't over yet.'

But Jean-Jacques hurried towards his cell, the guards following him.

Three weeks later, the name of Jean-Jacques Henri was back on the front pages of the newspapers. His murder trial was about to begin. It was going to be a high-profile hearing. The Palais de Justice was packed to the rafters – with journalists, patrons of the Tour d'Argent and curious townsfolk.

Jean-Jacques walked towards the witness stand.

'You may sit down, sir,' said the court orderly.

'I prefer to stand, sir, at least until the judge walks in.'

As he stood, he started drumming a rhythm on the wooden stand. Then he began chanting, his chant gaining in volume and momentum: '*Abelungu oswayini, basincintsh'itiye basibize ngoswayin'.*' *Whites are swine; they deny us tea, and then call us swine.*

'You can't do that,' said the court orderly, touching his truncheon.

But Jean-Jacques ignored him. He continued chanting. The public gallery went completely silent, the spectators mesmerised by the man's urgent chant.

Abelungu oswayini, basincintsh'itiye basibize ngoswayin'.

He was back in the forests of Arques-la-Bataille, chopping trees, breaking stones in the quarry, doing his bit for the war effort.

He walked out of the stand. The orderly tried to stop him, then changed his mind and reached instead for his truncheon. He clasped it firmly – but he made way, allowing Jean-Jacques to walk to the open space in front of the judge's bench, which stood on a raised platform. As Jean-Jacques scanned the crowd, he caught a glimpse of Jerry's familiar face, next to Thierry, in a gaggle of eager journalists. Then, facing the empty bench, Jean-Jacques lifted his hands in the air, his legs bent at the knees, in readiness to dance.

Still chanting '*Abelungu oswayin*', he raised his arms high, twirled about twice and then slammed his feet rhythmically on the wooden floorboards. Crying out with each slamming of the feet: 'AJI! AJI!'

As he stamped, he allowed his voice to soar above the excited murmurs from the public gallery. 'They might have emasculated me, they might have refused me a gun, they might have lied about their reasons for bringing me to Europe, they might have confined me to the kitchen, to tree-felling duty, to breaking stones at the quarry, but they couldn't stop me from dancing the death dance. Today I am dancing the death drill, I'm telling my story. Whether I die or not does not matter any more. No one can deny me my own dance of death – *Abelungu oswayin*'!'

When the judge appeared from a side door, the court orderly shouted, 'Order in the court. Order! Order!'

Jean-Jacques bowed respectfully before the judge but did not stop chanting and dancing. 'I know I'm going to die. I should have died on that ship. Should have died out there in Dieppe, from German bullets. I should have died before I was born.'

'ORDER! ORDER!'

'I should have died many times before. So what is death now? But my story must be heard.'

'ORDER! ORDER!'

'I am dancing my death drill. No one can take it away from me. This death drill is my truth. They made me leave my spear, my shield, back home those many years ago. So I am going to fight with my words, turn my words into bullets. This dance is my history, my heritage, my story that they tried to suppress. This is my death drill, my dance of death, my dance of truth.'

Like the men on the *Mendi*, he danced, the rhythmic slamming of feet gaining momentum with each movement. Slam-slam! Slam-slam!

AUTHOR'S NOTE

The story about the sinking of the ss *Mendi* has haunted me from the time I was a child. Unlike many childhood tales, I acquired this story not from the mouths of my paternal grandfather and my maternal grandmother, both of whom shaped my imagination through the tales they told me; this story first reached me through the medium of music.

As a young boy, I loved music so much that I became part of Ingede Higher Primary School choir as a tenor. We sang pieces by both European and African choral composers – everyone from Handel to R T Caluza, from Hayden to Myataza. We sang in isiZulu, my mother tongue, in Sesotho, isiXhosa, and even English, which was a language so foreign to us that even though we sang these foreign songs with gusto and confidence, most of the time we did not know what they were all about. We just concentrated on the notes, on the music, twisting our tongues around strange words.

Then we were introduced to a haunting dirge, 'Amagorha e*Mendi*'. Written in isiXhosa, the short, haunting piece of music was composed by Jabez Foley, one of the most illustrious black composers, in memory of the more than six hundred men who had gone down with the *Mendi* when it met its demise off the coast of the Isle of Wight.

Having internalised the song, I started hearing more stories about these soldiers. Maybe the stories had always been there – it was just that they did not make sense before then. The song had contextualised and humanised the lives of these men.

When I reached Standard Nine and read South African history at a more advanced level, reference was again made to the sinking of the ss *Mendi*. But it was just a footnote to a chapter on South Africa's involvement in the war. The ancestors whispering to me and my classmates through the pages of that book were silent on why black men had enlisted in a war that was clearly not theirs in the first place. Why would they throw in their lot with the British Crown, the very authorities who had not so long ago enacted the Native Land Act of 1913, which had seen the country's black majority being consigned to thirteen per cent of the land? The very Crown that had imposed countless taxes upon them? The very Crown that had put the final nail in the coffin of the Zulu Kingdom, the last such entity on the subcontinent? Why would they support a regime that had continuously denied them the right to vote, that had denied them a say in the affairs of the 'native' community, as blacks were still then called?

Years later, when I was already a journalist and novelist, I realised that the hooks of the *Mendi* story were digging deeper into my psyche. The story wouldn't leave me alone. I realised that, in order to exorcise myself of the *Mendi* demons, I simply had to write the story once and for all. But where to begin? Were the survivors still alive? How to locate them? Imagine my exhilaration, then, when, in 2004, I chanced upon a book by Norman Clothier called *Black Valour – The South African Native Labour Contingent, 1916–1918 and the Sinking of the Mendi*.

I wolfed down the 177-page book in one sitting, after which I wrote an opinion piece on the subject – for *Rapport* newspaper. A year later I, alongside John Battersby of the *Sunday Independent* and Chris More of the *Sowetan*, was invited by the French government (the Foreign Affairs department, to be exact) for a two-week briefing on that government's revised foreign affairs policy with specific reference to Africa. During our stay there, at no urging from our side, we were driven from Paris all the way to the coast, where we were given a tour of South African war graves. And there, in Dieppe, the graves of some of the members of the Native Labour Contingent were pointed out. Coincidence? Fate?

It was after having seen the battle scenes and the graves that I began thinking about taking Clothier's book further – by bringing to life the individual stories of these men; by creating something of an epic in memory of their selflessness and courage. It is no coincidence that South Africa's highest national order for bravery is the Order of Mendi. The story of the *Mendi* is at the heart of our nationhood, but we have yet to do justice to this narrative. This is my humble contribution towards this effort.

Now sadly out of print, Clothier's book served not only as an inspiration, but also as a lighthouse which always helped put me back on course whenever I got lost in the sea of this vast, sprawling narrative. Clothier kept me anchored, but also pointed me to further sources which helped immensely in putting matters into perspective and reading the story in its proper context. If I have misread or misinterpreted the sources, the fault is mine.

'Jantoni', referred to on page 62, alludes to John Dunn, a white hunter sheltered by King Cetshwayo, the last independent ruler of the Zulus, only to betray his protector and later proclaim himself a white Zulu chief, marrying hundreds of Zulu maidens.

The lines quoted on page 202 are from a letter written by Captain Louis Hertslet that appears in Norman Clothier's *Black Valour* (page 50). The King's speech on pages 254–5 is reproduced there as it appears in Clothier's book (page 140), as are the transcripts of Acland and Stump's dialogue on pages 258–9 and 260 (pages 86–8), and sections of the court's report quoted on pages 261–3 (pages 88–90).

On page 208, the lines 'We are drilling the death drill. I, a Xhosa, say you are my brothers. Zulus, Swazis, Pondos, Basutos, we die like brothers. We are the sons of Africa' appear. This piece of oratory is attributed to real-life character Reverend Isaac Wauchope Dyobha in oral accounts of the sinking. It has also been repeated in various written texts.

Details about 20 February 1917 that appear on page 258 are taken from the 1917 wreck report for *Mendi* and *Darro*, available at http://www.plimsoll.org/resourcess/SCCLibraries/WreckReports2002/21285a.asp.

Stimela Jason Jingoes, referred to on page 265, was a real-life character. His account of life with the Labour Contingent is captured in the book *A Chief Is a Chief by the People: An Autobiography of Stimela Jason Jingoes* (London: Oxford University Press, 1975), from which some of the quoted utterances are taken.

I am indebted to Professor Bill Nasson and Professor Albert Grundlingh, both history professors at Stellenbosch University at the time of writing, who shared with me their insight into and experience of the South African War and the sinking of the ss *Mendi* through their writings and informal chats with me. While I'm at it, let me express my heartfelt gratitude to the Stellenbosch Institute for Advanced Study where some chapters of this book were written. Thank you, Professor Hendrik Geyer and team.

This book probably wouldn't have been finished without the unstinting (but certainly stinging!) support of my colleagues at Wits University (MA Creative Writing class of 2013–2014). Thanks, especially, to my supervisor Dr Christopher Thurman, and to programme convenor Dr Gerrit Olivier, who gently but firmly put me back on course whenever I got seduced by the allure of the narrative at the expense of historical accuracy. My unreserved thanks also go to Dr Michelle Adler, also of Wits University, and Professor Michael Green, of Northumbria University, for their thorough and constructive comments on the manuscript.

A bow to my good friends Dr Danyela Demir of the University of Augsburg and Dr Meg Samuelson of the University of Cape Town for their detailed responses to my original text. Thanks to Professor Zakes Mda (*Enkosi Gatyeni*), Professor Kgomotso Michael Masemola (*Nazo-ke mf'ethu!*) of the University of South Africa, and Dr Grace Musila of Stellenbosch University for their faith in the project.

My wife Nomvuzo was a virtual widow during the writing of the bulk of this book – *Enkosi, MaMgebe omhle!* Thanks to my son Vusisizwe Freddy The Famous for reading my very long and sometimes long-winded first draft and giving me honest, detailed feedback. Son, you rock!

SOURCES AND SUGGESTED FURTHER READING

Clothier, N. *Black Valour - The South African Native Labour Contingent, 1916-1918 and the Sinking of the Mendi* (Pietermaritzburg: University of Natal Press, 1987)

Commonwealth War Graves Commission. *Let Us Die Like Brothers* (twenty-minute film about the ss *Mendi* disaster and the involvement of black South African men in the war), London, 2006

Grundlingh, A. 'Mutating Memories and the Making of a Myth: Remembering the ss *Mendi* Disaster 1917-2007', *South African History Journal*, Volume 63, Issue 1, 2011

Kay, J. *The Lament of the ss* Mendi, radio documentary, BBC Radio 4, London, 19 November 2008

Kessler, S. *The Black Concentration Camps of the Anglo-Boer War 1899-1902* (Bloemfontein: The War Museum of the Boer Republics, 2012)

Morris, W. *Off The Record* (animated short film), Flanders: The History Channel, 2008

Nasson, B. *Uyadela wen'osulapho: Black Participation in the Anglo-Boer War* (Johannesburg: Ravan Press, 1999)

Nasson, B. *The War for South Africa: The Anglo-Boer War (1899-1902)* (Cape Town: Tafelberg, 2010)